Two for Joy

Also by Mary Reed and Eric Mayer

One for Sorrow

Two for Joy

Mary Reed & Eric Mayer

Poisoned Pen Press
Scottsdale, AZ

Poisoned
Pen
Press

Copyright 2000 by Mary Reed and Eric Mayer

First Edition 2000

10 9 8 7 6 5 4 3 2 1

Library of Congress Catalog Card Number: 99-068851

ISBN: 1-890208-37-X

Poisoned Pen Press
6962 E. First Ave. Ste 103
Scottsdale, AZ 85251
www.poisonedpenpress.com
info@poisonedpenpress.com

Printed in the United States of America

Acknowledgments

Our grateful thanks to Adrian Cook, Sally Winchester and Dr. Robert Ousterhout for their generous assistance.

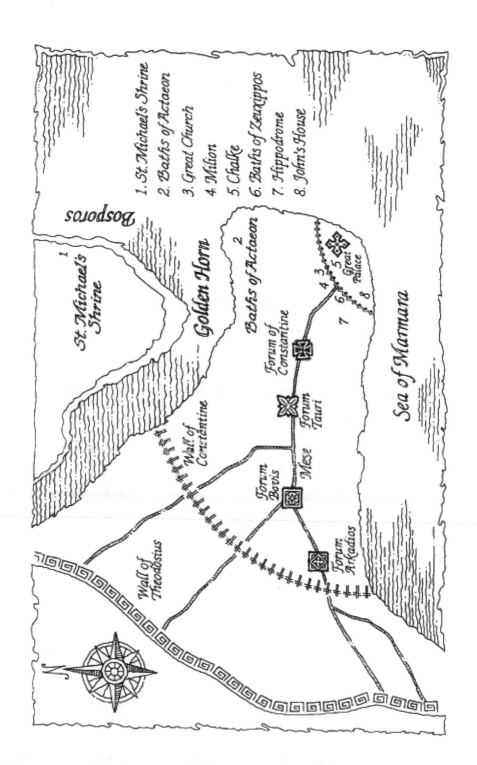

Chapter One

Where had the old man gone now?

A storm was moving in from the Sea of Marmara and prudent men should long since have headed home. Irritated, John, Lord Chamberlain to Emperor Justinian, tossed aside the skewer with the charred remnants of his simple meal of grilled fish and scanned the small colonnaded forum again.

Looking around through a throng of hawkers, loiterers, roughly dressed laborers, and clusters of dusty pilgrims, John quickly located the missing man. He was possibly the only living person in the entire city wearing an elaborately folded himation although numerous antique statues within its confines displayed fine examples of the same outmoded style of clothing.

John sighed. While it was true that Philo had journeyed far beyond his native Athens, this was his first visit to Constantinople. Under John's watchful eye he had spent the afternoon among the city's wonders, gawking and dawdling through its busy streets like a white bearded child. Unfortunately, it seemed he was also as trusting as a child, for he had now fallen into conversation with three young ne'er-do-wells sporting beards and mustaches after the Persian style.

John strode quickly through the gang of gulls fighting raucously over the scraps of his discarded fish. At the sight of his lean, sumptuously-robed figure and unmistakable military bearing, the three young men sauntered away.

Philo, however, was not so impressed by his former student.

"I was just about to ask that pleasant gentleman if he had any news from Khosrow's court. Word of my colleagues, perhaps," he said peevishly.

"They wouldn't know anything about the Persian court. They aren't Persians," John informed him. "They're members of the Blue faction. That's just the way they dress. They'd put a knife in your ribs as soon as look at you. This isn't the Academy, Philo. You must always be on your guard here. Always."

The crowd in the forum thinned rapidly as the storm neared land. Vendors complained loudly to each other as they doused their grills prior to setting them up again in some convenient portico offering shelter against the wavering curtain of rain advancing across the sullen swells. A freshening breeze dispersed the usual smells of commerce, a blend of fish and apples tinged by exotic spices mixed with the sour reek of spilled wine and sweat.

"We must go home now," John told his charge, "unless you want to get soaked."

"I've spent so many years in the desert, I wouldn't mind a little rain. But that column over there, it's home to another of your holy pillar sitters, isn't it? Perhaps we can discover how long the demented creature has been up there." Philo darted off again without waiting for John's reply.

The rough granite pillar standing in the middle of the forum rose to the height of several men. The ladder propped against its side and the empty baskets at its base gave mute testimony to offerings recently sent up to the occupant of the platform.

When John reached him, Philo was examining what appeared to be a misshapen coin. "It was lying in the dirt," he explained.

John nodded. "It's a pilgrim token. Acolytes make them from the earth around the pillar. Tokens like that are said to have powerful curative powers, so the faithful buy them at quite high prices."

"As high as these stylites sit, perhaps? They support quite a thriving industry, don't they?" Philo took a step back and craned his neck to gaze upwards.

The tangled hair and beard of the skeletal man perched above were streaming in the wind. So slight was the stylite's body that he looked as if he would be carried away by its force were it not for the heavy chains of penance weighing him down.

Two fat, cold raindrops broke against the back of John's thin hand. Others quickly followed. As they hit the ground they stirred up dust to mix with the sharp smell of animal dung and the briny tang of the sea. From nearby came the odor of freshly baked bread.

"We can discuss stylites once we're out of the storm," John said. "We can't linger here."

With obvious reluctance, Philo left the foot of the pillar. Light faded from the suddenly chilly air. From a church nearby came the drifting ebb and flow of chanting—or perhaps it was just the sound of the wind groaning among the colonnades edging the forum. A loose shop awning whipped upwards by a stronger gust and the warning patter of rain on tiled roofs heralded the approaching downpour.

John glanced back and caught a glimpse of the stylite outlined against dark clouds. He would not care to be standing up there in such weather. As if in response to the thought, a sheet of wind-driven rain swept across the forum. John grabbed a loose fold of Philo's voluminous clothing and hurried him faster across the rain-slick cobbles.

Philo's outraged protest at being handled in such an undignified manner was drowned by a ground-shuddering thunderclap shockingly close by. The rain quickened to a choking deluge as if an angry deity had picked up the sea and emptied it out onto the city.

Through the roar of the storm and the ringing in his ears John heard shouting and screams. Someone's been hit by lightning, he thought immediately. Then he realized he no longer grasped Philo's robe.

"Philo!" He turned back, convinced for an irrational instant that his companion had been struck. But Philo was a few paces away, staring up, shielding his eyes from the rain.

Others, heedless of the downpour, also looked toward the heavens, pointing. As his hearing recovered from the thunderclap, John could discern, amid the onlookers' curses and cries of terror, a frenzied, metallic clanking.

Atop the pillar, the stylite flailed his arms wildly, their motion whipping his chains against the platform's railing. The man's arms were on fire.

Even as John grasped the fact, rivulets of flame ran greedily across the stylite's robe. Glowing patches blossomed and spread in the man's straggling beard. A small dark shape—a rat—scuttled to the platform's edge and fell over.

The burning man tried to dowse the blaze, slapping at his chest. He began screaming only when his matted hair burst into an incandescent halo around his head.

The onlookers fell silent, horror etched on their faces.

The stylite's shrieks did not diminish as he careened around the platform, trying to escape the engulfing flames. Now he was a ghastly silhouette in a fiery nimbus. Sparks swirled away in the wind each time he struck the railing.

At last his legs gave way and he crumpled. His shrieks ended abruptly, leaving only a faint sound, a hissing and popping akin to the noise made by damp wood burning, discernible under the onslaught of the downpour. Mercifully, wind-swirled smoke obscured the platform.

John shivered as a sudden freezing gust of wind carried a familiar smell to him. For an instant, it made him think of street vendors. Then he realized why. It was the unmistakable odor of roasting flesh.

※ ※ ※

"Master! Thank the Lord you're home safe!"

Peter, John's elderly servant, stepped shakily away from the heavy nail-studded door. John entered, stamping soaked boots on the hall's tiled floor, closely followed by a grumbling Philo.

In the trembling light of Peter's oil lamp, the servant's lined face resembled those of mummies John had seen in Alexandria, their huge eyes blank rather than serene, as if terrified at the prospect of entering the afterworld.

Something was troubling Peter. "Ah, master," he lamented, "I fear I have just witnessed the beginning."

Philo closed the heavy door, abruptly muffling the rush of rain.

"The beginning? Of what, Peter?" John asked.

"Of the passing away of the world," was the cryptic reply.

"I shall be passing away myself if I don't get dry," complained Philo. Indeed, his garment was so sodden that he seemed barely able to drag himself up the narrow wooden stairs under its weight.

The air of the kitchen, warmed by a glowing brazier, carried a comfortingly familiar faint odor of onions and boiled poultry—and before long the dog-like smell of wet wool.

John hung his dripping cloak near the brazier. He glanced at the two aging men, Philo trembling from the chill, Peter obviously terrified, and he felt that stabbing awareness of mortality that more commonly beset him when he lay awake in the middle of the night.

"What precisely was it that you saw, Peter?" John went on more for Philo's benefit than to cheer Peter, "It must have been truly terrifying to upset a tough old camp cook like yourself."

"Please do try to be brief, if you would be so kind." Philo warmed his hands. "We've just had quite a shock ourselves."

John had tactfully left room near the brazier, but Peter evidently preferred to remain by the doorway. His gaze seemed inexorably drawn to the fogged rectangular panes of the kitchen window.

"It was this way, master. I had retired to my room," Peter finally began, "for I like to perform my devotions there. You can see all the crosses on the rooftops and the dome of the Great Church catches the light of the setting sun. A glorious sight it is too. But today the window panes were streaked with rain and darkness seemed to arrive earlier than usual."

He paused briefly to collect his thoughts.

"I had just began to sing a hymn," he went on. "It's a particular favorite of mine for it was written by the emperor himself. Then I heard a cry, a wailing that turned to a terrible keening as if some mighty hand had torn open the doorway to Hell and the lamentations of the damned were issuing forth."

"It's very windy," muttered Philo.

Peter appeared not to hear. "I peered out of my window," he continued. "What with it getting so dark and rainy, at first all I could see was the light shining from the dome of the Great Church. Then I began to pick out other bright flickerings here and there around the city. They were much brighter than torches, more like bonfires.

"And that seemed to me to be very strange, because the rain was still pouring down. It's such weather as Noah must have seen." The elderly man drew a deep breath. "It's buildings set on fire by lightning, I thought. Nothing unusual in that. But several at once? I feared that the whole city would be going up in flames, and my master and his guest out in the streets. But then the rain shifted and I could see the nearest fire more clearly. And I saw..."

The old man's gaze flickered up to the kitchen ceiling as his voice faded. His hand traced the sign of his religion.

"What was it you saw, Peter?" John persisted gently.

"The fire...it wasn't a burning building. It was hanging above the rooftops, up in the sky. And in the middle of the flames I could see the dark figure of a man."

Peter swayed and his legs seemed to give way. John leapt forward and caught his servant's shoulders, but as he lowered the limp body gently to the kitchen tiles Peter's haggard face turned ashen and his eyes closed.

"Mithra!" John muttered.

As he bent over the unconscious man it occurred to him that Peter must have seen the stylite he and Philo had observed. Burning like a torch, distorted by the rain-streaked window of his room, the sight must have been enough to frighten him almost to death.

"I'm going for a physician," John told Philo.

* * *

Outside, the rain was slackening. John did not waste time seeking help at the barracks across the square from his house. Gaius, the palace physician, lived some distance across the grounds but would arrive quickly if John personally summoned aid.

When John attended the Academy, Philo had constantly chided him about preferring its running paths to the sheltered walkways where students and teachers strolled serenely while engaged in leisurely debates.

"Perhaps you should leave us for a while, John," Philo had once counseled him. "Go out into the world. Run until you have tired your body. Then you will be more prepared to use your mind."

The words echoed in John's memory as he loped rapidly along meandering paths through the earthy smell of rain-soaked shrubbery.

Hair hanging in dripping rat tails and soaked to the skin, he presented a startling sight to the dark-haired servant girl who answered his frantic pounding on the physician's door.

She peeked out in terror. "He cannot assist you, excellency," she quavered, "He is engaged. That is to say, he is not here. He was summoned to see the emperor."

The distressed girl glanced over her shoulder into the murky depths of the house. John had noted the fresh bruise under one eye. It did not surprise him. Gaius was surly when intoxicated.

"Engaged in entertaining Bacchus, you mean!" John snapped, cursing that it would be this of all nights the otherwise competent physician had chosen to drink himself into a stupor. He was certain Gaius was lying in an addled heap inside, but even if he had hauled the physician out bodily, in such a condition he would be of no value to any patient.

Reining in his temper, John apologized to the girl for his abruptness and prepared to depart. "If you are able to tear your master away from his goblet," he said as he turned to go, "and get him back on his feet, be so kind as to impress upon him that there is a dying man who needs his assistance. At the Lord Chamberlain's house."

"The Lord Chamberlain...oh..." The girl gave a stricken moan.

※※※

John was not a man who believed in oracles or prophecies, but, as he rapped on his house door, he experienced a chill as if a cold draught had found a crack in his mental armor and penetrated to his soul. He abruptly knew, with an absolute and terrible certainty, that Peter was dead. So he was surprised to find his servant sitting at the kitchen table, drinking a cup of watered wine.

"Master," Peter reproached him, his voice weak but steady. "You should not have gone for help. You must have forgotten that I am the servant."

John looked at Philo.

"Remarkable, isn't it?" smiled his erstwhile tutor jovially. "When you insisted on running heedlessly off as usual, I gave the matter some consideration. Then I recalled that curious token I found beside the stylite's pillar. You'd mentioned it was of the sort used by the faithful as a medicinal remedy. I wasn't certain how to administer it, so I crumbled some of it into a cup of wine."

He paused, enjoying the telling of his story. "I managed to get Peter to take a few swallows of the mixture. You see the result."

It was indeed a remarkable transformation. Peter was still pale, but he was perfectly lucid and his hand barely shook as he lifted his cup.

"Thank Mithra," breathed John.

Peter's lips tightened. "Master, I would not call on that deity of yours," he frowned, "and especially not on this night, not now. Not after what I witnessed."

John sat down on a stool beside the servant. "What do you mean, Peter? And what exactly did you see? Was it a man on fire? There is doubtless a commonplace explanation for that unfortunate incident. We saw it ourselves."

Peter set down his cup on the scarred table top and looked at John, absolute certainty in his eyes.

"There is no need to seek an explanation, master, no. For what else could it have been but an archangel in his fiery chariot, returning to judge this sinful world?"

Chapter Two

By the next morning there were almost as many explanations for the stylite's fiery death as there were inhabitants of the city. Anatolius, secretary to Justinian, ached to be out in the forums soaking up the latest rumors. Only a hour before he'd learned from one of the house slaves, back from a market visit, that two other stylites had died in the same mystifying and terrifying manner.

Unfortunately, the young man had to answer a summons to his father's study. Senator Flavius Aurelius, it seemed, was displeased with his son. Again.

"Anatolius," Aurelius began in a weary tone, "as you will doubtless recall, we have had this conversation on numerous occasions. When are you going to desist from being so hasty in your speech?"

The silver-haired senator distractedly pushed a pile of scrolls and codices to one side of his desk, revealing the grinning skull depicted in its tiled top. It was a not so subtle reminder that when work was to be done there was no time to be wasted on fripperies or foolishness. The desk made an odd contrast to the cavorting cupids which the senator's wife had had painted on the walls of what had been her sitting room. The decorations had not been favored by Aurelius during his wife's lifetime, but now that she was dead, they served as a comforting reminder of her. Or so Anatolius supposed. Such sentiments were not the sort that his father would share with anyone.

The young man shifted his feet nervously and bowed his head, knowing better than to reply but wishing that his father would finish his latest speech about responsibility and respectability and not wearing his hair too long in the back. "You'll be mistaken for a Blue," was how his father usually expressed his disapproval.

"Take this latest nonsense, this 'Ode to An Empress,'" the senator was saying.

Anatolius looked up sharply.

A wry smile creased Aurelius' face. "Ah, I see I have finally managed to surprise my son. Yes, I heard about it."

Anatolius looked down again, studying the mosaic floor. Unlike the desk top, its purely decorative geometrical patterns had no comment to make on mortality.

"The emperor might well dismiss your patronizing the fleshpot where it was overheard as a worldly sin. But as to the verse itself...No doubt you will wish to know the identity of the person who informed me." Aurelius continued, "Let us just say that it was someone at court. The gods smiled on you, for the person who told me about it is a friend and can be relied upon to be discreet."

"Father, I only recited it to a few acquaintances. It was a jest." Anatolius looked hurt, because he was. Paternal lectures always had the effect of making him feel at least ten years younger, or perhaps even twenty.

"I do have some care for what I say in public. And in private."

The senator shook his head, pointing out that however private the room, in a house of that sort little went unnoticed and even less went unremarked.

"Yes, I suppose that's so," Anatolius admitted, "I'll be more careful next time."

"It would be best if you were careful all the time, for all our sakes. Everyone at court has enemies. Timothy, the vineyard owner who supplies the imperial table with much of its wine, has openly declared his designs on my country estate, for example. He, for one, would not be averse to seeing me fall from favor through your disgrace. Then, too, I have lately been hearing much gossip concerning Senator Balbinus distressing his wife by frequenting that very establishment where you recited your scurrilous verses. If that is indeed true, you are fortunate that he was not there to hear your sorry performance."

Anatolius frowned and began to speak but his father cut his words short.

"That particular young woman ceased to be your concern when she married Balbinus," he said. "What I want you to consider in this matter is that if he had overheard you, he would have been only too ready to use your ill-considered words to his own advantage. He and I have been much at odds lately. And need I say Balbinus and Timothy are but two opponents of many?" He nodded toward the documents on which he had been working when Anatolius arrived. "Some day you will have to deal with all this."

He sighed and gestured to the chair beside his desk. "Now sit down, Anatolius, and let us talk."

Anatolius, familiar with the course of his father's lectures, breathed a sigh of relief. Now, most likely, they would discuss chariot racing. After that he would be dismissed and be free to go to the Forum Constantine to hear what new embellishments had been added to the tale of the burning stylites. Better yet, his father had not yet inquired when he intended to visit the tonsor or wear more sober garments as befitted his official position, nor when he might be thinking of getting betrothed. He was not getting any younger, despite how his father could make him feel, and neither was his father.

"All the same," Anatolius said unrepentantly as he sat down, "it really was a marvelous epigram, rather than a poem. It began 'Theodora's father kept bears, now Theodora bare...'"

"Stop!" The senator rarely used that tone.

Anatolius regarded the floor again. He regretted his haste in speaking so lightly. Perhaps his father had a point.

"Now I must tell you that I have made a decision about your future, Anatolius. I believe you would do well in a legal career, and thus I have arranged for you to take up an appointment in the quaestor's office."

Anatolius looked at him in stupefied amazement. Surely his ears had deceived him. "The quaestor's office?"

His father, horribly, nodded confirmation.

"But it's practically worth my head to squeeze an occasional fine turn of phrase into the emperor's official correspondence," Anatolius blurted out. "How will I survive organizing dry old laws and drafting proclamations?"

Aurelius raised his hand slightly but imperiously, quelling his son's protests. Although the senatorial class lacked the political power it once possessed, its members still passed down to each generation the commanding presence of their ancient rank, not to mention their extensive land holdings.

"It's true that legal matters have more need of prosaic wherefore's and whereas's than of poetic seas that are wine dark," he admitted. "But it's time for you to fully enter the adult world, to become a respectable and responsible citizen." The senator glanced down at the tiled skull. "Not only that, I am getting older and I would like to see a grandson before I make my journey with the dark ferryman. But at least at this point I am not looking to arrange a good marriage for you."

"Thank Mithra for that," Anatolius muttered.

"No, Anatolius, for that you can thank your dear mother, who was always the romantic and opposed arranged marriages. And furthermore, you had best guard your speech when uttering an oath. One day your tongue will behead you, if it does not do worse. I will not always be here to smooth things over."

The older man frowned and Anatolius saw his lips tighten. Perhaps he was thinking of his deceased wife. Aurelius quickly resumed his composure, however, and continued brusquely. "But on to a more pleasant topic. I have decided to hold a banquet in honor of your appointment. The guests will be colleagues of mine, men of good reputation and prominent in their fields. It's of great assistance to a young man such as you, Anatolius, to have friends in high places, especially when trying to climb up to their level. They can offer you a helping hand."

"Or they can knock you down and plant their boot in your face," Anatolius retorted, "depending on which prominent person you mean and from which quarter the political wind happens to be blowing that particular day."

His father nodded gravely. "I see that you have at least begun to learn some caution, if you do not always exercise it. Remember, at the palace, although it's always necessary to look ahead and consider all possibilities, it is equally important to guard your back against the blade." He grimaced as he stood. Anatolius jumped up to offer assistance, resentment at the paternal lecture dissipating as he asked if his father were in pain.

The answer came with a shake of the head. "Just a stone which I hope to pass in due course. I would prefer to avoid having to submit to the surgeon's knife. Now, since I have urgent business to attend to, I've decided to place you in charge of making arrangements for this festive gathering I mentioned. I'm certain that it will be a credit to the household. Nothing too extravagant, of course."

The prospect of arranging a banquet was more to Anatolius' liking than that of joining the legal profession. "I'll consult with the Lord Chamberlain and ask for his advice, then," he said with a smile. Surely this ghastly whim of his father's would pass, most likely with the stone. He would enjoy the banquet at any rate. "Perhaps I could engage some of Isis' girls to entertain? In an appropriately genteel manner, of course."

Aurelius laughed. "You are incorrigible, Anatolius! But take care that whatever you arrange does not lead you—or any of us—into danger. There will be absolutely no recitation of scurrilous epigrams, for example."

Anatolius assured him that he would be very careful.

"Then I must be away," his father replied. "We shall discuss the banquet further tonight. You can tell me then, having consulted your friend John, how your arrangements are proceeding."

Aurelius departed, leaving his son sitting by the desk. Before leaving, Anatolius quickly pushed a codex over the skull that grinned up at him from the desk top with over much familiarity.

※ ※ ※

The face of death atop the stylite's column was less easy to ignore.

As John approached the platform where the stylite's charred remains lay, a flock of crows rose with raucous protests, forming a roiling black cloud in the bright morning sunlight. With the birds gone, he could hear the buzzing drone of flies, their smaller but no less busy companions.

Unfortunately even the brisk breeze blowing in from the sea could not quite dissipate the odor of burnt flesh emanating from the body in the middle of the confined space atop the column.

Suppressing a gag, John reached over the iron railing and, grasping Gaius' hand, helped the heavyset physician clamber up off the ladder. With both of them now on the narrow platform, it was difficult to avoid treading on the remains of Matthew the Pure. John looked away, out over tiled rooftops, but the white-capped swells of the sea visible beyond them did nothing to subdue his sudden nausea.

"In my time, I've buried the dead on battlefields, sometimes after they've been lying in the sun for a day or more," he remarked to the physician, "but this is far worse. At least a soldierly death is clean. This was not."

"I have yet to witness a clean death," replied Gaius bluntly. He vigorously shook the railing fencing in Matthew's own battlefield, dislodging chunks of rust. "But I have to say that if Matthew slept leaning against this, his deity must surely have had a hand on him."

Remembering how the burning stylite had flung himself vainly against the railing, John realized the rusty iron was stronger than it appeared, but said nothing. He glanced down. From this height, Felix, the excubitor captain standing guard below, resembled a small, poorly detailed mosaic figure. A curious crowd had already gathered in the forum. Justinian, John knew, would have the remains of Matthew and the other dead stylites spirited away during the coming night to avoid any further public commotion. But first the emperor had ordered John and Gaius to inspect the bodies where they lay in the hope of finding some pointer to the reason for their mysterious deaths.

It was all very well for Justinian to give orders, Gaius had grumbled on their way to the forum, but he didn't have to personally carry them out. Felix, with a wolfish grin, had pointed out that that was one of the advantages of being emperor. Someone else would handle unseemly matters or those liable to soil imperial hands. Felix, however, was now standing safely and cheerfully below. It was Gaius and John who were aloft, staring down at the blackened ruin of what had once been a man.

Grunting with effort, Gaius knelt heavily down beside the charred corpse. If the physician had indeed been inebriated the night before he showed no ill effects. John wondered if the maidservant had mentioned his futile visit to her master. Perhaps not. Both he and Gaius had awoken to a summons to an audience with Justinian. Now here they were, standing on a windswept platform high above the city, seeking an answer to an impossible death.

"Sanitary conditions up here should be much worse," noted Gaius, gesturing expansively with a curved bronze knife he had produced from his bag and barely missing John's hip. "But these holy men eat and drink very little and they evacuate dryly, like sheep."

John nodded silently.

The physician pushed aside one of the heavy chains lying across what remained of Matthew's body and continued his study. "I see that our ravenous winged friends have already begun my investigations for me," he commented.

John nodded again, then glanced at several large crows perched expectantly on the wooden crosses rising from the roofs of the nearest houses. He preferred looking at them to observing Gaius at work. After a moment, he forced his attention back to his own task, that of examining the departed Matthew's cramped living quarters.

There wasn't much to see. The platform was so small that it took but a few paces to cross it from one side to the other. It was obvious at a glance that there was nowhere a murderer could have concealed himself.

John voiced the thought while examining two wicker baskets beside the rusted railing. One basket held a few loaves of the bread whose enticing aroma John had smelled the afternoon before, the other a small heap of olives and figs. The hungry crows had touched neither bread nor fruit. It struck John that while the olive branch promised peace, for Matthew the Pure, the peace that comes with death had been hard won.

John squeezed sideways past Gaius, who, muttering a mild protest, continued wielding his knife intently. An impossibly filthy and tattered rag that had once been a tunic was tied to the railing. Perhaps it had been part of the stylite's wardrobe. John prodded at the disgusting scrap with his booted foot.

"It always amazes me how these stylites attain such advanced age, given their living conditions," remarked Gaius conversationally, glancing up. "A good many of my patients succumb to disease or accident by the time they're thirty, despite my ministrations and not, I hasten to add, because of them, no matter what you hear from the palace gossips." A smile briefly illuminated his ruddy face. "And yet," he continued thoughtfully as he returned his attention to the dead man, "Matthew lived up here for longer than that, half-naked, tormented by vermin, exposed to the elements. Of course, I am told that like our emperor, he abstained from meat. Perhaps that was his secret."

"Have you ascertained anything of use concerning his death?" John was eager to take his leave.

Gaius rubbed thoughtfully at the side of his bulbous purplish nose, the nose of a dedicated devotee of Bacchus. "Not much that wasn't obvious to begin with, John. Look, here." He pointed his knife at the dark cavity he and his assistants the crows had cut into the blackened corpse.

John leaned closer, waving away the swarming flies buzzing around his head. Matthew, or what remained of him, lay on his back. His head had canted to one side of his body and a large yellowish bone, a thigh bone, protruded slightly from a fire ravaged leg. The wet mess visible inside Gaius' investigative opening revealed nothing strange to John, who said as much.

"Our friend's innards, as you can see, are quite unharmed, barely cooked," Gaius replied in a matter of fact manner. "That's because the body is full of watery substances—blood, phlegm, bile—so although the outer parts may be burnt away, the inner organs tend to be protected. It's a very interesting and surprising effect. I regret to say that I have observed it more than once, but I suppose that's hardly to be wondered at given that builders will insist on constructing ill-made wooden tenements and then compounding their errors by getting tenants who tend towards carelessness with their braziers." He sighed. "But Matthew here burned from the outside. He had no brazier, and since there's nowhere an assailant could have concealed himself, the obvious conclusion is that he was struck by lightning. And so I shall report to Justinian."

"I would certainly agree, Gaius," John replied, "but for three stylites to be struck by lightning, at almost the same instant..."

"The storm was severe. The world can be a strange place. It is as simple as that," Gaius grunted as he struggled upright. "Steady the ladder, Felix!", he called down to the man below.

Pausing as he swung his foot out to the top rung, he grinned cheerily across at John. "We're done with Matthew now. Only two more to go."

Chapter Three

When John got home after a day spent examining the unpleasant habitations of the three burning victims he found Philo ensconced in his study. The philosopher had taken to that formerly private room like a stylite to a pillar, as Anatolius had remarked not long after Philo's arrival.

"You're late for your meal," announced the philosopher. He was studying the odd board game—shatranj, he called it—that he had brought back from his travels and which John, unthinkingly, had allowed to be placed on a table in the study.

"I cannot claim much of an appetite after the sights I've seen today," John replied softly. "I'd have arrived back earlier but I stayed somewhat longer than usual at the baths." He did not add that his long immersion in its tepid pool had not succeeded in making him feel any less soiled.

The chair usually set behind his desk had been pulled over to Philo's table. Suppressing a sigh, John sat down and regarded the game board. It looked to his eye much like a latrunculi board, but the heavy, carved jade pieces ranged stolidly upon its squares were unfamiliar. Alas, his mind had been occupied with other matters when Peter had brought up the question of the table Philo had requested. What had John told him? "Oh, put it anywhere."

Now John regretted his inattention, for the study was his sanctuary. He liked to sit there in the evenings when the sun's dying light, streaming in through its large window, lent a rusty hue to the bright tesserae of the mosaic that transformed the width of one wall into a bucolic scene. John had developed a special fondness for one of its figures, a girl with almond-shaped eyes. He had named her Zoe and had been known to have a word with her from time to time, much to Peter's distress.

Perhaps, John thought wryly, Peter had placed the table in the study to stop him from sitting in there talking to himself.

He realized he should ask Philo to move to some other room to contemplate the game. But the last time he had seen him, John had been a student, not his equal. Even though that had been a lifetime ago, the two weeks that had elapsed since Philo had accepted his hospitality had not been sufficient for John to overcome the long shadow of that accustomed relationship.

"How has Peter been today? Does he seem recovered?" he asked his guest.

"He's been going about his duties," Philo replied.

"And your day went well?"

Philo looked up. The expression of childish curiosity his face had displayed during their previous day's exploration of Constantinople had been replaced by the exhausted, hunted look increasingly familiar to John since his former mentor's unannounced arrival at his door.

"I spoke with Senator Aurelius as you advised me, John," the other said heavily. "He taught at the

Academy himself and yet still he refuses to offer me assistance."

John expressed his surprise.

"He treated me so curtly," Philo continued, moving pieces idly around the board, "that I thought my mere presence in his study was causing him pain." A frown nagged his bushy eyebrows.

"This is a wealthy city," he went on resentfully. "Its beggars don't ask for less than a follis. Every baker and mason and common laborer has the dignity of work. There are scribes laboring at the palace without knowing a word of Latin, or so I hear. And yet I am to believe there is no employment anywhere in the city or at Justinian's court for a philosopher, a man of learning such as myself."

John detected a bitterness in Philo's tone he had not heard before. But in the old days, this scholar, this man who had taught him to read and write and who, during John's own brief stay at the Academy, had imbued him with the taste for knowledge, had been little touched by the dark cares of the world. The man who had so recently arrived at John's door was almost a stranger. The carefully clipped beard and longish hair, now thinner and receding from the forehead, had turned white, the eyebrows were thicker, the eyes sunken, and the hawk-like nose more prominent. Philo had become the perfect physical embodiment of the ideal philosopher. Except for the gnawing bitterness.

"I would say, Philo," John replied, choosing his words with care, "that a philosopher such as yourself, a follower of Plato, should not perhaps be too shocked to find a less than warm reception at a Christian court in a Christian city."

Philo's lips tightened. "I recall quite well that Justinian ordered the Academy closed because of its alleged pagan teachings," he snapped. "Why do you suppose that Diomedes and I and the others who taught there spent this past seven or eight years in exile? King Khosrow at least is an open-minded patron of the arts and learning without, if I dare say so, our own emperor's religious agenda."

John thought it appropriate and necessary to warn Philo against voicing such sentiments in public and as he did so, he looked up into the calm, glassy eyes of the mosaic girl Zoe. He did not, however, voice his thoughts about that other Persian royal patron of the arts whose subjects had captured a young adventurer straying over the border years before and changed his fate forever. If not for them, he thought, he might have been simply John, a small landholder married to his Cornelia, raising a family in comfortable obscurity in some corner of the fertile Greek countryside.

"You must have realized that this lack of opportunity was possible when you chose to come back, Philo," he pointed out at the end of his cautionary comments.

"It didn't even occur to me! It's been five years since Justinian signed the Eternal Peace, the treaty giving us the right to come back. Some of my colleagues did so at once, of course. A few are still in the east and to tell the truth I thought about staying too, but I suppose I was homesick. That's why I returned. I'd forgotten that my only true home was the Academy."

"No matter the unfairness of Justinian's closing it, that's all in the past, Philo. Nothing can be done to change it. But at least you're no longer in exile. Perhaps that's all the justice you'll ever find. However little it is, it's more than many enjoy."

The other shook his head. "No, John, I cannot accept that. We've been allowed to come home and even given the right to practice our own religion, that's true. How often that's been pointed at as a demonstration of the emperor's boundless mercy. Merciful indeed, allowing some harmless old scholars to come creeping back to their homes!"

"But," John replied, "of such pagans as remain in the empire, you're the only ones having the emperor's official sanction, Philo. Consider, here I am, Justinian's Lord Chamberlain, sharing my house with a Christian servant and a licensed pagan, as it were, yet I'm the only one unable to legally profess my faith!"

Philo just shook his head more vehemently. "Don't make light of my sorry situation, John. Has the emperor returned to us the land or the assets he confiscated? Has he offered us compensation for all we lost? Of course not. Nor are we permitted to teach. What then is the point of allowing a man to live yet allowing him no way earn his living? It's my opinion that Justinian's mercy is nothing more than calculated cruelty. He seeks to increase our suffering by forcing us to wander like wraiths through a world in which we no longer have a place. He wants to see us in rags, begging in the streets. What pleasure that would give him!"

"It's unlikely Justinian will ever go walking about the streets observing beggars," John pointed out with a thin smile. "As a matter of fact, he rarely ventures out into the city except when in procession, and in that case the beggars are all removed from his route beforehand. You must realize, Philo, that the vast majority of the populace would probably have had you all flayed alive before agreeing to allow you to return. I hope your colleagues took a more realistic view of what most likely awaits them."

Philo thoughtfully tapped the board in front of him. "Perhaps it would be better for all if men conducted themselves by sensible rules such as those they're bound to follow when they play shatranj," he offered. "Now I admit that to the uninitiated, this is a game that may seem mysterious at first, but really it's akin to one of those secret codes used by spies or military couriers. That is to say, once you possess the key to the cipher, what looks like nonsense makes perfect sense."

He lifted one of the jade pieces. "This, for example, is an elephant. Its lot is to move two squares diagonally and it will never confound you by moving otherwise. Would not the ideal of life be to seek and hold to such a pattern of orderliness?"

John chuckled. "Unfortunately, life seems to more often resemble a game of knucklebones, where nothing can be predicted!"

Philo ignored John's remarks. "Do you suppose I might be permitted to teach this game at court?" he wondered. "It is new even in Persia. Surely Aurelius could arrange such a concession for me?"

"But do you not realize how little political power a senator now has?" John paused. It was not just consternation he saw in his old teacher's face, but fear as well. "Perhaps I should not tell you this," he said changing the subject, "but I know you are trustworthy and will keep silent upon the matter. At the order of the emperor I spent the day investigating the deaths of three stylites, the one we ourselves witnessed and two others, identical in their particulars. What do you think of the likelihood of all three being struck by lightning during the same storm? That is what Gaius believes happened."

Philo thought for a time. "I would agree with him. It isn't entirely surprising, considering how openly they presented themselves to the heavens. I see you are disappointed in my answer."

"I had hoped you might have some other explanation. Nevertheless, I intend to have the circumstances further investigated."

"Indeed? Then I should like to offer my assistance."

John shook his head. "I appreciate your offer, but I'm afraid what I have in mind isn't a philosophical task. I've already consulted Felix. He's the excubitor captain and knows the Prefect well, not to mention that he has a horde of well-paid informants in all parts of the city. Between them, they'll discover what is to be found soon enough."

"I thought the excubitors' duty was to guard the palace?" Philo displayed some surprise.

"Yes, but as Felix often says, the defense of the palace starts with control of the streets. So I've asked that he make inquiries about suspicious activities in the forums where the deaths occurred. I'm also rather hoping that the backgrounds of the dead will shed some light on how they came to meet their fate."

Philo pointed out that the trio of stylites would surely have long since lost contact with anyone from their past.

"Many would doubtless say the same," John replied, "but I think you will agree that our pasts have an exceedingly long reach."

Philo appeared eager to pursue questioning his former student, but was interrupted when Peter tapped at the study door and hesitantly entered the room.

"Forgive me for intruding, master, but it is almost dark. I kept food warming near the brazier for you." His gaunt face was pallid.

"Thank you, Peter, but I fear today's duties have upset my humors. Perhaps I shall eat a bite later, but meanwhile please bring us wine. Then, if you wish, go to bed."

Peter left and returned carrying a jug, a good ceramic cup for Philo and the cracked clay cup that was John's favorite, for it reminded him of the woman with whom he had shared it, some years after he left the Academy, the woman with whom he might even now be sharing his life had fate not intervened. He noticed Peter's hand trembling as the servant measured out first wine, then water. A few drops splashed on Philo's board and Peter wiped them away, murmuring apologies and knocking several of the carved pieces over as he did so.

As Peter turned to leave the room, Philo lifted his cup and asked loudly, "Why do you keep such a useless old man as your servant?"

John waited until Peter had shuffled out before replying. "When I asked you earlier how he had been today, Philo, you told me he was going about his duties. You neglected to tell me the effort it was costing him."

The sharpness in his tone seemed lost on the other. He had turned his attention back to his game, idling fingering first one piece, then another.

John said nothing more. His old mentor had described Peter as a useless old man, but it was clear that he might well have been thinking of himself.

＊＊＊

Abandoning his study to Philo, John sought solitude in the garden. He sat on the marble bench beside a pool whose rippled water was replenished by a slow trickle from the mouth of what had once been a splendidly sculpted creature, but was now worn down into a shapeless mass of lichened stone. There was to be no rest there either. The single olive tree near the pool insisted upon reminding him of groves of its ancient kin, which ringed around the Academy. Before he could shake the memory, Anatolius appeared.

"John," his friend called cheerfully as he approached, "Why are you lurking about out here? It's getting chilly. It's going to be a good night to be indoors."

The emperor's secretary was one of a very few allowed unquestioned access to John's house—the emperor himself would have been another in the unlikely event that he ever appeared at John's door—but this evening the Lord Chamberlain was in no mood for visitors. His dark gaze swept down from contemplating the sky above the colonnades surrounding the garden to scour Anatolius' face. He murmured a half-hearted greeting.

Anatolius plumped down beside him. "You look as if your humors need balancing, John. Has Justinian been particularly difficult today?" Before John could reply, the younger man rushed on. "My day was difficult indeed, I may say. I had an extremely trying interview with my father, who trotted out all his usual complaints. What's worse, though, is that he has arranged for my transfer to the quaestor's office." He sighed heavily. "I am hoping I can persuade him to change his mind, but meantime he has at least entrusted me with the final arrangements for a banquet he is holding shortly. I thought I'd consult you for appropriate guidance on certain matters relating to that, John. The matter of the entertainments, for example."

John nodded, relieved that Anatolius had not arrived to share the latest gossip concerning the spectacle of the stylites. He preferred to avoid that subject for a while if at all possible.

"I trust that you weren't contemplating anything too flamboyant, Anatolius?" he said. "Officially it's your father giving this banquet and I imagine many high officials and courtiers will be present. You should therefore be thinking of the less lively sorts of entertainment, if you take my meaning—as I am certain you do."

Anatolius evinced no surprise at John's statement. He was familiar with the Lord Chamberlain's uncanny ability to be aware of every event connected with the palace, not to mention much of what was occurring outside its walls.

"As it happens, I received an personal invitation from your father this morning," John went on, unwittingly destroying at least part of Anatolius' admiration of his powers. "So it will have to be a rather sober affair, I fear, if I am to be present in my official capacity, which I surmise is the intent."

"Well, it certainly won't be as lively as some banquets we could mention," the other grinned, tossing a pebble into the pool. "Now, I have in fact already planned part of the entertainment. It's a presentation certain to please those whose taste is refined, not to say stodgy. In short, it's a tribute to the Muses—singing, flute playing, recitation of poetry, that sort of thing."

"Yet doubtless there will be a few who will frown at a senator inviting actresses into his home," John pointed out with a slight smile.

"No need to worry about that. These aren't actresses. I've engaged Isis and some of her girls," Anatolius replied airily. "Their performance will be perfectly decorous, of course. After all, you know how Isis fancies herself a patroness of the arts."

"True enough. No doubt she'll be happy for an opportunity to show off some of her girls' more refined skills. Still, Anatolius, I must admit that I really don't think that your father would have engaged such entertainers himself. What else did you have in mind? Nothing too outrageous, I trust?"

"No, of course not. There'll be your usual mimes, jugglers, dancers, that sort of thing. But I was trying to think of something a little more unusual that would not shock the guests, and I though you might have heard of some troupe new to the city."

John's recent contretemps with Philo was still fresh in his mind. "Here is one suggestion," he replied. "As you know, my old philosophy tutor is currently my guest. He has been tormenting me with a new game he brought back from Persia. Shatranj, he calls it. It's something to do with trapping your opponent's king. The elephant moves this many squares in one direction and the ship so many in another. I'm afraid I've not shown much inclination to learn to play, so I'm vague about the details, but as it happens he just mentioned the idea that he might eke out a living teaching the game at court. Now, if you were to engage him to entertain at your banquet by demonstrating it to your guests, at the same time that might perhaps assist him in finding employment. And what's more, I do think it could be quite the talking point, without a hint of scandal attached to it. That would certainly please your father."

Anatolius leaned forward intently. "And nobody has seen this game yet, you say? That would certainly weigh heavily with the guests, wouldn't it?"

"The court always appreciates novelty." John hesitated before continuing. "I should caution you, however, that it's possible Philo may not feel inclined to accept your offer. To be blunt about it, he approached your father for assistance and was rebuffed."

"Well, my father might turn your old friend away but I shall certainly talk to him," Anatolius said firmly.

"If he hesitates, you might also consider mentioning that since many powerful men will be present, he may well meet someone willing to provide him with other sorts of employment. I'm certain he's chafing at depending on my hospitality for a roof over his head—that of course is how he sees the situation, not the way I view it. I'm happy to provide him with a home for as long as he wishes, although it's true that we do not always see eye to eye. In fact," John concluded, "he upset Peter with a very unfortunate remark hardly an hour ago."

"He upset Peter yesterday too," Anatolius told him in an interested tone. "Peter was just telling me about it when he let me in. For a man of philosophy, Philo can be very tactless, I must say. Apparently he was complaining the sauce for the duck was not thick enough. Of course, Peter pointed out to him that you preferred plain food and that he was not going to go against the master's preferences. It's probably just as well they are both civilized men, as there are always sharp knives on the kitchen table and even cooks and philosophers must surely be hotheaded at times."

John nodded, adding that Philo had risked all simply by venturing into the kitchen while Peter was cooking, since that something which the servant could not abide. He would have a word with Peter, he thought, and ask him to try to be forbearing. It struck John that it was fortunate he was not married or the ubiquitous philosopher would probably also have invaded his wife's apartments in addition to the study and Peter's kitchen.

"How long has he been here, John? More than two weeks, isn't it?"

John confirmed the fact, noting that Philo had arrived on the Ides of October.

"Well, now November has begun," Anatolius replied, "And it's a lucky month, so they say. Let's hope so, for all of us! But however did he know where to find you?"

"Apparently my fame has spread further afield than I realized," John replied with a frown. "He evidently heard of my good fortune at some time or other."

"Ah, that would explain it. A teacher never forgets those of his students who do well."

"Whether or not they did well as students." John paused, uncertain whether to voice the thought that had come to him. There were many things he shared only with the mosaic girl Zoe, upon whose discretion he could depend completely. Strangely, the only other person with whom he sometimes shared confidences was Anatolius, probably the least discreet man John knew. "It gave me a shock when Peter called me to the door and I saw Philo standing outside," he finally said, "for I had thought that all that part of my past life was dead, had died long ago."

Anatolius, looking interested, asked if Philo appeared very much different.

"He looks much the same. Older, of course. More somber, certainly. The perfect philosopher. You might say he now looks truer to his vision of himself, closer to the ideal image to which he aspires. My first reaction was to tell him to go away."

In the ensuing silence, the water trickling from the stone creature's mouth sounded louder as it splashed into the pool beside them. There was not enough light for John to see the question he knew was written across Anatolius' face.

"You are aware, Anatolius," he continued, "that I am not the person I once was. I have no desire to revisit the world where that other person lived. In fact, I have made every effort to forget my former life."

"But your past has a way of finding you, John," Anatolius pointed out, "which is not to be wondered at considering that you live at the very hub of the world. One seeking to escape his past would do better to dwell in the desert like these hermits the Christians are always gossiping about."

"Even hermits sometimes eventually find their way to Constantinople," John replied ruefully.

"Well, then, you would doubtless find the far reaches of the desert yet more congenial, without so much as an occasional wild-eyed zealot to interrupt your solitude. But why do you continue to harbor that prickly old rogue Philo? Surely he knows other people here that he could stay with until he is able to get an establishment of his own?"

"I don't believe Philo knows anyone else in Constantinople. He spent most of his life at the Academy in Athens and then in exile in the east. To tell the truth, Anatolius, I owe more than you realize to him, for it was he who taught me reading and writing and instilled some philosophy in me. Extending him hospitality for as long as he needs it is the least I can do, for while one cannot repay a kindness, one can at least pass it along by helping someone else."

Anatolius agreed that that was so. As Justinian's secretary he certainly understood the value of literacy. "For after all," he continued, "had it not been that you could read and write, when you arrived at the palace as a slave all those years ago you would not have had the opportunity to put your foot on the ladder that eventually led to your being appointed Lord Chamberlain."

"There is more than that," John said quietly. "Let me explain. You how I was captured by the Persians."

Anatolius nodded. "The gods should be ashamed for allowing such a fate to befall a young man seeking only to buy silks for his lover."

John gave a grim laugh. "Or at the very least the gods might have given me a map showing the location of the border, so that I would not have strayed over it. But then again, quite a few others had also been caught, between ambushes and skirmishes. But we became a burden and would have been killed except that Fortuna at least decided to show some kindness and sent a band of traders, to whom we were of some value if properly prepared. And thus was it done, and I became...a eunuch."

He had paused before spitting out the last two words. Now he sighed. Why was it so difficult for him to name the reality with which he lived every day, one that could never be changed?

"That part of the story you know," he said, forcing himself to continue. "But I have not told you what happened after we were sold to the traders. We set out for a large settlement, a long march away. But when we arrived, already half starved because supplies were not always easy to come by in that wild country, it was discovered that a contingent of captives from an overrun border city had just arrived. So there was no shortage of slaves for sale."

John paused and directed his gaze up to the sky, where bright stars were peering through high, wispy clouds. He continued to gaze at them as he resumed speaking in a near whisper. "We were assembled at the edge of the encampment and forced to kneel in the dirt. The leader of the traders addressed us, saying that since they could neither sell us nor feed us, we were to be freed. First, however, we were to sign an official acknowledgment of our debt to their merciful and magnanimous ruler and so on and so forth.

"He then made his way with kalamos and parchment along our ranks. Thanks to Philo I was able to sign my name. Almost all of the others, being illiterate, made only their marks. When the charade was done, all who could not write were beheaded on the spot."

He heard Anatolius' quick intake of breath.

"Those few of us who were literate were of course extremely valuable, so well worth the bit of gruel necessary to keep us alive until we were finally sold," John concluded quietly. "So as you see, Anatolius, I owe my life to Philo's tutoring."

※※※

Darius, doorkeeper for Madam Isis, hurried along a marble-floored corridor in his employer's establishment. It led from an entrance hall where the gold leaf decorating the capitals of Corinthian columns gleamed almost as brightly as the many coins that changed hands during commerce within the house.

He could not help feeling anxious now that darkness was drawing in. True, nightfall meant an increase in business but it also heralded more dangerous possibilities. Thus the bullish man bit back alarm when he knocked on the rosewood door of Isis' private sitting room and it swung open unaided to reveal a plump woman seated on a softly cushioned couch as she worked intently on her account book.

Tugging his black, curly beard in agitation, Darius stepped into an atmosphere so thick with incense it blanketed the smell of the perfume drenching his beard and long wavy hair. It was only when the door thudded shut that the woman noticed him and set down codex and kalamos next to the silver fruit bowl on the table beside her.

"You must keep your door locked, madam," he scolded. "I might have been an assassin."

"According to my accounts we don't seem to have that many disgruntled customers, Darius," she replied. "Besides, you're always nearby."

"I can't be everywhere at once! And there is much unrest in the streets on account of the strange deaths of those pillar sitters. Unrest outside inevitably finds its way inside, just like bad smells." He drew breath. "But you summoned me?"

The woman seemed lost in thought, caressing the thin gold marriage band she wore in Egyptian fashion on the middle finger of her left hand, although whether as a remembrance of her past or merely as a disguise she had never revealed. "Do you think this stylite business will dampen our customer's appetites?" she finally asked.

The big doorkeeper looked surprised.

"You have been with me for a long time," Isis said with a smile. "I would value your opinion. But before you give it, please sit down." She patted the couch beside her.

Looking even more surprised, Darius seated himself beside his employer. "Well, madam, since you ask I think some of our clients may hesitate to venture out at night if the streets become too unsafe."

"I wasn't thinking of that exactly," Isis admitted. "After all, men regularly throw away their lives for what we offer here. No, what concerns me more is the possibility of too many of our Christian friends developing a sudden fear of their god, who I hear frowns on every form of pleasure."

Darius remarked that unfortunately in that case he could not address the question since he was not a theologian.

Isis laughed. "Well, you are the only person in Constantinople who will admit that! Now, I realize the very idea sounds ludicrous but this very afternoon one of the girls informed me that her client leapt off her bed at a most inopportune moment crying out that he felt hot, that he was about to be consumed by the flames of sin inside him, or some nonsense of that sort. In my time, I've heard many things but I don't recall ever hearing anything like that, not even in my wilder days"

Darius shuffled his feet uncomfortably. Although he had been in Isis' employ for many years, it had been even longer since she had actually practiced the profession that had brought her not a little wealth and some measure of fame in the capital. It was difficult for him to believe this imposing matron must have once been nothing more than a pretty little thing, like the foolish girls in his care. To him she seemed more like a mother.

Changing the subject, he reminded her that she had wished to consult him on a matter of urgency.

Isis had picked up her codex and was looking at its notations. "Oh, yes. Yes, I will need you to accompany me and a few of the girls to a banquet," she informed him absently. "It's to be held at the home of Senator Aurelius. That young rogue Anatolius has engaged me to present a classical entertainment."

"I hesitate to say it, but if I may, I would strongly advise against attending," Darius replied worriedly. "It really is not safe on the streets after dark."

"If custom does in fact begin to drop significantly we may have to consider redecorating," Isis muttered, apparently oblivious to Darius' counsel. "We could adopt a new motif, get new costumes for the girls, offer something extra and different to lure more customers in. Now, what could that be?" She thoughtfully tapped at her small white teeth with her kalamos.

Darius began to repeat his warning, then stopped. He knew from experience that once Isis began reading her accounts nothing else could compete for her attention, not even classical entertainments or musical instruments. Not entirely a bad thing, he reminded himself, noting the largely unused hydra standing against one wall. He certainly did not care to hear again the cacophony of agony the merest touch of her fingers made groan from that instrument.

"What is so fascinating about those numbers, madam?" he asked, his chagrin at his employer's ignoring his advice momentarily overcoming his tact.

Isis ran her finger down a column in her account book, mumbled a few numbers to herself, and bit the full lower lip reddened with wine-dregs whose lush pout had helped accumulate the wealth whose extent she was now calculating. Finally she smiled and looked up.

"Well, my friend, numbers have their own beauty. Then too, my account book always makes me think of my father."

Darius could not conceal his look of surprise.

"He was a tax assessor in Alexandria," Isis explained. "He taught me about numbers. They balance, like lines in well-constructed verse. As I say, they have their own beauty."

"You would have made a fine tax assessor." Darius was thinking about Isis' shrewd evaluation of the girls so often brought to her doorway for sale by their destitute families.

"But that is not a woman's job, is it?" Isis put her account book down and took a handful of dried figs from the silver bowl beside her. "My father was often away from home, valuing estates and villages and such like. I had an uncle who sometimes visited while he was gone. He'd bring me trinkets and tell me stories about his travels for as long as I cared to allow him sit beside me with his hand on my knee."

She paused to chew thoughtfully for a moment or two on a fig. "This uncle of mine," she resumed, "had traveled all over the country and had even seen the high falls of the Nile. But the story that impressed me the most was about the Saraceni. Apparently they were nomads who didn't enter into matrimony as we understand it, but rather hired women to act as their wives for whatever length of time it was agreed the marriage would last. Well, you may say, that's not so very different from my business here. But it wasn't quite the same, really, for the so-called wife brought a dowry with her. More importantly, she had the right to leave her husband after a certain time, if that was what she wished."

"What sort of savages must these Saraceni be?" interrupted Darius.

Isis laughed. "Oh, that struck me as a much more civilized arrangement than the one my parents had. But I had an even better plan, Darius. By reducing the time agreed to and placing the burden of providing the dowry upon the man, I have done quite well. Of course, this uncle of mine, as I later learned, had only heard the tale at second hand and wouldn't have known the Saraceni from his sandals."

Isis finished her figs and licked her sticky fingers daintily. "And what of your family, Darius? Do you have one?"

"Indeed I do, madam, and by making my fortune in this rich city I have been able to be of some assistance to them by sending them what I can."

"But just lately I heard it rumored that you are the son of a village lord."

Darius' face reddened. So that explained his employer's unexpected reminiscences. She had hoped to draw him out.

He asked her where she had heard such a tale.

"From a lady friend of yours," Isis replied lightly. Then, her voice hardening, she added, "who is another employee of mine."

"Madam, I am sorry. I should..."

Isis raised an imperious hand. "Do not explain, Darius. We both know the only circumstances that could produce such ridiculous boasts. Adula will believe anything she is told, which is an attractive trait in our line of work. In my day, I had a great deal of difficulty appearing so credulous. But you are aware of my rule."

Darius hung his head, feeling as if he were being scolded by his mother. "I know, madam. And I assure you, I have not breached your rules before now."

"I know you haven't, Darius, or at least not too often. The wares we offer here would hardly be worth the price they are sold for if they were so poor that a man such as yourself could live among them without ever falling prey to temptation."

"Thank you, madam."

"But remember, although such indulgence might seem to cost my business nothing, unlike a baker's assistant stealing a loaf say, yet each transaction increases the likelihood of those complications which contribute to our expenses. And Gaius for one has been talking about raising his fees for necessary remedies."

Darius assured her that he would be careful not to break her rules again.

"You will have to be, Darius, for I fear Adula is quite smitten with you," Isis replied. "Now, as I said, I have been asked to provide refined entertainment at the senator's banquet. I've already chosen several of my most talented girls. They will represent the Muses and each will declaim poetry. I wish you to arrange for extra guards to look after the doors since you will accompany us because, as you just pointed out, the streets are unsafe right now. And of course even senators and their esteemed colleagues can become bestial after imbibing too freely. Besides," she added with an impish smile, "with a loincloth and a pair of gilded wings you'll make a most striking Eros. Rather a subtle advertisement for our business here, wouldn't you say?"

Chapter Four

As he entered the imperial reception hall with Senator Aurelius the next morning, John's quick eye noted that Justinian was wearing the scarlet boots that were his imperial prerogative. The boots formed an incongruous splash of color in the hall's cavernous marble space, one that always made John think of an enormous sarcophagus.

Whether Justinian's gaudy footwear had been chosen to reflect the importance of their audience or was simply an unfortunate result of inattention to dress, John could not say. Aside from the boots, Justinian was dressed in his usual careless manner which on this occasion meant a purple, gem-studded cloak thrown over a creased tunic that even from a distance looked as if it had been slept in.

"Leave us," Justinian ordered the two excubitors who escorted his visitors into the enormous hall. "These men are known to me. They present no danger."

He waved the guards away with the rolled parchment in his soft, heavily beringed hand. The excubitors withdrew but only as far the reception hall's great bronze doors. No man, however trustworthy he might have seemed a day or even an hour before, was to be left alone with the man who was supreme head of the Roman Empire and God's representative on earth.

The hall was chilly. Its green marble walls, graced by ivory panels webbed with delicate gold leaf traceries, soared up into the shadowed vault of the roof. The only other decorations were one or two statues of celebrated military figures. John had thought more than once that those fortunate enough to be permitted to approach the emperor's throne were in no need of such reminders of Justinian's absolute power over every living thing in the empire. Having observed countless such visitors approach and depart, John felt that most of them counted themselves fortunate to leave with their heads still on their shoulders. He, however, like all those serving at court, was continually camped very close to danger whether he was actually in Justinian's presence or not.

"Caesar," began John, but before he could approach the throne, a simple affair of inlaid wood looking as out of place as a shopkeeper's stool amidst the soaring magnificence of its setting, the emperor leapt up from it. The jeweled fibula fastening his purple cloak slipped, allowing the precious fabric to drag on the floor as he advanced to greet them.

"Lord Chamberlain, I regret I must ask you to put aside preparations for the formal opening of the Great Church for yet another day since I have another task for you. However, no doubt you will be relieved to hear that it will not require you to climb pillars."

Justinian's round, florid face bore its customary bland smile. Some of his enemies characterized that smile as the expression of an idiot, others considered it the blank mask of a demon yet to completely master aping the human form. And some called it both, but not too loudly.

Justinian turned toward Aurelius. "Word has reached my ear that you are not well, senator."

"A matter of minor import, Caesar, about which I did not wish to trouble you."

"I see," Justinian said. "But I do wish to say this. Doubtless you're aware that when physicians failed the ancients, oft times their patients visited the sanctuary of Asclepius. Our medical knowledge is much advanced since those days, but still it does not do to ignore the possibility of divine intervention, while bearing in mind that the faithful now petition Saint Michael rather than a pagan god." His tone clearly conveyed the promise that anyone addressing their petition to the latter could be guaranteed ill health as soon as the fact was discovered. "Perhaps," he continued, "you should consider making a visit to such a shrine."

Aurelius murmured his humble appreciation for the suggestion, which was the same advice he had already received from more than one of his acquaintances.

Justinian fell silent, staring into the vault of the ceiling and then pacing away, forcing his two visitors to follow. He never seemed to stand still. John, who dealt with the emperor nearly every day, could almost believe the popular rumor that Justinian never slept.

"But I shall smooth your way for you, my dear senator," the emperor went on. "I am sending you with the Lord Chamberlain here to visit the shrine of Saint Michael, the angelic physician himself. It is beside the Bosporos. You will have horses at your disposal within the hour."

Aurelius bowed his thanks.

"And now, my friends, we shall turn to the particulars of why you were summoned to see me." The emperor's tone hardened. "It so happens that a crowd of pilgrims has taken up temporary residence in and around that very shrine. It is a holy place, we are all agreed upon that, and therefore worthy of pilgrimage. However, their leader, who conveniently enough calls himself Michael, has apparently taken leave of his senses."

Justinian was off again, scarlet boots padding quietly across the marble floor as John and Aurelius trailed at a respectful distance.

"I received a communication from this Michael a few days ago demanding an audience, if you can believe such audacity!" he went on. "It also stated that certain dire events would soon come to pass if the demand was not met. As vaguely worded a prophecy as any, yet it appears to have been borne out by the deaths of the stylites."

John exchanged a glance with Aurelius before speaking. "Gaius will doubtless have apprised you of the results of our investigations into those deaths, excellency?"

"Indeed he has, and he is of the opinion that they were caused by lightning. He also informed me you are not quite so certain, Lord Chamberlain. Why is that?"

"Lightning does not usually strike so many places at once. Such a remarkable coincidence gave me pause."

"True enough, but then chance can confound our expectations." Justinian pointed out. "Recall that Emperor Carus was struck down by lightning during a military campaign. Even a prudent gambler, if such a person can be found, would happily have wagered the entire imperial treasury against half a follis that such an event would never happen."

"Unless of course the lightning was directed by a divine hand," Aurelius put in.

John glanced quickly at him. Apparently the senator's contemplation of a lengthy ride to the shrine of Saint Michael undertaken while suffering his painful condition had disconcerted him. Suggesting the possibility of divine retribution against an emperor was surely a statement the senator would normally not dream of making.

"I have heard it said that there might be a more worldly explanation for the emperor's death," John quickly remarked, "but most would dismiss that as mere gossip."

"No doubt, Lord Chamberlain, no doubt," Justinian agreed mildly. "But as for these poor holy men, I know you would prefer there was a mystery to be solved, and so would I, rather than suppose that this Michael person possesses the key to knowledge of the future. Thus, you will suspend your investigations and all your other duties for a day or so since there is a journey to undertake." He flourished the parchment he carried. "Here is a second communication from Michael, newly arrived. He again demands an audience, but this time he mentions something of his theology, which is extraordinary to say the least."

"Caesar, if I could have a copy of these messages, it might..." John quickly said.

Justinian waved the letter in a dismissive gesture. "Do you doubt my characterization of them?"

"Of course not." John knew well the folly of contradicting Justinian.

The emperor smiled coldly and continued. "Very well, then. You and Senator Aurelius will go to the shrine as my ambassadors. Meet with this Michael and ascertain all you can of his plans or any other information that will be useful to me. You are there officially as bearing my greetings, but I also wish you to ascertain whether he may be inclined to negotiation."

Justinian addressed Aurelius. "Now, senator, I would not tax your strength further. I will speak to my Lord Chamberlain alone."

As soon Aurelius had departed the hall, Justinian handed John the rolled parchment. "Since you were so interested in reading Michael's letters, you may examine this latest one. First of all, give me your general impressions," he ordered.

John rapidly scanned the proffered parchment. "I note that Michael writes in excellent Greek and his hand is fairly neat, but that his theology is not what the Patriarch would term orthodox."

"Yes, it is an interesting theory, is it not, this idea of theirs, what would you call it, not a Trinity but a Quaternity?" The emperor's lips twitched into what, for the first time since the audience began, might have been a genuine smile. "But this notion of a purely human Christ co-equal with the Trinity, that is the blackest of heresies." Justinian's smile did not waiver as he made this pronouncement. "Still, I intend to compose a thesis upon this startling suggestion. Perhaps we can discover some path to a mutual understanding with these Michaelites, as they apparently call themselves."

John did not doubt that the amount of understanding that might be discovered would depend heavily upon the number of followers Michael could claim. "If there is such common ground, I am certain you can find it, excellency," he said tactfully, "The Patriarch himself bows to your theological prowess."

"Thank you, Lord Chamberlain. And now a question for you personally. What is your opinion on this matter of an audience? Michael's theology is fascinating, if abhorrent, and I confess I am drawn to a dialogue. Perhaps his words are not so blasphemous as they seem at first glance, if we could only decipher their meaning correctly."

John bowed his head in thought. Few knew better than he how dangerous it was to give the emperor the wrong advice.

"Caesar," he said at last. "I would counsel most strongly against granting him an audience. What purpose do the land walls of our city serve but to keep out the enemy? If this Michael should be revealed as such, we should have thrown wide the city gates to let him in without so much as lifting a hand in our own defense."

"True enough, Lord Chamberlain."

John saw disappointment in Justinian's ruddy face and added quickly, "Doubtless you are aware that after Daniel the Stylite came down from his pillar and was allowed entrance to the city, Emperor Basiliscus was forced to flee to Hebdomon."

"Those events are known to me, of course. It is not so long since they took place, after all."

John paused, reluctant to say what he sensed had to be said. "And if I may draw your attention to the end of that particular story?"

Justinian's shoulders stiffened slightly. The eyes that looked out at his advisor from a pudgy mask of affability might have been the burning eyes of a demon. Then he averted his gaze and a strained laugh emerged from his lips.

"Thank you, John. I value your advice, as always. May you and the senator have better success with Michael than all Basiliscus' chamberlains and senators achieved with Daniel. You may depart now."

John's heart did not cease its clamorous pounding until he had bowed his way out of the reception hall into the fresh air of the palace gardens. Everyone in Constantinople was aware of the ending of that particular story, when, in the presence of much of the population of the city, Emperor Basiliscus and the Patriarch had humbly prostrated themselves at Daniel's feet.

❄❄❄

"I'm sure this Michael knows the story of Daniel and Basiliscus as well as anyone else," growled Felix after John had outlined his conversation with Justinian.

John could not help noticing that just the mention of an emperor's humiliation had sent the excubitor captain's scarred hand to the hilt of the short sword at his side, startling a passing clerk who immediately hastened his pace along the peristyle outside Felix' office.

The burly, bearded German directed a rumbling laugh at the retreating scribe's back. "What is it you want, John? Just so long as it doesn't involve me standing down wind of some dead stylites again..."

John assured him that he was not planning any more visits to stylites' columns. "I just wished to ask if you were able to secure any assistance from the Prefect?"

"He wasn't as helpful as usual." Felix frowned. "Perhaps we should discuss this matter elsewhere?" he added cautiously. Around them Justinian's administrative army had embarked on its daily march, ready to wield quill and writ against all enemies of the empire, treacherous tax delinquents, marauding purveyors of unlicensed silks, barbaric bakers asking an unregulated price for their loaves, and all their criminal brethren. Who could say who might be eavesdropping?

"I can't linger, Felix. I was ordered to leave almost immediately! But as to that, I know a route that will provide more privacy for our conversation."

When they were on a narrow path winding between thick plantings of yew trees Felix glanced casually over his broad shoulder and, seeing they had not been followed, took up the conversation while keeping his tone discreetly low. "The Prefect's resources have been stretched rather thin lately, John. The Blues have been growing bolder by the week and now they're hunting in packs. One of my guards was robbed outside the Inn of the Centaurs only three days ago. He was still in uniform and armed! If Justinian would only allow it, I'd be more than happy to hunt those Blues down like the cowardly vermin they are."

"At least the Greens have not yet dared confront them, and just as well, considering the riots that would be touched off if they did," John said grimly.

Felix wondered thoughtfully if the death of the stylites might provide the excuse the factions scarcely needed to be at each others' throats.

"I wouldn't think so," John replied. "But that is one reason I want the matter looked into very carefully. Exactly what aid did the Prefect feel able to offer?"

"He agreed to interrogate his patrols about anything odd or unusual they may have observed in the forums where the deaths occurred. Odd activities, fights, that sort of thing. But as far as questioning vendors and merchants, I fear to accomplish that I'd have to place some of my men on, shall we say, extended leave?"

"I have placed you in an uneasy position, Felix. Your superior is no friend of mine. I can see that that would be difficult."

"But on the other hand, the Master of the Offices is too consumed with political intrigues to take much notice of the work we are doing, so long as we do it quietly and without drawing attention." Felix briefly displayed his wolfish smile. "So perhaps we may be able to assist you more than seems possible at first glance."

John led the way through a garden and into an enormous rectangular building housing the imperial financial offices. Down a narrow, echoing hall they went, descending into the building's lower level. Finally, having navigated a labyrinth of passages that would have defeated the Minotaur, they emerged into a terraced garden from which the long profile of the Hippodrome was visible above a line of poplars planted alongside the palace walls.

"The remains of those poor stylites will have been removed from their pillars by now," John said thoughtfully, "I doubt their bodies have anything left to reveal, and in any event mens' lives are always more instructive than their deaths. Those men were not always perched up beyond the world's reach. Is there some common thread that links them?"

"We have plenty of informants among the religious orders." Felix offered, speaking in a normal tone now they were outside in the open. "It shouldn't be too difficult to ascertain their backgrounds. It might cost more than a follis or two, though."

John stared thoughtfully at the Hippodrome. "I will see that your expenses are discreetly reimbursed, Felix. Now, however, I must be on my way."

Felix tugged thoughtfully at his beard. "I think too much is being made of this Michael, John. Remember, in the end Daniel went back to his pillar. Perhaps Michael's just a simple holy man, like all the rest. I'd wager—if I were still a betting man, that is—he'll tell you that all he wants is permission for a triumphal procession down the Mese and an audience with Justinian."

"I hope you're right," John replied. "I'll know more at the end of my journey."

※ ※ ※

Peter had been beset with misgivings as he watched John and Senator Aurelius ride off on their diplomatic mission. The armed escort provided by the emperor had done nothing to reassure him. It merely pointed at the danger involved in his master's mysterious journey.

Nevertheless he was heartened when Philo departed the house soon afterwards, muttering that there had to be at least one person in this barbaric city who might have need of a man of learning. As a good Christian, Peter had offered a brief prayer on behalf of the philosopher that such a person would be found. He also offered a briefer prayer on his own behalf that such a patron would not be found until night arrived. Then he allowed himself to contemplate the pleasing prospect of a quiet day alone.

Thus when there was a knock on the door he answered it reluctantly. He was relieved to be greeted by a dark-eyed young Egyptian woman.

"Hypatia! It's been some time since you last visited. Come in! Come up to my kitchen."

They had met when Hypatia arrived to serve as gardener for Peter's former owner, Lady Anna. Following their mistress' untimely death, they had both been freed and now Hypatia worked in the imperial gardens, living on the palace grounds although in a house far less magnificent than John's.

The young woman set a basket of pears down on the scarred kitchen table. Reaching into the basket she pulled out an earthenware pot of honey.

"I heard that you have been unwell, Peter," she said, "so I brought along a small gift for you. Now, make certain that you eat it all yourself and don't use it in dishes for John!"

Peter peered under the lid, smiling his surprise and gratitude. The honey was the same golden brown as the woman's skin. "I do occasionally like to indulge in something sweet," he admitted. "Thank you for the gift and your concern, Hypatia. But I am better now, thanks be. And now tell me, how are things with you?"

"Well enough, Peter. Yet I must say that while the palace is certainly a place of luxury, lately there seem to suddenly be many dark corners. I'm grateful that my work keeps me outside in the sunlight, even on colder days."

Peter nodded. "There is indeed much darkness in the city," he agreed sadly, "and not always during the hours of night. Now, before you go back to digging and pruning and such like, sit down and take some wine."

"Why, Peter, can it be that you have taken to imbibing in your old age?" Hypatia asked affectionately, pulling a stool to the table.

Peter smiled again. "I would be offended beyond belief if we had not worked together for the Lady Anna, rest her soul, and I had the measure of your frivolous speech! No, this will be just a splash, for the humor's sake. Gaius prescribed it for a tonic as needed and the master insists that I follow his instructions."

He measured out two small libations.

Hypatia pushed her dark hair away from her face. "And has your kitchen lately been invaded by that young man Anatolius?" she asked with too careless inquisitiveness.

"Anatolius? He is often here, yes, although I sometimes wonder whether he visits to speak with the Lord Chamberlain or to steal my stuffed dates. And why do you inquire?"

The young woman blushed. "Oh, I was just curious. I sometimes see him passing by when I am working in the flower beds."

"Ah." Peter's thoughtful monosyllable had subtle shadings.

"But," she rushed on, "never mind about court dandies like Anatolius. Everyone is abuzz about these Michaelites."

"The emperor sent the master off to visit them," Peter said, "I must say that I do not think he would normally care to mingle over much with such people, a rabble by all I hear, despite their being led by a holy man. But then he must do his master's bidding, just as we must obey ours."

Hypatia took a sip of wine and asked for Peter's thoughts about the situation.

Peter paused to compose his reply. Elderly cooks were not often asked to explain matters of religion, much to his disappointment, and he was happy to have the opportunity to expound his theories.

"I know you worship the gods of Egypt, Hypatia, and so perhaps the finer points of theology do not intrude upon your reflections," he began, quickly adding "and I see you are valiantly trying to conceal your amusement at an old man's words. However, the beliefs of these Michaelites are rather unsettling, to say the least. Their deity, it would seem, is comprised of four parts, one entirely human. It's not so long since that they would have been immediately executed for daring to even breathe such a thing." His voice trembled slightly at the very thought.

"But," he went on, fortifying himself against such rank heresies with a sip of wine, "as to that, they say that this Michael has promised to rid the city of all unbelievers and that those houses about which decent men do not speak will be shuttered, and much else besides."

Hypatia commented that if this band of believers was able to achieve such lofty goals, they would have done what all of Justinian's laws had not yet been able to accomplish.

"True enough. Yet they seem to have had supernatural assistance. It is chilly in here, don't you think? Or perhaps I notice it more as I get older."

Peter got up stiffly and stirred the nearly dormant brazier back to life. "I only hope the Michaelites do not stir up a greater conflagration than this," he murmured.

"The merchant who sold me this honey said there was much disquiet expressed at the inn he patronizes," replied Hypatia. "When inns are awash with such talk you can be certain the streets will soon be equally flooded with trouble. And like you, he mentioned the supernatural. Do you know anything more about that?"

Peter sat down again. "Well, Hypatia, the evening before last," he began, "and I assure you that this is the perfect truth, I saw a fiery angel descending from the heavens. The master insists it was merely one of those unfortunate stylites who were struck by lightning, but that is not what I saw. And like you, I speak to people in the market place so I know that others trembled before the same vision."

Hypatia looked thoughtful rather than surprised. "And this angel, do you think he has arrived to battle on the side of Michael or to defend the city against him?"

"As to that," said Peter, "time will tell." He stared into the flames leaping above the brazier. A few moments before the kitchen had seemed cold, now it felt suffocatingly hot.

"That's true enough. But meantime perhaps you should try some of the honey, Peter? It's said Hippocrates recommended it for a variety of ailments as well as for making sweet confections, for bees distill whatever may be in the plants they visit. I've heard of soldiers poisoned by bees who feasted on rhododendron. But don't worry, those who labored to make this honey for you dined only upon the best wheat!"

Peter could not resist dipping his finger into the honey. "This makes for a better potion than wine," he said, lifting his finger to his lips. "But now tell me, how do their keepers persuade the bees to feed only on wheat or clover?"

"Oh, it's quite simple, really. The hives are placed in the middle of a wheat field or a patch of heather or other flowers, depending which flavor is desired. Bees do not stray far from their homes and so will only visit flowers within a certain area around them."

Peter smiled. "Perhaps we should all take note of the ways of the industrious bee, then, and if at all possible seek not to stray too far afield. If we settle our hearts in the midst of righteousness and remain close to home, then we will never taste evil."

He was discomfited to see that Hypatia suppressing a giggle.

"I'm sorry," she said, patting his hand affectionately. "But truly, when you've had perhaps a sip or two too much wine you could pass for a churchman."

Chapter Five

The crowds bustling through the bright sunlight and long morning shadows striping the colonnaded Mese were being regaled with a sight which, unlike the dining habits of bees, would soon be the subject of hundreds of excited conversations.

A mounted company of heavily armed imperial guards, twenty strong, was clattering along the wide street at a steady pace. In the midst of the contingent rode two men of obvious importance, one a silver-haired aristocrat with tightly drawn lips, the other a lean, somber looking man who might have been mistaken for an ascetic except for his elegant robes and the richly embroidered mantle lying over his shoulders. Passersby stopped to stare, as they might have paused to listen to distant thunder, while hoping that the storm surely being heralded would break over someone else's head.

John was aware of the faces gaping at him. A private man, their attention made him uncomfortable. He knew, however, that both route and escort were designed precisely to gain such attention. The emperor could have ordered his envoys ferried across the narrow mouth of the Golden Horn from where it was but a short ride to Saint Michael's shrine beside the Bosporos. But, John guessed, Justinian's agents were already spreading word of this diplomatic mission far and wide and before long, all over the city, people would be exclaiming that indeed it was true, the most pious of emperors had accorded Michael the respect due such a man. Hadn't they seen with their own eyes the lofty officials dispatched to visit him as Justinian's emissaries?

As to whether this display of magnanimity would serve to placate the restless populace as much as Justinian apparently imagined or would simply encourage further support for the heretics, John could not say.

So the showy entourage made its way through the bustle of the circular Forum of Constantine, past the rotunda of the senate house and the towering column surmounted not by some ragged stylite but a gleaming statue of the city's founder, and through the much smaller but still busy Forum Tauri beyond which the Mese forked. Here they turned not south, towards the Golden Gate and the Via Egnatia which would have taken them, after weeks of hard and dangerous travel, to the ancient capital Rome itself, but toward the west.

Only when they were beyond the inner city's wall and away from the crowds did John speak. "Do you wish to stop and rest for a time?" he asked Aurelius.

"I would rather continue and have the journey over with that much sooner." Although the senator spoke without taking his gaze from the flat stones of the roadway in front of them John could see the pallor of his face. Recalling Justinian's comment about sending the senator to the shrine for a cure, he couldn't help remembering Philo's reference to the emperor's cruel concept of mercy.

"Have you consulted Gaius about this ailment?" he asked, concerned.

"Unfortunately, yes. He had me taking a vile concoction of naphtha which, I have heard, can kill as easily as cure. But since it failed to render either service to me, he has demanded I fast for three days. If the stone has not passed by then, he intends to play the surgeon."

They were riding through one of the cemeteries that dominated the area between the inner and outer walls of the city. Modest burial mounds and grave markers were scattered around and between sheltering cypress trees. Aurelius waved his hand at the tranquil scene, adding in an undertone "If worse comes to worse, I'd as soon rest here in three days' time than lie under that drunkard's knife. The pain has been so desperate that I have actually contemplated visiting my country estate and sacrificing to Salus. On the other hand, now there's the matter of this shrine we're visiting. Many have dreamt cures for their ailments there, or so I have heard."

John remained silent.

Aurelius continued thoughtfully, as much to himself as to his companion. "Consider the well-known case of Aquilinus. He was starving to death after a fever because he was unable to keep nourishment in him. When his physician could do nothing, he went to St Michael's shrine, carried there, so they say, by one of his servants. And what happened but at the shrine Aquilinus dreamt he would be cured by dipping his foot into some strange sludge of wine and pepper and honey. Oh, his physician was doubtless much put out and, I am willing to wager, called it a cure flying in the face of medical knowledge and probably much worse. But since the man was half dead anyway, he determined he would do as he dreamt and did so and indeed was cured."

John pointed out sympathetically that as far as treating illness was concerned, sometimes in battling them it was necessary to face the knife.

Aurelius laughed harshly. "You preach to me in the same manner in which I lecture my son! What you say is true enough, John. But a warrior does not have his legs trussed up over his head while the physician standing behind him—how may I put this delicately—coaxes the cursed stone along in a fashion that would make even a powdered court page blush. I could endure the knife that follows without flinching, but not the indignity that precedes it."

"We can't always choose what we must endure. Indignity, at least, can be survived."

The senator realized that his words had been ill chosen and his expression grew even more stricken. He apologized.

"You don't have to excuse yourself for reminding me of what I have endured, Aurelius," John replied. "But although you might choose to leave us prematurely for your own reasons, think of Anatolius. He is certainly a man of many talents, but..."

"Yes, yes, I know," Aurelius muttered, sparing John the impossible task of finding some tactful phrase to describe Anatolius' dangerous blend of impetuosity and impracticality. "I'm sure he has informed you about his new prospects?"

"He went on at greater length about the banquet, but he did mention you are planning to launch him upon a legal career."

Aurelius winced, perhaps from the jolt of his horse stepping down harder than hitherto. "You sound almost as enthusiastic as my son about the prospect, John."

"It's a good plan, though. Anatolius tends to drift with his fancies and those ponderous legal phrases may serve to anchor him. However, he still needs occasional guidance."

Aurelius shook his head wearily. "Not guidance, John. Let us be honest. He still needs to be protected from himself."

The senator fell silent and few words were exchanged during the remainder of the tedious journey. Both men knew that just as they had been ordered to observe Michael and report back to Justinian, so one or more of their escorts would be under orders to observe the emissaries.

Having passed beyond the high mortar and stone walls built to protect Constantinople on its only side exposed to land attack, the mounted party proceeded northward around the end of the Golden Horn and then back east along that narrow drowned valley. The way was lined with small settlements alternating with fields and villas set amid country estates. The city they had left was visible across glassy water bristling with ship masts. Tenements and churches clung to the side of a long ridge whose highest points formed six of the seven hills of Constantine's new Rome.

Their journey was more rapid than John anticipated. Other riders, pedestrians and the drivers of carts and wagons, realizing at a glance that the company was about imperial business, readily vacated the narrow road at their approach. Although such highways were a boon to trade their real purpose was military, having been built wide enough to accommodate the passage of a single war chariot.

Only when they turned north in the direction of the Euxine Sea were the travelers forced to slow their pace as the road grew increasingly congested with people on foot, predominantly peasants and laborers by their simple tunics. As they neared the shrine, more than one slave-borne litter and even a covered carriage could be seen, swept along in the human tide flooding the road.

"This crowd reminds me of the day before a celebration," observed Aurelius, before leaning down to address a sturdy farmer leading a donkey burdened with baskets of fruit. "Shouldn't you be going in the other direction, to the market?"

The farmer looked up fearfully. "I would on any other day, excellency, but today I am taking an offering to Michael, to ask for his blessing upon me and my family."

"Justinian will not be pleased to learn how quickly the man's fame is spreading," John remarked.

The senator made no reply. His eyelids had narrowed to slits and his lips, drawn tight for hours now, looked nearly bloodless as his horse, made restive by the crowd, snorted and pawed at the ground, jolting its rider painfully.

The guards, who earlier had been talking and laughing in a relaxed manner, became as restive as the horses. They shouted warnings, shaking spears to underline them.

"Take care," John admonished the nearer of their guards. It would not take much to touch off a disturbance. A carelessly handled weapon drawing blood, for example.

They finally saw St Michael's shrine after cresting a long hill. A rectangular marble building with a flight of steps leading steeply up to its columned portico, the shrine sat at the far edge of a grassy open space where the ground dipped away from the road before dropping abruptly to the Bosporos. The building was indistinguishable from hundreds of other small temples, Christian and pagan alike, to be found in all parts of the empire, but it was here that the sluggish river of humanity spilled off the narrow road into a wide lake swirling around the shrine.

The company rode to the foot of the shrine's steps, forcing a path through the massed pilgrims. The murmur of the crowd gradually rose higher as it took note of the imperial party. When several excubitors had taken up posts at the shrine's doorway beside a pile of baskets, sacks and amphorae that had accumulated there, John quickly dismounted as Aurelius struggled off his horse, grimacing in pain.

"Well, John," the senator muttered, "I hope you know the proper ceremonial greetings when meeting some holy vagabond fresh off the road from who knows where, because this is something quite beyond my own experience."

A fresh breeze had been scouring the shrine with the sharp smell of the sea, but as it subsided momentarily John detected from within the building another odor, a disturbing blend of sweet perfume and the acrid smell of the sick. He had just noted it when an ruggedly-built man almost as tall as himself emerged from the shrine.

The man's size and the hard lines of his face suggested a military background, but he appeared unarmed and wore a long white robe. He offered no hint of a formal greeting nor did he make any effort to hide his disdain as he looked down the steps at the emperor's emissaries.

"I see Justinian has declined the opportunity to meet personally with the master. However, there is yet time enough for that. You may follow me," he instructed.

If John had intended to reply he would have had no opportunity because the acolyte, as he supposed the man to be, immediately vanished back into the building. Aurelius gave a grunt of displeasure. Their visit was not beginning well.

Inside the shrine, a long nave ran between two aisles accessible through archways. The shadowy aisles and their niches were filled with figures, some reclining on stone benches along the walls, others lying on straw pallets on the floor. A harsh cough echoed, then another. The rasp of labored breathing and low, monotonous moaning echoed around the stone walls. The smell of illness was overpowering.

"These poor creatures are seeking the aid of Saint Michael, the heavenly physician," noted the big acolyte. "And so by faith they shall be healed."

Dimly seen figures moved around, attending to the sick. A knot of acolytes, going by the fact that their robes were identical to that worn by their guide, stood conversing in the center of the nave. As he went by them, John noted the eastern eyes of a Persian, an Egyptian's hawk nose and wavy hair, a man in a himation who could have been Philo's brother, not to mention two men who looked to be of sturdy peasant stock, possibly farmers temporarily absent from their land. Michael's theology appeared to appeal to a dangerously heterogeneous group, it seemed.

John was weighing how he could best reveal this unfortunate discovery to Justinian as they reached the end of the nave, where a plain marble altar stood before a slitted window in the back wall. A dusty beam of sunlight lanced through the lazy coils arising from two perfumed candles, the only items adorning the altar.

The swirling smoke stung John's eyes. He blinked away tears and suddenly there was a figure standing in front of him.

Michael was not the begrimed, weather-beaten desert hermit John had half-expected. He was a slight man of elegant appearance, dressed in an immaculate white robe. His head was shaven, his face gaunt but smooth. Sunken eyes flashed in the candlelight like water at the bottom of a well as he inclined his head in silent greeting.

Why did an invisible hand wrench at John's vitals at the sight of this man? Fighting back his inexplicable unease, John made his formal salutation.

"The Emperor Justinian, conqueror, ever Caesar, conveys to the pious Michael his greetings. We stand before you as his eminent representatives, the revered Senator Flavius Aurelius and myself, John, Lord Chamberlain to the emperor."

Michael regarded his two visitors placidly. "I look forward to consulting you concerning the arrangements for my meeting with your most eminent emperor, Lord Chamberlain."

He spoke softly but even so could not disguise the unnatural timbre of his voice. John understood then what troubled him.

Michael was a eunuch.

"The emperor has graciously granted audiences to many pious men such as yourself," Aurelius said.

"I see," Michael replied with a slight smile. "So there have been many who were heralded by all-consuming holy fire?"

John stood silent for the length of several heartbeats. He abhorred dealing with other eunuchs, nearly all of whom had been maimed as children. He had reached manhood before being castrated and did not like the thought that many would mistake him for one of those effeminate creatures whose nature had been prevented from taking its proper course. Aurelius' suddenly raised voice abruptly brought his attention back to their mission.

"We regret that we have not been granted authority to escort you into the city at this time. The emperor has instructed us only to offer you his felicitations and the prospect of an audience to be arranged at his convenience, a boon that few receive and many would envy you."

"We must hope then that Justinian will be able to invite me into the city for an audience with him before the cleansing fire strikes again. When you return, please convey to him the matter we will be discussing when we finally meet."

"And what matter would that be?" Aurelius inquired stiffly.

"Concerning my ascending to the patriarchy and, of course, to co-equal rulership with Justinian." Michael replied calmly.

Aurelius stared at Michael in amazed disbelief.

John remained silent. He realized now that they were dealing not merely with a eunuch, but with a madman. Or at any rate, he reminded himself, a man who was obviously familiar with the story of Basiliscus prostrating himself at the feet of Daniel, and furthermore a man wise, or perhaps foolish, enough to attempt to use it to his own advantage.

It was obvious that there was nothing further to be learned today. John was preparing to make a formal farewell when, without warning, Michael stepped toward Aurelius and grasped the senator's shoulders.

"You have been unwell." Spoken in a whisper, the words took on an even more abnormal timbre. One could almost imagine that the voice did not emanate within the frame from which it emerged.

Michael closed his eyes for an instant, then stepped back quickly, causing the perfumed smoke to writhe about him. "Now, however, you are healed," he said. "Go back to the emperor with this miracle."

❊ ❊ ❊

On their homeward journey John and Aurelius rode for a long while in silence. They were proceeding back along the Golden Horn before John finally spoke.

"I judge this Michael to be a dangerous man indeed, Aurelius. All his talk about divine retribution and miracles is bound to stir up unrest."

"Considering that he seemed to be implying that could be more deaths, I have to agree," Aurelius said. "But surely you do not take his claims seriously?"

John lowered his voice before replying. "Fire is sacred to many religions and to be honest, I do not see it being used as a tool for divine retribution. Those stylites died by some human agency, I am certain of it. The sooner I can discover who murdered them the faster peoples' fears can be laid to rest. And also of course the sooner this fraud can be sent back to whatever desert he emerged from, if he is not executed, that is."

"You have allowed him to upset you, John." Aurelius observed. "Is it possible he is simply seeking to take advantage of some strange but natural occurrence that happened to kill those unfortunate stylites?"

John shook his head. "I think not, and considering the size of the crowd gathered around him, I wish I were already back on the other side of the water looking for the person who is really responsible."

Aurelius' gaze moved to the glittering waters of the Golden Horn and the city beyond. He too wished he were back there, if only to be spared the painful jolting of this seemingly endless ride.

"For all our sakes, I hope you're right, John," he said. "Yet despite my own religious inclinations I do wish the man possessed the powers he claims because the miracle he claimed for me would be exceedingly welcome, to say the least. But as to your investigation, didn't you mention Felix was continuing in your absence? Certainly he is a capable and trustworthy man. Perhaps he will have some information for you by the time we arrive back."

"True enough, Aurelius. As you say, investigations are proceeding in good hands."

Chapter Six

Philo was questioning yet another of the pilgrims among the crowd milling around the base of the column which had until recently been home to Matthew the Pure.

"Why, I was standing here on this very spot, as the Lord is my witness," declared the pilgrim, a middle-aged man with weather reddened skin, an unkempt beard and a cast in one eye. It seemed to Philo that the grubby traveler had looked flattered to be asked for assistance by such an obviously learned gentleman as he.

"I'd just arrived," the pilgrim went on, "having come all the way from Galatia. At least when I get home I shall certainly have a story to tell, no doubt about that. But I never heard Matthew preach!" he added petulantly.

"Just as well," declared a nearby crooked-nosed man leaning heavily on a stick. "You have seen proof of what Matthew's words were worth, which is to say nothing at all. He was consumed from within by his own evil, just as Michael said!" He began to quote scripture.

Philo sighed. These pilgrims, he had learned, were extremely eloquent on the subject of their beliefs but not overly forthcoming when it came to facts. Nevertheless, it was barely the ninth hour of the day and he had already visited the other two columns whose occupants had died so horribly. He was now completing his self-appointed task in the forum he and John had been passing through at the time of the deaths. He had certainly earned the coins Felix had paid him, he thought smugly. It had not been difficult to convince the gruff excubitor captain that John had recommended that his old mentor assist in the investigation and for only minimal remuneration. Certainly, given the success of his questioning, John would forgive him the small lie.

"Could you tell me what precisely you observed?" Philo asked the Galatian pilgrim, interrupting the nearby man's droning recitation of sacred verses.

"Just what everyone's been saying. He was consumed by fire from within. One moment he was looking down over the railing, spreading his arms in benediction, the next he was on fire. I saw it with my own eyes."

"You mean you think you saw, but you're half blind," put in a stout, clean-shaven man who had joined the growing cluster of curious spectators around Philo and his informant. "But what I heard was that a fiery hand reached down out of the clouds."

"Nonsense!" someone at the back of the group shouted. "I was right here at the time. The flames came out of his fingertips and ran up his arms."

"The fingertips of what?" inquired another voice. "Matthew's hand or the hand from the clouds?"

It was no different here than at the other columns. Everyone had seen it happen or had heard in detail about the event, but no one could agree on any of the particulars. Perhaps it was not surprising, thought

Philo. He had himself observed no more than anyone else since Matthew had already been on fire when he looked up.

"Do you know anything about Matthew's life?" Philo changed his line of questioning by contriving to appear a garrulous old gossip.

The pilgrim he addressed inclined his head slightly. "Why, I believe he was from Cappodacia, " he began vaguely. "What he did before he began to preach I couldn't say. But I did hear that before he journeyed here, he lived in an abandoned church on the road to Pergamom. A cousin of mine lives nearby and he told me about this church. Years ago, it was invaded by demons, so it seems, but Matthew entered it anyway and dared to spend that night and many subsequent nights. For weeks, it seems, the foul beings pelted the church with stones that appeared out of thin air, but finally he vanquished those ghastly beings." The pilgrim paused thoughtfully and a look of pain crossed his weathered features. "Yet it would seem he was actually having commerce with demons all the while. My wife will be sorely disappointed when she hears about that and I shudder to think what my cousin will say."

Several of those standing near Philo became engaged in arguments about the origin of the fire, the nature of the stylite and the exact wording of the scriptural verses recently recited. Philo shook his head. These Christians, he thought, could never agree upon anything.

Leaving them to their arguments, Philo paced thoughtfully around the granite column. It was the tallest of the three he had visited. This afternoon there were no baskets of offerings at its base, he noticed. The pilgrims had apparently gathered there out of curiosity or perhaps to share their stories, or possibly because they had undertaken long and arduous journeys with this destination in mind and wanted to rest for a while before returning to their distant homes with an astonishing tale to tell. Philo glanced around idly, not certain what it was that he sought.

The Galatian pilgrim had become embroiled in a loud dispute with the crooked-nosed man who had now apparently lost his need of the stick on which he had been leaning, considering how vigorously he was shaking it at his opponent.

"You question Michael?" shouted the stick waver. "Stand back, sir," he cautioned Philo, "for this evil one is about to erupt into flames. Move away for your own safety!"

"I was merely wondering about Michael's choice of sinners to strike down," countered the florid man hastily. "Matthews's secret heart may have been blackened with sin, but no-one can dispute that he suffered exposure upon his pillar, while some of his so-called brethren dwell in comfortable huts atop theirs. And," he added with a sniff of outrage, "Eutropius, as is well known, crawls through a trap door into the hollow of his pillar when darkness falls, there to spend the night well protected from unkind weather."

"Calumny!" raged the other. "Eutropius has braved the elements day and night these fifteen years!"

"It's merely thirteen—"

"Stand back, sir!" his opponent addressed Philo. "Guard your fine robe! Can't you see sparks beginning to emerge from this vile creature's ears?"

The philosopher could bear no more. He, a man who had spent his life debating the nature of beauty and order, was now cast adrift in a city where zealots came to blows to claim for their particular religious champions the most disgusting cases of extreme physical mortification. It was intolerable.

Still, hawkers in the streets did cook the most succulent piping hot peas, he reminded himself, having just noticed one such vendor on the opposite side of the forum.

After filling his stomach while hardly emptying his purse, Philo decided to abandon his investigation and turn his steps homeward. It was not a long walk to John's house. He had merely to go past the Church of the Holy Wisdom, a building that was certainly magnificent but, according to John, was not yet consecrated, then by the Baths of Zeuxippos, skirt the wall of the Hippodrome and so into the palace grounds. He would be back in plenty of time for the evening meal. Perhaps Peter had prepared duck again.

✷✷✷

Two hours later with the sun already grazing the roofs of the surrounding tenements, Philo was forced to admit to himself that he was lost. He had vainly tried to orient himself by the relentlessly dropping sun, but the streets and alleys he followed obstinately refused to lead him in the proper direction.

He was aware of the narrowness of the peninsula on which Constantinople was located. Simple logic, he told himself, proved that he was either moving in a circle, or had somehow turned inland—west—for otherwise, considering how long he had been walking, he would have already fallen into the sea. Logic, however, refused to reveal to him exactly where he was. And small as it was, Constantinople was enormous compared to the familiar grounds of the Academy with its ordered paths.

At first, from sheer stubbornness, he had refused to ask passersby for assistance. Now, he noted with alarm, he seemed to have wandered into a shabbier quarter. Its few pedestrians had a rough look about them, so since he thought it would be extremely imprudent to reveal himself as a stranger to the city, alone and lost, he kept walking.

The narrow street he was now traversing was rendered prematurely dusky by the overhanging tenements that crowded out the fading daylight. He strode along at the best pace he could muster, fighting off exhaustion and trying to appear confident of his destination rather than terrified. Lining the way there were only the blank walls of the tenements' lower floors and workshops already closed for the day, or perhaps shut forever, having ceased trading entirely. Looking ahead, he noticed a patch of sunlight where the street opened out on to another forum. He forced his suddenly shaking legs to move faster. Surely, at last, he was coming to some familiar landmark?

But when he emerged into the open space, he found only an empty, weed-infested expanse of flagstones. Atop a dry fountain set in their middle, some forgotten ruler surveyed the surrounding warehouses holding the empire's children with an imperious and uncaring marble gaze.

Philo had already walked past this fountain once.

Or had he?

Exhausted, he dropped down to sit on its rim, sending a rat skittering away.

Again his thoughts turned to the Academy. He had never expected to be cast out of those ordered and tranquil surroundings into the unruly and dangerous world beyond.

He commanded himself to settle his mind and consider the problem, as if he had become one of his own flighty students. Which had been the last place he had recognized? The Forum Constantine? Well, it was huge and circular and who could mistake the statue of the city's founder glittering atop its central pillar? He had considered going from there down the Mese, since he knew it would lead him straight to the Great Church.

Why hadn't he done so? He had been lost for some time before he stumbled into the Forum Constantine. But instead of thanking the gods for their favor, he had chosen instead to insult their kindness by electing to take what he foolishly thought would be a quicker route home. Thus, he had crossed the forum, plunged into an alley, and almost immediately lost his way again.

That moment of decision was so clear in his mind— and so maddeningly irretrievable. If only he could return to that time and rectify his mistake. Well, such was life, he told himself, realizing even as he muttered the words that if he were, indeed, still at the Academy, his erstwhile colleagues would scornfully demolish such a shallow and uninstructive bit of trite philosophizing.

Philo stood up and looked around. Since John's house was at the eastern end of the city he should be moving away from the sinking sun, which he now realized uneasily he would not have for guidance much longer. He had just started towards one of the streets radiating from the forum, one that seemed to run most nearly in that direction, when three figures appeared.

Their long hair and beards immediately put him in mind of the Persians among whom he had spent his years in exile. However, thanks to John's recent explanation he now realized that these were not foreigners, but rather fashionable members of the Blue faction.

Had they been following him? These were youths who had no compunction about robbing passersby in the middle of crowded forums, or so John had warned him.

The three Blues paused for a moment. Then one of them pointed toward Philo and called out. "Is it not the old man we were talking to a day or so ago? How fortunate we are to have found you by yourself. Come over here and we can resume the discussion your thin friend so rudely interrupted!"

The man's words sounded friendly enough, but Philo detected only mocking menace in his tone.

He ran away.

He was much too old to run so hard and a philosopher's voluminous and intricately draped himation was designed for thinking while pacing in a stately manner, rather than fleeing for one's life. But he ran anyway, cutting first down one alley and then into another, back and forth, like a rabbit racing before the fox.

He came to a gasping halt in a narrow passageway, closely resembling the others he had passed through by being darkened by overhanging buildings leaning overhead. The sun was now no more than a faint orange glow at its mouth, but at least as he stood trying to quiet his loud, ragged breathing, he could discern no sounds of pursuit.

Futilely he attempted to tuck his disordered robes back into some semblance of orderly neatness. Now that darkness was creeping in ever more quickly, he could think of nothing else to do but seek out some sheltered nook in which he could safely pass the night.

With this in mind, he continued slowly down the passageway, his tired eyes directed toward the rectangle of dimness marking its exit. He did not observe the dark shape huddled against the base of the right hand wall until he was suddenly made aware of it by its sickening stench. Revolted, he glanced down briefly as he scurried by.

But as always, he was ruled by his curiosity and after a few steps onwards, he went back to investigate.

Holding his breath, he bent over the shape.

It was the corpse of a severely burned man.

Philo gagged and backed away. Backed into a barrel chest as hard and unyielding as the dirty walls hemming him in.

He turned and looked up into the curly-bearded face of a huge man, who although doubtless in the process of planning an imminent attack upon Philo, was smiling jovially down at him.

❊❊❊

Felix had served the empire on many battlefields, from the forests of his far-off homeland of Germania to the no less dangerous streets of Constantinople. Few doubted his courage. Yet he looked strangely ill at ease lounging on the couch in Isis' lamp-lit sitting room.

The other occupant, a man even larger than Felix and perching incongruously on a tiny, gold-inlaid stool, took the liberty of pointing out this interesting fact.

"Well, Darius, it's one thing to visit Isis' house for pleasure," Felix growled bluntly, "but quite another when you realize you must make a special visit to inform your friends they're likely in danger. The streets are becoming worse by the hour, as you well know."

Although he had always been a military man and thus was accustomed to austerity, Felix had to admit the warmly perfumed room had a certain charm. Here it would be easy to sink into the soft embrace of the couch's red and gold pillows and let the outside world go to Hades in its own way. The problem was, of course, that the outside world was just as likely to take a detour and march loudly through this cozy sanctuary on its way to that place. He observed as much to Darius.

The other looked thoughtful. "Yes, the world certainly passes through madam's establishment, but of course it's usually bent on more pleasant matters than attempting to close it down. And you say that that could well happen if these Michaelites obtain the ear of the emperor?"

"So it seems. Of course, it won't just be this house that will be shuttered. After all, a place such as this is not everyone's idea of heaven!" Felix replied straight faced, since he, along with John, Anatolius and a number of others at court were of necessity secret followers of Mithra and Darius well knew it.

The burly captain leaned forward to pluck a small, fragrant apple from the silver bowl set on a small ivory table in front of the couch. He examined the fruit, put it back in the bowl and then looked unhappily around the room.

It had been a long day. He had spoken with numerous officials after a mercifully brief audience with the emperor and as he placed together a rumor heard here with news reported there, adding a scrap of privileged information inadvertently alluded to elsewhere, the picture slowly forming was indeed a frightening one. He was about to say as much to Darius when the door opened and Isis swept in.

Darius rose ponderously to place an upholstered chair for her near the couch. She sank into it in a cloud of perfume and a thankful wave of a beringed hand.

"My dear Felix," she began, helping herself to an apple. "Let us be blunt. Is it your opinion that Darius and I must now make plans concerning the safety of my house and my girls?"

Felix nodded. "Indeed it is. I was just discussing some general strategies with Darius and he agrees it would be an excellent plan to post two extra guards in the front hall as well as at the door into the back alley. And also I think it might be best to keep your shutters closed and secured at all times."

Isis grumbled that she would be forced to buy more olive oil for the extra lamps that would thus be rendered necessary. "Still, better the expense than stones through our windows," she concluded. "Perhaps I should also consider purchasing protection until this latest storm passes. What do you think?"

"The factions may provide such useful services, as they call it although most of us would call it extortion," replied Felix, "but I doubt that these religious zealots would even consider accepting any such useful financial arrangement."

"Are they so otherworldly they don't need a nomisma or two now and then?" Isis wondered. "If so, I fear those of us who are still corporeal may be facing difficult times indeed. But who knows, all this trouble might turn out to be the sort of cloudburst that dies before it's crossed the city walls."

"Perhaps, madam," Darius commented, "but may I also suggest that it would be wise to make such alternative arrangements in case it becomes necessary to abandon this house for a time? Of course, I would be honored to continue guarding you personally for as long as you wish."

Isis glanced up sharply from cutting her apple with a silver knife. Popping a sliver of fruit into her mouth, she chewed thoughtfully. "Yes, you are quite right," she finally said. "My girls all have special friends among their clients to whom they could go for temporary shelter if need be. As for myself and Darius, I wonder if I could impose upon John for hospitality if worse comes to worse?"

"I don't think he would refuse since he has recently opened a hostel for unemployed philosophers," Darius put in with a jovial smile. "I found one such not far off only an hour or so ago, hopelessly lost, and assisted him in returning safely to John's house. He talked all the way there!"

Felix uttered a mild oath. "Philo! He wasn't unemployed today, though, since he was working for me. He told me John had recommended his services. But now I doubt he was able to find much information when he couldn't even find his way home."

"I would not say that," replied Darius. "In fact, he'd just stumbled on a charred corpse."

"Corpses are a common affliction, I fear." Isis' spoke lightly but her expression betrayed fear. Fire anywhere nearby was a matter of the gravest concern. For every sturdy brick structure that Constantinople boasted, ten shoddy wooden buildings were piled like kindling around splendid forums and public buildings.

"I've already notified the Prefect of the discovery," Darius said.

"Do you think it has something to do with this Michael?" Isis wondered.

"I would hardly think so," Felix answered. "Why should he or his deity wish to inflict such a death upon some poor soul in an alley?"

Chapter Seven

"Death by fire is certainly not a pretty sight," said Philo, between bites of one of the honey-sweetened cakes piled on the platter Peter had just set down on the kitchen table. "John, no doubt you'll recall that Plotinus was of the opinion that of all material things, fire possesses the most splendor. However, if he had witnessed two such deaths in a span of three days I believe he might well have changed his mind."

The heat from the cheerfully glowing brazier had steamed the window panes, obscuring their view of the waking city. With the rising wind came the clatter of carts and the cries of gulls. John sat across the table, sipping the cup of water that was all he customarily took in the mornings.

"But this beggar," Philo rattled on, "for surely he must have been a beggar to die in such circumstances, what evil could he have committed to bring such wrath upon himself? The poor have so much less opportunity for evil doing, do they not? Could he perhaps have been a murderer? Yet the city must be full of rich and powerful people who have committed many crimes, crimes that would be beyond the capacity of a beggar and equally worthy of punishment."

"The man started a fire for warmth on a chilly night and fell asleep too close to the flames. It is not uncommon." John set down his empty cup.

"Now, you were telling me what you learned about the three dead stylites," he went on. "There was Matthew, who braved the stone throwing demons in an abandoned church, but what of the other two?" John had been horrified to learn of Philo's adventure but since the deed was done it seemed best to attempt to derive some benefit from it.

"Well, John," Philo began eagerly. "I haven't imparted to you even half of all that I learned. Peter, I must say that these are excellent honey cakes. They remind me that Virgil said that a bee contains a particle of divine intelligence."

Peter turned away from rearranging utensils and bowls on the kitchen shelves. "If he is correct then you must contain more than a particle of intelligence yourself, sir, because you have partaken much of the work of those intelligent creatures. These cakes are quite tasty, master. Perhaps you should try one." The look he directed at Philo clearly added "before he eats them all."

John declined politely. He found it difficult to face food before midday. "You ascertained the other stylites were called Gregory and Luke?"

"That is correct." Philo studied the platter of cakes before selecting another. "Several of the pilgrims I interviewed knew of Gregory. He was reputedly a small landholder near Tyana. Then one day he was bitten by a snake and fell into a deep trance. His doctors gave him up for dead. Then—you will never guess—a miracle occurred. Isn't that always the case in these tales? Anyhow, it seems he suddenly awoke but unfortunately he was paralyzed."

As Philo paused in his narration to take another bite, Peter seized his opportunity. "Wasn't Gregory the one they carried to a nest of snakes? A friend of mine has taken much comfort from his sermons. He'll have to find solace at another pillar now."

Philo frowned. "Your servant, who has so kindly interrupted us, is essentially correct, John. It seems that as soon as Gregory awoke he imparted to his grief-stricken family a vision he had had of a nest of snakes in a certain grove of trees outside the town and requested to be taken there. And when they came to the place they found it to be so, and once among the snakes Gregory miraculously recovered, there was much rejoicing and many hosannas, all that sort of thing. He stayed there, and as word spread he preached with amazing eloquence to multitudes of pilgrims who, of course, kept at a respectful distance although personally I suspect that was more because they could not rely upon another miracle should one of them get bitten."

"But he who has seen the Lord is armored even against the serpent's fangs," Peter put in, making his religion's mystical sign.

"I prefer your servant's culinary efforts to his philosophy," Philo muttered to John.

"Yet if it were not for Matthew's token, which you administered to me yourself, I would not be here to cook for you," Peter pointed out sharply.

Philo sniffed. "Yes, well, that was an interesting coincidence, wasn't it? Perhaps the foulness of the medication revived you? But to resume my tale, after several years' journey along a regular thoroughfare of vermin-infested caves and ruins, Gregory finally found his way to Constantinople, where no doubt he found himself immediately surrounded by more snakes than populate the deserts of Arabia and all equally deadly, despite possessing legs."

John smiled thinly. "And concerning Luke?"

"He arrived here more recently than Gregory, who ascended his pillar about four years ago. I wasn't able to learn what Luke did before he took up mortification of the flesh but I did ascertain that he began his vocation near Antioch. A man who owned extensive olive groves there awoke one morning to find that someone had erected a column during the night on his land, something of a wonder in itself if you ask me given the short time available. But in any event, the sun rose and there sat Luke, already in residence atop the column."

"It was a great honor to the olive grove owner," Peter protested.

"He was outraged, apparently," snapped Philo, without deigning to look at the servant, "and no wonder. You can't have strangers taking up residence on your property on a whim, after all. But before he was able to convince the appropriate authorities of the necessity of investigating the matter, the silver tongued-stylite—for that is what they called him, Luke of the silver tongue—had begun to attract large and potentially riotous crowds."

"Wherever there's a crowd of followers, there's always the possibility of a riot," agreed John, thinking of the crowds outside the shrine where Michael and his acolytes were encamped. "But what was the outcome?"

Peter, who had finished ordering the shelves and was now wiping the steamy window panes clean, jumped into the conversation once again. "I have heard that the olive grove owner underwent a change of heart and became one of Luke's followers."

"More likely the authorities made the stylite's tenancy worthwhile to the landowner," countered Philo. "It's remarkable what these stylites can get away with, really it is. In fact, since neither Senator Aurelius nor anyone else in this city seems to perceive a need for my services, perhaps I should climb up one of those recently vacated columns and earn a crust by preaching to the multitudes." He finished his honey cake. "I will admit that asceticism, in moderation, is not to be derided. It is considered a virtue by nearly all philosophies and one I try to practice myself."

"I am glad to hear it," said Peter, whisking the platter of cakes away from Philo's descending hand.

※※※

"Philo perched atop a column, preaching about beauty to a crowd of unwashed pilgrims? Now that's something I'd like to see! In fact, I'd gladly pay my father to continue refusing his entreaties for aid just to witness such a spectacle. Or rather, I would suggest such payment if I could maintain a civil conversation with the august Senator Flavius Aurelius long enough to make the offer." Anatolius ran a hand irritably through the unruly black curls of his still-damp hair as he and John emerged from the Baths of Zeuxippos. Behind them, a faint fog of steam escaped through the uncovered gymnasium in the center of the sprawling building, coiling up into a gray, leaden sky.

Anatolius shivered. "This cold is unseasonable," he complained. "Perhaps the Christians' god wasn't angry at those stylites but just wanted to warm his hands."

The sight of the Great Church facing them across the square apparently struck him as a rebuke, because he added quickly, "You truly believe this Michael could have caused their horrible deaths?"

John, who had related the results of Philo's investigations to Anatolius, nodded. "Caused them, or, if not, has certainly sought to take advantage of them."

"But this first message you mentioned, didn't it predict their deaths?"

"So Justinian said. Unfortunately, I have been unable to read the letter itself, nor am I likely to, since the emperor apparently construed my request to inspect it as a direct criticism of his powers of description."

"And once he has spoken on a matter it is closed. Not unlike my father," Anatolius replied with a scowl. "But surely the emperor can read well enough? Why do you suppose that he overlooked some important fact or other?"

"It's been my experience that the most magical aspect of prophecies is how much clearer they appear in retrospect. There might have been something useful to be gleaned by examining that letter."

They had crossed the square and were now walking down a street behind the Great Church.

"I shall be going home momentarily," John continued, "but first I wanted to inspect where Philo stumbled across the dead beggar. Felix gave me directions this morning, having got them from Darius, who, by the way, says that on your last visit to Isis' house a certain composition was very well received. I understand her girls are all hoping you will write poetry for them too. You seem to be quite a popular young man with the ladies, Anatolius."

Anatolius, who appeared preoccupied, muttered a noncommittal comment. He tended to be intolerably voluble during one of his frequent periods of longing after a lady, but when his love was requited he became belatedly discreet. This consummation occurred far less frequently than anyone would have guessed, given his rank, poetic turn of mind and a face that might have been chiseled by a sculptor of the classical era—one who wasn't busy creating statues of wise old philosophers. But it was no puzzle to John, who had observed over the years how his friend invariably set his heart on women who were either hopelessly below or too far above him in the city's stratified society and therefore well out of reach.

One day, John feared, Anatolius would suffer the misfortune of actually making an unsuitable match.

They passed through a small forum where one of the city's ubiquitous stylites still preached, for the mysterious deaths of the three had not come near to even decimating their population. Soon they plunged into one of Constantinople's countless narrow byways. There was a lingering aura of darkness about it, as though the previous night had not quite seeped away but remained puddled along the base of the walls hemming in its narrow length. They paced up and down for a time, kicking at reeking piles of refuse that yielded up only a few outraged rats.

Anatolius asked John what it was that he sought.

"I don't know. The poor die in alleyways all the time. I thought if I examined..." John's voice trailed off. "Nothing suggests itself, I'm afraid."

A moment or so later they had regained the sunlight. John's spirits lifted somewhat as he recounted what Felix had imparted when he stopped briefly at John's house that morning, not long after Philo had completed detailing his investigations.

"According to the information Felix received, no one in the vicinity of the columns saw anything out of the ordinary when the stylites burst into flame—unless you count a brawl between a Blue and a Green a few hours before not far from where Luke stood, although you could hardly call that out of the ordinary."

Anatolius laughed. "In other words, Philo has thus far uncovered about as much useful information as the captain of the excubitors and all his informants and in a shorter time. Perhaps my father could use Philo's services after all—to spy on me! He may uncover some shortcomings I have as yet unguessed!"

John finally allowed himself to comment on his friend's foul humor. "You have argued with your father again?"

"Why not ask if the sun has risen? We are so unlike in character, John, that I sometimes wonder if I am not my late mother's bastard child and that is why he despises me so."

"All men disappoint their fathers, or at least suppose that they do."

"Even you, John? A man who is Justinian's Lord Chamberlain?"

"I do not care to speak of my own family. I left that life behind long ago." John's tone was uncharacteristically curt. "But you, Anatolius, although you are young, you are already a man of substance. As secretary to Justinian, privy to so much of the emperor's confidential correspondence, you hold a most responsible position. You have also risen to the rank of Soldier of Mithra. You have been anointed with the blood of the Great Bull. Your father is proud of you, I am certain, although he may but rarely say so."

"No, John, I am derided for acting like a boy. I am told I do not carry myself with the appropriate gravity. When my father strides naked through the baths men address him as senator! Senator! As if that title means anything these days. A senator's worth as much as the land he holds and nothing more."

※※※

When they arrived at John's house, he invited Anatolius into the quiet garden. "If we go upstairs I am afraid Philo will insist on regaling us with another of his orations. I am too tired for that at the moment."

"An intruder in your own home," Anatolius remarked, not even attempting to make a jest of it.

"I can't bring myself to say so. He was my tutor once, after all. But it certainly feels that way."

"Unfortunately, I must be off, John. I would not idle away more of my time. After all, there must be some grand task I can accomplish, some act of manly bravery. I must go forth and search for it."

"Put your efforts into seeing that the banquet goes well, my friend, and don't brood too much over your father's harsh words. He's had much difficulty with that bladder stone and Gaius tells me the pain it brings can be hellish. And of course these Michaelites pose a real threat to us all. Such trials would make any man's temper short."

"But my father, the senator, will of course set the situation to rights," was the sarcastic reply, "and that is as certain as it is obvious that I never could accomplish such a thing, given my supposed hot headedness and hasty tongue."

Anatolius turned to go but John placed his hand on his friend's shoulder. "Wait. I hesitated to mention this, but now I think I must. Don't you see why Justinian chose your father to assist in his negotiations with these people?"

Anatolius gave John a questioning look.

"It is because he is a pagan," John said. "After all, although such things are never publicly acknowledged at court, there is no doubt that they are known. And he is from old and aristocratic Roman stock so such beliefs would almost be expected, if not talked about too loudly. But nevertheless, just as we ourselves both are, he is a pagan in a city where only Christianity is officially recognized."

Despite the fading light, John could see horrified understanding draining the color from Anatolius' face.

"You have grasped the situation correctly," John said evenly. "If negotiations with Michael fail, your father, as an extremely high ranking official—but a pagan—will make a convenient sacrifice. If worst comes to worst, Justinian will have no hesitation in ascertaining if the mob can be placated with a senator's blood."

❊❊❊

After the shaken Anatolius had departed, John remained sitting beside the garden pool, listening to its soothing, hypnotic trickle. Around him, the garden's friendly darkness rustled as night creatures ventured out. He sighed. What he really wished to do was sit in his study and commune with Zoe. Was it possible Philo might have put his game aside and retired early?

He had just decided to go indoors and find out when an indistinct figure drifted like a white mist towards him, having appeared from behind a large clump of lavender bushes.

"Philo! What are you doing?"

"My apologies to be barging about your flower beds, John. I seem to have lost my path in the dark."

"My garden lately seems to offer all the privacy of the Forum Constantine. No matter," John said quickly, hearing in the philosopher's long pause the promise of a lengthy classical quotation that would be trotted out as surely as the flight of an arrow follows the groan of the bow. "Were you looking for me?"

"Yes. There's something I wish to ask you."

"Well, come inside and we can talk about it."

Philo instead lowered himself onto the bench. "No, I prefer that we discuss it out here. It's a matter I wanted to mention this morning, but I didn't think it proper with that inquisitive servant of yours flapping his ears so obviously."

A cold breeze rustled the shrubbery, bringing with it a hint of frost as well as the sweetly clinging scent of the herb. "I'm afraid you'll have to be brief, Philo," John said. "It grows cool and I'd like to warm my hands. What is it?"

He could barely see Philo fidgeting, smoothing down the baggy himation that had been disordered by his stumbling progress through the bushes. His white hair and beard and pale clothing gave him a spectral appearance.

"It is this, John," he finally said, choosing his words with care. "As I was talking to people in the street during my investigations, I was shocked to hear the way some of them spoke. More than one beggar referred to the empress as 'Theodora from the Brothel.' They didn't even seem to intend it is an insult."

"What is it you want to ask?" asked John, suspecting he had already guessed.

"And others referred to the Lord Chamberlain as 'John the Eunuch'."

"It is true, Philo," John confirmed, wondering how Philo, who was used to dealing with perfect and ethereal ideas than disorderly physical reality, would react.

Philo noted only that John had said nothing to him about it.

"Why would I? If you ever left your bed early enough to attend the baths when I do, you would have known. And your next question will doubtless be 'how?'"

"I am truly sorry, John."

The Lord Chamberlain no longer felt cold. Anger flushed his cheeks. "I will spare you the details, Philo. In short, you may recall I was a less than diligent student. Finally I took your advice and left the Academy to see the world. The world, it happened, was home to a woman with whom I fell in love. One night I determined I would seek a special gift for her. But unfortunately in my search, I strayed over the border."

Philo's clothing rustled as he shifted uneasily on the hard bench throughout John's sparse account of his capture and subsequent fate.

"There is, as you probably know, a market for castrated men," John concluded, "and to slave traders a captive's value is measured only in nomismata, not in whether there is a woman who loves him or not. Or whether he is soon to be a father, even if he does not know it at the time. And so I was prepared for market.

"That young man, Cornelia's lover, the son of a mother and father, the father of a daughter, your student, the former mercenary, all that that man was died when the curved blade did its work. A new being was born then and has lived on to become this eminent personage whose hospitality you sought out under the mistaken belief that you once knew him."

"An interesting theory," Philo said gruffly, "but I do not think we can shed our past as easily as you appear to believe. However, I now clearly see why you have been attracted to a god as austere as Mithra, since he is a deity who values the uncomplaining endurance of hardship."

John did not reply, contemplating Philo's insight, but his old tutor, as usual, quickly filled the silence.

"I cannot help seeing the irony in this terrible tale, John. It's well-known that eunuchs are valued precisely because their lack of family insures their loyalty to their masters, yet you say you have a daughter..."

"I will not speak further of my past." John's voice was colder than the breeze wandering through the garden.

Philo apologized for his tactlessness. "You say you departed the Academy because of my advice?" he continued thoughtfully. "If so, I feel a great deal of responsibility for the tragedy that befell you."

"You did not wield the blade. It was not your fault. Nor, for that matter, was it mine, either for taking your advice or losing my way in a foreign land. The fault lies solely in the hearts of those who would take from a man everything he is for the sake of getting a few more coins for him when they sell him into slavery."

"But are you not surrounded by such heartless men in this very city? Even if they do not trade in human flesh, still...you even serve beside them at court."

"Your old student may not have approved, Philo. But remember, that impetuous youth died long ago."

Chapter Eight

An hour or two before the banquet, Anatolius stopped by the palace office where he spent most of his work days. He was surprised to find Empress Theodora glancing through the correspondence piled on the plain wooden desk.

He stood quietly just inside the doorway. If he did not know Theodora he might have mistaken her for one of Isis' girls playing the part of an empress. Caught unaware, she was simply a short, attractive woman, her complexion carefully lightened by chalk, her deep set eyes accentuated by artful application of kohl, as if she depended upon enticement to work her will, rather than command. Surely the smooth pearls glistening along the edge of her mantle must be milky glass droplets, the brooches pinning her elaborately draped silk robes more common stones cleverly aping emeralds.

Yes, he thought as Theodora looked up from the untidy pile of letters and fixed him with a cold gaze like an adder's, it would be an extremely easy mistake to make. And a fatal one.

"The emperor will not be needing your assistance today," Theodora began. "I am here to retrieve your draft of his reply to the bishop of Antioch but it does not seem to be among these documents."

Anatolius did not tell her he had not been expected, having been excused from his duties on account of the banquet. "I do not recall seeing that, highness, but I have some copying to do today, so if I discover it I will have it carried to Justinian immediately. I trust the emperor is well?"

"Do not concern yourself. The emperor isn't ill. He is engaged in composing a theological treatise seeking to reconcile these Michaelites' curious beliefs with more orthodox views." Theodora's lovely mouth curled into a sickle of a smile. "A difficult exercise, I would imagine."

And one with which she would have no sympathy whatsoever, thought Anatolius, for she was a well-known champion of the Monophysites, despite the fact that their theology was also less than orthodox.

"A challenge worthy of our beloved emperor's wisdom," he replied tactfully. "It is far better to reconcile our philosophies than to shed blood. The pen can defeat the sword if wielded with sufficient skill."

"Now you declaim like the emperor." Theodora's smile turned into a small grimace of disappointment. She moved away from the desk and Anatolius found himself enveloped in her scent, so like a summer garden after rain, the smell of musky blossoms and damp earth. "And indeed I confess that it is a statement I could almost wish to see tested on the floor of the Hippodrome, kalamos against spatha."

Anatolius tried to suppress a shudder. Even the most extravagant whims of the imperial couple had a nasty way of becoming reality.

Theodora laughed and lowered her darkened eyelids. "Don't worry, Anatolius. I would not want to see those black rebellious curls matted with dust and blood."

She reached out and touched his hair. Anatolius could not be certain whether the ice he felt brush his temple was one of the empress' rings or her flesh.

"I appreciate your...uh...kind thought, highness," he stammered.

Theodora gave a girlish laugh. "And now, tell me, where is my poem, Anatolius? I have been waiting."

With panic the young man recalled the scurrilous verse which had so alarmed his father. "Your poem?"

"Why do you look so surprised? Every lady at court has had a verse, and not a few of the servants as well by all I hear. Have you then nothing left for your empress?"

Anatolius' relief was short-lived. Theodora took another step toward him, bringing her near enough so he could feel the warmth of her breath, faintly fragrant with some spice exotic beyond his experience and certainly one not to be found in the public markets or even at the table of a senator. She was wearing a heavy gold necklace, a chain of interlocking dolphins. Were those kindly sea creatures not said to bring good fortune? Perhaps not for him, not under these circumstances. He stared at the faint pulse in her slim white neck.

"If it is the wish of the empress I would welcome the opportunity to compose a panegyric."

"A panegyric? They are for emperors and architecture. I would prefer a love poem," she pouted.

"As you command, highness."

"And not about the empress bare either."

Anatolius tried to reply but could not. He half expected the tread of military boots in the hallway and the prod of iron between his shoulder blades announcing he was to be hauled off to the dungeons.

But Theodora just laughed again. Not a girlish laugh this time but the coarse sort of guffaw sometimes heard emanating from behind closed doors at Isis' house.

"Oh, don't worry, I quite enjoyed your little verse. But your evocation of my talents left something to be desired. Perhaps your sensibilities are much too delicate, Anatolius. But a pretty love poem, that's what I'll have from you."

Her slightly upturned face was near to his. He knew he must back away from her. Were Justinian to arrive at the door there would be no time for explanation. But he could not force himself to move, even though his heart pounded with fear.

"It is indeed a pity," she whispered, her piquant breath hot against his face. "that you are presently spoken for. I am sorely tempted to inform the lady's husband and claim you for myself."

Anatolius stared at her lips, stained fashionably red, the furtive movements of her tongue visible behind dainty teeth. Then she leaned forward and her lips touched his so lightly he would wonder afterwards if he had only imagined it. Before he could respond she was turning away towards the door.

"The poem, dear Anatolius," she said, firmly. "You won't forget, will you?"

He was left alone with the wraith of her perfume.

In a daze, he moved to the cluttered desk where he would sit writing as Justinian restlessly paced the small room, dictating letters carried by imperial couriers to all corners of the empire. Clearly the empress was playing with him. But to what end? Had his verse angered her so much? Was he to be made to suffer before his inevitable demise? Or did she have some other purpose?

He forced himself to look quickly through the correspondence on his desk. Her scent seemed to cling to him, reminding him that it was everywhere rumored that the empress' lovers were often of a much lower class than a senator's son. But a senator's son...

Immediately Anatolius was horrified that he could even allow himself such speculation. Perhaps it would be safer were he, like John, beyond such unthinkable folly. He became aware of the sour odor of his sweat.

He found the missive he sought and sat thankfully down.

His hand trembled as he put kalamos to a scrap of parchment. An errant blob of ink spidered across one corner of the original document. It did not matter, Anatolius told himself as he started to work. All John needed was a verbatim copy of the first message delivered from Michael.

❊❊❊

Hektor the court page was bored. It was his job, along with the other boys who served as pages, to ornament Justinian's court. Elaborately and fancifully dressed, lounging and strolling about the palace and its grounds, they served their emperor as small, glittering gems in the splendid tapestry of imperial power, tales of whose splendor awed ambassadors would carry back to their distant homelands.

"For all its vast magnificence, the Great Church would be but a dark cavern if not for the ten thousand lamps burning inside," the Master of the Offices had told the boys. "Likewise, each one of you is a shining lamp in your emperor's court."

The pompous old fool had not added that pretty perfumed boys could also perform certain services for palace officials that shining lamps, not to mention in many cases the officials' wives, could or would not.

However, the religious zealots camped on the other side of the Golden Horn were casting a gloomy shadow into the palace. Receptions were delayed, banquets cancelled and foreign emissaries sent away while court officials prowled about with long faces. It was as if that ghastly holy man was already in charge, thought Hektor.

So he was bored—and that usually heralded trouble.

Already he had painted and repainted his face and tried on four different garments before making his final choice of finery for the day. Then he had ruined his azure tunic by lying in ambush in one of the palace gardens for a hour, hoping to catch the small brown cat he had seen hunting there. No doubt a captive cat would have afforded the inventive boy a hour or two of pleasure. However the animal had not hunted that morning. Perhaps it had succumbed to religious fever and rejected meat, as had the emperor long ago.

He wandered idly through the well-kept grounds until he arrived at the menagerie, not far from the stables. Most of the enclosures were empty, the imperial couple having temporarily lost interest in exotic fauna, but the largest cage was still occupied.

The boy snapped a branch from one of the carefully pruned ornamental trees clustered nearby and banged it furiously at its bars.

"Hey, Felix!" he shrieked, that being the name he had given the caged bear.

The shaggy animal shifted sluggishly in its shady corner and emitted a half-hearted deep rumble. It seemed hardly more awake than a mosaic.

Disappointed, Hektor poked through the branch through the cage bars, jabbing at the bear. The animal raised its furry head tiredly but made no effort to lash out

"Ah, Felix, you're a sorry excuse for a murderous beast," Hektor grumbled. It was hard to believe the huge animal had killed a man. That was why Theodora had insisted it be brought to the palace, or so Hektor's fellow page Tarquin had claimed. But that wasn't so surprising, was it, considering that the empress had an affinity for bears. After all, her father had been a bearkeeper for the Greens and she must have spent a good deal of time around them as a girl.

Spent time with both bears and Greens, Hektor thought with a pleased smile. No doubt that was where she had acquired some at least of her more violent tendencies. Unfortunately, two years or so of captivity seemed to have taken its toll on Felix's murderous instincts.

"If I were to set you free, would you show your claws?" Hektor asked the bear, darting around the side of the cage and jabbing his branch sharply into the bear's face. The animal snarled more in dismay than anger but the boy at least got a glimpse of the long yellow teeth that had torn out a human throat. He wondered, idly, what it would feel like to take a man's life. He felt certain he would appreciate the experience more than a bear ever could.

Still bored, Hektor bid farewell to the animal and wandered away in the afternoon sunshine, eventually venturing into that part of the palace Justinian used for his offices, a place where there was seldom much call for pages.

As he strolled along the corridor, the boy's thoughts wandered back to his thwarted interrogation of the hateful cat, which had now transformed itself in his imagination into a heavily disguised spy, a cunning and evil foe to be dealt with most severely when apprehended. But his daydreaming ceased abruptly when he saw Theodora emerging from one of the offices.

Hektor quickly retreated around a corner to the shelter of the nearest doorway. As skilled as he was at being conspicuous he had an even better facility for hiding, both exceedingly useful talents at the court in conjunction with an well-developed instinct for knowing when, where and in which circumstances to employ each.

Theodora, he was certain, did not notice him as she swept away in the other direction. He immediately crept around the corner and moved stealthily back through the trail of her perfume to the room from which she had emerged.

What Hektor saw when he peeked inside made him forget the nefarious spy disguised as a cat. There sat Anatolius, looking dazed. Anatolius, of course, was just a harmless fool, but the fool's eunuch friend John had spoken most impertinently to Hektor on more than one occasion.

The eunuch had made a grave mistake, the boy thought, his mouth tightening at the humiliating recollection of those slights. Hektor might yet be young but he knew much. He was aware, for instance, of Theodora's deep enmity toward John. It sprang, he suspected, from jealousy. How often had he had seen her glare at John as he departed after a private conference with Justinian, her angry look touched with panic? After all, she had made it plain to all that the emperor's opinion was for her alone to influence. What the emperor truly believed, what actions he intended to take, these were in the nature of marital secrets. Yes, the empress would certainly richly reward the person who found a means to end the unseemly intimacy between her husband and the eunuch John. That was something else Hektor knew.

So it was with special interest that he observed Anatolius sitting at his desk copying something. It was not an unusual task for a secretary, but Hektor's court-sharpened instincts immediately detected something amiss. Perhaps it was the man's posture or possibly a subliminal hint of his sour, nervous sweat.

Hektor peered more intently around the door post. There was a blotch of spilt ink on the corner of the document Anatolius was rapidly copying. Moving quietly back down the corridor, the boy smiled to himself. He would wait for Anatolius to depart and then read whatever he had been transcribing. Perhaps he would discover something that could be used against him and his friend the eunuch. Yes, he thought, he would obviously have to keep a close eye on John's movements for the next few days. Suddenly, he was no longer bored.

Chapter Nine

Senator Aurelius beamed with satisfaction as he strolled through his atrium with Anatolius. The banquet was underway. Around the central impluvium sat graceful vases holding huge bunches of the white roses sacred to Venus. The splendid garments of his guests captured the sweet scent of juniper garlands woven with leaves of ivy and grapevines, those ancient symbols of hospitality, looped around the doorways. The happy sound of his well-fed guests' conversation and laughter swirled around them. Yes, the scene was perfect. How could it not be? That morning the senator had finally passed his painful bladder stone.

"Anatolius, I am well pleased with your efforts," Aurelius commented, nodding benignly at a cluster of senators discussing the yields of their vineyards. "The menu was completely appropriate, restrained but with a hint of exotica. I was especially impressed by the various wildfowl in plum sauce, not to mention the braised lamb. And the entertainments the same, no dwarfs dancing on the table knocking jugs flying or stepping into the platters, for example."

For the first time in days the senator was seeing the world through eyes unclouded by pain. "The roast venison was particularly well received, I noticed," he continued, "Did you steal away imperial cooks and do I thus face financial ruin for the honor of benefiting from their labors?" He gave his son a paternal smile, intended to remove any sting from his words.

Anatolius reddened. "I borrowed the services of John's cook to oversee the kitchen for this occasion, father. He was more than happy to oblige. John prefers the plainest of foods, but Peter does enjoy the occasional challenge to his culinary skills."

Father and son had paused by the impluvium. Glancing into it, Aurelius was startled to see golden fish swimming in the clear water.

Anatolius followed his gaze and smiled proudly. "A little surprise for later. Toward the end of the evening, your guests can try to catch them and the person who succeeds in capturing the one with the black spotted tail will be presented with a small golden fish suitable for wearing on a chain."

His father regarded him with affection. "It appears that the poet can imagine something other than mooning over lost maidens," he said. "It will certainly be more than interesting to see Senator Epirus, for one, trying to land a fish, especially after one too many cups of wine. Or better yet, Gaius. He's already intoxicated enough to pay the fee for one of those imperial cooks you didn't hire."

Anatolius reminded his father of the strange fortune-telling rhyme that John had once mentioned, something about one meaning sorrow and two, joy.

"Could it not equally apply to wine?" he continued, "For certainly two cups bring merriment but not enough to provoke the uninhibited sort that leaves the Furies in the head and scandalous stories circulating around the court next day."

They continued their tour of the crowded house. The noise was intense, but it was the sound of voices loud with enthusiasm rather than raised in anger. The senator smiled when he saw that now the house slaves had cleared away the remains of the banquet there was, in fact, a dwarf dancing on the long dining room table, tumbling and tripping for an enthusiastic audience. Nearby, a group of acrobats twisted themselves into impossible positions for knots of amazed guests.

Aurelius noted with approval that his son had sensibly employed Felix and several excubitors in the event of any sort of unpleasantness, but had instructed them to circulate quietly, dressed as guests. He complimented Anatolius on his arrangements, and, again, upon the carefully chosen floral decorations.

"About those tubs of linden trees. I was just explaining to Senator Epirus that they represent the legend of the hospitable Philemon and Baucis. Ever the cynic, he said that he doubted we are acting as unwitting hosts to Zeus and Hermes, however powerful many of our guests may be. But surely the palace gardeners needed some persuasion to loan such choice items?"

"Oh," Anatolius shrugged, "I happen to know one of them, and she was happy to assist. Her name's Hypatia and she also provided the very choice pears Peter baked for us, not to mention the excellent vegetables. She's an accomplished herbalist as well, and indeed I had asked her about a potion for your infirmity. Fortunately now I shall be able to tell her that it will not be required."

"Send her to me tomorrow, Anatolius. I can inform her myself and I'd also like to reward her suitably for the aid she has rendered in making this such a wonderfully successful evening."

As they circulated, sparing a word for this or that courtier, Senator Aurelius smiled with pride. Perhaps Anatolius would not disgrace the family name after all, despite the concerns his, Anatolius', mother had often expressed during the boy's somewhat turbulent youth. Thinking of Penelope, gone these ten years, brought unexpected moisture to Aurelius' eyes. Such emotion was not for public display, and he was happy to see John enter the atrium because it gave him an opportunity furtively to wipe his brimming eyes as he turned away from Anatolius to greet the new arrival.

John apologized for his late arrival. "Unless I am ordered otherwise, I must assume the emperor still intends the Great Church to be officially dedicated in a few weeks. I am to arrange all the secular ceremonies and I fear I have been much occupied with other matters."

"Let us not speak of those other matters tonight," Aurelius replied.

Anatolius grinned widely. "And do enjoy some wine now that you're here, John, although I'm afraid there's none of that dreadful Egyptian vintage you insist on serving at your house."

John accepted a cup from the servant who appeared at a gesture from Aurelius, commenting on the latter's cheerful appearance.

"I'm a new man, John." He explained the amazing improvement in his health. "Were I a credulous sort I would probably be barefoot and on my way to prostrate myself before Michael at this very moment. I've been regaling my friends with my cure. It makes an amusing story, don't you think? An old pagan healed by a Christian holy man. A cosmic jest indeed! Not that I really believe it is, of course."

"Gaius thinks you do," John told him. "On my way in, I heard him complaining bitterly, saying you are trying to ruin him by telling people that weeks of his treatments aren't as effective as a single touch from a charlatan."

Aurelius was charitable. "Gaius imbibes too much upon occasion, and when he does his appreciation of humor deserts him. But if he continues to worship Bacchus so ardently, would he blame his patients for preferring to find their cures by sleeping in shrines?

He will be in better spirits tomorrow and no doubt regret what he has said tonight, if he even remembers it, which personally I doubt."

John agreed that going by past experience such would certainly be the case.

"Let's not concern ourselves with Gaius, then. And don't worry about your crotchety old house guest either, John," Aurelius went on. "He's having a marvelous time eating dried apricots and demonstrating this peculiar new game of his to some of the soberer guests in my sitting room. That was another excellent notion, Anatolius," he added. "Not that I would actually employ someone to tutor me in such a frivolous pursuit, as I made plain to him, but I'm pleased with the interesting diversion he's offering. Although I must admit, I wouldn't have engaged those girls we were talking about at table."

"They're here to offer livelier entertainment than a board game, are they?" wondered John, giving a quick smile.

"On this occasion, no," Anatolius grinned. "Now, John, you may have missed the prawns and partridges by arriving so late, but there are still delicacies to be admired. But only from a distance, you understand. As I was saying to my father, these ladies are as pure as Vestal virgins."

Aurelius laughed. "Remember, my boy, I know the nature of the temple where our lady visitors reside."

Anatolius grinned again. "Ah, but these particular handmaidens have many talents."

"And they may need them soon. One of my colleagues mentioned to me earlier that there is some thought of proposing to Justinian that he immediately shut down all those storehouses of talent wherein such ladies as we are discussing dwell. Apparently the thought is that it might be one of the easiest ways to appease the religious zealots camped by the Bosporos."

"Is the Senate really considering making such a recommendation?" John's tone was thoughtful.

Aurelius said that it might well be just rumor.

"Well, be that as it may," Anatolius said, "tonight the ladies will be showing off talents which, in their usual employment, are probably the only things they keep hidden! They will be dressed as the Muses, attributes and all, and each will give a recitation from the classics, to musical accompaniment provided by Euterpe, muse of music and joy. That is to say, by our friend Isis."

John laughed at the very thought. "Isis? Playing on that hydra of hers?"

Anatolius shook his head. "Oh, no. No, I would have needed to engage a carter to drag that contraption over here. She has taken up playing the flute. It's her newest pastime, apparently. Don't worry, father," he added quickly. "She will be veiled most modestly. No-one will recognize her, or if anyone does, they won't be too eager to admit it."

"My son has even had the foresight to protect the reputation of my house. I never thought to see the day!"

"If you are so pleased, perhaps you will think again about this matter of my laboring with the quaestor?"

Aurelius chuckled. "Now how could I disappoint all my guests? Your poetic imagination will be treating us to some remarkable sights and sounds this evening, but I wager that tomorrow no one will be talking about your earthy Muses, your flute-playing Euterpe, your prize-awarding pisceans or even Philo's exotic game. No, I predict the chatterers will talk only of how an old senator's stubborn and wayward son was transformed, as if by magick, into a man of substance by his new appointment!"

They had emerged into the peristyle surrounding the inner garden. Clusters of men strolled along graveled pathways winding around and between flower beds filled with more vases of roses whose heavy perfume sweetened the cooling air. Here and there, deep emerald sprays of ferns soberly emphasized the flaring trumpets of the pale pillars of lilies gleaming in terracotta pots. Shallow bowls of violets glowed purple against the clipped yews forming a somber background for the marble statues and busts set about the garden.

"I will address my guests shortly," said Aurelius, "but first I must retrieve the notes for my speech. John, after Euterpe and her companions have entertained, if you would be good enough to say a preliminary word of introduction? And then after I announce your august new position, Anatolius, my guests can begin fishing."

❋❋❋

Aurelius made his way down the hall, glancing in as he passed by the sitting room where Philo was still entertaining several guests. The senator's study was deserted but only because, he supposed as he picked up his notes, it offered neither entertainment nor a convenient couch upon which to rest.

The painted cupids on the walls reminded him of happier times when Anatolius was a baby and Penelope was still alive. This room was where their only child had taken his first unaided, tottering steps. Here, he still hoped, one day he would see a grandson take his first steps across the same mosaic floor on which Anatolius had played under Penelope's fond care. How quickly the years had marched inexorably along, lately seemingly attended as much by sorrows as by joys.

Now, as the sun fell behind the rooftops of the city, the cupids were illuminated by lamplight. Some of the chubby godlings were playing musical instruments, others drove chariots pulled by donkeys. Penelope's artistic taste had not favored the classical school of painting. Perhaps it was her influence that had made their only child so tender-hearted, so flighty, Aurelius thought. And this being so, she had spent her last years agonizing over how a poet would survive life in the palace.

This room, so full of memories tonight, was the warmest in the house except the kitchen, and since he had become an old man he had grown to detest the cold. But, although he would admit it to no man, that was not the only reason he had made it his study.

Tears began to sting his eyes and he could not read the words on the parchment. It was not a seemly thing to weep, he knew; he was reacting as Penelope would have reacted. The thought brought her closer, as if she had momentarily come back to him from the shadowy land beyond the Styx.

He filled a cup from the jug of wine on the side table. A few days ago he had not been certain he would see this day, given the agony he had been suffering and those damnable Michaelites. Now the pain at least had vanished.

Aurelius raised his cup toward the cupids. He could feel Penelope's presence as strongly as if she stood behind him. "This is our proudest night, my dearest wife," he whispered.

Let the Michaelites fulminate outside the city walls, he thought. On this glorious evening, he would banish them from his thoughts.

※ ※ ※

Standing under the portico of the shrine beside the Bosporos, Michael was preaching a sermon. The sun, it's rusty red light no longer finding its way to bless the festivities in the garden of Senator Aurelius' home, was still visible. Unimpeded by Constantinople's walls and buildings it cast a ruddy glow across the rapt faces of Michael's audience.

"What do you witness today within the great walls of the city?" Michael was asking. Despite not possessing the booming voice of an orator, his words carried easily out from the steps of the shrine into the attentive crowd gathered at their foot and on the grassy incline leading up to the road.

"Everywhere demons holding their orgies, everywhere citadels of the evil one, everywhere fornication decked with wreaths of honor," Michael continued. "Even as I speak, the powerful and the godless are gathering to celebrate their own iniquity. But I say to you that these offenses against heaven will draw unto themselves a fiery wrath."

A woman scanned the faces of the people pressing around the shrine steps. All classes and conditions were represented, a cross section of society—and the dregs of society for that matter.

"We light our lamps and praise the heat and the light cast by the flame. We praise the oil from which the flame draws sustenance. But what of the humble clay vessel which is necessary to hold the oil?"

As the words flowed on, fear nagged at the woman's vitals. Could her husband have followed her, found her despite all the care she had taken to obscure her path once she had fled their country estate, taking only her jewelry and a few coins? Again she felt a pang of pity for the slaves. They would doubtless have been interrogated mercilessly as to her whereabouts. Although a gentle man in many ways, her husband had always been very conscious of his social position and it would certainly not be enhanced by his wife running away while he was in the city. She glanced at the wound of the sunset, welcoming the approaching darkness that would help her hide her face more securely for another night.

"Those wealthy men in fine robes who measure the Lord's riches by the weight of gold on their altars declare me to be a heretic," Michael continued, "and because I say to you who are gathered here by the roadside that we should venerate not only the Father and the Son and the Spirit but also the Vessel of the Spirit, they accuse me of blasphemously worshipping mere flesh."

The woman looked up into the fast-darkening sky above the crowd of pilgrims milling around the shrine, reminding herself that she must be ceaselessly vigilant. Discovery was possible at any time, one slip, one error, a careless word, and she would be caught.

What, she wondered, had brought the sturdy peasant family clustered nearby to the shrine? They looked healthy enough, brown skinned from laboring in vineyards or fields. A farmer, perhaps even freed slaves? The man was tall, bearded, his face as bony as the hand that rested on his wife's shoulder. She was short, with child and very near her time. Looking at the high swell of the stomach under a dusty gray tunic and the small chubby-faced boy sucking on a dirty thumb as he peeked at her from between his parents, his eyes mirrors of a blue summer sky, she felt a familiar stab of pain.

The poor, it seemed, bred as easily as brute animals. In the country there was room for all the little ones. But in Constantinople, did they never pause to consider that here was another mouth to feed, another dweller in a city already bursting with humanity, swarming with people crammed into tiny rooms and spilling out into the raucous streets? Children needed light and air and space, not dirty hovels and cramped rooms, scrabbling for food and growing old before their time.

She found herself wondering what the grubby little boy would look like, playing happily in the garden of her husband's villa. If only she had not lost the child she was carrying just a few short months after her marriage. Her husband had been overjoyed when she returned from the physician with confirmation of their happy suspicions. "Now I have two reasons for joy," he had said, stroking her still flat stomach fondly. "A wife and a child. I am a rich man indeed!"

Still Michael's words flowed on as the crowd murmured to each other, some nodding, others looking around them as they listened. Were their thoughts wandering as much as hers?

"Yet how can there be anything, even mere flesh, which does not proceed from God, who created all?" Michael asked. "And how can that which is created by Him not partake of His own being? Now still there are those of you who may not be fully convinced. But consider the woman who brings forth a child. Is it argued that the babe arrived by cart from another place, or that it is somehow different in substance and in nature from its mother although arising from her?"

The words brought a pang to the woman. She was not meant to be a mother. She felt gnawing pain again, a lamentation in the dark space that dwelt in her heart. She had lost their child and they had turned away from each other. Her husband became distant, not acknowledging or apparently even realizing how much she needed his comfort. Oh, he did not begin to drink too much wine to drown his sorrow and he was always icily courteous. But he became a stony-faced stranger who said little and spent less and less time with her, pleading the polite fiction that official business kept him in the city.

And then one night he had arrived home intoxicated and cursed her as barren, screaming his rage, taking pleasure in revealing in obscene detail that he had consorted with women from the gutter and enjoyed it. Yes, and enjoyed it more than anything he had had with her.

In the morning, when he was sober, he had tried to apologize. But it was too late. The drunken words that had flowed like poisoned wine had done their work too well.

"They believe they are safe," Michael was saying, "like beasts in their dark dens, yet the sacred fire will reach inside their luxurious houses with their beautiful furniture and painted walls."

Painted walls. Yes, she had taken to spending most of her time sitting in her room, staring at the frescoes. The finest craftsmen had come from Constantinople to decorate her husband's villa and their handiwork was exquisite. A meticulously painted window deceived the eyes into believing that it opened out into a classical landscape graced by a temple to Venus, whose symbols were seamlessly blended into the tranquil scene.

Here was a serenely flowing river, clear enough to see the rounded stones over which it gurgled and sang, dancing between grassy banks graced by willows and fringed with violets and roses. There, two stately swans swam in the shallows and on the far side of the water, a young couple walked hand in hand up the slight incline of a hill toward a small temple to the goddess. Two doves hovered over its tiled rotunda, pomegranate trees bloomed outside its open door. Beyond, wooded hills rolled into a misty distance.

It was a beautiful scene, or at least she had thought so when she arrived as a new bride. In the mornings they would lie in bed and spin each other stories about the young couple and what had happened to them and all the other supplicants who visited the temple to offer a sacrifice to Venus or perhaps to ask for divine assistance on the field of love.

And they had discussed the names that their first child would be given. But the child had died before he was born and now there would be no more chances.

Was it not strange that here she was, standing beside another shrine? Perhaps someone outside this world was lying on their bed looking in through a window painted upon their wall, seeing her and all the others and spinning romantic stories about their lives.

"I tell you that each human being is a part of God," Michael went on, "so that the murderer offends not merely flesh but also God. And so too the jurist offends who sentences an innocent to the axe and the husband who beats his wife and those who administer all manner of injustices. Look into the palaces and churches and the houses of the wealthy. They are filled with vessels of gold. But the flame burning in a vessel of clay burns no less brightly. It burns no less hotly."

The words seemed oddly distant.

The little boy hid his face in the folds of his mother's rough tunic. The woman became aware that she had been staring at him. She looked away, then glanced back quickly. He was peeking at her, a smile wreathing what could be seen of his face. She felt an answering smile begin to form.

Yet what was Michael saying? "On this very night, God's holy fire will once again consume those who offend Him."

Chapter Ten

After Senator Aurelius left the garden to prepare for the short oration he planned to give to commemorate the occasion, John and Anatolius—the latter the subject of the senator's speech—lingered under the peristyle. John noticed the fountain, like the rest of the house and garden, was lavishly decorated by white roses. They almost, but not quite, succeeded in diverting the eye from the rotund bronze Eros at the fountain's center.

John commented that he was glad to see Aurelius was pleased with Anatolius' efforts.

"Or pleased that he is about to dispose of my future according to his own ideas of propriety." Anatolius' voice betrayed fatigue quite at odds with his demeanor. "But never mind, who knows what may yet happen? Perhaps these Michaelites will march into the city and promulgate their own laws and have no need of my services!"

"That might save you from joining the office of the quaestor but I doubt there would be much room for your preferred kind of verse in a city ruled by zealots such as them."

"You're probably right, unfortunately. By the way, have you had time to read that letter I copied out for you? I left it at your house earlier today."

John was puzzled. A letter? A chill of understanding came to him, like a sudden draught from an open window. He recalled mentioning to Anatolius that first communication from Michael, the letter Justinian had not permitted him to examine. "Anatolius, you didn't place yourself in danger, did you?"

But Anatolius was already stepping forward, raising his hands to draw attention.

"My dear friends, thank you for joining us this evening." His voice had regained its usual ebullience. "I understand my father intends to say a few words shortly, but for now the entertainment will continue with a presentation of the Address of the Muses after the fashion of the ancients."

A murmur of interest rose from the guests. Several settled down on the peristyle's marble benches while others lounged against its columns.

When all was quiet except for the hiss and pop of torches fending off growing darkness, Anatolius clapped his hands sharply.

A procession of the nine Muses, modestly dressed in elaborately folded robes, appeared from the shadows. They were led by Isis in the guise of Euterpe. Her chubby fingers coaxed a passably grave melody from the flute disappearing beneath the billowing veil disguising her face. The huge semi-naked figure of Darius, sporting tiny gilded wings on his broad shoulders, followed in their wake. A murmur of admiration rose from the spectators as the little procession stopped beside the fountain overseen by Darius' bronze colleague.

"I thought Darius disposed of those absurd wings when Isis abandoned her Temple of Aphrodite décor?" Anatolius had rejoined John.

"I do think she should occasionally restrain her taste for the theatrical however good it is for business," John muttered back. "Surely Darius must find the ridiculous costumes he's obliged to wear very demeaning, even if it is part of his job?"

"But then we all have our jobs to do," Anatolius said in a disgruntled tone, "whether we like them or not."

John changed the subject. "When I was a young man at the Academy, Philo once warned us that Aristotle considered flutes to be immoral because their music was overly exciting. This struck me as so ridiculous that I have never forgotten it, but perhaps Aristotle and Isis are privy to knowledge unknown to me."

"In that case, I'm surprised that Isis does not have whole companies of flautists serenading her clients," Anatolius replied as the plaintive melody changed to an emphatic keening.

One of the Muses, surely Calliope judging from the wax tablet and stylus she carried, stepped forward and began her recitation. John noted wryly how Anatolius' attention focused immediately on the meticulously metered words—or perhaps it was on the meticulously painted mouth from which they were emerging. Realizing any comments he might make could never compete with such attractions, he said nothing.

As Calliope continued declaiming, he found himself thinking that there was a comforting familiarity about these soporific entertainments. Epic verse was something John preferred to read for himself in the solitude of his study, uncolored by another's interpretation and, for that matter, unsweetened by pretty lips.

His attention wandered up to the night sky. The breeze felt cold on his face, reminding him that the seasons turned more rapidly every year, or so it seemed. His thoughts drifted away on the liquid notes of the flute.

A terrible wail yanked his attention back to the performance. At first he thought it was some impossible, piercing noise Isis had managed to wrest from her instrument.

Then he realized it was a scream.

Pandemonium broke out in the garden as a pillar of flame blazed up from the fountain. A dark figure writhed in its midst. Darius had grabbed a vase and was throwing water and roses onto the burning girl, trying futilely to douse the conflagration.

John leapt forward as Isis began to beat at the flames with her bare hands. Shouting a warning in her native tongue, he pushed her aside before her billowing veil could catch fire. She fell to the ground. The Muses shrieked hysterically as John tore off his heavy cloak and threw it over the girl, hoping to dampen the flames. Then, leaping into the shallow basin of the fountain, hardly aware of the cold water splashing around his knees, he helped Darius thrust the girl deeper into the water.

By the time the flames were dowsed and the girl been pulled from the fountain it was much too late.

It was not Calliope, who stood nearby covering her face with her hands and sobbing, but another.

"Adula," Darius whispered and then began shouting a string of curses in Persian, so dire as to confound John's considerable powers of translation. One tiny gilded wing still clung to Darius' broad back. Screaming obscenities, he ripped off the gauzy conceit and hurled it away in a fury, as if wearing the wings had somehow rendered him impotent to avert the tragedy.

Isis stood beside her charge, shaking and pale, apparently oblivious to the ugly burns already blistering her hands and arms.

"She just burst into flames," one of the senators said loudly in an incredulous tone. Others shouted their agreement. The silence that had initially descended on the garden in the face of the horrible spectacle gave way to a cacophony of agitated conversation.

"Master," came Peter's familiar but trembling voice. He had appeared from the kitchen, Hypatia at his side.

"It was heaven's judgment," he went on, his voice rising. "Heaven's judgment upon those who practice an unchaste profession."

Isis looked at him with hatred.

"You're burnt, Isis," John said quickly. "Where is Gaius? He can treat you immediately."

"I saw him a few moments ago, unconscious in a corner like a common reveler in the gutter," a nearby senator remarked. He had been staring down, fascinated, at the charred form. John directed a look at the speaker that caused the man to slink hastily away.

"Perhaps Hypatia can make a poultice to treat your burns until Gaius can be roused," John said to Isis. "You really shouldn't have tried to beat those flames out with your bare hands, Isis."

"I had no choice." She stifled a sob. "I had to try to save my investment, didn't I?"

John looked around the torch lit garden, struck by a sense that he had overlooked something. He realized what it was. Felix remained inexplicably absent.

"Mithra!" John muttered. "Has something happened to him as well?"

As if summoned by the question, the man's bear-like figure appeared. To John's surprise, Felix walked right past the dead girl and stopped in front of Anatolius. The excubitor's bearded face was grim.

The young man stared at him with alarm. "What is it, Felix?"

Felix paused. His gaze dropped to the ground for an instant and then he forced himself to look up again into Anatolius' eyes.

"My friend," Felix said gruffly, "it is your father. He is dead."

After Felix had placed the exits of the senator's house under guard and sent one of his men to the Prefect to report the deaths, John accompanied a dazed Anatolius to Aurelius' study.

The senator was slumped over his desk, under the merry gaze of the frolicking cupids so beloved by the wife with whom he was now reunited. Beneath his hand lay the notes for the speech that would have announced his son's new appointment. He had planned it to be but the first step toward armoring Anatolius for that dangerous future when the frivolous young man would be left alone to fend for himself. Now, shockingly, that future was already upon him.

John could see that the room was undisturbed. Aurelius' bluish lips revealed to John what he needed to know.

The senator had been poisoned.

❊❊❊

By the time the rising sun turned night into the first day that would go unseen by the senator and the prostitute, the throng of banquet guests had been reduced to a group of excubitors, the Lord Chamberlain and a stocky, petulant shoemaker.

"As I have already told you," the latter was whining, "my name is Kalus. Surely you must have noticed my large workshops not far from the Forum Bovis. How could you miss them?"

The man's breath formed a faint mist in the chilly air of the garden. John was grateful for the cold. It was helping him stay alert, for he and Felix had spent the night questioning senators and courtiers one by one before permitting them to leave. Most, he noticed, had been more disgruntled by their personal inconvenience than grief-stricken over their host's murder. Perhaps it was as well that Anatolius had withdrawn into the house. Now, standing beside Felix, John looked on as the bearded excubitor captain patiently made another notation on Calliope's tablet.

"Have you written that down correctly this time?" demanded the shoemaker. His fleshy face was red with irritation and his double chin waggled indignantly. "I spoke only briefly to Senator Aurelius last night. As I have already explained, we discussed the possibility of a mutual investment in a shipment of olive oil. I'd thought to use the profits to pay for the family mausoleum I'm having built. Why would I murder a potential business partner?"

"No one suspects you," John put in soothingly. "Please understand, we need to ascertain if anyone saw anything... "

"And since I am just a common shoemaker, of course I was detained to the very end. That's always the way, isn't it?" Kalus puffed out his chest, a pugnacious pose that would doubtless be immortalized in marble in the mausoleum the man had mentioned.

"How do you suppose the emperor's soldiers would fare against their foes were they to go into battle barefoot?" Kalus railed at them. "At least Justinian knows the value of a good shoemaker."

"The emperor can always find more shoemakers if he needs them," growled Felix.

"You questioned those senators right away," Kalus complained. "Epirus, now, when did he leave? I am worth twice what he can boast, yet he already sleeps in his own warm bed. I have an army of craftsman under my command. I employ six eunuchs at my summer villa alone."

"You are free to go," John said curtly, wondering if the man was trying to be provocative or was just extremely careless in his manner of speaking.

Felix glanced questioningly at John as the shoemaker marched off. "He didn't say anything about the girl, you notice. Should I summon him back?"

John shook his head tiredly. "We don't think we need hear anyone else tell us one instant they were listening to Calliope's recitation and the next Adula was on fire. As if by magick, or as if the hand of God had struck her down, or she was consumed from within, whichever way they wished to put it."

Hearing John repeat the same descriptions they had been listening to all night, Felix admitted he supposed that John was right.

Looking around the garden which had seemed so festive only a few hours before, John noticed a small bird perched on one of the ivy garlands decorating the peristyle. For the bird it was a morning like any other. Its world was no different. It was fortunate indeed, John thought. The subtle political maze through which the court moved changed each time a person of rank died. What had once been an open path might be blocked, a former barrier perhaps removed. What had the senator's death changed? It was too early to ascertain.

The bird took flight, vanishing into the sky, and John, wishing he could fly off as easily, forced his attention back to the matter at hand.

"Nor do we need anyone else to assure us that they never left the public rooms, Felix," he said, "Not to mention that of course they had no notion of where Aurelius had gone, let alone which room he used for his study. Was it a politically motivated murder, do you suppose?"

Felix scratched his unruly beard. "Aurelius' death? The method would suggest it. It's been my experience that the ambitious resort to the blade only after lawyers and poisons have failed."

"Poison also suggests premeditation. But what of the girl Adula?"

"A obvious diversion, most probably inspired by the fiery deaths of those stylites."

"There's also the senator's diplomatic mission to be considered. There may well be some in this city who would prefer not to see any negotiations at all carried out. But it could also have been a purely personal affair," John suggested.

"You're thinking of Gaius, aren't you? I heard him arguing with Aurelius myself. But we both know Gaius is a drunkard, not a murderer."

John nodded agreement. "However, I fear he can be a violent drunkard. I have noticed his servants bruised on more than one occasion and I suspect he beats them when he is in the arms of Bacchus."

"Not praiseworthy, perhaps, but violence toward a slave can't be compared with violence toward a senator. The former is an owner's prerogative, after all."

John admitted that that unfortunately was true.

"You might as well suspect that old man you've been harboring," the excubitor captain continued. "He was grumbling bitterly about Aurelius to anyone who would listen. A foolish man for a philosopher, if you ask me. Athens must have been a safe place indeed for his tongue to have survived to such an age."

"I'll caution Philo again about that when I get home. He certainly poses a danger, but only to himself."

Felix nodded and called out an order to one of his men.

"I'll keep guards at the outer doors while we search the house, John, but the rest of my men can go back to the barracks now that we're almost done here." He paused. "Thank Mithra that Anatolius' mother did not live to see this."

"As you say, Felix," John replied. "But before I leave, I must attempt to speak with Anatolius again."

The youthful servant Anatolius had left to guard the study door replied to John's query as he had to all those made earlier. The master was in mourning and wished to be alone with his thoughts.

As the youth recited the rote message his gaze darted back and forth as if he were looking for a place to hide. Clearly he was terrified of offending the Lord Chamberlain. However, he remained at his station by the door.

"I must respect his wishes, of course," John told him. "What is your name?"

The servant looked even more terrified. "It's Simon," he stammered.

"Well, Simon, when I do finally speak to your master I shall tell him that you carried out a difficult task very diligently. He will be pleased, and since he is now head of the household, this tragic night may well serve to start you on the way to a bright future."

To John's surprise Simon's face clouded with disappointment before he replied, his voice breaking. "Pardon, your highness sir, but I had hoped the old master would free me in his will."

"Yes, of course. He may just have done so," John told him, then added gently, "But there are thousands of freed men in this city who labor at far worse jobs than serving a man like Anatolius."

Before the servant could reply, a strident voice echoed from the entrance hall, demanding that Senator Aurelius come out of hiding without delay.

John arrived at the hall to find Felix arguing with a man whose patrician features were familiar to everyone at the palace. And not only his features. Senator Balbinus' orations were renowned for being as noisy as the slapping of thongs against the oracular brass plate at Dodona.

"As I have been trying to tell you," Felix was saying, "the senator will not be seeing anyone again. He is dead."

Senator Balbinus abruptly ceased fulminating and his face settled into a frown. John noted the dark smudges under the eyes and the half-healed wound, a long scratch, running along one cheekbone.

"It's true that we had our differences of opinion," Balbinus said. "but still, I am very sorry to hear this most shocking news. A great loss to the senate and to the empire. But if I may inquire…"

"There will be an official announcement in due course," said John. "And now tell me, senator, what business did you intend to conduct here at such an early hour?"

"It was of a personal nature." Balbinus' hand moved to the nascent scar on his cheekbone. Catching the glance exchanged between the other two men, he blustered on red-faced. "The streets become more unsafe every day. A couple of Blues set upon me within sight of the Chalke. The factions grow bolder by the hour. Where are those engaged to protect good citizens like me?"

"I'm sure those ruffians took to their heels when you unleashed your oratory at them," snapped Felix, taking the senator's question as a personal insult.

Balbinus ignored his remark. "Please extend my sincere condolences to his son. He is a most astute young man, for a poet."

After Balbinus departed, Felix made as if to spit his disgust but looked at the artfully patterned tile floor and refrained. "There's one who'll obviously be happy to deal with the son rather than the father," he said tartly.

"There are plenty of others like him," observed John. "They might be surprised when the time comes."

"I hope so," sighed Felix. "But I wouldn't bet on it. If I were still a betting man, that is."

Chapter Eleven

It took longer than John might have guessed to examine Aurelius' house in the brighter but no more revealing light of day. With the task completed, he went directly to the palace, where he was kept waiting for hours before being informed that the emperor was not available. Exhausted, John returned home. The short nap he intended to take turned into a death-like sleep that lasted until the next morning.

Despite his chagrin at such weakness, it did not matter because that day Justinian was still receiving no one. The emperor's instructions were that all communications were to be conveyed to him through Theodora, who was also authorized to act in his stead on matters of urgency with his full knowledge and approval.

The elderly silentiary who recited this information gave John a toothless smirk. Both men knew very well that when Justinian was engrossed in theology he wouldn't notice Satan squatting atop the dome of the Great Church. Although whether Theodora was likely to issue orders that would gain the emperor's attention too late, was, John thought, an open question.

"I imagine that a number of officials have decided it is an excellent time to visit their country estates," remarked John evenly after he received heard the news.

The silentiary chuckled. "Isn't that always the case when the political weather changes? But as far as that goes, I've heard it said that heavenly fire is but a candle flame compared to the wrath of the empress."

With a brooding sense of foreboding John made his way across the palace grounds, past deserted pavilions, the richly decorated houses of court dignitaries, and half bare flower beds waiting for summer to bring back their colorful displays of blooms. His destination was the Hormisdas Palace where, as the silentiary had informed him, Theodora was holding audience that morning.

The smoky corridors in the Hormisdas were as crowded and noisy as the city streets, and just as malodorous. Theodora had lived here with Justinian before he became emperor, but now the rambling building housed the empress' collection of heretics.

No one could say whether the religious refugees sheltered there owed their temporary good fortune to the empress' sympathy for the downtrodden, her tolerance for various beliefs, her political machinations or to simple perversity. What was certain was that Justinian was, as always, ready to indulge his wife's whims. Thus, between the high ceilings and floral mosaic floors of rooms ringing with a babble of prayer, chanting, and disputation, fleshy bishops rubbed shoulders with their emaciated and hobbling lesser brethren.

John walked swiftly down a corridor on whose bright walls unfolded the progress of a tiger hunt. The striped fur of the stately beast blended with the lush foliage through which its hunters pursued it, the thick undergrowth concealing not just the tiger but the ever present danger it posed to those that sought to catch it. It was, John thought, a fitting decoration for one of the most dangerous buildings in the city, the more so as the tiger, endlessly pursued, yet remained free. Many laboring in the tangled warren that was Justinian's court must surely envy it.

Passing under the elaborately carved lintel of the tall door at the far end of the corridor, John stepped into Theodora's gilded audience hall. A wild-eyed man, clad only in a yellow loincloth, bowed away from Theodora's elevated throne as John approached, almost colliding with him. The half-naked man gasped in terror and hastily stumbled out.

Theodora emitted a sharp laugh. "Jubal appears to believe that he's still in the desert. He probably mistook you for a scorpion, Lord Chamberlain. How could he know you have no sting?"

"Highness, I had hoped the emperor would grant me an audience," John replied, bowing his head to her.

"I regret that is not possible," Theodora replied, an amused expression in her eyes. "But of course you must feel free to discuss matters with me as you would with him. That should not present a problem. You are granted audiences so often that such consultations will be second nature to you." The scimitar of her smile wordlessly informed John that it would be extremely foolhardy for him to speak to her in as straightforward a manner as he did to the emperor. "And now tell me, what business of the empire is it that brings you here today?"

"In part it concerns my investigation of the three stylites who recently died so mysteriously."

Before he had was able to complete what he had intended to say, the empress swept past him in a rustle of stiffly embroidered garments and musky perfume. "I have matters to which I must attend elsewhere, Lord Chamberlain, but you may accompany me and tell me of your inquiries. Have they been successful in ascertaining the cause of those deaths?"

"Alas, I fear not," John replied, following her along the corridor, past the tiger hunt.

"Then I assure you that you have nothing to say on the matter that would be of interest to the emperor."

"I have also appointed the captain of the excubitors to assist the Prefect in this matter, highness. Between us we will uncover the answers, given time."

"Time is a thing that the emperor may easily take from a man but something that, alas, even the emperor cannot have newly minted."

Theodora lapsed into silence. As they followed a circuitous route through the crowded corridors, she occasionally bestowed an imperious nod or a few words of greeting. The Hormisdas had undergone extensive changes since she and Justinian had made it their home, with numerous wooden and plaster partitions haphazardly erected, creating small rooms for its new inhabitants while simultaneously turning much of the building into a confusing labyrinth.

Most of those residing here, being Monophysites, were fortunate to have such a sanctuary, John thought. As a practicing Mithran, he was interested in such theological debates because they shaped the political terrain across which he and the rest of Justinian's court traveled. Nevertheless, he was not quite so dismissive of such beliefs as some. Anatolius, for example.

"When theologians start debating how exactly to cut up their deity's nature they remind me of butchers arguing over the best way to carve a cow," Anatolius had once rashly remarked, luckily far from imperial hearing. Justinian and his wife might disagree on theology but they would no doubt have been united in seeing blasphemy where Anatolius saw only wit.

John broached the matter on which he had wished to speak to Justinian. "You are doubtless aware that Senator Aurelius died very suddenly the night before last, highness?"

"The unfortunate incident has indeed come to my attention," Theodora replied shortly, "The quaestor's office examined his will this very morning. It is amazing how negligent some of these senators have been in regards to such matters of late. Such a shame for his son. He's such a handsome boy, have you ever noticed, Lord Chamberlain?"

John was not certain whether the empress was commiserating with Anatolius over his loss or whether she was referring to defects in his father's will. The quaestor's office, it was increasingly rumored, had been finding many such defects in wills resulting in more than one estate passing by legal default into imperial possession.

Theodora bent down to address a few quick words to what appeared to be a bundle of rags lying untidily in a corner where the corridor branched into three. The bundle moved and a bony hand with mottled skin emerged to stroke the empress' amethyst and pearl-studded shoe.

It was as well that all who dwelt in the Hormisdas enjoyed Theodora's personal protection, John thought, for anyone who dared to touch her outside its walls, even in such an innocent fashion, would have been arrested immediately. Their execution, however, would not have been as swift, however much they begged for it.

"You see, Lord Chamberlain, how much our subjects love us?" Theodora remarked, removing a ring and pressing it into the dirty palm of the extended hand. The bony fingers closed over their treasure and the hand disappeared back into concealment.

Somewhere in the hot, overpopulated rooms around them, a hoarse voice began to recite verses, presumably scriptural in nature, in a near scream that hovered vulture-like above the general hubbub.

The empress continued on her way, entirely unperturbed by the unseemly tumult all around her. Perhaps it was not surprising, John thought with a measure of grudging respect. After all, she was a bear-keeper's daughter and had lived as both an actress and a prostitute, which amounted to much the same professions. She would naturally be equally at home prowling these untidy, crowded corridors as attending a banquet in the imperial dining hall.

"There is little more I can do at present concerning the matter of the stylites," John continued. "However, once I have further information from various informants I can resume those investigations. Until then I had hoped for the emperor's gracious permission to devote my energies to looking into the death of Senator Aurelius."

Theodora stopped abruptly and pinned John in her unwinking gaze. "Absolutely not, Lord Chamberlain. The emperor and I must have an explanation for these stylites' deaths before this wretched heretic Michael uses them further to his advantage. After all, the Greens and Blues and whole legions of religious factions are not ready to riot in the streets over the death of your friend's father, however regrettable a loss it is to him and to you."

"But they may well be prepared to riot over the death of a girl who also died at Aurelius' home that night, since it would appear that she was consumed by the same supernatural fire that claimed the stylites," John responded. "No doubt this has also occurred to you, highness."

"I have, of course, been informed of her death, and I fully expect the Michaelites will seek to take credit for it. However, I have dismissed the possibility as of little consequence."

"Highness, I have asked myself how could there be no connection between her death and that of Aurelius, in the same house during the same hour? And then Aurelius was Justinian's emissary to Michael, as was I myself. I am absolutely certain there it is all linked together and so by looking into these two latest deaths, I will gain insight into the others."

"If the Michaelites wanted to murder Aurelius they would have done so by fire, wouldn't they?" Theodora said impatiently. "And that being so, let us go further and ask ourselves why they would choose to demonstrate their supposed power by killing only a little whore nobody will miss? Concentrate on the dead stylites, Lord Chamberlain. Find out what or who killed them, for it was certainly not the hand of God. We wish for this Michael to be completely discredited. Only then will calm be restored to the streets."

John bowed slightly. "I would not seek to confound your wishes, highness."

"Your tone already does, it is so cold," Theodora replied. "Anatolius was much warmer to me."

John made no comment. Theodora was obviously toying with him by making the merest hint of such an indiscretion. Surely even Anatolius could not have become so thoughtlessly reckless as to covet the affections of the empress?

Theodora appeared to read his thoughts. Her scarlet lipped smile bloomed again. "What would you know of the longings of the heart?" she asked rhetorically. "But to return to the matter under discussion," she went on after a slight pause, "I omitted to point out one thing to you, Lord Chamberlain, which is that in your negotiations with Michael your shortcomings will serve us well."

John was silent.

The empress looked disappointed. "I have been told that Michael is one such as yourself," she said, giving a cold smile as John's cheekbones flushed red. "So now that Senator Aurelius is gone, you alone will continue these discussions with Michael until you obtain such evidence as is needed to expose him for the fraudulent blasphemer that he is. And at that time the only negotiations involved will be his futile pleas for his miserable life."

"I will do my utmost, highness, but I feel I must point out that I am not the seasoned diplomat Senator Aurelius was."

"But like Michael and unlike poor Aurelius, you are a eunuch. I expect you and Michael have the measure of each other."

Chapter Twelve

*U*nlike Justinian, Anatolius finally agreed to speak to John. He would not, however, emerge from the study in which his father had died.

As John entered the room, Anatolius raised his head. His drawn face and red rimmed eyes formed a sad contrast to the uncaring riot of cheerful godlings going about their merry business on the painted walls.

John sat down and the two friends looked at each other in silence for a long time.

Finally Anatolius spoke. "Well, then, is it not ironic that Fortuna would grant my father's wish in such a strange fashion?"

His voice sounded lifeless, the result, thought John, of that freezing numbness that the kindly gods send to the bereaved for the first few days after a death, lest the too heavy burden of grief snap mind and spirit under its inescapable oppression.

There was nothing he felt he could say to help Anatolius cope with his loss. He could only listen to him and in that way permit his friend to give rein to his feelings. Public displays of these were not considered manly, it was true, but Anatolius, newly orphaned, had not yet learnt the emotional control which circumstances and years at court had thrust upon John.

"Just a day or so ago," Anatolius went on, tears pooling in his bloodshot eyes, "I sat in that very chair you're in, John, listening to my father talk about respectability and how he wished I would become more responsible, before I brought danger upon him and others." He buried his wan face in his hands. "And I brought his death here," he said, his voice muffled. "Now he is gone and I have gained all the respectability and responsibility he could have wished, because now I am the head of the household. If only I wasn't! If only he were still alive!"

John felt moisture seeping into his own eyes in sympathy with the grief-stricken man before him, who was now valiantly trying to swipe tears discreetly away with his knuckles.

"Yes, Anatolius," he replied quietly. "It is a fact that, by virtue of his being your father, he was always part of your world. And now he is gone, and that world is changed forever. It can never be the same. I think that now you are bitterly regretting all your hasty words to him, your disrespect. Wishing, too, that you had told him you loved him more often than you did."

Anatolius looked at his friend in a wondering fashion.

John nodded. "That is exactly how I felt when my father died," he said, "although I would never speak of it outside this room. Although it's hard to believe now, time will smooth out the jagged edges of the pain in your heart, just as it has since your mother died."

"There is not a day passes that I do not think of her, John," Anatolius admitted, "although I rarely talk about her."

"That is the way of it," John nodded. "We speak little of the departed, even though our memories of them are our only comfort once they are gone. And as to your father, he was a good man and I know you will conduct yourself well when the time comes for the funeral rites. I'd be happy to assist you with those, if you wish."

"Thank you," Anatolius said listlessly, leaning his chin on his hand and staring down at the inlaid skull peering up at him from the desk top.

"But," John went on, "one thing, Anatolius. You must not blame yourself for his death. A senator, indeed any man, always has enemies of whom he is not aware. It is part of life. Nothing that you did could possibly have caused his death."

Anatolius looked up, a flash of anger in his tired eyes. "But I did, John. He gave me free hand with the banquet. I sent out the invitations. Therefore I must take the blame."

John sighed, realizing it was too soon for him to attempt to persuade his friend that his reasoning was faulty.

"And the odd thing is," Anatolius continued, hunching his shoulders and wrapping his arms around himself as if he was cold, despite the warmth of the room. "I was very careful not to invite persons whose presence might embarrass or distress my father. Senator Balbinus, for example. There'd been bad blood between them for some time. And there were one or two others, but you see, there must have been one that I somehow overlooked, the bastard who ate and drank and laughed with us and then murdered..." His voice trailed away and he looked down in dumb misery.

"Your father has been ferried over the Styx earlier than any of us could have foreseen," John said, "but can you not try to think how happy he was about your appointment to the quaestor's office? Many men must live beyond their time of happiness and die looking back on their lives with regret and bitterness. He was proud of you and although perhaps he rarely said so, he loved you. He has left you an honorable name and an excellent example of civic duty."

"And surely Lord Mithra smiles on him for that alone," Anatolius murmured.

John nodded. It seemed that their conversation was helping Anatolius somewhat, so he cast about for further topics. Inspiration struck him. "Anatolius, here is an odd coincidence. From what Philo has been telling me, if I had attended the Academy a few years later than I did, your father might well have been one of my tutors."

Anatolius looked surprised. "That's an odd thought indeed. He used to talk occasionally about his days at the Academy, but after a while, you know how it is, the stories all become over familiar and you don't listen too closely. Of course, he left the Academy years before Justinian ordered it closed. Yet despite what Justinian claims, I never formed the impression that theology was much discussed there, pagan or otherwise. I know my father lectured on the nature of justice, for one thing, and he did once attempt to explain the mathematical proof for the existence of the aether, or some such theory. I was not much interested, I am sorry to say."

"I wasn't either," John admitted. "I was hasty of nature, I fear, wishing to learn but not wanting to take the time necessary to acquire knowledge. That was why I left. Had Clotho spun my life differently, no doubt I would have trodden an entirely different path to the one that brought me eventually to Constantinople."

"You would have been happier, John. Yet I can't imagine you being an inattentive student."

Anatolius got up and began pacing from the desk to the door and back again. John thought it was an encouraging sign that the younger man was restless. Upon arrival, John had questioned Simon and learnt that Anatolius, having ordered his father's body prepared for burial, had locked himself into the study on the night of the banquet and remained there ever since, drinking only water and refusing food.

Anatolius stopped his pacing and looked at John. There was a strange expression in his eyes. "I believe," he announced, "that the dead can speak to us from Hades."

John wondered if the other had become light-headed from lack of nourishment.

"And," Anatolius continued serenely, "that the method by which they communicate with the living is through dreams. So I have slept here, in the last place my father saw before he left this world, hoping that he would appear in my dreams and tell me who murdered him."

John asked if he had received any such visitation.

"No, my father did not come back," Anatolius frowned. "But my mother did. Yet I cannot remember exactly what she said, however hard I try." He looked stricken at his admission. "It seems to me that she bade me to open my eyes, to be ever vigilant and guard my back against the blade, just as my father said to me in this very room not so long ago. I asked her if she could name his murderer and suddenly she was gone."

"Then it was but a dream," John said gently. "And we must labor in this world to find the culprit." He stood and laid his thin hand on Anatolius' arm. For an instant he recalled his recent audience with Theodora and her order that he devote himself solely to investigating the deaths of the stylites. He pushed the unpleasant recollection aside.

"I give you my solemn oath, Anatolius, as a Runner of the Sun, as a fellow initiate of Lord Mithra, that I will help you find the man responsible for your father's death and ensure that he pays the price for it."

⁂

Following his discussion with Anatolius, John made his way home through unusually congested streets, his thoughts restlessly circling the mystery of Senator Aurelius' death. He was so preoccupied that he had pounded at his own front door long enough to attract a curious stare from the guard lounging outside the excubitors' barracks across the square before he realized that Peter was not attending to his duties. When he tested the nail-studded door he found it secured from within.

Faced with the unexpected problem of how to get into his own home, he stepped back and surveyed its brick front. The first floor was a blank wall in the usual fashion and the windows ranged along the second floor were well beyond his reach. A single rap on the door usually brought Peter, if not on the run, as near to it as to it as he could manage. But Peter had not been himself recently and John now found himself imagining the elderly servant lying helpless inside, unable to move or be heard calling for assistance. Perhaps he had fallen down the narrow stairs and now lay unconscious only a step or two away on the other side of the door on which his master had lately been pounding.

Suddenly the bolt was drawn back and the door swung open, revealing Peter's leathery, lined face peering out. He apologized for the time it had taken for him to answer his master's summons.

"I laid down to rest for a while and fell asleep," he explained as he rebolted the door. Hardly were the words spoken when his legs gave way. John barely caught his arm in time to prevent him from pitching forward and breaking his gray head open on the tiled floor.

It was all John could do to assist Peter up the two flights of stairs to the servant's room. Although Peter was too feeble to walk unaided he nevertheless protested and resisted John's assistance, as drowning men will sometimes struggle against their rescuers.

"I can't lie about all day, master, I have work in the kitchen," Peter fretted when John insisted he rest.

"Bread and cheese will feed me well enough for now, and those I can get for myself." John glanced at the large wooden cross on the wall behind Peter's narrow cot. It struck him anew how ironic it was that a servant could display the symbols of his beliefs openly, whereas his powerful and high placed master could not afford the risk of having any symbol of Mithra in his home.

"You see," said Peter, catching the direction of John's glance, "you need not fear. I do not believe my time has come yet, but if it has, then surely He will send another to look after you in my place."

"That may be, but for now you need rest and that is what you must have. I shall ask Gaius to visit you and perhaps he can prescribe something to help you recuperate more quickly."

"That physician will have no stronger medicine than the one I am taking already."

Peter nodded at the plate on a small table in the corner. It held what remained of Matthew the Pure's pilgrim token, the sight of which reminded John of the dangerous speed at which another holy man's reputation was growing.

※ ※ ※

He took bread from the basket on the kitchen table. Peter had not been well enough to go to market that morning, it seemed, for no cheese was to be found. Instead, John contented himself with a plain chunk of bread and a cup of water in what had been his study but with the arrival of Philo had been transformed into a shatranj room.

After its outing to Aurelius' banquet, the exotic game sat once again on its borrowed table, its heavily carved playing pieces arrayed against each other in orderly ranks.

He picked up a finely wrought ship. It reminded him of his long ago journey to the chilly, misty land of Bretania at the very edge of the civilized world. The memory of crossing the choppy seas in the teeth of a gale was not a pleasant one and he set the piece back down quickly.

Thankful for solitude, he sat quietly and allowed his gaze to wander across the mosaic wall of his study.

At this hour, the girl Zoe slumbered quietly behind her tesseraed eyes, waiting for the flickering light of a lamp to awaken and animate her. Yet the world in which she lived still spoke to John.

Beneath the heavenly riot of pagan gods, who like Zoe were nightly given life by lamplight although life of a much coarser nature, was the familiar bucolic scene. Staring at the bent-backed farmer plodding along behind a patient ox as he plowed his field, John's thoughts strayed to the palace gardener, Hypatia.

Suddenly, he saw a solution to the problem of what to do concerning Peter. He would enlist Hypatia to assist with the household duties, temporarily at least. Doubtless he would still have to order Peter to accept her help, particularly since he did like anyone in his kitchen when he was cooking, but on the other hand, he suspected that his proud servant would not resist too strongly since Hypatia was a friend who had once served with him in the same household.

The sound of Philo clattering upstairs intruded upon this happy thought.

"John! I am glad to see you've returned!" Philo said, breezily barging into the study. "Because although as you know I am not one to complain, I visited the kitchen earlier and it's not quite what I would expect to find in a Lord Chamberlain's household. No roast venison, no lark's tongues or stuffed peacocks, none of those exotic fruits and spices which we all know courtiers dine upon every night! What is that servant of yours up to, anyway? It took him long enough to answer the door, I noticed."

"You were here when I arrived?"

"I was in the garden, contemplating philosophical theories. Anyway, I was wondering if perhaps we could dine upon duck again tonight, although Peter needs to make a richer sauce as I was telling him just the other day. I don't think he appreciated the suggestion, to be honest."

"He will not be cooking anything tonight. He is unwell," John said.

"I see," Philo was peeved. "Perhaps you should consider engaging another servant. After all, we replace our boots when they are no longer serviceable, do we not?"

Philo's hand went unerringly to the ship John had moved. "I see you have been examining my game. My demonstration at Aurelius' banquet certainly attracted a good deal of interest, but I doubt if anyone will remember it now, considering all the excitement over the senator's unfortunate death, not to mention that disreputable girl's."

Philo continued to prattle on about his prospects of tutoring would-be shatranj players, but had lost John's sympathetic ear after his outrageous suggestion that Peter be tossed aside like worn-out footwear.

"Philo," John finally cut in sharply, "Peter is my trusted servant and I will deal with his difficulties in the manner of a just master. But as for yourself, I must deal with you as master of this house. I must insist that from now on, while you are enjoying my hospitality, you will not venture outside alone. It would be foolish, since the streets are becoming extremely dangerous even for those who are familiar the city."

Philo glared at his former student. "You have no right to speak to me in that manner, John."

"There is no one except for the emperor to whom I may not speak in any manner I wish," John replied coldly. "And I am ordering you to remain inside this house for your own safety."

The harsh words stuck in his throat, or perhaps it was the last crumbs of bread. He reminded himself it had been many years since Philo had been his tutor and further that he had no right to speak of Peter in the manner that he had used.

"Very well, John. After all, I am in no position to argue with my benefactor." Philo replaced the shatranj ship on the board with enough force to send several smaller pieces to the floor.

The mention of Aurelius' banquet reminded John of another matter and his anger at Philo was now directed at himself. How could he have forgotten something so important? He, the Lord Chamberlain who owed his position and his continued life largely to his unerring attention to every detail, no matter how minor it seemed in the richly woven carpet of court life.

"To change the subject, Philo," he began, "Anatolius said he left a document here on the day of the banquet."

"He would have left it with your servant. Why are you asking me about it?"

"Peter was not here then, being at work directing the slaves in Aurelius' kitchen."

Philo looked at the ceiling. "I know nothing of any such document. You have intimated that I am foolish. Would you now call me a liar as well?"

John had spoken plainly on many occasions to satraps and senators and the highest officials of the empire. But those powerful men had not taught him to decipher the magic of the written word nor walked with him along the shaded paths of the Academy, opening his mind to the wonders of history and philosophy. He could not bring himself to do it.

"No, Philo," he finally admitted with a sigh. "I cannot call you a liar. But I must now go out, so please remain here and see that Peter does not try to over-exert himself. I have inquiries to make."

Chapter Thirteen

John found the first person he sought standing under the portico of the senate house on the north side of the Forum Constantine.

Senator Balbinus looked as if he'd not slept since he'd appeared at Aurelius' house hotly demanding to speak to his recently murdered colleague concerning certain mysterious matters whose details he had refused to divulge.

On this occasion, however, Balbinus' anger was directed elsewhere.

"The senators were ordered to convene here in the very midst of the mob," he complained, "and furthermore, we've been forbidden to leave the city." His tired gaze moved past John out into the forum.

The crowd of raucous humanity eddying past the base of the Column of Constantine was the usual mixture of roughly clad laborers interspersed with an occasional better robed aristocrat. Customers jostled each other in front of the shops lining the upper and lower levels of the colonnades surrounding the forum.

Nothing in the scene seemed out of the ordinary. Still, on his way over, John had sensed impending violence. Was the collective breath of the city sourer with wine, were its citizens talking louder than normal?

"No doubt the emperor fears the sight of the entire senate scattering to their estates would cause a panic," John commented.

"It has nothing to do with Justinian. It's Theodora who's holding us hostage." Balbinus replied. "There's no doubt that this order is her doing. The emperor is a reasonable man, except when he chooses to wrestle with the angels. Not that we don't all support his theological efforts, of course," he added hastily, "Yet even the Patriarch has fled the city, or so I hear."

The two men were conversing beside one of portico's four towering columns, taking advantage of the scant warmth offered by weak early afternoon sunlight. John inquired politely about security measures at Balbinus' country estates and vineyards and the senator grumbled and muttered his replies in irritated tones.

"Do you think ne'er do wells in the country aren't aware that we are being detained here?" he demanded. "Do you suppose they won't be swift to take advantage of the situation if violence breaks out in the city? We are all men of property. Businessmen. It is intolerable that we should not be permitted to look after our assets at such a time as this."

John found himself wondering if it had been an illegal business arrangement that had led one senator to murder another. Yet powerful men did not usually find it necessary to personally resort to murder to dispose of their rivals. They had more subtle means at their disposal. Nevertheless, Balbinus' visit to Aurelius had been just ill-timed and inexplicable enough to pique John's curiosity.

Then too, he could not help noticing that as Balbinus spoke he kept the side of his face presented toward his visitor. Certainly, John thought, it was a regal profile that would have looked more fitting on a follis than Justinian's commoner cast of features. Was it the practiced vanity of a thoroughly professional politician or was the man trying to distract attention from the partially healed wound running along one cheekbone?

"Was it affairs of business that brought you to Aurelius' door?" he asked.

Balbinus' hesitation was slight enough that few but John would have noted it. "Of a sort," he finally admitted.

"Is it then a new arrangement that men of property normally discuss such matters at the first light of dawn?"

"My visit concerned something I prefer not to discuss, Lord Chamberlain."

"Perhaps you would rather discuss it with the Prefect?"

Balbinus looked puzzled. "What do you mean?"

Now it was John who paused. The senator's surprise seemed genuine. Could the man truly be such an innocent? Didn't he realize the implications to be drawn from the odd hour of his visit to Aurelius' home?

"I mean no offense, senator, but your colleague Aurelius was murdered. The Prefect will naturally be interested in, let us not say an enemy, let us say a colleague with whom he had fallen out, who arrived uninvited at the victim's doorstep shortly thereafter."

Balbinus affected a half-hearted laugh. "If I'd had the old rascal murdered why would I come calling? To ascertain whether the poison had had the desired effect? The whole affair is the talk of the senate."

Several senators emerged from the busy throng and nodded familiarly to Balbinus as they passed by on their way into the senate house. John did not recognize any of them, not surprisingly since most of the landholders who comprised the senatorial class visited the city only very occasionally. Aurelius was one of the few who lived there. Or had lived there, he corrected himself.

Balbinus scowled. "Now that my colleagues have seen us talking, they'll be asking me what fresh gossip I have from the palace."

"Senator, I must ask you again about your business with Aurelius. Let me also assure you that I am a much more discreet man than the Prefect."

"But you can't suspect me, surely? I am a senator!"

"I am not implying that, but surely you will understand that under the circumstances you are almost certainly already under suspicion so far as the Prefect is concerned?"

"So you consider that's a possibility? Well, then, it seems I must speak after all. It strikes me that if I'm thrown into the dungeons you can take over my job here, Lord Chamberlain. You certainly have the persuasive tongue for it!"

Balbinus stared out into the forum for a few moments, deep in thought. One hand went absently to the reddened wound on his face, then drew away quickly.

"My business with Aurelius was personal and of a very delicate nature," he finally said. "My wife Lucretia has been missing these past few days. I thought I might find her at his house."

Balbinus' reluctant words not only explained his interest in speaking to Aurelius but also strongly indicated the feminine hand that had inflicted the half healed scratch that marred the senatorial face, John thought. "You had reason to believe that you would find her at Senator Aurelius' house?"

"I did. She was, however, not there and is still missing."

"I see. You have, of course, alerted the Prefect to her disappearance?"

"No. I intend to take care of the matter myself. Do you think I have no resources at my disposal?"

"If she wandered off…"

"Lucretia did not wander off. She is a capable woman although young. And very beautiful. Any man half my age would be proud to claim her as his wife!"

One of the men who had recently arrived emerged from the senate house. "Balbinus, we need your assistance. Several of us are composing a petition to the emperor, pointing out that if our estates are sacked while we are detained here against our will, the imperial treasury will suffer mightily since compensation will be due and most certainly sought."

John silently admired their courage in even contemplating presenting such a petition to Justinian.

"I have to attend to this, Lord Chamberlain," Balbinus said. "So if you will permit me? There is nothing more I can tell you, at any rate. I do not need to say, I trust, that I rely upon your discretion regarding what I have just told you."

John nodded, adding "And if anything else occurs to you, I am not difficult to find."

John remained standing under the portico after Balbinus had gone inside. Again he noticed that the eddying crowds seemed louder than usual, and few beggars could be seen prodding charitable purses by displaying their malformed bodies or ghastly sores. That was strange, he thought, since more often than not society's outcasts were at the forefront when unrest fermented in dark alleys and darker lives boiled over from a scalding cauldron of noise and hate, its flood sweeping all before it. He must mention this sudden curious lack of mendicants to Felix.

John made his way quickly across the forum. At the Column of Constantine he glanced up briefly at its mounted statue of the first Christian emperor. A smile flickered over John's sunburnt face as he recalled one of Anatolius' more unfortunate remarks, to the effect that the emperor's statue should have been placed on a lower pedestal because there wasn't a single inhabitant of Constantinople who, having seen its glory once, would bother to make the effort to crane their neck to observe it a second time.

He sighed as he resumed his swift lope, realizing he could not avoid further investigation of Balbinus' suspicious appearance at Aurelius' house. But there were other interviews to be conducted first.

***

Following John unobserved had been child's play. Tall and lean and wrapped on this chilly afternoon in a heavy black cloak, he made a striking figure, his dress and bearing clearing him an easy path through swarming humanity. There had been no danger of losing sight of him in the common throng while still being able to maintain a safe distance. It would be simpler than expected to close the space between them when the time came, thought the pursuer, a smug smile crossing his face.

The narrow street they were now traversing was lined with brick buildings, not tenements but obviously divided into apartments. Their first floors were taken up by the customary merchants' establishments. The smell of fruit too long unsold mingled with the odor of boiled fish and cabbage emitted from open windows. Several workshops rang with the sound of hammering, but the street's occupants were apparently even less inclined to labor than usual, since several establishments were shuttered. Here and there, men clustered in stray patches of pale sunlight, conversing in strident tones but falling ominously silent as the two strangers, pursued and pursuer, approached.

John's swift stride took him past the mouths of several alleys, narrower than the street into which they yawned and largely deserted at this time of day except for the occasional foraging rat, skittering about their gloomy length.

Philo had already decided that he would draw closer to his prey and risk the possibility of revealing his pursuit if John should turn aside into an alley since he had no wish to become lost anywhere in that warren of narrow, dark ways a second time. He had therefore been chagrined when John led him at last to the Forum Constantine. That enormous open space made it impossible for him to sidle close enough to the senate house's portico to overhear John's conversation with the important-looking man he was addressing. He was thus forced to lurk under one of the ornamental archways leading into the forum, peering out now and then while wondering where John might go next.

Yes, he thought, John would not be at all pleased if he discovered that Philo had ventured out of the house. But who was he to order Philo about as if he were an ignorant student? There again, hadn't Philo already garnered more about the dead stylites than the Prefect's men had managed to uncover? And, no doubt, an innocent-looking old gentleman could easily extract more information from one suspected of murder than could an intimidating Lord Chamberlain. He had only to find out who John suspected and then talk to them. And how else to do that but by following John, however distasteful such deceit might be?

Yet, he thought, John would thank him in the end, when he was presented with those vital scraps of fact necessary to solving the murders. Not to mention the matter of deciphering that most peculiar letter from the leader of the Michaelites. The guilt he might have felt at concealing his possession of the hastily scribbled copy Anatolius had left, in order to study it for carefully hidden meanings, had been assuaged by John's totally unwarranted tone with him. What right did he have to speak to him in that manner? He might indeed be Lord Chamberlain to Emperor Justinian but Philo remembered a time when John was an unlettered student from the country, rough and awkward in his manner although certainly intelligent, if overly hasty in making decisions.

Peeking around the edge of the archway, Philo was suddenly assailed by the sweet scent of roses. It was unexpected here, amidst the odor of the crowd and the bitter smell of animal dung. Not to mention the acridly lingering memory of the beggars who had relieved themselves in the relative privacy of the archway under bas reliefs commemorating forgotten military victories.

Philo was reminded of Senator Aurelius' banquet, at which the gentle fragrance of roses had hung sweetly in the air. He looked around.

A heavily perfumed child glared up at him with the black eyes of Cerberus, red-painted lips drawn back in an expression that was not exactly a smile.

"You, old man! Tell me quickly why I should not call the Prefect and have you thrown into an imperial dungeon immediately!"

Philo drew back in alarm and confusion, staring at the apparition. The boy, for it was a boy despite the heavy layer of chalk on its face, kohl rimmed eyes and the cloyingly heavy rose perfume, was dressed in a short plain brown tunic which blended in with the garb of the majority of the crowd around them. The bright yellow leggings he wore did not. Philo had occasionally glimpsed exotic beings such as this on the palace grounds. The lad was obviously one of dozens of decorative court pages.

"What do you mean?" stammered Philo, for once finding himself at a loss for words.

"Oh dear, what do I mean?" mimicked the boy, making his voice quaver. "Don't think to play the innocent with me, I warn you, or you'll be lying on top of dead men at the bottom of a pit within the hour. I don't suppose you'd last long down there. Even an old gizzard like yours might be palatable to the crows."

Philo retreated another step, not caring when he felt one of the befouled bas reliefs imprint its triumphant scene upon his himation. "Who are you, to accuse me like this?" he demanded, outraged.

The boy gave a harsh laugh. "My name is Hektor," he said. "And I am well-known in high circles. The very highest."

Philo protested weakly that he was guilty of no wrong doing, having merely been taking a stroll around the city.

"You have been following the Lord Chamberlain," Hektor broke in impatiently.

"That's ridiculous!"

"You've been creeping along behind him ever since he left his house."

"How would you know that?" Philo demanded. Had he been so obvious in his shadowing that even a child had deduced his plan?

"When you both came out of the same house and took the same path, yet you did not hail the Lord Chamberlain, I said to myself, now, that is interesting. Why would that wretched old scoundrel be skulking along following the highly placed official whose hospitality he has been enjoying? It was quite obvious that was what you were doing, for when he paused, so did you. So I followed you both. After all, who knows what your design might be? Under that billowing, pretentious thing you're wearing, are you an assassin in an old man's clothing waiting for your opportunity to murder our dear Lord Chamberlain?"

Hektor stepped forward, extending one hand to grasp Philo's shoulder as the old man cringed backwards, trapped by the befouled wall behind him. When the boy's delicate hand mercifully stopped short and drew back, Philo noticed its fingernails were painted.

Philo paled, feeling his heart squirming fearfully in his chest. "I am an acquaintance of the Lord Chamberlain and indeed, as you say, I am enjoying his hospitality, as is well known."

"Ah, but how do I know that you are not a spy who has ingratiated himself by some subterfuge into the Lord Chamberlain's household?"

"I have known John for years. He was..."

"Never mind." Hektor waved his dainty hand in a gesture of dismissal. "I shall allow you to live. Count yourself fortunate that I am in a merciful mood today." A scowl marred the boy's beautiful face. "You seem harmless enough. You may go now."

Philo departed hastily. As he left the forum at as quick a pace as he could manage, he berated himself for the irrational fear he had felt of the absurdly painted creature, yet it was a fear he could not shake off. He glanced back once more before going around a corner and leaving the forum blessedly out of sight. From that distance, from the back, as Hektor craned his neck to see over the crowd, he looked like any other boy.

❄❄❄

"Yes, Lucretia, I remember it was always your favorite game as a child. You loved to hide for me to find you," Nonna recalled, a smile blossoming along the well-worn lines of her face.

The elderly woman was in full flood of happy reminiscences. Chattering like a magpie, she only paused now and then to spoon up boiled wheat from her dented silver bowl, a gift from her former owners upon her manumission and retirement.

Lucretia was perched nearby on a low chair finely inlaid with rosewood nearby. It had been another parting gift from her parents to her former nursemaid. Nonna seemed unchanged, she thought, or was this strange effect of time leaving no traces of its inexorable passing merely an illusion? To a child, all adults look elderly. Yet now that Lucretia was a woman, Nonna, although more stooped and slower in her movements, looked scarcely a day older. The only real difference was that her hair had thinned to little more than a gray nimbus.

The young woman nervously patted at her own glossy black hair, such a contrast to her milk white skin as more than one poetic suitor had remarked.

"I always hid under the kitchen table, didn't I?" she recalled.

Nonna nodded, smiling. "Yes, and I had such a bad memory even then that that was always the last place I looked. And of course with being rather hard of hearing, naturally I could never hear you giggling, not even when I came in to ask the cook if he had seen you."

Lucretia smiled wordlessly, enjoying Nonna's little fictions, happy to listen to the old woman's soothing flow of words, as sweet as the honey with which Nonna had cured the tickle in her throat whenever she had a cough.

The narrow, sunwashed room in which they were conversing was on the top floor of a sturdy house on a side street leading from the Forum Constantine. The room served as Nonna's bedroom, kitchen and general living space. Despite its cramped dimensions, it was pleasing to her, particularly as it was part of a building of solid masonry construction rather than one of the dilapidated wooden tenements in which the city's truly impoverished congregated.

The large unshuttered window by which Lucretia sat admitted street sounds floating up from four stories below, a running stream of noise that diminished only slightly with each setting of the sun. There was always people out and about after darkness fell, although not necessarily to do good works.

A hoarse shout caught Lucretia's attention and she shifted quickly in her chair to scan the scene below. No, that wasn't Balbinus' voice. It had probably emanated from the ne'er-do-wells conversing loudly as they lounged like dusty tomcats in a patch of sunlight at the house front.

"But hide and seek is a child's game," remarked Nonna. "It is not a game for a proper young woman. I'm glad you are here rather than walking on dusty roads or at that shrine you say you visited. Did they sing hymns?"

"Not while I was there," Lucretia said. "But speaking of hymns, I recall that whenever we were going home after attending a church service, if I started to sing them in the street, you always admonished me very severely."

Nonna sniffed. "Girls who sing in the streets grow up to be prostitutes, selling themselves in dark corners. Everyone knows that."

"I would never prostitute myself," Lucretia said firmly. "Besides, Michael will stop all singing in the streets."

Nonna took another spoonful from her bowl. "You were always my favorite, Lucretia, of all the children I have looked after. I had high hopes for you, my dear. I still do. You are so beautiful, so intelligent, and yet I confess there have been times when I feared you were about to make a terrible mistake. Anatolius, for example. A handsome young man and pleasant enough, but really not at all a suitable match for you."

"Anatolius is the son of a senator," Lucretia pointed out.

"But Balbinus is himself a senator and a man of substance. Not a landless boy like Anatolius."

"But a woman should marry for love, don't you think?"

"Oh, my dear," Nonna gave a nervous laugh and her weather-beaten face reddened. "Love? Well, there is poetry and then again there is life."

"I will not be bought and sold," Lucretia said quietly.

She was bitterly disappointed. She had expected Nonna to take her part, just as she always had, or at least in Lucretia's memory. It had been some years now since her nursemaid had been granted freedom and a small pension and given this tiny apartment. Lucretia had visited her many times in the intervening interval. But not lately, not since Balbinus had turned out the attendant who accompanied her around the city. He had done it out of spite, she was certain.

Nonna sighed. "Lucretia," she began gently, "You will understand that I am saying this only for your own good. And that is just how I would begin when you were a child and you were going to hear something you'd consider unpleasant, yes, yes, I can see you thinking it now."

Lucretia smiled sadly. "You are going to tell me that I must go back to my husband, who is doubtless pacing the floor wondering where I am and worrying about my safety."

Nonna nodded. "Yes. I could not refuse you shelter in my humble home but it has been long enough now. You must be aware that rumors will be circulating. This will not reflect well upon you or your husband, or for that matter on your own family."

"I do not want to cause difficulties, Nonna. I will seek some other place to go."

Nonna clucked scoldingly. "What do you know of fending for yourself, child? The city is a dangerous place and grows more so every day. You are fortunate indeed to have a man like Balbinus to take care of you."

"And I thought you would understand!"

"You have not been very married long, Lucretia. You seemed happy enough. What demons have been whispering in your ear? Or does your husband mistreat you? I have a strong suspicion that my little lamb is not telling Nonna the entire story."

Lucretia shook her head. She realized she could not bring herself to speak of it, tell Nonna that the senator's ring burned her finger as if the circlet was fresh from the goldsmith. She could not accept her duty as other women did. Hadn't she tried, for more than two years? Even after she had realized that it was an agony that would never end.

Then she had heard Michael's preaching and something in the man's words, something she could not identify, called insistently to her.

"Well, if you are indeed concealing something from me," Nonna was saying, "still, you are from a noble family and therefore need no instruction on these matters. Would it not be possible to overcome the difficulty? Perhaps Balbinus could talk to your father about it?" She paused, considering how best to phrase what she had to say. "If you will permit an old woman who in her humble way loves you to speak plainly, whatever marital problems you are experiencing, Balbinus does love you and he must be very worried. It surprises me that he has not already been here looking for you."

"The only way he could learn of your whereabouts is by questioning my father. To do that, he would have to admit that I had left him, and he would never do that. He is after all a man in the public eye and must be ever careful of his reputation."

"And what about your own reputation, Lucretia? Do you not think that your servants are not wagging their tongues and nodding very wisely as they discuss the identity of your lover? Or lovers?"

The stern look on the old woman's face relaxed. "Well, now," she continued with a chuckle, "I see that setting of the jaw that I remember so well from your childhood. Nonna has said enough, yes, yes. But no doubt you accept the wisdom of my words, just as you always did when you were a little girl, so let's enjoy a last few quiet hours together before you're on your way home."

She wiped a crust of bread around her silver bowl to sop up the last scraps of boiled wheat. "You were blessed not to be assaulted when you went to visit that shrine, Lucretia, for even in that wretched old tunic you are as beautiful as a dove and it is a miracle you did not attract unwanted attention. Perhaps it would be safest to convey a message to Senator Balbinus so that he can come to take you back, or at the very least send a couple of brawny servants to accompany you home."

Lucretia stared down into the busy street, panic welling in her breast. A thin girl passed along below, carrying a basket of vegetables. Slaves had more freedom than well-born women. A beggar could roam the city without an escort.

The world was such a large place and so full of wonders and life, how could she spend all her days confined in the dark, windowless cell of a loveless marriage?

Chapter Fourteen

ohn was startled by a high-pitched scream sliding upwards until the voice cracked and gave out. "The master is attending a patient," explained the maidservant who had just admitted him to Gaius' house. The bruise under her eye, newly blossoming when he had called on Gaius the night Peter had been taken ill, had faded to a yellowish discoloration.

"Don't worry, the master isn't inflicting unnecessary suffering," the girl rattled on. "A good loud scream is always a hopeful sign. When there's no sound from the surgery, that's when the poor things are carted out on boards."

John crossed the atrium to the room where Gaius conducted his professional consultations. The ruddy-faced physician was tending to a young man seated on the edge of a long wooden table. Gaius looked up from the man's right arm, which was already firmly swathed in bandages from wrist to shoulder, to acknowledge John's arrival with an amiable nod. The contents of a small clay pot set on the table beside his patient filled the sunny room with a rancid smell. The injured man's face was the color of an unpainted marble statue and set just as rigidly.

"You are fortunate you broke the upper bone," Gaius informed his patient, "It's possible that you might be left with a slight deformity when it's healed, but you have good muscles and a little extra flesh there, so if you are, your injury won't show at all. The ladies will love you as much as ever!"

He secured the last length of linen strip and the man climbed gingerly off the table.

"Now whatever you do, don't try to bend that arm too soon," Gaius instructed. "I once treated someone who took no notice of this advice and the jagged end of the bone not only broke through the skin but the bandaging as well."

The patient fumbled at the pouch on his belt with his useful hand. "I am sorry but I have few nummi," he said hoarsely. "I hope these will be sufficient?"

Gaius waved away his offer of payment. "Never mind. Put them towards buying yourself a jug of wine. In a couple of hours you'll need it. You'll think Cerberus' teeth are chewing on that bone," he replied cheerfully. "Pain isn't so bad. Just think of it as a sign you're alive."

Gaius shook his head when the man had departed. "That poor young man is a plasterer, John. He was working on the new banqueting hall's ceiling when the scaffolding gave way. Fortunately an excubitor was passing by and brought him here immediately."

"He will recover full use of his arm?"

"Oh, I have set the bone well, John. It will certainly heal well if he follows my instructions. But until it does, how he will feed himself and his family, if he has one, with just one good arm, I cannot say."

Gaius wiped unguent from the leaf-shaped blade of the spathomele lying next to the clay pot and bustled off with both through an archway into the small storeroom opening off his surgery. Glancing into the other room, John noted two walls of shelves crowded with pots, jars and wooden boxes. A large, low table holding trays of probes, forceps and scalpels and a selection of basins of various sizes stood against the third wall.

"That's was a foul smelling concoction you were using, Gaius," John remarked, following him into the storeroom.

"Cerate, that's what it was. It's compounded mostly of lard and wax. Marvelously effective for dressings."

John picked up a mortar partly filled with pulped leaves.

"Comfrey," Gaius told him. "Another excellent medication for knitting together broken bones, but in fact when that young man arrived I was preparing it for burns."

"You are expecting to be treating them, then?"

"The entire city is expecting fires, I would imagine. If not of the supernatural sort, then the kind set by the sort of fools driven to violence by superstitious fear."

John set down the mortar and fingered a stoppered jar containing a dried herb he could not identify. "I suspect many of your ingredients are poisonous?"

"Practically everything in this room is poisonous, if you do not administer it correctly," Gaius confirmed, "or if you mix it with another ingredient or two. Take hellebore for example, which is what you're fiddling with, by the way. Hypatia brought me that from the palace gardens only last week. She says the empress always stops to admire its flowers, which is rather amusing since we both know the plant is poisonous and doubtless so does Theodora. I've asked Hypatia if she can supply me with rue. I'm beginning to run out."

John, grasping his opportunity, asked about the course of treatment the physician had prescribed for Aurelius.

"When he first came to me with his bladder complaint I prescribed warm naphtha, the usual thing for that sort of discomfort. But when that didn't heal him, I realized he was suffering from a bladder stone."

Gaius' expression darkened. "John, why are you questioning me so closely?"

"Simply put, the senator was poisoned—and here is a room full of poisons."

"He hadn't taken naphtha for three or four days, if you're implying that I tampered with his medication. He was fasting, or at least he should have been, because had he not passed the stone, I would have had to resort to surgery."

"He was telling everyone at the banquet he had been cured by Michael's blessing."

"I heard him," Gaius said shortly. "Regrettably, it resulted in heated words between us. Strange how it hadn't occurred to him that his miraculous cure may have simply been my ministrations taking effect. As I pointed out to him, unlike miracles which are instantaneous, medical treatments often take some time to work their full effect."

"However unfair he might have seemed by crediting your cure to Michael, still, it's undeniable that the two of you argued before he was murdered."

"That was the wine talking."

"If wine can talk, doubtless it can also wield a weapon, and while some men find Lethe in their cups, others find the Furies. Did you think I would not notice your servant's face the other night? Her bruising was as purple as your nose and its cause was the same."

Gaius looked ashamed. "I regret striking the girl, John. I have apologized to her. But surely you don't really think I murdered Aurelius?"

"You informed half the guests at the banquet that he was bent on ruining you by telling everyone they could be cured immediately by going to visit Michael. Your devotion to Bacchus is common knowledge, Gaius. It's already cost you a number of your patients. You can't afford to lose the rest."

"That's ridiculous, John! To murder a man, a senator, because—" Gaius face reddened with anger.

"Too much wine makes men do ridiculous things. Or murderous things," John pointed out.

"Indeed? And did the senator's most excellent wine also make me set fire to that poor girl from Isis' house? I was certainly not responsible for either death. You're grilling me like St Lawrence or a street vendor's fish," Gaius concluded plaintively, "and I considered you a friend."

"I am your friend," John replied quietly. "But as a physician you will know that cures necessitate investigation and investigations are not always painless."

Gaius turned away. Grabbing a heavy pestle, he angrily pounded it down into the mortar.

"You misunderstand, Gaius," John assured him. "I must speak to all who attended Aurelius' banquet. I am going now to question Isis further."

"Good!" Gaius did not look up as he ground the mixture in the mortar to smoother consistency. "And while you're there you can inform her that her girls will have to soak their contraceptive pessaries in olive oil for a while, since I can't spare lead ointment for them right now. On the other hand, I shall soon should have rue enough to mix into abortion potions. That'll certainly please her."

❊❊❊

Madam Isis was outraged. "Soak them in olive oil! As if that would do any good! What's he trying to do, ruin me?" She paused, reflecting for a moment. "Ah, I have it, John. There's a honey seller just off the Forum Tauri. Honey can be got a lot cheaper than Gaius' services, and it's better than olive oil for the intended task. Since the honey seller visits my girls often, I'm certain we could arrange to exchange services. I'll send Darius around to ask about that right away. Now why didn't I think of this before? Think of the money I'd have saved!"

Isis was about to sweep out of her luxurious sitting room in her usual maelstrom of colored silks and exotic perfume when John stopped her. "There was another guard at the door when I arrived."

"I sent Darius out to purchase stronger locks and more bars for the windows. Iron bars. If he's back, he'll be outside further securing the house."

The madam left the room long enough to give instructions.

"Not that there haven't been one or two of my girls who, honey or not, have been rather careless," Isis told John upon her return. "And then there's poor Darius, he's absolutely distraught about Adula. Confidentially, John, he'd become very fond of the girl. Of course, she doted on him. And it was a terrible death." She glanced down at the burns on her hands, mute witnesses to her fruitless attempts to save Adula.

John moved uncomfortably in his chair. It was padded much too amply for his spartan tastes. "Isis, I'm here to speak to you about that very girl. You say her name was Adula?"

"Yes, or at least that was what we called her. What she was called by her father, or in any event the man who claimed to be her father when he showed up at my door trying to hawk her for twice as much as I was willing to pay, who can say? He never told me." Isis half reclined on her couch. The delicate table beside it bore its customary jug of wine and silver bowl filled with fruit. On this occasion, she did not seem inclined to sample either.

"You mentioned Darius was very fond of the girl. There was a special relationship with her, perhaps?"

"Special?" Isis laughed. "Darius frets over all of us. He's a regular mother hen. He did admit to taking some liberties with Adula, but there's nothing unusual in that, men are men and always will be. If it were otherwise, I'd be out of business. He'll recover his spirits soon enough."

"Can you tell me anything about Adula's background?"

Isis shook her head. Her cheeks were hollower than John had seen in the years he had known her. While it was true that her thinner features hinted at the finely chiseled face that had made her a rare beauty before she "retired to a desk post", as she liked to put it, they more strongly suggested incipient exhaustion.

"She was from one of those peasant families scrabbling to survive, or so said her father or whoever he was."

"Did she entertain any regular clients? Any particular favorites?"

"Favorites? Well, Senator Aurelius has never frequented this house, if that's what you're thinking. As for his son, I'm not aware he ever visited with her. Everyone knows he's attracted to the aristocratic type, and he's quite willing to put down an extra coin or two for one who can play the part well," she concluded.

John nodded, embarrassed that Anatolius' private preferences in such matters were a well known matter of commerce in Isis' house. "So there was no particular reason you chose her to be among those accompanying you to the senator's banquet?"

"Nothing beyond talent and enthusiasm. Besides, it is good for a country girl to see how wealthier citizens live, don't you think? It gives them an indication of what is possible in Constantinople. After all, we all know what Theodora was before she married Justinian, don't we?"

John agreed, adding "Of course, there were many men at that banquet who might have been here at one time or another, even though they all professed ignorance of your house when questioned."

Isis waved her beringed hand. "Please, John. You know I cannot answer the questions you are about to ask. My livelihood depends upon my being discreet even when my clients are not. But I will tell you this," she continued, "Just looking over the guests I recognized enough familiar faces to keep you busy interviewing for, well, for much longer than I suspect you have available to solve the matter."

John asked her to recount whatever she had observed of Adula's death. Unfortunately, Isis had been too intent on her flute-playing to notice anything until the screaming began. John made a mental note to request that one of the Prefect's men interview the other girls who had been present. Suspecting such questioning would be fruitless, he did not wish to waste his time on it. People tended to see what they expected to see. And unexpected events, catching them unready, were seldom carefully observed.

He asked Isis once more if she were certain she had no information to offer.

She shook her head. "Nothing except that I hear that around the city it's being said she was struck down because of her evil ways. If that's true, I might well be next."

John murmured that he doubted it, the sins of her house were not the worst in Constantinople by any means, and concluded with a slight smile, "Indeed, compared to some, your girls are still innocents."

Isis leaned forward intently. "At least, they are innocent of anything but quenching the natural fires of the fleshly sort. Personally, I don't believe those other fires had anything but a human origin and I suspect that you agree with me."

"Of course I do, but then neither of us are Christians."

"But how does one's religious beliefs change deductions arising from the facts?" A shadow passed over her face. "To tell you the truth, I blame myself for it," she said, dabbing at her suddenly wet eyes.

John looked at her questioningly.

"Isn't it obvious what happened? There were torches everywhere, in the corridors and rooms, along the colonnade. And I insisted my girls wear those elaborate costumes. A spark must have fallen into the folds of Adula's clothing and smoldered there until it burst into flame. And now those zealots are taking credit for what was nothing but a terrible accident!"

Before John could reply there was a brisk rap on the door. A blonde girl dressed in a softly folded, short linen skirt and little else padded barefoot in. Her sapphire colored eyes betrayed lively interest in this richly dressed man in her owner's private sitting room.

"I found Darius and he has departed to the honey seller's shop as directed, madam," she said respectfully.

"I shall have to talk to Darius at some point, Isis, but for now I must be away myself, since I have others to consult upon this matter," John said, concealing a smile at the girl's obvious curiosity. "Besides, you are becoming too philosophical for me, especially since there is a talkative old Greek philosopher living under my roof at the moment."

Isis laughed. "Come and see me again soon, then. I promise you I shall have some of that awful Egyptian wine you love and we'll talk only about the old days in Alexandria and the latest palace gossip."

John nodded gravely. It was a long standing jest, for although years before they had both lived in Alexandria at the same time, their paths had never crossed in that huge city.

On their way down the hall, the barefoot girl giggled nervously. He glanced quizzically at her, asking what was amusing her.

She looked at him in panic. "Oh, sir, excellency, I mean, I beg your pardon. It is just that, well, there's an old Greek philosopher visits me every market day, as regular as the sunrise, and I couldn't help laughing, thinking about him. I shouldn't say anything. Madam will be furious that I talked about one of my clients. It's against her rules."

"I won't betray you, don't worry. But what makes you think he is a philosopher?"

The girl looked nervously back at the door of Isis' sitting room, caught between the known perils of her imperious employer and the possible dangers that could emanate from angering this obviously important stranger.

"I would not offend you," she began hesitantly.

"I doubt you could offend me. I'm just curious," John assured her with a slight smile.

"Well, it's this, excellency. When he comes up to my room he watches while I get undressed. But after that...well...he has me pose, like a statue, this way and that." She demonstrated, flapping her arms, looking more like a small, ungainly bird than any classical sculpture John had ever seen. "He keeps me at it until the last drop runs out of the water clock. After an hour, or sometimes two, my arms feel ready to fall off."

"And so you think he's a philosopher because he has you pose like a statue?" John asked, thinking that the girl would get far stranger demands if she stayed very long in Isis' house.

The girl giggled again, her light blue eyes bright. "Oh, no, excellency. I know he's a philosopher because he just sits on the edge of my bed for the entire time and drivels on about various ancients' theories on the nature of beauty. And that's all that happens."

✳ ✳ ✳

"I've never set foot inside a house like that in my life!" Philo angrily grabbed a thick stick from a pile of kindling in the corner of the kitchen.

John, seated at the table, half-expected him to bring the stout stick down on his knuckles as he had once or twice when John had misbehaved in his student days. However, Philo contented himself with vigorously stirring up the brazier, sending golden sparks floating ethereally upward. "I am shocked that you could even consider accusing me of such base licentiousness, John."

The sun had just set. It had been a weary day and John's mind was moving much too slowly to keep a proper guard on his words. Too late, he regretted mentioning the young prostitute's remarks.

"I was concerned about your safety, Philo, that's all," he explained tiredly. "How a man conducts such personal matters is entirely his own business."

Philo threw the slightly charred stick back on the pile. "As well it should be. And to change the subject entirely, that old scoundrel Peter is still lying abed."

John had already noted that the kitchen smelled merely of smoke. Only a ghostly trace remained of the welcoming fragrance of simmering meats and sauces that normally greeted him each evening.

"You really must do something about him, John." Philo sat down on the stool he'd pulled closer to the brazier and warmed his hands. "When he did not appear this afternoon, I eventually went up to see how he was feeling."

"He was still resting as I had instructed?"

"Ah, so you had ordered him to stay abed? However, we did have some words."

"Peter is my servant, Philo, not yours. And, if may I remind you, a free man," John pointed out shortly.

"I meant it in the sense that we had some fascinating discourse, John. In fact, we had quite a long and most interesting conversation. He insisted on trying to explain to me how this god of his can possess distinct but inseparable natures. Nothing but convoluted word play in my opinion, but I do believe we might have gained a good orator there if he'd had some proper training as a young man."

After his tiring and tedious investigations John did not care to consider such a spectacle, so he contented himself with commenting that he was happy that the pair had found something in common.

"Oh, he's a veritable library of knowledge on religious heresies. Eutychianism, Manichaeism, Docetism... It's quite remarkable how many ways they have found to slice up that deity of theirs. Yet sink a knife into some poor dumb beast to honor an older god and you are immediately called a blasphemer of the highest order!" Philo rubbed his hands together. John was not certain whether he was still trying to warm them or was simply enthused by the topic under discussion.

"Anatolius has made similar comments but he is young and often careless in his speech," John said. "I hope you are old enough to know better than voice such opinions too loudly."

"Do you think I'm that much of a fool with these Michaelites stirring trouble up for all of us with their odd ideas?"

John shrugged. "I'm amazed that Justinian would think he can reconcile their beliefs with orthodoxy. Perhaps he sees some subtle shading we do not. But," he continued wearily, rubbing his eyes. "it's been a difficult day. I will be retiring early, I think."

He got up. As they had been talking the last embers of sunset had faded. The flickering orange light of the cheerful brazier danced across the room's plain plaster walls.

Philo also stood. "John," he began hesitantly, "I have something to confess. I went out earlier. I followed you." He quickly recounted his meeting with Hektor. "I'm ashamed to say it, but the child frightened me so much I came back immediately and sat in your garden to compose myself. It took some time, I fear."

John no longer felt tired. Hektor would not be spying for any good reason. Had the boy somehow discovered Theodora had ordered John to desist from investigating Senator Aurelius' death and intended to ferment trouble?

"No need to feel ashamed, Philo," he finally said, "You have good reason to beware of Hektor, and so do I."

"John, if I have put you in any danger..."

"No. Not at all. In fact, it's fortunate you followed me, because now I'm forewarned about Hektor's sudden interest in my movements. But, please, don't follow me again. You were a wonderful tutor, Philo. I owe my life to you. But take my counsel on this and stay inside in relative safety from now on."

Philo replied with uncharacteristic hesitancy. "One thing more. I...found that message Anatolius copied and left here on the day of the banquet."

He led John to the study and removed a piece of parchment from beneath the shatranj board.

"An unfortunate place to lose it," John remarked, "considering how unlikely it is that I'd ever touch that wretched game of yours."

Philo, looking sheepish, handed the document to him. "I thought Michael might have concealed some meaning within the text. I was trying to decipher it for you."

"Before you lost it?"

John read the copy letter quickly. It contained the usual lengthy honorifics, followed by a demand for an audience. Then came the dire prophecies Justinian had described. John sighed. There seemed little to be learned from it. Had Anatolius placed himself in danger to no gain?

"Of course," Philo was saying, "Anatolius may have copied the words accurately but not their arrangement. These things can be very subtle indeed. Not everyone grasps this significant detail."

John's attention was suddenly snagged by one of the sentences. He reread it, half aware of Philo droning on beside him, having realized that by seeking cryptic hidden clues the philosopher had seemingly overlooked the content of the message itself.

"Philo, did you notice this?"

The old man glanced at the letter.

"It is this sentence," John pointed, "'And lo for each of these holy entities the heavenly fire shall claim a sinner, so that all the world shall rejoice in the might of the True Number.'..."

"That must refer to some formula," ventured Philo, eyes brightening at the prospect of a mathematical puzzle to solve.

"No, Philo, I don't think so. According to the second letter, these Michaelites worship a fourth holy entity, the human vessel, that they consider co-equal with the usual trinity. That makes four. So their so-called True Number must be the same. Thus this supposed heavenly fire was prophesied as taking four lives. But on that night only three died."

Philo understood immediately. "Could the girl at Aurelius' house have been the fourth?"

"Possibly. But possibly not, for I heard Michael predicted more fiery deaths in a sermon the same evening as Aurelius' banquet."

"Then what can it mean?"

John was about to reply when there was a thunderous knock on the house door. Going downstairs, he curled his fingers around the hilt of the dagger at his belt.

Cracking the door open cautiously, he was surprised to see Darius looming outside.

"Madam informed that you wanted to question me, so I thought I should attend at once."

John let him in and shut the door against the windy night.

Philo had vanished when they entered the kitchen. Since he could not have avoided hearing Darius' distinctive voice booming up from the entrance hall, perhaps he was not anxious to have one of Isis' employees confirm his recently denied patronage of her establishment.

"It's a bitter night and I would have been happy to speak to you tomorrow," John said, gesturing Darius to take a seat.

It was obvious from his visitor's red eyelids and blotched features that Darius had been weeping and was attempting, with little success, to suppress more sobs. "I was right next to her, Lord Chamberlain," he said. "It was my job to guard madam and the girls and I could not even do that."

"You did all you could." John looked pointedly at Darius' enormous hands. They were covered in blisters from his efforts to extinguish the fire that had killed Adula. He hoped Gaius would not charge too steep a fee for the amount of unguent that would be needed for those burns. Better still, he thought, he would arrange for it to be given to Darius at no charge and pay the cost himself. "You will display the scars from your brave efforts for the rest of your life. And rest assured, we will find out who is responsible for her death."

"No. No, I fear not." Darius' eyes glistened. "It was surely the work of some dreadful and malign deity."

"I am certain that there was no such intervention involved, Darius. Now, reflect. You were closer to the girl than anyone else. Perhaps you saw something unusual, something strange, that might be helpful in discovering the villain responsible?"

Darius shook his head. "I've spent hours thinking about it, over and over, trying to remember exactly how it was. But all I can remember is that one instant I was standing there and the next, there was a terrible scream. I looked at Adula and already she was being consumed by flames."

John went to the kitchen window. Its glass was opaque with condensation. He ran a finger around one of the small rectangular panes and the lights of the city leapt into view.

"Everyone has said that, that the fire was suddenly just there. Yet it must have originated somewhere."

"I believe it came from within, John. Her eyes... they looked as if there was an inferno raging behind them. I can't forget that..."

"Perhaps you heard something?"

"Well, there was madam's flute, poetry being declaimed, people talking and laughing. Just the usual things you would expect to hear at a gathering such as that."

As Darius wiped his eyes with the heel of his hand, his sleeve slipped back to reveal oozing burns on his wrists. Most men with such wounded flesh, John reflected, would be crying from pain rather than with grief.

"It is a strange world, Lord Chamberlain," Darius went on. "Everyone knows that you and Senator Aurelius were sent on a diplomatic mission to Michael. And now the senator is gone. He is not the only one dead, either. If I was asked, I would tell the emperor that if he wants these deaths to stop he should make peace with Michael. No human hand can stop him."

✳✳✳

Having secured the house after Darius' departure, John retired. On the way to his bedroom, he paused for a moment at the doorway of his study. For once, his gaze was drawn not to the mosaic girl Zoe but to the pagan gods cavorting lustily in the heavens above the bucolic scene. As the flickering light from the lamp he carried gave lewd animation to the figures, he wondered afresh. Had that subtly shifting scene been specified in its owner's original commission or was it a sly joke on the part of the artisan, directed at the despised tax collector who had owned the house until his head was sacrificed by Justinian in an attempt to placate an enraged populace?

The old gods in the mosaic reminded John of Aurelius, a staunch pagan yet, he sensed, despite his jesting almost convinced he had been granted a miraculous cure by a man whose religion he did not follow. Darius likewise was no believer and certainly no coward, yet he was already frightened sufficiently to counsel immediate surrender. It was obvious that if Michael could so easily persuade the minds of men like those, it was equally certain that Justinian would not be able to control Constantinople's largely Christian population for very much longer.

John's last glance around his study touched the shatranj board. A thin smile briefly illuminated John's lean face. During his brief discussion with Darius, it had occurred to him that small though the scrap of parchment that had been hidden under it was, it was the only thing offering a shred of hope. Its message demonstrated that Michael was not as all-knowing as everyone appeared to believe.

Chapter Fifteen

y first light next day John was standing in the long shadow of a stylite's pillar set at the center of a nondescript forum not far from the docks. Unlike three other columns in the city, this pillar was still occupied.

As red-gold light crept over the surrounding rooftops, the stylite, a tall figure dressed in a long black tunic, addressed the knot of pilgrims who had already gathered, despite the early hour. A cool breeze carried the rank smell of decomposing fish around the spacious forum along with the elevated man's ornate phrases. This morning he warned of divine retribution against imposters who mounted pillars and subsequently preached falsehoods to pious pilgrims.

At John's approach some of the faithful drifted away. He had dressed in a simple white tunic and thrown a dark woolen cloak over his shoulders, yet there was something in the quality of his clothing, perhaps the hint of silver thread along the hem of his cloak, that, coupled with his bearing, alerted even these simple travelers to at least some suspicion of his rank. And, John reflected ruefully, no matter how much senators and high court officials might boast of their efforts to better the lot of the general populace, those thronging the streets sensed their enemies as instinctively as a rabbit knows the fox. It was a pity that many ordinary folk apparently suspected anyone holding rank as inevitably harboring rancor directed against those lower on the social scale.

John accosted one of the retreating pilgrims. "What is the name of the man up there?"

"He is known as Joseph, master," his informant answered without breaking stride, increasing his pace as he hurried away.

A few of those who had lingered were talking in undertones, casting furtive looks in John's direction. It was as if they assumed he was there with some official and thus doubtless regrettable purpose in mind rather than just passing through on his way elsewhere.

Perhaps it was therefore not too surprising that the young man who had just removed a large empty basket from atop the pillar seemed to be in an extreme hurry to remove the heavy ladder he had just descended, which reached only as far as cast iron footholds embedded in the brickwork supporting Joseph's perch. Acolytes would have to be nimble indeed to haul offerings up there, John thought as he stepped forward and offered assistance.

"May I ask you a few questions?" he asked after the ladder had been laid safely down on the trampled earth at the pillar's base.

The acolyte glanced upwards before replying hesitantly in a low voice. "We are permitted to cooperate with worldly authorities."

John asked how many served the man Joseph.

"Seven, master," was the brief answer.

"You have not lost any of your number recently?"

"Lost? My brothers were all here earlier." The acolyte was little more than a boy. Fresh nicks on his head showed he had recently shaved off all his hair but his chin was perfectly smooth, not yet in need of such ministrations.

"Do you know anything of an unfortunate man who burned to death not far from here?"

"What would I know about that?" The acolyte was puzzled rather than defensive.

"Have any of those who frequent this forum lately been absent?"

"I would not know, master. My eyes are turned ever toward heaven." He picked up the empty basket. "I am sorry, but I must now go to market for we have not yet supped."

John looked up at the stylite. "Perhaps he may have observed something unusual?"

The other shook his head. "Our most revered Joseph saw nothing, for it has pleased heaven to spare him the burden of having to look upon the sinfulness of this city or of the world. He is blind."

After the boy departed John focused his attention to pilgrims and increasing numbers of passersby. After an hour of fruitless questioning, he decided wryly that no-one crossed the forum who was not blind or deaf and as near to dumb as fear of authority would allow them to be without inviting arrest. He realized that he would have to employ someone less obviously associated with officialdom than himself if he was to learn anything useful. One of Felix's paid informers, perhaps? Yes, he would broach the matter with the excubitor captain immediately.

John turned his steps toward the palace. As he strode along, he became aware of a rising, sullen murmur. It might have been mistaken for storm-driven waves breaking against the sea walls but John recognized the sound immediately.

One glance as he reached the street corner confirmed his conclusion.

From his vantage point, he could see a torrent of humanity surging down the Mese, moving toward him in a flood wide enough to spill under the colonnades hemming the broad street. Hundreds of excited conversations punctuated with shouts and hoarse exhortations rose to affront the bright sky, mingling in an unintelligible roar growing ever louder.

A grocer who was swiftly closing up his shutters a few paces back from the corner called out to John.

"I wouldn't go any further if I was you, sir. It's those accursed Michaelites. You should get home as soon as you can." He stooped to lock the shutters into iron rings set near ground level in the wall of his shop. "They'll keep looters out, but as for the rest...." He made the sign of his faith and hurried inside, thudding the shop door shut. Bolts grated home.

John was fully aware of the dangers of allowing himself to be caught up in the treacherous currents of any mob. He quickly retreated back down the street and plunged into a narrow passageway. As he moved swiftly along parallel to the Mese, his progress was shadowed by the grumbling unrest of the crowd and the occasional bang of a window slamming shut or a mother's call, summoning her child hastily indoors.

As a mercenary in Bretania he had often followed the course of an unseen stream through the thickets and brush of dense forest in the same manner, staying just within earshot of its rushing waters. In those days his objective had been to creep up stealthily on some streamside encampment. Today he wanted to reach the Chalke as soon as possible, and without hindrance.

The small forum into which he finally emerged was eerily deserted. Everything were closed and shuttered, as if it were the dead of night rather than a bright morning. The only sign of life was a skeletal mongrel dog nosing around unperturbed in a pile of offal in the gutter, a canine feast doubtless discarded by some nearby butcher.

Suddenly the muffled roar of the unseen mob swelled into an explosion of sound, as if a Hippodrome crowd were saluting some favorite charioteer of the

Greens or Blues who had just emerged from its great bronze gates to parade around the huge arena.

John crossed the deserted space quickly as the roar subsided into silence, then rose again, hanging malignantly on the air. Clearly the mob was responding to someone addressing them.

Just as he plunged into a final dark passageway that debouched into the Mese, a group of grim-faced excubitors came racing down the narrow alley toward him, swords drawn. John recognized one of them, a dark, stocky fellow who regularly guarded the entrance to the excubitor barracks across from his house.

The excubitor stopped in his tracks, his face transformed by surprise, as his comrades in arms ran past John.

"Lord Chamberlain! What are you doing here?" He drew a quick breath. "I wouldn't get any closer to that than you are now!" He pointed his sword back. "We're off to help secure the Great Church, just in case somebody decides to burn it down again." He turned to follow his companions but the touch of John's hand on his shoulder detained him.

"What's the situation on the Mese?"

"Well, Lord Chamberlain, a so-called ambassador from Michael managed to slip into the city undetected."

"That would be easy enough for one man, but it sounds as if this ambassador has developed an extremely large following rather quickly."

The excubitor shrugged. "Right now the mob will follow anyone claiming to speak for Michael. In fact, it's escorted him right to the gates of the palace. He claims to have a message to deliver to Justinian."

John commented that it was unfortunate that the emperor was not receiving anyone.

"His message wasn't really intended for Justinian," the other noted shrewdly. "The brazen little bastard is doubtless happy enough to be able to stand in front of the Chalke and read it to them that escorted him there."

"What did he say?"

"I was at the edge of the crowd, so I didn't catch all the details, but as near as I could tell he said that Michael had grown weary with waiting for Justinian's answer regarding certain matters of what he called mutual interest." The excubitor paused to look, frowning, past John. His companions had vanished.

"And what else?" John prompted. "I shall ensure that you do not suffer from being delayed by my questions."

"Thank you, Lord Chamberlain. As I was saying, then, I was at some distance and the shouting got rather loud, as usually happens in these situations, so I may not have heard all the man's words correctly. But if what he said is true, we are going to have a lot more than a relatively good-natured mob to cope with tomorrow. He proclaimed that if Michael's demands were not met by tomorrow night, his god will set the waters of the Bosporos aflame. Impossible of course, but tell them that...." He gave a quick nod in the direction he'd come from. As if in response, the crowd roared again even louder than before.

The dog John had seen rooting in the gutter trotted quickly past the entrance to the passageway, holding a large bloody scrap of flesh in its teeth. Had John been a superstitious man, he would have regarded that as a very ominous omen.

"If you heard correctly," John said thoughtfully, "then it would appear that our time is growing very short indeed."

❉ ❉ ❉

Striding through the austere warren of imperial administrative offices, John found himself noticing the water clocks set in niches and corners to regulate the labors of those not content to depend on the sun. The level of water in the receiving bowls made it abundantly clear that it had taken him far too long to make his way through the boisterous crowd swirling about outside the Chalke.

Felix was not in his office when John finally reached it. It seemed he had been called away to a meeting with the empress. But when John made his way to the Hormisdas, she had gone and so had Felix.

"The excubitor captain was here," confirmed the silentiary still on guard outside Theodora's now empty audience hall. "He left in a hurry, looking very grim. I'd guess there was some military action afoot, though it'd only be a guess, since my hearing isn't what it once was—and of course I wouldn't be eavesdropping at any rate. We guards are nothing if not discreet."

John thanked the man for his garrulous discretion with a coin. He knew immediately where he would find Felix.

* * *

Once by tradition but now of necessity, the mithraeum was concealed in the bowels of an imperial storehouse in a less traveled part of the palace grounds. A casual visitor who might by accident penetrate far through the maze of winding passages to arrive at the stout door allowing entry into the holy place would have been intercepted by the guards stationed there, their constant presence easily explained by the valuable goods stored in similar stone cellars under the rambling building. Politely escorted back to the upper level, such visitors would doubtless be just as happy to see sunlight. Who knew how many had entered and never emerged back in the days when enemies of the state or those who had fallen from the emperor's favor had been imprisoned in those underground rooms?

But the guards stepped aside, knowing John was a fellow adept. Closing the stout door behind him, John quickly walked down the flight of steps into the shadowed mithraeum. Tonight there would be no celebration, no ceremonial meal, no ritual to mark a follower's joyous advancement another degree up the seven-runged ladder, drawing ever closer to Lord

Mithra. Tonight there was only a lone man, his bushy haired head bowed, seated on a stone bench.

John sat down next to him.

"Well, John," Felix said, evincing no surprise at the Lord Chamberlain's arrival, "I'm shortly off to visit the Michaelites."

"And not with peaceful intent it seems, for I see you are girded for battle," John replied with a nod at the helmet set on the stone flagged floor.

The two men were silent for a time, gazing at the marble bas relief behind the altar. Light from the torches bracketing it glanced off the deeply carved details of the familiar scene—the Phrygian cap Lord Mithra wore, the sharp edge of his raised blade, the powerful shoulders and curled tail of the huge bull he was about to sacrifice to bring forth life.

It was a scene which never failed to move John to the core of his being.

The low cave-like ceiling of the narrow mithraeum was painted with gleaming stars, but its walls were beyond the reach of the torches' pool of light. Thus it ever was. Moreover, it seemed to John that deeper shadows, more evil than those held at bay by torchlight or by the sacred fires kindled on the altar when ceremonies were to be held, were pressing in around them, inky doubles of the dark chaos engulfing the city above them.

Felix frowned fiercely.

"You're worried about something more than an engagement of arms, Felix," John observed. "Perhaps you have come to ask Lord Mithra for guidance? If so, I would be happy to leave."

The big captain nodded. "You're right, John, but in fact it's something I would like to discuss with you."

John listened closely as Felix continued. "I'm on the horns of a dilemma as sharp as those of the Great Bull," he said. "I am a soldier, it's my duty to follow orders, whether it be to fall upon the enemy and dispatch him or guard some soft and simpering ambassador from whatever evil he thinks he will encounter while going about his business at court."

He paused, folding his arms on his brawny chest. "I have just been ordered by the empress to ride with my men to the shrine where the Michaelites are gathered. And when we arrive there, we are to dispose of Michael immediately along with such of his followers as may seek to prevent us carrying out our orders."

"You have been ordered to kill him?"

Felix nodded. "You would think that Theodora must realize that to murder the man will inflame passions to such a degree that riots will break out as soon as news reaches the city. All of Justinian's generals would have refused, I imagine, mutinous although it would be. But my men and I, barracked within the palace grounds, well, we can hardly fail to do the empress' bidding, because generals would certainly not balk at putting down a rebellion by mere excubitors!"

"She must have made her decision immediately she knew of Michael's threat to set the Bosporos on fire."

Seeing Felix' look of disbelief John related what he had learned not long before.

Felix uttered a string of lurid curses. "She never mentioned that, but why would she? I armed myself, gave my orders and then came straight here to reflect for a few moments. You barely caught me, John. I must leave shortly to finalize arrangements."

"Perhaps Theodora is convinced that such a supernatural occurrence as Michael has promised will set off riots anyway and would rather they occurred without him to direct them?"

Felix nodded unhappily. "Excellent strategy to remove their leader, but the very notion of killing an unarmed man disturbs me greatly." He frowned. "I can't believe Justinian would order this rash action."

John considered the matter briefly. "That's probably so, Felix. There are women at the shrine, women and children both. I saw them myself when I was there with Aurelius. There going to be a blood bath of the innocent if there's any resistance and both of us know perfectly well that there will be."

"Oh, Theodora realizes that all right. When I received my orders, she remarked that baptism in blood might be just what the heretics needed. The bitch is as hard as one of those horse hoof breastplates the Sauromatae wore. But," Felix continued, "I'm glad you arrived, as I had intended to leave a message with Peter when I go to meet my men at the barracks. If you were not at home, I mean. It's this. If I should fall in the field, John, I would like you to attend to the rites. With no family..."

"I understand," John assured him, "and you have my oath on it."

Felix thanked him. "And there's one thing more, John," he went on hesitantly. "I ask you to give me your blessing as a Runner of the Sun and therefore a more senior adept than me."

Looking uncomfortable, he stared at the floor as he continued. "I don't fear the blade, but what of this fiery magick? It claimed the stylites and Isis' girl as well, and that within Aurelius' house as my men and I stood guard. So if you would...?"

This night was bristling with as many surprises as a crafty wild boar, John thought. Felix had achieved the Mithraic rank of Lion, just two below that which he himself held, and had never made such a request before. Perhaps his unease about the task he had been ordered to undertake was more profound even than he had indicated.

"But of course," John said, "if that is what you wish."

Felix donned his helmet and they took the few steps necessary to stand reverently before the altar. The big, bear-like man bowed his head as John addressed the torch-lit image of their god.

"Mithra, Lord of Light," John began, "Slayer of the Great Bull, I approach to humbly petition thy blessing upon thy servant Felix, who will soon march forth to soldier."

Torchlight wavered across Felix's bearded face, as he glanced briefly up.

"Grant that his eye be keen, his judgment sound and his sword arm strong." John paused. It did not seem appropriate to be offering a prayer of such a militant nature, given the unarmed pilgrims Felix and his men would be facing. Inspiration touched him.

"Keep him in the shelter of thy starry cloak," John continued, "and give him wisdom in directing the engagement, that it be conducted in a way that is honorable to thee, his lord. But if it must be that he climb the seven-runged ladder and leave this world, grant this, that he depart with grace and that his memory be considered worthy and fitting for one who faithfully followed thee."

Turning, John laid his hands on the captain's bowed head. "And now with this blessing, go forth and soldier, Felix, captain of the excubitors and adept of the rank of Lion."

"And may Lord Mithra guard me on the field of battle," the captain replied in the traditional response.

John lingered for a few moments after Felix left the mithraeum. It was growing late. There was no question now of engaging an informant or one of Felix' spies. If there was anything useful to be learnt, John would have to discover it for himself.

Chapter Sixteen

Philo had spent a lifetime studying philosophy. He had read countless dialogs and listened to endless discourses. But he had never received such a pointed and sorry lesson in human nature as he received while standing near an apple seller's stall not far from Isis' house.

The succession of well-dressed men he observed slinking down the side alley leading to the brothel's back door spoke more eloquently of the baseness of human nature than the most imaginative and perverse theologian ever could.

"Another apple?" The old woman, nigh as wizened as the dried fruit she was hawking, glanced down at the coins on Philo's palm. "I don't mind taking your trade, but if I may say so, you'd find it cheaper, not to say much better for your humors, to summon up your courage and just give a quick rap on the door. Darius will let you in as quick as a wink. Do you think anyone takes any notice of the traffic in and out of that house?

All sorts of people go there at all hours. It's like the procession of beasts to Noah's ark. Except, of course, all the beasts going into that house are male."

Philo flushed. It had been humiliating finding his way to the establishment but at least he had only needed to ask a couple of people before he was able to obtain directions. Evidently the house he sought was one of the best known in Constantinople.

"I assure you, I have never entered such a place nor do I intend to," he said. Even as he protested, he wondered why he should care what an apple seller might think of him. But his statement was true enough and so he had been extremely offended when John had more or less accused him of patronizing such a place. Mulling it over later, though, he could not help wondering who might have been mistaken for him. John had mentioned the man always called on market days. So, this being market day, Philo had chosen to lie, or rather stand about, in wait to see if he could find out.

His encounter with Hektor still weighed heavily on his mind, but as always, notwithstanding John's warnings, his curiosity was stronger than his caution. Besides, he did not think he would find Hektor frequenting such a house. At least, he sincerely hoped not.

He pressed a coin into the fruit seller's palm and took another apple.

"Perhaps you've loitered here so long because you want to talk to me?" the woman suggested with a lewd cackle. "Don't be shy, deary. We're both of an age, you know. Why should youngsters have all of love's delight, that's what I always say."

A man selling lumps of stringy meat of indeterminate origin from a stall a few paces away overheard her badinage and bellowed an obscene suggestion in their direction, illustrating his words with graphic gestures.

Far from being outraged, the apple seller yelled back an even lewder reply.

Philo drew away a few paces. How many hours had he been standing here, watching that house? The fruit he had consumed was beginning to make him feel queasy. How could he have been reduced to this? How could his years at the Academy have fled so quickly?

He could remember his leave-taking so clearly. His few belongings, with those of his friends, were packed and loaded on the cart ready to take them all to Piraeus as soon their escort arrived to accompany them to the docks and so into exile.

It had been a morning of bright sunshine. He had left the others waiting at the Academy gate and walked back through the well planted grounds. These cloistered gardens and beautiful groves had been his world. He knew the winding pattern of the flagstone paths as well as he knew his own soul. The sudden warmth of the sunlight into which he emerged from the stand of murmuring, gloomy firs beside the gymnasium he had felt many times before.

But he would not feel it again.

The gymnasium was empty. The students had gone as soon as Justinian's edict was handed down. All that remained of their boisterous activities was a mildewed leather ball lying in one corner of the exercise area.

He left the deserted building and walked slowly to the far end of the Academy grounds, realizing that this walk, one he had taken so many times before, would be the last. Ever since Justinian had ordered the Academy closed Philo had been aware of many such last things. Thus, in the midst of a discourse on Plotinus he had thought "This is the last time I will lecture students about beauty." As students trickled away to their homes he had told himself "I will never again meet a new student fresh from Athens".

And all the time, although he told himself he was preparing for his departure, still he clung to enumerating the last week, the last day, the last hour.

Now the time to leave had finally come. He stood in the ancient, weed-overgrown burial ground just beyond the back wall of the grounds. Concealed in a stately palm tree, a bird trilled sweetly. Doubtless it would sing the next morning as well, and the following week, and the month after that, but, Philo thought, he would not be there to hear it.

He had often come to this quiet place in the mornings. He liked to contemplate the grave markers, some simple slabs, others in the shape of amphorae, weathered beyond recognition. On a few, patches of lichen clung to half-eroded inscriptions—perhaps because moisture gathered there—allowing a meaningless letter or two to be made out. The graves might have been a thousand years old. Philo had thought himself as likely to leave the familiar precincts of the Academy as were the crumbling bones lying under the mossy earth.

Loud voices interrupted his thoughts. Two men, young and intoxicated enough not to care about being observed leaving through Isis' front door, staggered loudly past.

Tears stung Philo's eyes. He could he possibly live in this terrible city. He blinked the tears away, angry at himself. He was too old for self pity. His past was gone. It had no more substance than a dream. Crossing the Aegean the day after he had left the Academy forever, the life he had lost had been etched in his memory. It had remained so for his first year at Khosrow's court, and during his second. But though time healed wounds, it also wore away memory. The only thing about his past life that seemed real now, Philo reflected bitterly, was his leaving of it.

It was at that point he finally sighted his prey emerging from Isis' front door. His sorrow was replaced by a mixture of shock and relief that what he had dared hope might be was actually, incredibly, true.

Himation flapping, Philo ran after the man now walking briskly away.

"Diomedes!" he called out. "Wait! Wait, old friend!"

※ ※ ※

Peter fretted. It was late and John hadn't returned. His concern was not borne of self-interest, for as a freed man and an excellent cook, he could be certain of obtaining a good post should he ever find himself unemployed. Cooks, after all, were everywhere more in demand than philosophers. Occasionally he had wondered what it would be like to work for a less ascetic employer, especially when John regaled him with tales of the exotic dishes he had sampled at the tables of some of the wealthier inhabitants of the city. It was true that his master's simple tastes rarely presented a challenge to culinary skills but inevitably loyalty, and perhaps more than a pinch of distaste for such ostentatious fare, kept Peter in John's employ.

And John, he admitted to himself, was kind enough even if his theology was both mistaken and dangerous. Sooner or later it would bring grief upon his master, as if he had not already suffered enough. Unless, of course, he eventually saw the error of his beliefs, as Peter fervently prayed he would. The possibility that his master's beliefs would also visit fury upon his own head he dismissed. He was elderly now, but John still had many years left in him. And yet…and yet it sometimes seemed to Peter that John almost willfully sought out situations where he would have to place himself in danger.

However, Peter thought, with these Michaelites stirring the city into a turmoil as fiery as his kitchen brazier, there was no telling what might happen. And whereas John habitually carried a blade about his person, as did all sensible men including himself, there had definitely been an increase in violence in Constantinople over the past few days. Not to mention the undeniable fact that two or three thugs working together could out-stab even the nimblest person, especially if they thought it would gain them a few nomismata. Since there was anonymity in a multitude, it was unlikely ruffians like that would ever be caught. Yes, it was a dangerous time to be abroad alone.

What concerned him most was that John invariably sent a messenger if he expected to be delayed an hour or two beyond the time of the evening meal. Now it was nearly dusk and no word had arrived. This unusual event, coupled with occasional bursts of that angry, distant growling that told of the rising appetite of a mob working themselves up to committing who knows what crimes, suggested to Peter that it was quite likely that John had fallen afoul of some anonymous cut throat.

Shuffling about his duties while straining his ears for the sound of John's familiar rap on the door, Peter offered a quiet prayer for his master's safe arrival home. Having thus left the matter in heavenly hands, he began chopping onions. Their pungent odor made tears flow down his walnut brown and similarly wrinkled face.

❋ ❋ ❋

The beggar knew it was time to seek shelter for the night. Already the tide of darkness had filled the byways with shadows.

During the warmer months he preferred to claim a sheltered corner where he could doze in solitude without fear of being robbed or assaulted. But the increasing chill in the night air reminded him that he would soon be needing better protection from the elements. Unfortunately, in such refuges as were available to him others would also be gathering, many of them untrustworthy, violent or even deranged, and all of them filthy and vermin infested.

He intended to avoid such accommodations for as long as the weather and his fraying garments would allow. In the life snatched away from him, now all but forgotten, the beggar had been a private and fastidious man.

He set off for his night quarters, a cozy niche underneath a huge yew tree that grew near the aqueduct through the burial grounds between the city's walls. The decently buried dead were quiet companions and since few ventured into their settlement after dark, it was one of the safest places in Constantinople.

Yes, he thought, as he stepped out smartly for his destination, after the tumult of the day he would appreciate the serenity waiting there. Having observed the enormous crowd flooding the Mese that afternoon he had sensed the city was ready to explode into rioting. It had happened before. The prospect filled him with a mixture of eagerness and dread. Once bricks and fire opened the houses and shops of the wealthy to such as himself, he might again taste a peach he had not found half eaten in a gutter. Perhaps he could find sandals whose soles were unbroken or a warm tunic for the winter. Those were excellent possibilities to consider. But there would also be human packs roaming uncontrolled, more vicious than starving dogs. That was something he did not like to contemplate. He had lost his workshop and his former life to just such a riot. Fortunately, he had not been married nor had a daughter or he might well have lost even more.

He shuddered and turned his thoughts firmly to the refuge he had chosen. It was some distance away, at least by the route he was planning to take. He intended to avoid certain streets likely to be frequented by Blues or Greens and give a wide berth to particular alleys he knew to be deadly.

As he passed swiftly along his way, he stayed close to the shuttered shops edging the streets, wary as a cat of open spaces where he was away from a wall to have at his back if the need arose.

He came to a wide avenue lit by the wall-mounted torches that merchants kept burning outside their places of business at night. A dark shape on the cobbles ahead caught his attention. Was it some unconscious intoxicated person? A corpse? If it were, it was too small to be human, he decided. A dead animal perhaps? There were enough of those to be found in the streets.

He crept forward slowly, ready to flee if necessary. It was not human, he realized with a sudden rush of relief. It was discarded clothing, a cloak.

The beggar snatched it off the ground, clutching its heavy folds to his thin chest. He could almost hear his heart pounding against his rib cage. The cloak was made of finely woven wool. Even in his former life he had never owned anything of such richness and value.

Belatedly, a terrible suspicion occurred to him. He looked around in panic. Was this the trick of some cruel Blue or Green who would materialize out of the shadows, blade in hand, to reclaim his possession from a thief? But neither faction needed an excuse to kill a beggar. Perhaps it belonged to a courtier? Certain tales concerning them were commonly bandied about the streets. If only half of them were true, would it not please such a person to have a beggar like him handed over to the imperial torturers?

Other horrible possibilities, each worse than the last, raced in a mad riot through his head. Should he even have picked the cloak up, thus placing himself in danger? He shivered, looking around, waiting for the hand on the shoulder that heralded....who knew what? Yet, as time passed he still stood unmolested, clutching his newly found treasure to his chest with shaking hands.

Examining the cloak in the light of the nearest torch, he realized that, however it had come to be there, it was certainly of great value.

His thoughts were swirling as wildly the debris blown around by the chilly wind now guttering the lonely flares of the torches. How much food would the cloak be worth if he sold it? And if he kept it, how many cold nights would it allow him to remain safely in his hidden corner, well away from the communal refuges he so dreaded?

He pulled the cloak over his shoulders, noting with satisfaction how warm he felt. Its hem dragged behind him a little as he set off down the deserted avenue with much springier steps than those that had brought him there. The cloak had been made for a taller man. What fate had befallen him?

Chapter Seventeen

Lucretia awoke in darkness to the sound of muffled thunder.

Someone was pounding at the front door of Nonna's apartment building. Balbinus? Her heart leapt, an animal trying to escape from a trap. It's only a nightmare, Lucretia told herself. How many times had she had that same awful dream since fleeing her husband?

A sleepy tenant shouted from a window below, castigating the nocturnal caller for waking everyone in the house. The visitor replied with a yet more inventive string of curses. Familiar curses, bellowed in a familiar voice.

As Nonna stirred sleepily nearby, Lucretia dressed in frantic haste, grabbing the first clothing her hand encountered in the dark. She ran out on to the landing, her mind still dazed with sleep.

There was a door at the back of the building's first floor. If she reached it quickly enough she could escape before the argument going on at the front of the house was finished. Running downstairs in a panic, she caught the toe of her sandal on a loose board and fell heavily to the floor on the landing.

From below came the rattle of a bolt drawn, the bang of the front door flung open. More shouting. More foul language. For an instant she was paralyzed, huddled on the floor by the door to the communal lavatory. Terrible words she had hoped never to hear again came booming up the stair well.

Heavy footsteps pounded upwards.

Lucretia pushed herself to her feet. No time to escape now. She jerked open the lavatory door and crouched down in the cramped, malodorous cubicle. Insults continued to be shouted upstairs after Balbinus. His footsteps crossed the landing, past her temporary sanctuary.

As soon as she heard him rapping at the door of Nonna's room on the floor above, Lucretia flung herself downstairs and escaped out the front door. Her heart pounded faster than her feet on the slippery cobbles as she dashed into the alley across the street, heedless of danger, seeking any concealment she could find.

With laboring breath, she traversed the dark length of the narrow way and ran across the open space beyond. Torches guttered here and there at shuttered shop fronts. Down another street she went, pulling away in fright from the grasping hand of a woman sitting in a doorway, and finally stumbled into a marketplace.

Boisterous stallholders were already setting out wares for their expected customers, comparing competitors' offerings in the light of torches, loudly finding them the worst rubbish they had ever had the misfortune to observe and having little better to say about each other's ancestors and sexual practices.

She glanced back down the shadowed street from which she's just emerged. Was that someone running after her? She whirled and fled, straight into the side of an ox cart.

The next thing she knew she was being dragged to her feet. She tried to pull away, lashing out toward her captor's face at the same time. A strong hand gripped her wrist.

"Stop it! I'm not going to hurt you!"

It was a ruddy faced carter, about her age or perhaps a year or two younger.

"Where are you running to, lady?" he asked.

"I'm sorry," Lucretia stammered. "I was just careless...."

"A lady wouldn't be roaming the streets at this hour without good reason. You're in trouble, aren't you?"

Lucretia protested feebly that it was not so, but the carter would not be convinced. It struck her that he was young enough to grasp eagerly at the adventurous prospect of assisting a pretty woman in obvious distress without giving much thought to the possible consequences. Certain that her husband would burst into the marketplace at any moment she blurted out her destination.

The carter grinned. "Well, there's a miracle for you! I'm just on my way to that very shrine!"

As he quickly cleared a space for her amid the sacks of onions and amphorae of olive oil piled in his cart, he pointed out that those encamped out there needed to eat and have light just like everyone else." I do well enough from their trade," he went on, "even though I charge a bit less than some, what with them being pilgrims and all."

Lucretia thanked the young man. She did not reveal that although she had contemplated joining Michael's followers she also feared what that would entail— cutting herself off forever from her former life, from her friends and family. Her mind had finally been made up only when Balbinus arrived bellowing at the house door.

As soon as she was safely aboard, the carter urged his ox forward.

"It could be good for future business too," he shouted back to her loudly enough to be heard over the rattling of wheels, "since they'll remember their friends if they should take over the city. And it might help me in the afterlife as well, you never know. Yes, it's certainly been excellent for trade, although not so good for public order. There's an uneasy feeling in the air, fermenting like demon's wine as you might say, but isn't that usually the case? Always somebody stirring up trouble, always somebody else suffering for it." He was quite the philosopher, it seemed.

"But," he went on, "although personally I don't know what to make of it all, there's a lot of talk when the wine jug's been emptied a few times about how things will be different when Michael's in charge. I'll believe that when I see it, though."

Before long they had passed out of the city gates. The guards scarcely glanced at the heavily loaded cart. They were obviously concerned not with who might be openly leaving the city but rather with those trying to enter it by stealth.

❋ ❋ ❋

Lucretia suppressed a startled cry as she was jolted awake by the sudden, lurching halt of the cart. She had been dozing uneasily and peering warily over its side was relieved to see neither her husband nor a pursuing Prefect. There was, however, a white-haired man lying a short distance away beside the unruly line of brush running along the edge of a field.

Her benefactor was already investigating. Lucretia leaned forward, staring. Surely the man on the ground had not been set about by robbers? Even from a distance, she could see from his rough clothes and malnourished look he had nothing worth stealing. Dark patches of blood stained his tunic. Perhaps he had been beaten for the sport of it?

Helped into a sitting position, the old man spoke for a time but Lucretia could not hear what was being said.

When he returned to her side, the young carter looked grim. "Nothing to be afraid of here, lady. But there's been an attack at the shrine. He says he barely escaped with his life."

Lucretia asked who could have been responsible for such a terrible act.

Her companion spat into the dust. "Our beloved emperor sent a company of excubitors. Apparently they showed up before dawn. Their captain ordered the pilgrims to get out while they still could. Most of them did, scattered like leaves in the wind, it seems. Not much faith there, you may say, but what is faith against the sword? Still, it seems there were plenty who wouldn't, who wanted to defend their precious Michael so that poor old fellow told me."

Lucretia paled. "What happened?" she asked, knowing what the answer would be.

The answer was as stark and simple as she had expected. "A massacre. He doesn't know what happened to Michael but thinks he probably escaped disguised as one of his own followers." He spat again. "Not but what apparently some of them pilgrims gave good accounts of themselves. There's more than one of Justinian's men who isn't going to be marching back to Constantinople to get drunk or go wenching tonight— or any other night."

"Is that old man badly hurt?" Lucretia asked, noting that he had remained seated on the ground.

"It's only a scalp wound, looks worse than it is," was the dismissive reply. "He probably got a quick cut just to remind him unorthodoxy is severely frowned upon. He was lucky."

From her uncomfortable position Lucretia looked along the narrow road pointing back toward the city.

"So," the carter was saying, "do you want to ride back with me? There's no use going there now. The only people left at the shrine are either dead or wounded or excubitors, and what with all them soldiers being there, to be blunt, well, it could be dangerous for you, you know how it is..." He trailed off.

"If everyone else has run away help will be needed with the wounded," Lucretia said firmly. "I will go on."

"It's a mistake, it really is," he replied with a frown, "and I hope you don't live to regret it."

Lucretia watched the cart rattle out of sight towards the city. The Bosporos was hidden from this stretch of road but the fog rising from its hidden waters sent white, wispy fingers inland to clutch damply at her.

She had no choice, she told herself, wiping away her tears. She must continue onward, despite the fact that her only refuge had now been destroyed.

Trudging down the narrow road, she wondered briefly if Nonna had sent someone from the building to notify Balbinus of where his wife could be found. Doubtless coins changed hands. Would her old nursemaid have betrayed her? It seemed the only explanation, for there were thousands of doors in Constantinople, too many to bring Balbinus knocking at that particular one by chance.

And, of course, Nonna always knew best, she thought with a grim smile, just as she had always known what was best for Lucretia all through her childhood. And Nonna thought that Lucretia was dishonoring her family by fleeing and, yes, it was possible that the strict old woman had taken steps to ensure that Lucretia took the right, the honorable course. Unless, perhaps, Balbinus had finally gone to her father and discovered her possible whereabouts. She could imagine the sort of statements her father would have made when he was informed of her flight. Duty would doubtless have been the first thing mentioned.

"A dutiful daughter," she chanted softly to herself, as she plodded along the road, through the mist. "A dutiful wife. A dutiful daughter. A dutiful wife..."

※※※

The sun had burnt off the fog by the time she neared the shrine. During her journey, several groups of pilgrims had rushed by her, going in the opposite direction. There were also groups of men who did not appear to belong to the military, being unarmored and dressed in plain tunics, and yet they carried swords or spears. They seemed to take no notice of her but when, looking back over her shoulder from the crest of a rise along the way, she glimpsed a large band of such men moving toward her destination, she was grateful that they quickly outpaced her and vanished around a bend in the road. Perhaps they were arriving to reinforce the excubitors already holding the shrine, or, she thought, her stomach churning, perhaps they had been sent out to hunt down such acolytes as had escaped from their clutches.

Limping as she crested the final hill before the shrine, she gasped in shock and horror.

Where during Michael's sermons there had been a pool of humanity filling the space in front of the building, there was now only a scene of desolation. Bodies lay strewn across the trampled grass. A few excubitors paced around, poking at the fallen with their swords. Some of their colleagues assisted wounded comrades. The small group of acolytes clustered at the foot of the steps leading up to the shrine's columned portico were under heavy guard. Lucretia fervently thanked the Lord that she could not see Michael among the captives.

Surely they were not going to murder the survivors, she thought, looking again at the excubitors prodding swords at the figures on the ground.

From here and there on what must have lately resembled a slaughtering pen rather than a battlefield, an occasional hoarse shout rose to hang on the morning air. At each shout, one of the fallen was quickly picked up by a pair of brawny excubitors and carried, none too tenderly, into the shrine. So they were finding and tending to the living, she thought. She could be of assistance after all. That had been her first impulse. What she would do afterwards, where she would go, she couldn't say.

"Guard me, Lord, and keep me safe," she prayed softly, not certain if she feared detection by her pursuing husband more than the possibility of assault. She quickly walked down the hill.

Soon she was stooping, checking those lying in her path. The first person she found alive was a woman holding her gashed arm, lying on her back staring blank-eyed into the morning sky.

"Tear a strip off your tunic and bind your wound," Lucretia urged her. "Then come and help with the others."

The woman smiled benignly, patting Lucretia's arm with a bloody hand. "But of course I will, my dear. Just as soon as Michael heals me."

Lucretia looked around in desperation. "I don't see him here. He could be dead. He may have run away."

The woman's smile broadened. "Oh, no, not him," she contradicted, looking at Lucretia with obvious pity for such lack of faith. "No, he would never abandon us, my dear. Why, we followed him all the way from Sinope. Yes, me and my husband left what little we had. My husband. Where..." Her voice rose to a shriek. "Where is my husband? Is he dead?"

The woman scrambled to her feet and began a frantic search, rolling bodies over to look at their faces. Lucretia trudged after her. One or two other women appeared, also obviously seeking loved ones, stony-faced shuttles weaving back and forth across a tapestry of agony.

Flies were already buzzing at the feast. From here and there came soft whimperings of pain, a muttered curse, fragments of prayers. One woman discovered her lover, another her child, the one still living, the other dead.

Lucretia arrived at the shrine. The acolytes had been herded into the building, from which the sound of low chanting now emerged. Several excubitors sat on the steps. Silent, heads hanging, they stared at the marble beneath their feet with that blank gaze of the physically and emotionally exhausted.

Lucretia looked up at them. They had murdered her only chance of escape. It was suddenly too much for her to bear.

"You call yourself brave men, you call yourself heroes!" she screamed. "You miserable excuses for men, you filthy bastards! Creeping about in the night to do Justinian's foul work!"

She could not stop her tirade. All the bitterness and anger and fear of the past few days fueled it as she berated the group of excubitors staring down at her if she had been suddenly struck insane.

"You've murdered women! Children, babies even!" she shrieked, wild-eyed. "Pilgrims, people who had done you no harm! May the fire from heaven strike you down! May it roast your eyes out while you live to endure its agonies! May you die of the pox! And may Justinian suffer every agony he and that whore of a wife of his have brought down upon these innocent people, suffer them ten times over!" Her voice had risen to screaming so shrill that, fortunately for her, her words could hardly be understood.

One of the men leapt down the steps and grabbed her tightly by her elbows, fingers digging painfully into her flesh. "Be quiet, you fool!" He shook her roughly. "You'll cause yourself trouble."

Lucretia spat in his face. "Ah, so the murderer fears trouble, does he? From an unarmed woman! You coward! What would your mother think, to see her son carrying out the devil's work?"

The man dealt her a hard slap. His companions started to laugh, calling out obscene suggestions.

Her stinging face brought Lucretia to her senses as the man began dragging her away toward the edge of the grassy space, where bushes clustered along the banks of a small stream. The coarse laughter of his companions followed them, growing louder as Lucretia struggled to escape his grip. He stopped and struck her again, a harder slap. She jerked away and darted around him. His companions' bawdy shouts changed into jeering. Two of them stood to follow with obvious purpose.

But the man was fast on his feet. He caught Lucretia easily and turned triumphantly back toward his companions. "Stay where you are," he shouted at the two men approaching. "Find your own prize. This one's mine and I don't need your help with it." He then proceeded to describe in particularly foul detail exactly what he didn't need their help with.

Lucretia screamed again, provoking another burst of laughter from the two excubitors, who nonetheless went back to their perch on the shrine's steps.

The man threw Lucretia roughly down behind the bushes.

Before she could think, he was bending over her, his breath hot on her face. "Leave, woman! Go before you get hurt!"

She gazed up at him, dumbfounded. He knelt down beside her. "Don't you understand? We didn't kill any women or children. Our captain ordered the pilgrims to go. They were permitted to leave unharmed. The ones who stayed..."

"But I saw children dead on the grass, there were children..."

"In panicked flight people get hurt, children most of all. Most of the pilgrims fled, fortunately for them since our captain's wounded and has lost a lot of blood. I doubt he can keep order now and not all of my comrades were pleased to see the women escape. A couple weren't too happy to see the children get away either." Deep disgust was displayed on his face and in his voice.

Lucretia sat up. The bushes shielded them from sight of the shrine. As the man had dragged her boastfully away she thought she had understood his intent perfectly, but this odd behavior confused her.

"But what you shouted you were going to do just now...why would you want to help me?" she asked suspiciously.

"It is not a Mithran's way to force a woman. Now, leave."

"But what about Michael? Is he dead?"

"He wasn't with those we cornered inside the shrine," was the reply. "But if he's dead, at least he chose to stand and fight."

"You're lying! He escaped and you know it. I saw your men on the road. They were looking for him, weren't they?"

The excubitor denied her accusation.

Lucretia grabbed his arm. "But I saw armed men coming in this direction," she insisted.

Shouts came from the road as she spoke. Alarm washed over her companion's face. He peered through the concealment of the thick bushes toward the road.

Lucretia looked over his shoulder.

An angry crowd was pouring down the hill. Among them she saw some of the simply dressed but well-armed men she had seen along the road.

The excubitor cursed. His companions at arms were already jumping up, reaching for their weapons. Even Lucretia, totally unskilled in military matters, immediately realized her rescuer's concerns. This was a different situation altogether.

Before Lucretia could gather her thoughts she heard a familiar voice drifting across the open space.

Michael was standing on the brow of the hill. From where they crouched, she could not hear exactly what he was shouting.

It didn't matter. He was alive!

More excubitors emerged from the shrine, moving quickly to take up their positions, shaking off their weariness. The scattered group of exhausted soldiers was again transforming itself into a fighting unit.

Several acolytes appeared in the portico of the shrine.

"I must rejoin my comrades immediately," her companion said, unsheathing his sword.

Lucretia pointed out that they were outnumbered at least ten to one.

"But we are Justinian's men and they are just a rabble," he replied.

It was then that Michael raised his hands to the heavens.

A lightning bolt seemed to strike the foot of the shrine's stairs, sending gouts of flame toward the cloudless sky. Two excubitors broke formation, slapping at the flames crackling along their arms.

A second bolt exploded against the side of the shrine.

Now the mob of pilgrims was running, surging across the open space, shrieking and waving weapons with most unholy intent as they trampled over dead and wounded alike in their haste to attack the excubitors.

Lucretia saw nothing more. After the man who had rescued her raced off to carry out his duty, she covered her ears and cowered down behind the sheltering bushes, trying blot out the sound of hoarse oaths and screams and all the obscene sounds of a battle that was soon over.

When a terrible silence fell, she raised her head, weeping. She had come here seeking refuge and had found only hell instead.

Chapter Eighteen

John surfaced from the deep, dark waters of slumber, his hand moving to the blade at his belt. Something was wrong. He felt a rough surface against his cheek. Bricks. He was half seated, leaning against bricks. He was cold and his left arm, pinned between him and the wall, was numb. His thoughts winged briefly back to distant memories of military encampments, of waking on frozen ground in a cramped tent.

In an instant he realized he was not in an encampment. He was in Constantinople and had become a beggar, or as near to one as he could manage. And like many beggars, he had spent the night dozing out of doors.

He climbed stiffly to his feet in the hospitable doorway where he had found refuge. A few tatters of mist swirled low along the ground. A mangy black cat inspecting breakfast possibilities in rotting refuse piled nearby glanced at him with calm yellow eyes and then trotted away briskly on its three remaining legs.

John shook the numbness out of his arm. His heavy cloak was gone, discarded on the street after he'd left the palace grounds after his brief meeting with Felix in the mithraeum.

After hearing of Michael's threats to set the Bosporos afire and subsequently learning from Felix about the imminent attack on the shrine, John had realized the situation was too urgent. There was no time to engage informants, let alone wait for them to do their work.

He would have to do the job himself.

So he had discarded his cloak, torn his tunic, rubbed dirt into his hair and on his face and hands. He hoped, by posing as a beggar himself, to gain the confidence of, and confidences from, those who were afraid to speak to the authorities.

As yet, however, his disguise had gained him nothing. The people nesting in corners and clustered around small fires in alleys were as wary of dirty strangers as they were of officials, although less frightened. After all, they were many and he was but one.

The morning was eerily quiet, with none of the usual noisy bustle of merchants opening their shops. No doubt their businesses would remain shuttered today. He wondered about Felix's raid, muttering a brief prayer to Mithra that the burly captain was unharmed. Whatever had happened, it was obvious that word had not yet been carried back to the city. Otherwise it would not be so quiet.

As for Michael, John thought it more than likely he was dead. He doubted anyone at the palace would feel much sorrow at the ascetic eunuch's demise. It was commonly bandied about that those deprived of the opportunity to be men had strong tendencies toward treachery. No doubt it was a result of the gross imbalance in their humors. John himself had too often been labeled such a creature.

Unfortunately, it had apparently not occurred to Theodora that martyrs were the worst sort of foes with which to have to grapple.

Pursued by that bleak thought, John set out toward the forum graced by the pillar occupied by the stylite Joseph.

❊❊❊

John spent the morning and early afternoon loitering at the edge of the forum in which Joseph's pillar stood, observing the stylite and the intermittent stream of pilgrims arriving to pay their respects and place offerings in the baskets there.

In mid morning, a vendor set up his brazier and the tempting smell of cooking fish made John's stomach grumble with hunger. But a beggar, of course, did not have the wherewithal to purchase cooked fish.

Occasionally Joseph would embark on a garbled homily. These half-heard addresses seemed to bear no relation to the number of listeners gathered, if any. But then, John reminded himself, the man was blind.

Regretfully concluding that his vigil had produced nothing of value, John was contemplating going home when a figure loitering in the shadows of the nearby colonnade suddenly emerged into the sunlight. John turned quickly, catching the movement out of the corner of his eye.

"Greetings, excellency. It's so kind of you to visit us," it rasped hoarsely.

A demon, without a face, just as Justinian was rumored to be. That was John's immediate impression as it stepped toward him. Then he realized he was looking not at some supernatural being but a horribly disfigured woman.

"How may we accommodate you, excellency?"

One side of her face had melted and puddled into a formless mass like a candle left too long alight. Her cheek and temple were a reddened ruin in which sat a useless, opaque eye. But tilting her head to look at John with her good eye the speaker revealed that the other half of her face had the delicate features of an attractive woman not yet middle-aged.

"I think you mistake me for someone else," John replied.

She laughed, setting into motion myriad scraps of brightly colored ribbon tied in her matted black hair. Her laughter was as grating as her voice.

"Not at all," she said. "It's obvious to a person with one eye you're from a wealthy household!" Her filthy but dainty finger pointed at the gold embroidery on the wrist of John's tunic. "That is very fine workmanship. I'm familiar with fine garments, although you would not think so to look at me now."

She stepped forward another pace, spreading her thin arms slightly to show off her clothing, a gaudy assemblage of layers of draped and knotted tatters that might have passed for some exotic costume from a less civilized country.

"And how is your master, excellency?" she smiled. "Is he in good health or did you crack open his head before running off with his valuables?"

"I chanced upon these clothes at the baths," John said, grasping her implication. Perhaps he had not been discovered after all.

"What? And left your rags in their place so that here is a beggar dressed as an aristocrat while an aristocrat skulks home in rags?" Again the hoarse laugh, although whether because she thought John's explanation comical or extremely unlikely it was difficult to say.

"No doubt you have heard stranger tales," John replied.

The woman tilted her head, regarding him pointedly. "My name's Pulcheria, my friend. You're fortunate that the Prefect is too occupied with other matters to be hunting down runaway slaves right now."

John said that he supposed he had Michael to thank for that.

"And what sort of employment do you plan to follow now that you are free?" Pulcheria asked him.

John admitted he had not given it much thought.

Pulcheria nodded wisely. "You won't last long here, I'm afraid. I've been watching you. This is all a mystery to you, isn't it?"

John shrugged uneasily, unaware that he had been observed.

"Oh, I've seen the way you've been peering about," she went on. "I may not know who you are, but I do know you aren't telling the truth. In my line of work my clients lie to me as a matter of course. After a while you get a sense for it."

"I assure you…"

"Don't think you can fool a whore! I see you doubt me? Oh, I was pretty enough once, until a customer threw a lamp full of burning oil in my face. As if it was my fault he was too drunk to take what he'd paid for." She sighed heavily. "But then, it's always the innocent that suffer."

John agreed with the sentiment, adding that he was sorry to hear her sad tale.

"Are you?" Her tone was doubtful. "And have you also suffered, my soft-hearted friend?"

"Not all of us are ready to blurt out our lives to the first stranger we meet, Pulcheria," he said. "But I will admit, as you so rightly say, that this new life is a mystery to me. I fear I may have won myself only the freedom to starve to death, if I don't freeze first."

"And here I thought to earn myself a crust from such a fine-looking gentlemen. Perhaps, I thought to myself, perhaps he stole the master's purse as well as his clothes. That's what I'd hoped." Her face brightened. "However, if you're interested, I can turn my poor face away or present myself from whatever angle appeals to you the most. Whatever you choose will be nothing new to me."

"I regret I am not able to take advantage of your offer," John replied gently.

The human side of Pulcheria's face frowned. "If your purse is truly empty then I must find myself another lover, it seems. Still, I like to think of myself as a kind person, so before I do I'll tell you a few things you need to know. They might allow you to live long enough to earn a nummus or two and then you will remember Pulcheria kindly and perhaps pay me a visit. I am usually to be found here. Now, pay attention."

She pointed toward the fish seller who had unknowingly tormented John with the enticing smell of grilling fish.

"Now there's a mean bastard," the woman advised. "Packs up all his scraps and takes them away with him every night. Nothing tossed away that we could eat, no, not even the gulls can get so much as a fish head from him. No chance of stealing one, either. He watches those miserable fish of his like a patriarch admiring an actress. We call him the Guardian of the Fish."

John listened intently as she went on to praise the charitable character of a fruit seller whose stall was a few paces beyond the parsimonious seller of Neptune's bounty.

"That man now, he'll occasionally drop a fig or an apricot or some such and he never bothers to pick them up. Doesn't seem to mind if anyone else does, either, you can just go over there and get them as bold as you please. A good man."

John allowed himself to be led around her world. It was one that revolved around the stylite's pillar. Joseph was the sun and rain from which all those living near or in the forum gained their sustenance—not only the beggars but also the shopkeepers and artisans whose shops edged the open space. Although their establishments were shuttered today they had prospered thanks to pilgrims' purchases augmenting those of their city-dwelling customers.

"And as for me, travelers have the same needs as anyone else," Pulcheria concluded, "especially after their long, lonely journeys."

Having completed their tour, they were now sitting in the shady portico of what had originally been a civic building that was now, she said, reduced to functioning as a warehouse for an importer of wool. From her colorful motley of garments, she produced a scrap of sacking that unrolled to reveal a few shriveled bits of unidentifiable dried fruit. They shared the simple repast, John accepting her generosity gratefully. The three-legged cat he had seen earlier suddenly reappeared. It disdainfully rejected the scrap of mummified fruit Pulcheria offered but accepted a pat on its scabby head before limping rapidly away about its business.

"We call it Tripod," Pulcheria said with a fond smile. "And there's our Angel." She pointed to a shaggy-headed boy darting across the forum to the pillar.

At first glance John thought the boy was about to attack the pilgrims gathered there but then saw that it was a flute rather than a stick the lad was brandishing.

"This tune was composed by Emperor Justinian himself," the boy announced in a piercing voice. He commenced blowing out a melody that to some may have sounded akin to the noises made by a cat being strangled but also bore some faint resemblance to the melancholy dirge Peter often hummed as he went about his work.

John listened uneasily to the boy's playing, his discomfort partially brought about by the raucous squealing of the instrument but stemming as much from the realization that the last time he had heard a flute, it had been at Senator Aurelius' banquet and violent death had soon followed.

A man leaving the forum stopped to speak as he drew level with them.

"Good people, it is truly a wonder to find oneself in a city of such holiness that even unwashed urchins in the streets praise heaven with hymns written by the emperor."

After he had departed, Pulcheria observed it was a pity he had not acknowledged such an amazing event by tossing the boy a coin before he went on his way.

This reminded the woman that certain beggars took advantage of pilgrims' generosity. For example, there was the man called the Soldier, an ancient with only one leg who spent his days perched in a wall niche next to the entrance of the workshop of a seller of leather goods. His cozy alcove had doubtless once held a mute marble likeness of some notable or other but its newest occupant declaimed long-winded accounts of his military service in the Arabian desert to any pass-ersby he could persuade to listen. His concluding remarks always stressed that it was out there in the barbaric wilderness that he had lost his leg, thus lead-ing to his current struggle to support a large family on a small pension. His audience was inevitably generous in their contributions towards defraying the ex-soldier's expenses.

John was about to comment on the man's sacrifice for the empire when Pulcheria revealed that in fact the Captain had never set foot in Arabia but rather had lost his leg as the result of a knife wound that mortified.

"He was lucky he didn't lose his life," she sniffed, "and luckier still he didn't discover from bitter experi-ence that if he'd had the girl he was fighting over she would have given him a very nasty gift he wouldn't want to take home with him. He's the happiest of her suitors, the one who lost the argument. Of course, he will never admit that. It's a gripping tale he spins, though. He does well enough for sitting around all day doing nothing."

John said he admired the Captain's ingenuity.

"That's right, excellency, you do have to have a good story," Pulcheria replied

Pulling a piece of the tattered material swathing her body over the unburned side of her face, she turned the milky orb of her injured eye toward John and continued his instruction.

"But it has to be something different," she said. "Every other beggar these days claims to be a widow or an orphan or some worker crippled in a terrible accident and thrown out on the street with his wife about to produce a child, to boot." She paused, coughed throatily and then gave a piteous moan before saying in a wheedling tone "Oh, master, spare a copper for a poor blind lady who never did nobody no harm."

John admitted she certainly gave a convincing performance.

"It would be easy living, don't you think?" she said, rearranging her tatters. "But I prefer to give something in return for payment."

"Beggars do provide pilgrims a chance to demonstrate their charity, do they not?" John observed thoughtfully.

"Are you considering taking up begging, then? Or will you follow a lower occupation?"

John, puzzled, asked her what she had in mind.

"Thieving," Pulcheria informed him matter of factly, but only after some prompting would she elaborate. Of those thieves with whom she admitted personal acquaintance most stole from merchants who were thought well able to afford it, while one or two concentrated on pilgrims. "At least thieving does require skill," she conceded. "But a fine man like yourself, you can do better."

"You say there are those who prey on pilgrims?"

Pulcheria had been keeping her good side toward John but now she turned her full face toward him. Her sightless eye stared without expression as her good one narrowed suspiciously. "Even thieves have a right make a living. You aren't here to bring harm to us, are you?"

"No," John reassured her. "On that you have my word."

"I believe you, even though I know you're lying about something. Still, since you ask, yes, there are some. Remember, many of these travel-begrimed folk are wealthy men despite the humble guise they adopt for their journeys. And wisely so, I would say. Now, mind, I've never actually seen anyone robbed at knifepoint hereabouts, although I'm sure it happens in less pleasant parts of the city. But even so, since pilgrims aren't likely to stay in Constantinople very long, the Prefect tends not take much interest in catching those that rob them. Not but what there's a few innkeepers we could mention that do the same—but they do it with a smile and a flourish and an overcooked meal they sell at twice what it's worth. After all, what do travelers know of a strange city?"

"If thieves aren't caught, they'd probably do quite well, wouldn't they?" John remarked.

The woman cackled hoarsely, apparently amused at the idea of this lean stranger as an apprentice thief. "Some might. You're a bit too conspicuous, though. You don't blend in with the crowd, excellency. But then, I must say, I do like a tall man." She put her hand on his arm, her multicolored wrappings brushing the sleeve of his torn tunic.

John ignored the familiarity. "Do you have any more advice for me, Pulcheria? For I fear I must leave soon."

The pretty half of her mouth formed a pout. The effect was quite horrible. "Well, if you'd been here a few days ago you could have asked the Basket Man. He knew how to steal when people were distracted, he could whip the pouch right off your belt while you were listening to Joseph, so he could. You need a lot of people around you if you're up to no good, that's what he'd tell you. He was always quite honest about thieving."

John asked how the man had received such a curious nickname.

"The Basket Man? He was one of them that used to steal from the offerings always being sent up to the Crow."

"The Crow?"

Pulcheria gestured up at the stylite's column. "That squawking bird of ill omen perched up there. But he didn't actually steal from Joseph. He stole from those leeches who call themselves acolytes. Keep your eye open, like I do, and you'll soon see that most of the offerings the faithful put in the basket for Joseph never reach him. To be fair, the Crow couldn't keep the smallest portion of all the gifts he gets. It would take a miracle to find room for them all up there and miracles, as you've doubtless already gathered, are not in common supply around here."

"You said this Basket Man used to steal. He's stopped?"

"Oh, yes. Forever."

Pulcheria's expression was grim. John realized she must have been very fond of the rogue.

"He died, excellency," she continued. "Died in a horrible way. He never liked cold. It got into his bones, he'd say. He got hold of this lamp, and we won't inquire too closely how he did. Not that a little lamp flame is going to keep you warm in an windy alley on a freezing night, it was more the idea of warmth, you know? Something to warm his hands at or to see what he was eating if he'd managed to get a scrap of food from somewhere. Well, he dozed off, knocked the lamp over or something like that. Who knows? Anyhow, he set fire to himself." She wiped her tear filled eyes quickly with the back of her hand.

John was thinking of the body Philo had discovered. Could it have been the man of whom Pulcheria was speaking? It was worth asking. "He died near here?"

Pulcheria nodded. "Only a few days ago. Such a shame, it was. He'd just got a nice warm tunic as well. Why, he thought that heaven had smiled on him at last."

"A tunic stolen from Joseph's basket?"

The woman rushed to the dead man's defense. "The Crow doesn't need any more. He gets enough given to him in a week to wear a different tunic every day and three on feast days. Hang around here long enough and you'll realize that quick enough."

Apparently Joseph was one of those rare stylites who did not wear clothing until it rotted and fell off him, John thought. "Your friend, did he die on the night those stylites burned to death?"

Pulcheria scowled. "Those stylites were struck down by the hand of God, everybody knows that. You aren't saying that he died just for stealing, are you? He was just trying to survive as best he could, like all of us."

Glancing sideways at her, John saw the opaque orb of her blind eye welling with fresh tears that flowed down the reddened, melted flesh that had once been a rounded cheek, matching the shiny tracks meandering from the lowered eyelid of her good eye.

❊❊❊

It was already after dark as Hypatia, carrying a heavy basket, made her way through the excited crowds lining the high sea wall along Constantinople's northern shore. According to the wild rumor swirling in the streets, this was where Michael's promised fire would consume the waters.

The Egyptian gardener often shopped here, having found that the daily market in front of the Baths of Actaeon was unusually well stocked with those herbs she could not grow but needed for cooking or for preparing potions for Gaius. And she enjoyed the view, a spectacular panorama sweeping from near the tip of the seven-hilled peninsula on which Constantine had built his capital to the junction of the Bosporos and the Golden Horn.

Her tawny, dark-eyed face with its frame of black hair attracted bold stares from men passing by. Of course, no respectable Roman woman would be seen in the streets unaccompanied during the day, let alone at night, but the young woman cared little for the customs of a city that was foreign to her. Now, however, she almost regretted succumbing to her curiosity.

Perhaps she would have been wiser to go home after her customary haggling with various sellers of this and that. Instead she had lingered until after night fell, curious to see if the event the hawkers of herbs and vendors of vegetables and chickens were all talking about would actually come to pass, if the water really would be set afire.

She shifted her grip on the basket. Two large cabbages, several shiny green apples and small bundles of herbs made it heavier than usual, but she felt some satisfaction in having completed her marketing by beating the herb seller down to a more acceptable price for the fennel she'd purchased for Gaius, who lately seemed to be treating a higher than usual number of patients suffering from gastric disturbances.

She found the mens' appraising looks less disturbing than the scraps of conversation overheard as she strolled around the crowded market. The beggars limping through the throng, the gossips sitting on the worn stone steps of the baths or clustered along the sea wall, all had their opinions and did not hesitate to voice them.

Yes, surely the cowardly villains who had ambushed those peaceful pilgrims would also be smitten down, a purveyor of onions was informing his customer as Hypatia passed by. And punishment would not stop at boiling away the waters was the considered opinion of his neighbor, shouted across a fine array of ducks whose limp feet dangled pathetically over the end of his rickety wooden table. It would consume the entire city and everyone in it, chimed in the maker of lamps, who went on at some length, claiming himself to be more an expert on fire by virtue of his trade than sellers of ducks or onions.

A dandy sporting the long hair of a Blue, his finely worked leather belt displaying a conspicuous blade, padded past Hypatia, addressing his equally fashionable companion loudly. "If those treacherous demons in the Great Palace are still alive when the sun rises tomorrow," he declared, "we shall just have to see to the matter ourselves."

His companion gave a laugh that was more of a snarl as he roughly pushed aside a beggar who had had the temerity to appeal to their charity. The elegant pair swaggered away, laughing.

The man's mention of the palace reminded Hypatia of the question John had recently posed to her. Would she wish to come to live at his house to assist her old friend Peter? On a temporary basis, of course. But then, she wondered, could a Lord Chamberlain's offer be regarded as anything other than an order?

She did not want to leave her work among the fragrant groves, the lush flower beds and shaded walkways of the imperial gardens, but winter was almost upon them and then there would be less work for her to do anyway. And if her stay was to be only until Peter regained his usual health, then she would doubtless be back at her accustomed job before it was time to begin the spring plantings.

But there was also the question of the potions she had agreed to supply to Gaius. Peter would not appreciate such concoctions bubbling in his kitchen, that she knew. Not to mention his detestation of anyone else being present while he cooked. If she accepted the temporary job, she would need all her diplomacy and tact. Still, Peter was not well and they had been friends for quite some time.

Someone bumped roughly against her.

The man was saying "Pardon, lady," even as his hand was slipping, like that of a stealthy lover, along her belt. Hypatia sank her fingernails into his wrist.

"I'm not stupid enough to carry my purse at my waist," she snapped, infuriated at his gall. "Shall we go and find the Prefect to discuss the matter?"

The young man pulled his hand away. He had the straw blonde hair and pale skin of one from the northern part of the empire. "I should think he'd have better things to do right now," he said quickly. "A beautiful woman like you shouldn't be out on the street by yourself, you know. It isn't safe." He rubbed his wounded wrist, looking at her reproachfully.

"And I suppose you were seeking payment in advance for acting as my bodyguard?"

"I didn't intend to rob you," the man denied half-heartedly. "But as for being your bodyguard—well, I wouldn't require even half a nummus to accompany a lady such as yourself. Though I might accept an apple, for the temporary rental of my blade just in case it's needed."

Hypatia laughed and handed him an apple. "You are hired, then. What is your name, in case I have to scream for help?"

The man looked down at the fruit in his hand. "My parents, as good Christians, gave me a good Christian name," he said, hesitantly. "It's Michael."

Hypatia managed to keep a straight face. "Well then, I shall feel very safe indeed with you guarding me. Now, help me find a good place to look over the sea," she said. "If the world is indeed going to end I want a good view of its departure."

Her new companion did not seem particularly adept at clearing her way, but the stares she attracted, with a man at her side, did not linger as long. When they reached the sea wall she leaned against it, admiring the view afresh. It looked very different from the one she had seen so often in daylight.

The breeze blowing gently on her face carried a hint of coolness and the sharp smell of the sea. Below, dozens of torches burned along the docks. Their twins on the ships riding at anchor were doubled in the black mirror of the water. Further away, the scattered lights marking other ships floated star-like in a dark void. A cluster to the northwest, glittering like the empress' jeweled mantle, marked inhabited areas lying peaceful and unknowing across the Golden Horn.

"It's like looking downwards into the night sky on a cold desert night," Hypatia remarked appreciatively. "Yet the god Ra himself never glimpses such a sight."

Her companion took a quick bite from his apple. "I would have thought that a god could see whatever he liked," he observed, chewing the crisp flesh of the fruit.

"True enough, but you see, each night Ra is guiding the sun's barque through the underworld. So he does not see the stars."

"I wonder if these are the last stars I will see, if this apple will be the last I ever taste?" It was obvious from his tone that he did not believe there would be anything worth seeing, at least of a supernatural nature, no matter how long they lingered at the sea wall. "But there again, water doesn't burn, so we should be quite safe." He took another crunching bite of his apple.

Hypatia leaned further out over the wall, enjoying the freshening breeze. As they both fell silent, she became aware of the press of the crowd behind them, the acrid tang of fear in the air, their tense voices.

Her companion finished his apple and tossed the core over the sea wall.

The fiery hand of God descended to the waters.

There was a brilliant flash that hurt their eyes, followed by a line of crackling, leaping flames, snaking out of the mouth of the Bosporos and into the Golden Horn. A spitting, fizzling roar, the sound of a jug of water thrown onto a hot brazier, accompanied it but so loud that it echoed back off the dome of heaven.

The fire leapt greedily upwards, taller than the height of two men. Ships floating at anchor and the cluttered docks at which they rode were suddenly alive with running figures starkly illuminated by the advancing wall of flames.

The roar of the approaching conflagration formed a terrible duet with the screams from the crowd and the men below.

Heat slapped Hypatia's face. She blinked, her eyes dazzled. Steam gouted from the water, swirling in wild, hellish shapes as if a demon army were pouring up out of the underworld. Ships caught fire as the inferno spread its deadly tendrils along the shoreline. A sail burst into flames, ripped loose from its blazing mast and came spinning upward, a wayward spark in the maelstrom.

A choking cloud of thick smoke rolled into their faces, mercifully obscuring the carnage below, but the screaming could still be heard.

A man pushed by them and climbed onto the sea wall.

"Look," he screamed. "It's coming for us. It's coming for us!"

He flung himself over the edge, his thin wail trailing away as he disappeared into the fiery hell below.

Behind them the crowd was running, screaming, pushing to get away. Belatedly aware of her dangerous position, Hypatia struggled to move back from the sea wall before she fell or was pushed over it. A heavyset man knocked her sideways as he fled. She went down to her knees, dropping her basket. Another man kicked her back down as she struggled to get up, shouting obscenities at her. She screamed, afraid she would be trampled in the general panic.

A muscular hand latched firmly onto one wrist and she was pulled upright, sobbing.

"When you get home tonight, lady," her blonde bodyguard informed her, shouting to be heard above the noise of the panicked crowd, "tell your family that your life was saved at the cost of but one apple. I think they'll agree that a better bargain could not be found in the entire city."

Chapter Nineteen

Anatolius burst out of the study, disheveled and as pale as a demon. The young servant half asleep on the floor by the doorway scrambled to his feet in alarm.

"Simon," Anatolius said rapidly. "I am going out shortly. Ensure that a watch is kept every hour of the day. Under no circumstances is anyone to be admitted until I return except John or Felix." His voice was hoarse, his eyelids red.

"Master," Simon stammered. "The streets were filled with rioting all night." He looked around in sleepy confusion. "It is still night."

"I have business that can't wait on the sun."

"But..."

"You have your orders. Besides, we're still alive and the house isn't a smoking ruin yet, so it would seem the Prefect's men are containing the worst of it."

"But your father?"

"His rites can wait! I'll see him avenged before they are held, for now I know the murderer. I intend to take care of this matter myself. Even if the authorities caught up with the cowardly bastard…well, justice is a fickle thing. Besides, I'm looking forward to blessing my blade with his blood."

"Justice is the Prefect's work, master. Shall I fetch him?"

"No, Simon. This is something that I must attend to myself. My father's shade will be proud of me!"

※※※

The sun had barely risen above the rooftops as Peter hastened to open the heavy nail-studded door. Had John finally returned home or did the thunderous knocking echoing up the stairs announce some terrible explanation for his master's absence?

He was shocked to find Madam Isis standing outside. A bloodied Darius loomed over her with a large sack dangling from one huge hand.

"Let us in," Isis begged. "We're not expected but we've had no time to arrange better quarters."

Peter admitted them, pity for their state overtaking his umbrage at Isis' unwitting insult to his master's house. After all, she was acquainted with his master in a perfectly chaste manner. And he could hardly refuse refuge to one of the master's friends. Still…

Isis looked very different than she had when he'd seen her passing by Senator Aurelius' kitchen on the night of the fatal banquet. Then she had been perfumed and dressed in fine silks. Now her clothing was ripped and her unpinned hair fell in a tangle over plump shoulders.

"There's violence everywhere," Darius muttered. He limped as he crossed the hall.

"And the master has been away for two nights now," Peter replied heavily, ushering them upstairs to the kitchen.

Darius uttered an oath to some deity whose name Peter did not recognize. He pretended not to hear.

"The master's guest was up half the night, looking out the windows," Peter went on, "trying to guess from the smoke and glare where the worst rioting was breaking out. What's been happening? How are the streets?"

Darius shoved the sack under the kitchen table as he sat down. "Yesterday," he began, "we heard some confused tales about an attack on the Michaelites. First Michael was supposed to be dead. Then the attackers had been driven off by heavenly hosts. Nobody knows exactly what happened except that much blood was spilled."

Peter made the sign of his religion. "This is dreadful, dreadful," he said in a shaking voice.

"Not as dreadful as what happened next," Darius told him. "The Prefect had been managing to keep things more or less under control, with assistance from the military, that is. But last night the Bosporos caught fire, just as predicted. It was the hand of God, so they say. Naturally the streets immediately went up in flames, except of course that was the work of a thousand human hands."

Isis wiped her eyes. Kohl had streaked darkly down her cheeks. Despite his disapproval of her profession, Peter found himself asking about the safety of her employees.

"My girls?" Isis said. "They've all gone to their special friends. They're safe enough for now."

"All but one. All but Adula," added Darius mournfully.

Peter noticed the bruise rising in imperial purple on Isis' cheekbone. Her ears were bloodied. Intercepting his stare, she fingered one ear gingerly. "Darius suffered worse. If it wasn't for him, we'd never have escaped with our lives. He's a hero."

Slumped on his stool, Darius grunted disagreement. "A hero? My job is to guard your door, not to flee for my life with you."

Isis reached across the table to lay her small hand across Darius' bloodied knuckles. "No one could have done more than you did, Darius. These zealots have opened a Pandora's box with their damnable threats and holy fires."

"But surely they would not engage in violence?" Peter was genuinely shocked.

"Perhaps not," admitted Darius, "But there are always scum ready to take advantage, skulking about the back ways and waiting in the shadows. Too cowardly to fight but brave enough to rob and steal the weak while others are engaged upon matters of war."

"And unfortunately that sort always survives to go back to its lair and see another day," Isis put in gloomily, straightening her torn clothing.

Peter thought about John again, gone for two days. He tried to direct his attention to other concerns. "What of your house?" he asked.

Isis rubbed her face, smearing kohl further. "Just after I sent the last of my girls away, Darius and I were discussing where we could find sanctuary for the next few days. We should have decided that already, of course, but I had arranged for my house to be guarded by some Blues." She shook her head. "Well, Peter—it is Peter, isn't it?—you may wonder at that, for it's true their faction may lose its running battle with the Greens, but you have even odds that they won't. So your property has a good chance of being safe, at least."

Peter said that that seemed a reasonable assumption, given the circumstances.

"At any rate," Isis went on, "I was collecting up a few things to take with me as we discussed where to go, but a gang of ruffians broke in and surprised us."

"We shouldn't have sent the other guards away before the Blues arrived, madam," Darius pointed out.

"Perhaps not, but I was thinking of their safety rather than mine," Isis replied. "But Darius kept the bastards busy while I fled out the back door. After they had finished beating him, they threw him out after me. I crept back, and found to my relief—not to mention my surprise—that he was still alive. So we took to our heels. Fortunately, the guards at the Chalke had seen me often enough under happier circumstances. They let us into the palace grounds and so, here we are. Now you see why I say Darius is a hero."

Darius smiled wanly. "Yes, Peter, I was extremely heroic while being beaten, just as madam said."

"You must have been outnumbered ten to one," Isis said. "And, Peter, it seems by the time they'd finished with him, they'd had enough fun for the time being and I'd apparently been quite forgotten. And lucky that was for me, since you could easily have run away and left me to their mercy, or what there was of it." The woman shuddered.

Darius declared firmly that a man did not desert his family. "Or, he added quickly, "his employer. And what do you think that we have here, Peter?" He nodded at the sack under the table.

Peter had no notion what one might try to save from a house such as Isis'. "Candlesticks? Statues? Jewelry?"

At the last word Isis let out a strangled sob and dabbed afresh at her eyes. "Jewelry? We had no time to gather up my jewelry. I even lost the earrings I was wearing. Some bastard accosted us in the street and ripped them right out of my ears. They were my favorites too, understated but elegant. Gold wire amphorae with a pearl inside each one. And now they're probably decorating some low class tart's filthy ears." The irony of her words struck her and she gave a small, snuffling laugh.

Peter noticed for the first time that her throat was marred by the red imprint of splayed fingers.

"Oh, dear," Isis went on, wiping away tears of mixed merriment and grief, "what a fool I am to worry about earrings at a time like this. But then again, no doubt some will be vastly amused to hear that I, the owner of the one of the richest houses of its kind in

Constantinople, fled from it with only a sack and the clothes on my back, exactly what I had when I first arrived here from Alexandria. And that was longer ago than I care to remember."

"Christians do not mock the afflicted," Peter noted stiffly.

Isis looked unconvinced. "I'm glad to hear that. You may be asking yourself what I managed to save? Well, there's two silver dishes and the djeds I brought with me when I came to the city."

Peter murmured sympathetically, wondering what a djed might be. Something barbaric, no doubt.

"And," Isis snuffled, "more importantly, my silver fruit knife and…" Tears began to roll down her bruised face, "…and an apple. So these are the only things all my years of labor have gained me—two silver dishes, a knife and an apple."

Trying to think of some words of comfort, Peter hesitated and then asked awkwardly. "But surely your house at least is safe, if not its contents?"

Isis could not stop the flow of tears.

Peter looked helplessly toward Darius, who had turned away to stare out the window as if he could not bear to look at his distraught employer.

"They set fire to the house, of course," he muttered to Peter. "As we ran for our lives, we looked back and saw the flames."

❄❄❄

Peter had scarcely returned to the kitchen from escorting the weeping Isis to a bedroom to rest when a blessedly familiar rap echoed in the entrance hall.

He hurried downstairs as fast as his aging legs could carry him, throwing the stout outer door wide open to welcome his employer home. The fear and anxiety of the past two days was forgotten, a heavy weight lifted from his bent back—or at least for the short time it took to register that he was admitting not a well-dressed court dignitary but a haggard man, wearing a filthy tunic reeking of smoke and the gutter.

John looked at Peter with eyes red-rimmed with fatigue. "Please heat water and find me clean clothing, Peter," he said quietly. "But before you see to that, I would like some wine." Noting the other's aghast expression, a smile skittered across his weary face. "You are not to worry. We will be quite safe here."

"Master, that is as well. Madam Isis and the man Darius arrived not long ago, fleeing for their lives. The poor things." He hesitated. "I wasn't certain what to do, but, well, I thought you would wish them be admitted."

John secured the door, telling his servant that he had indeed done what John would have wished and concluding by remarking that doubtless Philo was having plenty to say to the new arrivals.

"He went out not long ago," Peter said reluctantly. "He said he had an appointment."

"At this hour? In these conditions?" John was extremely angry, Peter realized, despite his even tone. Not that he blamed him.

"The meeting was arranged for the first hour after dawn, he said. He claimed that the situation had calmed by the time he had to leave."

"Of course, that's exactly what he would say if he wanted to go out badly enough." John's shoulders had sagged at the news. "Keeping Philo from placing himself in harm's way is proving more difficult than undoing the Gordian knot of these murders. Unfortunately I cannot emulate Alexander and solve the mystery by slicing it in half, since the solution is concealed somewhere in its coils." He muttered a curse. "Did the old fool mention where he was going?"

Peter was shocked to hear his master speak of Philo in that fashion, and valiantly strove to conceal it. "Opposite the Chalke, it seems. He claimed that the unrest wouldn't be allowed to approach so near to the palace."

"A forlorn hope, considering the mob was all but battering its way through the Chalke not that long ago. And the rioting is all over the city. There's no pattern at all, you never know what's waiting for you around the next corner. It took me most of the night to make my way home. At times the situation was so dangerous that I had to take shelter and wait for my chance to move on."

"Come and sit in the kitchen, master." Peter said. "You look exhausted. You need to rest."

"Not yet, Peter. I'll have to go out and bring Philo back before he gets hurt. Thank Mithra Anatolius has sequestered himself, or he'd probably be wandering around unarmed in the thick of it, gathering impressions for an epic verse to rival the Iliad."

Darius appeared at the top of the stairs.

"Lord Chamberlain! I couldn't help overhearing. Will you allow me to rescue your straying guest? We came through the Chalke not long ago and he wasn't there then. He's probably wandering around the Mese. Very foolish if you ask me. You're dead on your feet and as for me, well, if anyone's looking for a fight, I'm more than ready to accommodate them." The smile that broadened his bloodied mouth was not a pleasant one, despite his light tone.

"You seem to be making a habit of rescuing Philo, Darius,' John observed. "Very well. I'd welcome your help. Since surely even Philo has the wisdom to stay fairly close to the palace, he shouldn't be too hard to find. Now, is there news of Felix?"

Peter shook his head wordlessly.

※※※

John leaned his folded arms on the kitchen table, nestled his head down on them and immediately fell asleep. Happy to see his master safely home, Peter charitably overlooked the fact that John's filthy hair was straggling on to his well scrubbed table. That could be set to rights later.

The elderly servant stirred up the brazier as quietly as possible. Honey cakes, he thought, now I wonder if the master would like a honey cake when he wakes up? Of course, he did not normally indulge in sweet confections, but who knew what he had been eating in the past couple of days? By the look of him, not very much.

But as soon as Darius got back with the errant Philo and sanity and order were restored within the household, they could all retire and have a good night's rest. Yes, it would be good to sleep snugly abed. If they could slumber at all, that was, what with the sound of distant and not so distant violence beating at their windows. It was quieter now but, having spent many years in the city, Peter fully expected the disorder to break out with renewed force when night again fell and darkness cloaked evil deeds.

As if summoned by the very thought, the ugly undercurrent of sound that had droned all day long swelled louder into a brief cacophony of shouts and cries before falling back into a sullen muttering. Peter glanced uneasily out. Here and there columns of smoke marked another house or workshop looted and set on fire. It was as if the city, having convinced itself it was next to suffer, was not content to cower while waiting for heavenly fire to descend upon it, but rather was undertaking to cleanse itself voluntarily.

He busied himself setting the last few honey cakes out on a platter and filled the wine jug as he pondered how he would feed this sudden influx of house guests, not having ventured to market that morning. He could not very well instruct an excubitor from the barracks across the way to go out and ask the first market stall holder he found to demonstrate his allegiance to Justinian by provisioning the Lord Chamberlain's household.

Thinking of excubitors reminded Peter of Felix and he briefly wondered what had happened to him before returning to the vexed question of feeding the recent arrivals. He thought of vegetables and meandered naturally from that topic to his friend Hypatia. Thank the Lord she would be safe in her house on the palace grounds.

***

A loud knocking echoed upstairs.

John leapt awake, blade in hand before his eyes were fully open. How long had he been asleep? Probably only a short time.

"I will attend to that," he said, striding out of the room before Peter could reply.

The heavy knock reverberated again, underlined by Darius' hoarse shouts for admittance. Isis called anxiously from her room, as if she too had been startled awake by the commotion.

John yanked the door open. Darius lumbered past him, a limp form over his shoulder. Dumping his burden unceremoniously on the tiles, Darius rushed out into the garden, retching.

For an instant John feared that Philo had been harmed before Darius reached him but the bloodied body on the tiles groaned and muttered something unintelligible. The voice belonged not to Philo but to Anatolius.

Peter would be extremely unhappy about all the blood and mud that was being tracked into the house he kept so spotless, John thought as he helped Anatolius to his feet.

Isis was back in the kitchen and with Peter, John and now Anatolius there as well, even before an ashen-faced Darius staggered in, the cramped, hot room seemed very crowded.

"I couldn't find Philo, Lord Chamberlain," Darius confessed, wiping his mouth with the back of his hand. "But I did see a woman. Or what had been a woman. A beautiful young..." He rushed into the lavatory that opened off the kitchen and vomited again.

John's mouth tightened. He looked around the kitchen, as yet untouched physically by the riots yet full of human flotsam fleeing them. "I will have to seek Philo then," he muttered. "and I pray to Mithra this will be the last time I'll have to warn him about heedlessly courting danger."

Chapter Twenty

Lord Mithra answered John's prayer, although not in a manner he would have desired.

Philo lay on the table in Gaius' surgery so recently occupied by the plasterer with the broken arm, but unlike that particular patient he was beyond feeling pain.

If only he had found his old mentor before his murderer had struck, thought John. But then, he reminded himself, Philo might have been lying dead in the alley where the Prefect's men found him even while John vainly searched the area near the Chalke.

John forced himself to walk over to the table and look down at the old man, who was decently covered by a linen sheet pulled up to his waist. Philo's lined face looked serene, his white hair and beard neat. The bruising on his neck and the narrow wound in his ribs told the manner in which his shade had been set free to fly to eternity, there to discover the answers to those vexing questions that bedevil all who live, farmers and philosophers alike.

But he could not offer an answer as to why or by whom he had been murdered.

A ripe oath and the crash of breaking pottery emerged from the next room, followed by Gaius. "I fear that Bacchus is again interfering with my ability to carry out my calling," he muttered. "I cannot seem to get my thoughts to flow correctly this morning."

"If I may trouble you for such information as has been revealed by your examination?"

"Yes, you'll want to know about Philo, naturally." Gaius rubbed his temples. "Very well, then. Since it was apparent how he died, I did not carry out any internal investigation of the body."

John was grateful to hear that. Philo had always been at pains to maintain his dignity and would have been horrified at the thought of his remains being violated by the physician's sharp and disrespectful knives.

So far as his death was concerned, it had been clean enough as such things went. He had been spared the sort of obscene wounds John had seen in his time as a mercenary, wounds suffered by men who left their homes and loved ones whole but oft times came back maimed and occasionally half insane. Nor, his treacherous memory reminded him, was it only in times of war that this could happen...but he turned his attention firmly away from that dark river as the physician continued speaking, still massaging his forehead.

"In this particular instance," Gaius was saying, "you would have been able to ascertain as much as I and that with a quick glance. By the bruising on Philo's throat, I suspect that the assassin crept up from behind and choked him to render him helpless and muffle his cries. Then a quick stab, a shove to the ground, and a hasty departure to avoid discovery."

"That is the coward's way, to creep up on an old man."

"No more cowardly than poison, John."

"But still I would like to think that it was not as easy as killing a chicken for the evening meal. And then too, I would have wished him a more dignified death."

"You mean, you hope he had the opportunity to die fighting? That is the former mercenary speaking! One thing, however. Although I rather suspect Philo wielded the blade he carried only at table, his dagger was under his body. We'd probably both like to think he marked his assailant, but even so it must have been over very quickly and mercifully so."

"So it's possible he at least had a chance to defend himself?"

Gaius picked up Philo's cold hand. "Briefly, perhaps. You see these wounds?" He pointed to gashes on the dead man's palm.

John bent down to examine the deep cuts. "Isn't it strange, Gaius, that they appear so regular?"

Gaius shrugged. "Those who are attacked commonly put their hands up to defend themselves against the stabbing and slashing."

"And yet..."

"Our minds seek meaning in the meaningless, John. Do we not see strange and wonderful shapes in summer clouds?" Gaius pointed out.

"Perhaps you're right," John admitted. What was obvious enough was that someone had taken advantage of the violence to slaughter an old man in cold blood.

"It's just too commonplace a death for Philo," he went on. "I wonder what other adventures he had in his wanderings and why Atropos wielded her inexorable shears and cut the thread of his life here instead of somewhere else."

"If it's any comfort, I would say that a blade wielded as expertly as in this instance provides an easier death than one by poison or fire."

John agreed, adding that apart from the other six recent deaths of which he was personally aware, there must have been many more who had died in the inferno at the docks.

"Yes, indeed. But you mean five deaths, don't you, John? Aurelius, the three stylites we examined, and that girl belonging to Isis?"

"There was also the burnt body Philo stumbled over," John reminded him.

"Yes, well, that's true. But there'll be more than a few like that once the weather gets really cold and they doze off too close to their fires."

"Gaius, I have a strong suspicion there is a connection between all of these deaths."

The physician looked down at Philo. "Well, I didn't see the man Philo found, but as for the stylites, as I said, they all burnt from the outside, notwithstanding people raving about fires from within, hands from heaven, and the like."

John thoughtfully traced the gashes on Philo's palm.

"But what about the matter of Philo's funeral?" Gaius asked after a short pause. "It seems you're going to be responsible, John, since obviously he has no family here to carry out his rites."

John nodded, adding "Although at the moment the dead will be fortunate to be buried with only a hurried prayer at their graveside. And Philo would not want that."

Gaius gently smoothed Philo's white hair but remained silent.

❋❋❋

The sun was setting as John lit a lamp and carried it into what had been Philo's bedroom. It was spartanly furnished, hardly fit for an Athenian, as Philo had remarked on more than one occasion with what John had taken to be an attempt at humor.

The room held few reminders of its former occupant. One or two letters Philo had been writing lay on a desk in front of the window and a pair of his well worn boots stood beside the one chair provided for the comfort of visitors.

Apart from artfully painted garlands of intertwined ivy, yew, and cypress branches hanging in dark green loops just above head height around its white plastered walls, the room's only decoration was its mosaic floor.

Glancing down at it, John found himself wondering how Philo had regarded the throng of rioting sea creatures frolicking around, on and under the mosaic's foaming sea swells, endlessly crashing ashore in frozen waves. The sun's dying light coupled with the window panes' small irregularities gave an eerie quality to blue, green and black portraits of octopi, dolphins, and other denizens of the deep. Had they reminded Philo of the long journey he had taken from Greece to the eastern wildernesses and then half way back to his home land?

John sat down and pensively contemplated the now ownerless boots. Philo had been willing to endure the bulky himation of the philosopher, but not the sandals.

What was he to make of this most recent death? Was it really just a terrible incident during the riots? If not, who would have wanted to murder an innocent stranger, a man likely to be executed when official tolerance suddenly evaporated for reasons of state, or, as had been John's experience, at a whim of Justinian's?

Or of Justinian's wife Theodora, he reminded himself.

Soon he would have to arrange a funeral. What sort of rite would Philo wish? Cremation, perhaps, after the ancient custom. It would have to be done outside the city. Perhaps at Anatolius' newly acquired country estate?

He thought of Aurelius. So far as the senator was concerned, there was a cornucopia of possibilities as to the person responsible for his death. Staring at the ceiling, John began to enumerate them. Perhaps the exercise would open his mind to inspiration or a flash of insight that would set his feet on the right path.

"Well, then," he muttered to himself, regretting that in this room he could not address his musings to the mosaic girl Zoe. "Let us consider. There are often reasons aplenty for murder but sometimes none at all. But assuming that it was done with deliberate intent, who would benefit by Aurelius' death?"

He stood and began to pace back and forth across the small room. Glancing out, he noted that some of the glare reflected in far off windows was not from their catching the rays of the setting sun. The violent hysteria gripping the city was worsening. Could it be the result of an alliance between the factions? During his night journey home he had several times observed what appeared to be Blues and Greens fighting shoulder to shoulder, rather than with each other.

And this led to another thought. Was it too outlandish to suspect that certain courtiers might have encouraged civic disorder by large, well-placed bribes and secret meetings with the factions' leaders for their own reasons, although these might not necessarily include deposing the emperor?

"Think more about that later," he chided himself, sitting down again. "For now, concentrate on who might wish to murder Aurelius. And drawing upon the training instilled by Philo, examine not just that, but also who had the opportunity to carry out the deed."

He stared at a particularly lively dolphin disporting in the silent waves crashing at his feet.

Among those at the banquet there were certainly many who, behind smiling faces and animated conversations, must have privately disapproved of the senator's role in the Michaelite negotiations, ignoring the imperial edict forcing it upon him. Perhaps they ought rather to have been grateful, John thought, that they had not been ordered to undertake the delicate task. But did they feel strongly enough to kill—and to what purpose?

The reasons for murder were surprisingly few. Unbalanced humors, lust, a desire for power or revenge, gaining wealth or social position.

Certainly Aurelius would have had professional or business rivals who might well have been happy to seize a chance to dispose of him. John would have expected a less public attack, but on the other hand, in a gathering of many suspects there lay anonymity and thus better odds of escaping justice. Then too, over abundant wine inhibited the reasoning capacities. One cup too many, unchecked hatred boils over and a man is dead.

But poison strongly suggests premeditation, he argued with himself, not to mention some degree of familiarity with its preparation and administration. Well, there were two people in Aurelius' house that night who immediately suggested themselves. Gaius, whose professional knowledge of herbs was by necessity far better than many gave him credit for, and Hypatia, who had been assisting Peter in Aurelius' kitchen, not that the girl had any motive.

Ah, but then again perhaps the poison had been intended for another victim and in the excitement of the occasion the wrong jug had been set out in Aurelius' study?

Speculating on the possibility, he leaned over and picked up the letters Philo had left behind.

One requested a meeting with a senator. Now that would never take place. The other was unfinished, written in florid Latin with hastily formed letters and many scratchings-out. John scanned it rapidly and soon found himself wondering if Philo had uncharacteristically imbibed too freely before he composed it.

As John read, he wondered anew at Philo's foolishness. If certain eyes had read the letter, the philosopher would have been immediately arrested and incarcerated in the imperial dungeons and the person to whom it was addressed—Aurelius—arrested along with him.

It was a scandalous document, to say the least.

> Philo to the honorable Senator Flavius Aurelius, greetings!
> Concerning they who sit in bejeweled radiance on gem-encrusted thrones, Justinian and the woman rightly known as Theodora of

the Brothel. This befouled pair are, and I am willing to demonstrate the truth of this statement with many instances, demons copulating in spiritual darkness. Truly, not even the filthiest and most broken-down whores fornicating in the worst alleys of this benighted city can approach the wickedness of the empress, whose gleeful delight in her public and obscene lewdness offends the heavens themselves.

Yet even so, what surprise the common folks appear to feel that wrath is descending upon them all, from innocent babes to the most respectable elders such as ourselves, because of the evil rotting at the heart of the empire. But they, by which I mean Justinian and Theodora, would take great delight in personally cutting out your tongue and ordering you starved until you ate your words, or rather the organ that declaims them, did you but dare to whisper concerning their guilt in bringing death and disaster upon this city. I do not say this from mere anger but as a reasoned observation, while pleading again, old friend, that as a former Academician you help me find some way to escape this sinister city.

The secrets of what lies beyond the grave will soon enough be revealed to me, but I am too old to make the long journey home to die in Greece, and although John has been kind, in fact more than generous, I feel I cannot avail myself of his hospitality forever. Perhaps you could inquire among landowners with estates near yours and thereby find some suitable post for an educated person such as myself? Between Michaelites and the demons in human form who rule the empire, Constantinople is a city under a murderous siege and you are fortunate indeed to have a bucolic sanctuary in which to take refuge. I regret I find there is little call for a tutor of my brilliance despite many inquiries, and I despair of ever finding such a place.

Indeed, where should prudent men such as us place our loyalties at this time? Certainly not supporting Michael and his rabble, who themselves are an affront to any reasonable mind and conscience, you may well reply. Yet from what I have seen and heard here, it seems more than likely that soon he will be in power and when that terrible day dawns, pagans such as you and I will be in the gravest of dangers.

Now, you may suspect that I have lost my senses, but I assure you that not only is this not so but that I have much of great interest to reveal. This Michael is but one subject upon which I would like to converse with you, but I prefer not to commit more than that to writing for reasons that will surely be evident to us both as men of the world. Senator, we must beware always of those imperial spies who...

John laid down the letter thoughtfully. For a self-described man of the world, Philo had certainly written much more than was wise. Obviously he had hoped to obtain another interview with the senator by intriguing him with vaguely worded hints about matters of great import. After all, Theodora's character, and for that matter her affairs, were common knowledge in Constantinople, even if Justinian remained—or pretended to remain—blissfully ignorant about them.

An unwelcome thought struck John. Had Philo stumbled upon more information and concealed it from him? Information so dangerous to possess that a man could be murdered to keep it secret? It would certainly be in keeping with the philosopher's secretive nature, and yet...

Peter interrupted his chain of thought.

"Lord Chamberlain," he said, peering around the door with a disapproving expression, "a summons has arrived from our most gracious empress."

The servant's demeanor and formal method of address alerted John that the message-bearer was within earshot. He nodded silent thanks and emerged into the hall to see Hektor, resplendent in yellow tunic and emerald hose, lounging a few paces away near the top of the stairs, turning one foot this way and that as he admired his exquisite yellow boots. He looked up with a gleeful grin as John appeared.

John said nothing. He had a strong suspicion that the lad had not arrived to bring good tidings. He was not mistaken.

"Well, my dear Lord Chamberlain," the boy began with a sneer, "you will have to explain yourself to the empress. I for one will be very interested to see what possible explanation you can make up to save yourself this time."

"Indeed?" John replied, ignoring the boy's studied insolence. Fortunately Peter had shuffled off to the kitchen and was not present to be outraged at the manner in which his master was being addressed by this perfumed creature.

"Indeed, indeed," Hektor echoed mockingly. "You are to go immediately to the empress. And just in case you were thinking of suddenly taking a trip to the country, there's a detachment of excubitors here to ensure that you make all possible haste to obey her summons."

A loud pounding at the front door reinforced his statement.

"Then I shall go immediately." John replied, refusing to give Hektor the satisfaction of inquiring as to Theodora's reasons for requiring his presence. "It is not often that the empress sends a mere page to announce such a summons, although I seem to recall that it has been known to happen on odd occasions in matters of extremely minor import. And your detachment of excubitors seems to have lagged behind somewhat. You must have stepped out smartly to have arrived here before they did."

Hektor bridled. "I did not say that I was actually with them." Raised voices echoed up from the entrance hall as he continued. "I arrived ahead of them in a sort of unofficial manner, because," an unpleasant smile spread over his small face as a heavily armed excubitor loomed at the top of the stairs, "I thought it kinder to inform you quietly that your dear friend Anatolius has just been arrested for the murder of your other dear friend, the philosopher Philo. My most sincere commiseration upon this tragic event, dear Lord Chamberlain."

Chapter Twenty-one

A natolius was not squeamish about sleeping in strange beds. He had spent the night in many—and not alone—perhaps in more than he would have felt comfortable admitting even to John. But until now he had never had to contemplate sleeping on what his poetic imagination had once dubbed the altar to Hypnos, slumber's personification, in such depressing circumstances and surroundings. Not even Ovid, he thought, would have been able to find any hint of romance in the emperor's dungeons.

It did not seem so long ago that he had been sitting in John's warm kitchen rather than on a cold stone floor. When John went in search of the missing Philo, Anatolius had insisted he accompany him. But John would not hear of it. Anatolius was to rest, he had said, and although he and the others certainly wanted to know the story behind Anatolius' sorry, blood-spattered condition, it could wait until Philo was back and they were all safe under one roof.

Would it have made any difference, Anatolius wondered, if had he remained there rather than departing on John's heels? He had had no desire to relate the less than heroic events that had culminated in his being carted to safety over Darius' shoulder, as if he were a sack of grain. Besides, he had to be certain his home had not suffered the same fate as Isis' establishment.

When he reached his house he discovered it had remained untouched. Moreover, on the way there he ascertained that the disturbances had been quelled, at least along the Mese and in the immediate vicinity of the palace. So, discarding his ruined tunic he hastily donned fresh clothing and set off for the baths, determined to enjoy that luxury while it was still available. He suspected the unorchestrated riots that had swept the city were but petty upheavals compared to the organized chaos that was surely being planned. And who could say if the new day might not bring further miracles of destruction?

Returning home again refreshed in body and spirit, he had almost reached his front door when it swung open and an excubitor stepped outside. Simon followed. His cringing bearing conveyed his abject fear before he even spotted Anatolius.

"Master," he cried, distressed, "we could not refuse them entry!"

The excubutor's appraising stare at the approaching Anatolius took on a harder edge. The man was holding the bloodied tunic Anatolius had lately discarded.

"Why are you here?" Anatolius demanded hotly as more armed men emerged from his house.

"By imperial order and in the name of the emperor, we are here to arrest you," the man holding the tunic declared. Despite his firm tone and hard look, there was a hint of uncertainty on his face. Perhaps he was not yet accustomed to arresting members of the court. "You are under suspicion of murdering a certain man by the name of Philo," he added, completing the formalities.

"Philo?" Anatolius was incredulous. "But surely he's at the Lord Chamberlain's house?"

It was obviously a ghastly misunderstanding, he thought. With all the disorder in the city someone along the chain of command had received garbled instructions. But his father would soon set things right. No, he corrected himself quickly with a deep pang of pain, his father was no longer able to aid him. But there again John would be able to straighten matters out just as swiftly.

"I suggest that you consult the Lord Chamberlain on this matter," Anatolius said, "for it is quite evident that a mistake has been made."

"Our orders are to arrest you. They are our only orders," the excubitor replied, resting a hand suggestively upon the hilt of his sword.

Anatolius demanded to know who had made the accusation.

The excubitor did not reply but looked pointedly down at the reddened tunic hanging over his arm.

Anatolius was marched smartly away through the dark and unhealthy network of narrow lanes pressing closely around the wall encircling the Great Palace. Even as he was escorted to a row of cells beneath the ruins of a small temple left picturesquely intact in a less frequented part of the palace grounds, he remained convinced that his detention was an error. Mistaken identity, perhaps, or some other simply explained misunderstanding. Had Felix been in charge of the excubitor detachment sent to arrest him, it would all have been cleared up in the wink of an eye.

Now, hours later, leaning against the rough wall of his cell, he wondered if he would be released soon or if he would be forced to make his bed that night upon the cold floor. No sound came from the corridor. He might as well have been already buried and forgotten.

Thinking of burials gave birth to unfortunate recollections of certain rumors and gossip. One day a courtier was received with smiling favor, the next he found himself ordered confined to his home until he died or hastened his own death. Had imperial policy changed, become yet stricter? Were such unfortunates locked away from the world now, left to starve to death with none knowing where they were hidden away?

Anatolius knew as little of the law as he cared to—which was almost nothing. As he recalled, Romans were seldom sentenced to imprisonment but rather to fines, forfeitures or death. The thought did not cheer him.

He rubbed his gritty eyelids. Why should the emperor, whom he saw nearly every day, whose words he worked diligently to embellish, treat his trusted secretary in such a barbaric manner?

He reminded himself at present it was Theodora who was in charge although the orders issued bore Justinian's name. He recalled Theodora's exotic scent, her warm breath on his face. Had she perhaps detected some forbidden interest in her in his demeanor?

Of course, he'd also copied out Michael's letter for John. Could Theodora have learned of that? Did it explain her sudden animus? She would need little excuse or reason, in fact none at all, to strike out at a close friend of her enemy the Lord Chamberlain, especially when that friend's execution would result in his newly acquired estate reverting to the coffers of the empire.

Yet he would not hold an estate were it not for the death of his father. The thought brought another of those sudden floods of shocked recollection to cut through the foggy miasma that seemed to be afflicting his reasoning. The pain of his loss, realized anew, was as sharp as it had been when he first saw his father lying dead.

"Oh, father," he whispered to the empty air, "if only you were here to help me now."

But there again, Justinian could not remain in seclusion for much longer and the absence of a man of Anatolius' stature would soon be noticed at court, unless everyone assumed he had abandoned his city house and fled to the safety of the country.

Ah, but then what of the household slaves? Well, the gossips would say, they would naturally have been left in Constantinople to guard the house. Or possibly the more charitable of his acquaintances would declare that in their opinion he was mourning in seclusion, refusing to receive visitors. And his slaves would not dare say anything. After all, once it was established their master had disappeared, they would be suspected of doing away with him under cover of the general disorder.

He rested his head on his drawn-up knees, clasping his arms around his legs. At least his cell was dry. He wondered what its original purpose had been. Perhaps it had once been occupied by a temple servant. He resolved when he was released he would sacrifice to whichever deity his temporary quarters honored as well as to Lord Mithra. Indeed, the underground room in which he was sitting reminded him of the mithraeum.

"Courage, Anatolius", he told himself loudly, "You have achieved the rank of Soldier of Mithra. Do not disgrace yourself and your companions at arms."

But even as he spoke, there came to his mind an image of the bear Theodora kept caged. Would he and the bear ever be free again?

The dark image was banished by a thud at the door. He leapt up, startled, heart racing. If only he had a blade! Was this where his life would end? But it would be sold dearly, he promised himself, moving swiftly to the corner that would be concealed by the door, now opening to admit the flickering light of a lamp. The cell's rough wall was reassuringly solid against his back. If he could grab that lamp and throw the burning oil into his visitor's face, it might offer an opportunity to flee down the corridor. He leaned forward, coiled ready to leap as the door swung fully back and a tall man stepped into the small room.

It was John.

Anatolius felt nauseated with the rush of relief.

The excubitor who had unlocked the cell looked in briefly before shutting the heavy door. He remained outside.

"I'll tell you what's happening as quickly as I can, Anatolius," John said, setting the lamp on the floor. "No doubt word's already on its way to Theodora that I'm here—and I would hate to find myself taking up residence in the next cell!" A quick smile curved his thin lips.

"But how did you know I'd been arrested? Did one of my servants rush to tell you?"

"A summons to Theodora," John said shortly. "brought by Hektor, who is less skilful at concealing his delight at your downfall than the empress. I must admit I did catch a glimpse of glee in those cold eyes of hers."

Anatolius shuddered. He did not tell John that the last time he had seen those eyes had been from a much closer viewpoint than John had enjoyed at his recent interview with the empress. "But why did she wish to inform you personally?"

"What can say? But it gave me an opportunity to petition that you be released into house arrest, either at your home or mine. She refused, naturally. Here you were and here you would stay, she said, and it made no difference if there was rape and riot in the streets, holy fire or bloodshed, while she was ordering imperial affairs, justice would continue to be served and the guilty punished."

Anatolius, feeling hysteria overwhelming him, gave a husky giggle.

"Calm, Anatolius, you must say calm!" John said sharply. "Lose your head now and you'll lose it in truth!"

Stifling the giggle that now threatened to change into a sob, the other nodded.

"I visited the Prefect before I came here," John continued rapidly. "I didn't learn much. Your accuser remains anonymous, and now the Prefect's busy gathering evidence against you. He's already interviewed some who claim they saw you this morning close to where Philo was discovered. And then there's this matter of your tunic. I'm hoping to discover something to tip the scales in your favor."

Anatolius did not care for his friend's grim tone. "Then Philo really is dead?"

John gave a curt nod and continued. "Now, one of your slaves told the Prefect that you left your house this morning before dawn in a raging fury, to seek out the man you thought responsible for your father's death. You had in fact declared your intent to kill the culprit. Is this true?"

Anatolius admitted that it had been so. "For my thought at the time was how pleasing it would be to slip my blade between his miserable ribs and twist it until his life painful bled away," he went on, "But when my humors had cooled a little, I thought better of it. A far sweeter revenge would be the humiliation of public accusation and arrest, for surely justice would be served and he would pay the supreme penalty? And of course when he paid it, I would be there to observe the rendering of the account, a thought I must confess I reveled in and still do." He did not need to point out the irony of his now himself being accused of murder and imprisoned in an imperial dungeon.

"I can see how you came to suspect Philo, Anatolius. He was certainly extremely angry with your father for refusing to help him find a post. He had spoken much of that and, of course, everyone who attended the banquet knows he was in the house when your father died. And then again you had personally invited him to provide entertainment. You said that you felt responsible...and your impetuous nature is well known."

The realization that John also suspected him was as if a bottomless pit had opened at Anatolius' feet.

"No, John, absolutely not! You have misunderstood entirely!" he protested. "The man I mean is Senator

Balbinus. He and my father were much at odds. While I was sequestered in the study I looked through the papers on my father's desk. Some were legal threats, concerning a land dispute with a neighboring estate owner, a dispute in which Balbinus had apparently seen fit to involve himself."

"And so you think that was the reason he murdered your father?"

Anatolius repeated that it had been Balbinus he had sought, not Philo.

John pointed out that Balbinus had not been present at the banquet on the night of Aurelius' death.

"He wasn't invited, John," Anatolius said wearily. "But don't forget that guests were arriving and departing from the house for several hours. Every public room was crowded. With all the comings and goings that evening, he could have somehow slipped in and out unnoticed. He or perhaps his accomplice."

John frowned as Anatolius' frantic rush of words echoed around the cell. "Is the truth at the heart of this matter that you have taken up with Lucretia again, despite the fact that she is now married? Is that why your rage was directed at Balbinus?"

"Of course not!" Anatolius was hurt. "You would have known about Lucretia if that had been the case. You know I can't keep confidences like that, even though doubtless you would have lectured me about morality."

John smiled grimly. "That at least is true. But I also remember certain statements you made not long after she and Balbinus married."

Anatolius looked at him in amazement.

"Do you think that, once uttered, our words vanish, never to return to our detriment, no matter how ill considered those words might be?" John asked.

Anatolius pondered the question briefly before replying. "As a fellow adept of Lord Mithra, you have my solemn oath that I did not murder Philo. He must have been the victim of some cut throat or other. After all, some will kill for the sport of it, some get caught up in hysteria and others kill from blood lust. There are stranger people about even than that, those who kill for pleasure. You did well to warn him of the dangers of going out alone. It's a pity he paid such a terrible price for failing to heed your advice."

Anatolius paused. "It's too easy to stumble over something people don't want trumpeted abroad." he said. "There's plenty of people with secrets that don't particularly interest us, but they'll kill to guard them. After all, how can they be certain that some inquisitive old man is not an imperial spy? There's enough of them around."

John said that unfortunately that was certainly so.

"I can tell you something I thought it prudent not to reveal when I was arrested, though," Anatolius replied, "and it's this. Although I did not find the man I was seeking, I did see Philo just before dawn this morning. He was standing outside the Chalke in very close conversation with a foreign looking fellow. I am wagering that's the man the Prefect should be looking for. The question is, will anyone believe me when I say I saw this man?"

John asked Anatolius why he had not tried to persuade Philo to go back home immediately.

"I would have, except, well, that was when a gang of Blues set about some Greens that were unlucky enough to be outnumbered. I got caught in the brawl and by the time I extricated myself, Philo and the other man had vanished."

"No doubt this was when you were bloodied?"

"Oh, that. Yes. Well, I fell and hit my head on the cobbles. It split my scalp open and I bled like a skewered ox. In fact, I lost consciousness."

John observed that it did not sound too convincing a tale.

"True. I can hardly remember all of what happened myself," Anatolius admitted. "But how long will I have to be here? Perhaps if you tell Theodora what I've just told you, she might relent?"

"It would do no good."

Anatolius mumbled something complimentary about John having a gift for reasoned argument.

"Yes, so Philo used to tell me," was the reply. "but he inevitably added that what I had was the potential for it if only I would apply myself more diligently…Alas that I did not, for at my recent audience with Theodora my powers of persuasion gained me nothing except orders to another audience with Michael. I am to be off to the shrine with the sunrise tomorrow, there to deliver a message I would normally term a capitulation except on this occasion Theodora is obviously hoping to gain time to lay further plans. As soon as I get back I will again attempt to see Justinian on your behalf."

Anatolius could not control the quaver in his voice. "There's no justice, John! There is no reason at all for me to be kept here!"

"Justice is the first casualty of war and that's the point we're rapidly approaching. Fortunately for you, your guards are fellow adepts, so for now at least you can expect reasonable treatment. The one outside told me that a few excubitors have deserted. Most of them have remained steady and so the palace is safe for now, but what will happen once they're outnumbered by a mob baying for blood, anybody's blood?"

"So perhaps it will indeed all end in fire and bloodshed," Anatolius muttered. "And as for me, it appears I am fated to remain hidden away here until the accusations against me are finally heard. If they are ever heard."

After John left Anatolius lay down. He could faintly hear the steady beating of waves, as if the sound of the sea was communicating with him through the earth upon which the building sat.

Then he realized it was the beating of his heart that was thrumming in his ears. He tried to pretend that the cold floor was just another of the many beds he had known. Uninvited, old lovers arrived to whisper to him. He forced them from his thoughts. But there was one more insistent than the rest. Anatolius was not able to convince her to depart. Lucretia seemed to kneel beside him, intent on comforting him, but his vision of her brought only further torment to this terrible place.

Chapter Twenty-two

Lucretia wiped her forehead ineffectually with the back of a grimy hand. She was exhausted. The quiet shrine where she had hoped to find refuge was now a crowded hospital, its fetid air filled with the sounds of pain and hope, prayers and curses. She could barely pick her way through the crush of the sick still hoping to dream cures and the wounded who had so recently fought on the field of battle outside the building.

Michael's acolytes had changed residence to a nearby villa in order to make more room for the patients. Michael himself, however, had remained at the shrine and so as Lucretia went about her work, she occasionally glimpsed him moving silently among the afflicted, bending to bestow a blessing or to gently touch a palsied limb or a horribly twisted face.

Lucretia had no blessings to bestow, only her labor. She spent her time washing and feeding, sweeping and carrying. Sweat glued her hair to her aching head and her tunic was stained and splotched. Her knees ached from kneeling beside straw pallets and her back had begun to twinge in sympathy, a protest against unaccustomed lifting.

Suppressing a sigh, she stooped to examine a cluster of sufferers. Her glance swept across them, past a man leaning against the wall but unnaturally still and over a younger man sprawled at his side, his ragged breath slowing gasp by gasp. They were beyond help now. But between them and another unconscious man huddled under a cloak lay a woman whose lips moved feebly. Lucretia set her basin of water down and knelt. She gently began to sponge the feverish face.

"We've been here two nights already and she's dying."

Lucretia looked up, startled by the growling voice. The speaker, a peasant by his callused hands and coarsely woven garment, was hunkered down in the shadows. His long face and straggling hair gave him a feral look.

"I'm afraid my woman isn't long for this world unless she dreams a cure more quickly," he went on.

Lucretia nodded and resumed her ministrations.

He launched on a narrative of how they came to be there. "We expected we'd have to make a sacrifice. That was the custom in Oropos in the old days. They say those who wanted a cure went there and made an offering of gold or silver to the sacred spring. Then they had to sacrifice a ram and sleep in its skin. We thought it might be the same here. We couldn't have afforded that." His voice was harsh but as he spoke he gently stroked the semiconscious woman's hand. "We were desperate. Somehow she found the strength to walk here. They said they didn't need gold and silver. She had only to pray and when she slept a cure would be revealed."

The woman seemed less restless now. Had she fallen into a refreshing sleep or begun her journey along the poppy-edged road leading to the bank where the dark ferryman waited to row the dead over the river Styx?

Why had that pagan image come into her head, Lucretia wondered. It was something the poetic Anatolius might have said. This was a Christian shrine but still she could sense the inexorable undercurrent of ancient belief that everywhere seemed to run just below the surface of life. Why would these Christian peasants have expected a cure to require the sacrifice of a brute beast? Why did they hope for the sort of dreams ancient healers had dealt in?

"Tell me," she asked the man, "have you heard of anyone being healed here?"

The peasant nodded his head. "Oh, yes, indeed. Only a day or so before we arrived, so I was told, there was a man who had suffered some terrible accident or other. I don't know any of the details, but anyhow after only one night here he arose from his pallet and declared to all that would listen that he had dreamed of a certain cure for his condition."

Lucretia inquired about the prescription.

The man barked out a laugh. "That he should marry a rich woman and live thereafter in idle luxury! Those who have wealth need never fear illness or getting old, for what they cannot do for themselves, their servants will do on their behalf."

Lucretia was about to rebuke the man for his harsh words but his unpleasant smile had been replaced by a look of grief that immediately stayed her tongue. She averted her gaze. Was this how her servants had felt? Surely not.

The sick woman gave a weak cry and flung out her arm, knocking over Lucretia's basin. The man leaned closer, holding her hands between his grubby palms until she lay still again.

"I'll get more water," Lucretia told him, beginning to rise. But he stopped her.

"Let me get it, lady," he offered.

Before she could protest he had scooped up the basin and slipped away. As she turned her attention back to the woman she saw that the man lying next to her patient had regained consciousness and was staring at her.

"Lucretia?"

She looked at him in alarm. The broad, bearded face, marred with bruises, was hauntingly familiar.

"Lucretia, what are you doing here? Does Anatolius know?"

"Anatolius? That was a long time ago..."

Felix blinked and let out a ragged sigh. "Of course, you're married now. Senator Balbinus." He tried to lift his hand but the effort was too much. The clotted blood clinging around the broad gash above his left ear told its own story.

"It's Felix, isn't it? Anatolius' friend?"

"Yes. But what are you doing here? Were you here during the attack?"

Lucretia admitted that she had been present.

"But what was your husband thinking of, to put you into such danger?"

Lucretia bit her lip. "I...I'm not living with Balbinus any more."

Felix closed his eyes and Lucretia thought he had drifted into unconsciousness. But then he was looking up at her again.

"You ran away," he stated. "to join a holy order! Mithra! The bastard beats you?"

Lucretia denied it. "No. Never. What makes you think that?"

"The bruises on your face, for a start. And for what other reason does a wife leave her husband?"

Lucretia did not have the heart to tell the captain that one of his own men was responsible for the condition of her face, although the blows had been struck in order to save her from worse.

"I am not a thing to be bought and sold," was all she said. It barely expressed the desperate revulsion she felt at her arranged marriage. Not that Felix looked to be in any condition to grasp a fuller explanation, even if she had been inclined to give one.

Felix muttered almost too quietly for her to catch his words. "When I am back on my feet, I'll tell Anatolius. He'll make sure that Balbinus pays, senator or not."

His voice trailed off as his eyes closed again.

"Felix?"

There was no answer but at least he was breathing.

Her attention was engaged by a sudden clamor in the aisle. She heard voices raised tremulously, beseechingly, as the peasant reappeared. He was accompanied by Michael.

She had seen him only from a distance, not daring to approach closer. He was slight of build and not much taller than herself. Strange to think that such powerful words could issue from the mouth of such a man.

"My woman is dying," the peasant saying. "You must heal her. We walked a long way. You owe it to her."

Michael bent and touched the sick woman's flushed forehead. Ignoring the peasant's passionate stream of pleas and entreaties, Michael next passed his hands over face of the dying man next to Felix. Then he moved on to the excubitor captain, gently touching the head wound.

"You must understand," Michael said, "that mercy must extend even to those who attack the innocent."

And now he addressed Lucretia directly. "A new handmaiden, I see, come to serve the lowliest. You will surely be rewarded, my sister."

Lucretia looked up into his dark, compassionate eyes, huge under the bald head. How could she doubt him?

"Holy one," she faltered, "the only reward that I ask is your blessing."

Michael laid his hand upon her head. "That you have. But your soul is troubled. May you gain peace of mind at least, if you do not find whatever you believe you are seeking here."

The peasant was kneeling also, asking Michael's blessing for himself and the woman he loved. Michael granted his request and moved away.

Her companion quickly looked down at the sick woman.

"Doesn't look that much different, does she?" he said harshly, a hint of yellowing teeth showing again. "If you ask me, she looks worse. Perhaps nothing can bring her back to me now. Not that I'm all that surprised," he concluded.

Lucretia, surreptitiously wiping her eyes, asked him what he meant.

"Didn't you see? If this Michael has really been blessed with his saintly namesake's healing powers, for that's what folks around here are starting to say, why does he have half-healed sores around his ankle?"

Smiling at her startled expression, he nodded importantly. "Oh, yes, you just look. He's coming back this way."

Michael was moving down the aisle again, blessing the unfortunates crowding the narrow space. As he passed by Lucretia bowed her head. It was not her right to question, but, hating herself for it, she quickly glanced at the thin ankles visible beneath the hem of his robe.

It was just as the peasant had said. She suddenly felt soiled, as she had with Balbinus.

"You saw, didn't you?" the peasant was asking her. "And by the look of them dark bits, his flesh is starting to mortify. A few days from now, his leg will be blowing up and he'll be smelling like a dead cow left out in the sun."

He leaned forward to confide in a whisper. "I'll tell you what I think, lady. He's an imposter. I've seen that sort of sore before. He's been held in shackles and that very recently. But why is he out here and what does he really want?"

Lucretia had no answer, nor did she care to ponder the question. She struggled to her feet and staggered outdoors. She needed fresh air. She felt very ill.

Chapter Twenty-three

The rhythmic swaying of John's mount as he rode up the Mese would have been almost soothing had it not been for his lingering vision of Anatolius' bleak cell.

He wondered how long Anatolius' stoicism would endure. Soldiers who had silently borne the most grievous battlefield wounds could be reduced to whimpering madness by extended periods of enforced hopelessness. It was something John had witnessed on several occasions. And more than once, out of mercy, he had counseled Justinian to sentence a miscreant to death rather than imprisonment. He prayed to Mithra he would not have to counsel such kindness on behalf of his friend.

His black thoughts about Anatolius' confinement, circling like birds of ill omen, were not all that distinguished this second diplomatic mission to Michael from the first. John's world had changed since then. Senator Aurelius, his companion on that first occasion, was dead. So was Philo. Felix was missing.

Isis and Darius had been reduced to refugees, the madam's girls were scattered, one had been horribly murdered. Even the reliable Peter was no longer his usual self, beset as he was by ill health.

The city seemed to reflect the ruins of John's life. He and the handful of guards accompanying him rode through wide blackened swathes, where fire had claimed the ill built buildings which crowded closely behind the colonnaded main thoroughfare. As they passed along the way, the hooves of their horses stirred up clouds of ashes. The acrid dust burned eyes and nostrils. Everywhere the air brought the sharp taste of smoke to the back of the throat.

If he accomplished his mission, would Theodora look more kindly on his entreaties on behalf of Anatolius?

John urged his mount forward. It was not until the shouts of his guards broke through his dark musings that he realized he had, for some time, been racing madly down the Mese at a full gallop.

❊❊❊

"Michael has agreed to an audience," the acolyte announced.

Outside the shrine, John had observed the scattered remains of cooking fires, shattered pottery, a sandal lying abandoned on the churned earth, things that together with the remarkable abundance of stones around the shrine's steps informed his trained eye of stealthy attack, a panicked route, and a determined counter-attack. Mute confirmation was provided by the dried blood staining the ground here and there. The number of the mounds of fresh earth ranged beside the nearby stream bore witness to the cost. He would not have buried the dead beside an encampment's water supply, he thought. Despite the Michaelites' recent martial success, it was obvious that their leader had had no military training.

Now, as he followed his guide through the crowded building, John glanced around its packed interior, searching for a glimpse of Felix.

Michael had not chosen to meet him in front of the altar this time. Instead, the acolyte led him to a small room in the back of the shrine. "This is the master's chamber," he revealed, before announcing John.

The room resembled a cell, but unlike Anatolius', it possessed an unlocked door and a tiny, square window overlooking the Bosporos.

Michael turned away from the view to face John. "I was sorry to hear of the death of your friend the senator," he said before John had a chance to speak.

"Your miraculous cure was short-lived, I fear," John observed tartly.

"It was not my cure, Lord Chamberlain. I am only an instrument for the heavenly physician."

The shaven-headed eunuch appeared to John even thinner than at their first meeting. Perhaps it was the increased gauntness of the smooth, ascetic face, the tired stoop of the narrow shoulders.

John began to offer the empress' felicitations but Michael interrupted the formal recitation. "She might have presented these greetings before she sent her excubitors."

"The empress also wishes to express her sincere regrets regarding the undisciplined conduct of certain of the imperial excubitors," John replied.

"They were, indeed, undisciplined," the other agreed. "And now let us dispense with all these flowery ceremonial greetings and waste no more time. Can you tell me why I would wish to hear anything from one who sought to destroy me and my followers?"

John repeated the communication Theodora had ordered him to deliver. "Emperor Justinian has been cloistered, seeking to reconcile your theological views with those of the orthodox persuasion. He left the empress in charge." He paused. Deception was not something he enjoyed but, like the sword, its use was sometimes necessary, if only in defense of one's self and one's friends. "I should not have to tell you," he finally said, still repeating Theodora's own words, "that the empress, as a woman, does not have the tight rein on the imperial military that..."

Michael raised his hand, again interrupting John. "Lord Chamberlain, let us speak freely. Do you really believe an empress cannot control those under her command? I most certainly do not. I notice you are extremely uncomfortable repeating this message from your gracious empress and I draw my own conclusions so far as that goes. But as for Justinian's attempts at constructing a compromise...as has already been proved, we are not timid nor do we balk at the logical conclusions to be drawn from our beliefs. In short, if orthodoxy cannot encompass a Quaternity then there is no compromise to be found. It is as simple as that. "

Michael half turned to look out of the window again. The sun shimmering on the restless waters of the Bosporos threw a rectangle of bright light across the stone floor, swept bare of even a single stalk of straw from the lumpy pallet in the corner.

"The empress wishes you to understand," John said, "that in such a large empire as this there is room for many differing shades of belief, although not necessarily within the confines of one city's walls. She wishes me also to point out to you that the patriarchy of Alexandria is an exceedingly high office."

Michael's pale, sexless face was framed by a nimbus of sunlight. John wondered if this was how others saw the person they so lightly referred to as 'John the eunuch,' not as a man who had been grievously wounded but as a creature neither man nor woman and, thus, a being not quite human or natural. His stomach tightened at the thought.

"Can it be that Empress Theodora is offering me the patriarchate of Alexandria providing that I abandon my followers and slink away in the night? Is that even an office that is hers to award?"

"The empress wields tremendous influence," John replied truthfully, thinking of Anatolius' plight as he spoke.

"Indeed? You have finally said something I can believe. But there again perhaps you can tell me why I should not simply remain here and take the patriarchy of Constantinople itself?"

John pointed out that continued stubbornness in the matter would eventually bring much larger detachments of military men with which to contend.

"Certainly in that case there is no doubt that they would prevail," Michael said with a slight smile. "But it would be a pyrrhic victory indeed. Need I remind you that the mob in the street vastly outnumber all of the emperor's men?"

"Will the mob follow one who is dead?" John countered.

"More readily than one who is alive."

It was true enough, John thought ruefully. He knew he was not speaking persuasively, yet having delivered Theodora's communication as ordered, he now wanted only to escape the other's unsettling presence.

Michael rested his hand on the stone sill. His sleeve slid down, revealing a skeletal wrist. John was struck by the impression that he was observing a prisoner yearning for unobtainable freedom. It occurred to him that quite possibly Michael would be happy to die.

Michael spoke in a near whisper. "Do not your emperor and empress possess eyes, Lord Chamberlain? Did they not see the holy fire strike down preachers of blasphemy atop their columns and reach inside the houses of the wealthy to destroy their whores? Did they not observe how the waters burned?"

John did not reply.

"Then carry back this message. Should Emperor Justinian wish to convey his views to me personally, I will listen," Michael continued. "But I see little point in you and I speaking further on this matter."

John bowed and began to leave, but then paused. "If I may ask, is there a man here by the name of Felix? A big, bearded soldier?"

"We took in all the wounded and are nursing even our assailants back to health, Lord Chamberlain. I believe I know the great bear you mention. He may go back with you, as a token of our mercy. He is, I think, just about recovered enough to travel. One of our sisters has taken special pains to nurse him." Michael stepped forward to look directly into John's face, as if he were searching for something in those lean, sunburnt features. "I fear, however, that you are beyond our healing power."

Before John could frame a reply, the other continued. "I was not thinking of the physical infirmity we share, Lord Chamberlain. I meant I could not exorcise the demons I see behind your eyes. You need a god who is as forgiving as he is demanding."

Chapter Twenty-four

Perhaps there was heavenly intervention even so, for John was spared the ordeal of reporting his failure to Theodora. When he arrived at the palace, she was inexplicably absent. He went home and awaited a summons which never came.

The arrival of a courier the next morning explained the mystery. Justinian had emerged from his theological labors to repossess the reins of power. His Lord Chamberlain was to attend an audience immediately.

On his way, John debated how he could inform Justinian about his investigations into the deaths of the stylites, not to mention that of the beggar, without revealing that he had been alerted to a possible connection by perusing, albeit at second hand, Michael's initial letter. Justinian had a tenacious memory and John could be certain that he would recall exactly what he had and had not revealed to John at their last meeting. Then too, more urgent yet was the plight of Anatolius.

As he entered the reception hall, John glanced at its bronze doors. Their depiction of a procession of nations presenting tribute to an impossibly handsome and elaborately garbed and crowned emperor was so familiar that he usually did not give them a second thought. This morning however he could not help noting the bronze emperor's towering stature and wondered if this flattering portrait was calculated to personify imperial glory or to save the hands and eyesight of some exceedingly shrewd craftsmen.

He realized that he would need to exercise more than his usual degree of shrewd discretion himself. Luckily, the emperor's demeanor was almost cheerful despite his tired eyes.

"Caesar," John began, "my felicitations. May I take it that congratulations on an imperial victory on the harrowing battlefield of theology are in order?"

"Alas, no, Lord Chamberlain," came Justinian's surprising reply. "After much reflection, I have come to the conclusion that attempting to join Michael's heresy to orthodoxy would be more difficult than sewing feet to a flounder." He laughed heartily.

"I am most sorry to hear that." John kept his voice level. He had been about to begin his plea on behalf of Anatolius. Now he was wary. To what could Justinian's apparent good humor be attributed if his efforts to reconcile religious viewpoints had come to nothing?

"The city is in a ferment." Justinian waved away a fly buzzing at his face and heaved a sigh that belied the strange lack of urgency in his tone. "In addition, I have received disturbing information to the effect that some of my excubitors are deserting their emperor. Such disloyalty pains me, but in due course it will pain them much more, I assure you."

John bowed his head. There was no doubt that Justinian would be aware that one high ranking excubitor was even now recuperating at John's house. Or had Felix already been arrested? "It is my understanding that the majority of the men have remained at their posts," he ventured.

Justinian waved his hand airily. "For how long, Lord Chamberlain, for how long? We both know the seductive power of a rampaging mob, just as we are both aware that stern measures are required to contain it. We have had to take such measures before, as you will doubtless recall."

He sighed again. "But," he went on briskly, "emperors must be subtle as well as wise. Brute force of arms is not the only way to rule. At times, my subjects are like children, appeased with golden toys, a delightful entertainment, unaccustomed delicacies to eat, a handful of coins. Failing that, there are always sterner measures of persuasion, such as the removal of their ringleader's head. After all, if their leader cannot keep his, what chance have his miserable followers?"

John remained silent. Was the emperor about to order a second attack on the pilgrims' encampment or would he require John to return to the shrine and personally remove Michael's head? With Justinian, anything was possible. Perhaps the emperor's mention of coins indicated he had decided to purchase a peaceful solution, as with the Persians who had been rattling their spears at the gates of the empire for years.

The emperor's hand flashed out. The drone of the fly stopped abruptly and he dropped its tiny carcass to the floor.

"That is how such agitators should be dealt with," Justinian remarked casually, "but unfortunately with a host as large as is buzzing in the streets, there are neither fists big nor numerous enough to catch them all. And so, dear Lord Chamberlain, given such a dilemma, what action would you take were you emperor?"

So that accounted for the emperor's cheerful manner, John realized. Although his theological efforts had failed, he had formed another plan of attack and for some reason wished the Lord Chamberlain to venture guesses at it, a childish game carried on in a marble sarcophagus while a lawless populace continued roaming the streets.

Justinian laughed. "I see that you are puzzled, John. Then I shall give you a hint. The house that you live in. What happened to its former owner?"

An icy hand squeezed John's heart. The hated tax collector's head had been handed to the mob. It was suddenly and horrifyingly clear that Justinian proposed to solve his current problems by utilizing the same method.

Mithra! John thought. He had endured so much. Could not he have been rewarded with a soldier's death? To be bound and sacrificed like a lamb or a dove at the self-serving altar of the man in whose service he had labored so long, and all because of a Christian holy man. It was ironic beyond belief—so ironic that, to his own amazement as much as Justinian's, he burst into laughter.

Justinian began chuckling himself. His amusement lasted longer than John's, whose brief merriment ended as abruptly as it had begun when it occurred to him that Theodora at least would certainly be vastly entertained to see him dead. He was absolutely convinced, as if the emperor had just announced it to him personally, that she had been apprised of his disobedience of her orders. It was just as certain that his disobedience had more than a little to do with what was now to be his fate.

Justinian slapped John's thin shoulder lightly.

"I have always admired your self-control, Lord Chamberlain," he said, "and now I stand in awe of it. When you heard your death sentence pronounced, your expression scarcely wavered, or at least not until you laughed." He chuckled again. "But you are not quite so cunning that I cannot follow your reasoning nor detect that hint of relief, however much you try to hide it."

"Caesar?" John forced out through dry lips.

The emperor looking amused. "Yes, yes, you cannot conceal it. You know me too well. It's true indeed that ordinarily by now your head would no longer be attached to your body and the rabble would already be praising me for dispatching the treacherous advisor who undermined my efforts to negotiate with Michael." He paused, contemplating the prospect. "Still, as a man of honor," he continued, gently nudging the dead fly with the toe of his scarlet boot, "despite the undeniable fact that it would be the easiest and swiftest solution to my dilemma, I find myself reluctant to use it. No, it has been my gracious decision that in view of your long service and discreet laboring on my behalf in many delicate matters you will go immediately into exile. Before the third hour hence, leave the city. Do not linger. My generous mood may be short-lived. After all, my next cup of wine may be sour or I may find, dare I say it, a fly on my plate."

He turned away. The audience was at an end.

John bowed to the emperor's back. How tempting a target it presented. But of course nobody was allowed into the imperial presence without surrendering any weapon carried upon their person. And the guards stationed by the doors, out of ear shot but well within sight, would swiftly fall upon anyone attempting to harm the emperor and, quite possibly, upon one who merely appeared to be contemplating doing so.

"Caesar, my felicitations," he said quietly.

"Goodbye, John," Justinian replied over his shoulder.

***

"I hope John's audience with the emperor has gone well," Isis remarked. "I do think it's a good omen that Justinian has decided to put his theological studies aside and take personal control of the empire again. Justinian you have at least half a chance of outguessing, but Theodora, well..."

Sunlight splashed over Isis as she sat at the kitchen table eating dried apricots and talking to Peter. It was that quiet time when the midday meal was over and the kitchen not busy with preparations for the evening. Now that she had washed and changed into a modest woolen robe, the madam could have passed for a respectable woman except for the barbaric lapis lazuli amulet suspended from a gold chain around her neck.

Peter commented that she had been fortunate that the bauble had not been stolen in her flight to John's door. His expression of distaste belied his words, however.

"Ah, Peter, you must give me credit," Isis replied, finishing the last piece of fruit. "As soon as I realized the possibility I took it off and concealed it about my person." To spare his sensibilities she did not say where it had been concealed.

Peter complimented her upon her ingenuity. "But tell me," he went on, "that amulet, it's a smaller version of that djed object that you have in your bedroom. Is it intended to protect?"

Isis weighed her words. She was well aware of Peter's faith and did not wish to offend the elderly man. He had been kind to her since her precipitous arrival, cast up on the doorstep like seaweed after a storm in the Sea of Marmara. In fact, Peter had obtained her respectable garment from a matron of his church and, although she did not care much for the hymns which he sang in a tuneless voice as he prepared food over the brazier, she was grateful for his concern.

"Well, it's Egyptian," she explained carefully. "Some call it a fertility charm, others the backbone of the god Osiris. Yet others claim it represents the tree in which my namesake discovered Osiris' hidden body. But whatever you choose to call it, a djed is considered very lucky. I would feel quite naked without mine."

Peter sniffed disdainfully. "Egyptian, you say? No offence intended, but they do have some very odd ideas. Why, they mummify cats and crocodiles and such and bury them with heathen rites, don't they?"

With a slight smile, Isis confirmed the truth of his information.

"The master lived in Alexandria a long time ago," Peter went on thoughtfully. "Do you think he would consider it impudent if I asked him to tell me more about it? It sounds like a very exotic and unusual place."

"No more so than Constantinople, Peter," was the reply. "We just become inured to what surrounds us. Why do you suppose that we scarcely notice the beggars crowding around the Milion? Sometimes it takes a stranger's eyes to see what is clearly before us yet to which we are blind."

As she finished speaking Darius came into the kitchen, escorting Hypatia, who was carrying a basket of leeks. She set it on the table and smiled at Isis. "Salutations, my lady. I am Hypatia."

Isis' drawn face lit up at the sound of her voice. "You're Egyptian! How wonderful to hear that accent again! Sit down, my dear. Tell me what is happening there. Have you been in the city long?"

Hypatia blushed. "You are too kind. I have been here only three or four years. Peter and I served the Lady Anna. Perhaps you knew her? When she died, we were both freed."

Darius had pulled a stool forward for the girl. She frowned at him, shaking her head slightly, apparently uneasy about taking it. Darius shrugged and left the room. Peter busied himself sweeping the kitchen floor.

"Sit down, my dear, sit down," Isis urged again. "It is a long time since I left Alexandria. A lovely city indeed. Not to say that Constantinople is not also a city of beauty." Her professional eye had already noted the girl's unblemished tawny skin and regular features. What an asset to her establishment she would be, if she was ever able to rebuild it.

At Isis' urging Hypatia sat and talked about her work in the imperial gardens and her continuing studies of herbs and their uses, both for medicinal purposes and as beauty aids.

"A herbalist?" Isis was thoughtful, thinking of several ways such knowledge would be useful in her house. She really must try to persuade the girl to work for her.

"Now tell me, Hypatia," she said with a smile, "are you open to persuasion concerning a change of occupation? Are you contented with your work, despite being constantly exposed to the elements and ruining that pretty skin? Perhaps you might consider employment with a private individual? Though few will admit it, not everyone enjoys working at the palace."

Hypatia looked surprised at the other woman's blunt manner of speaking. "Well, at the moment, yes, I am quite happy where I am, thank you. It is good to work in the sun and leave the rest to those who know more about the ways of the world than I do. Besides, for the next few weeks I have agreed to serve the Lord Chamberlain."

Isis chuckled. "Well, if you reconsider and decide you would like to work for me, Peter can tell you where I can be found, if I am not still in residence here. Now I must go and see if I can find something to do. Perhaps I shall go and sit in the garden with Darius for a while. You were very brave to come here unaccompanied, Hypatia."

"I live on the palace grounds and there is safety here, at least in daylight," the young woman replied.

Isis nodded and bid her farewell. Getting up to go, she knocked the basket and several leeks fell to the floor. Hypatia hastened to pick them up for her and, with a quick word of thanks, Isis left the room.

❋❋❋

"Peter," Hypatia burst out. "About that lady. I was wondering what a respectable woman would be doing wearing that amulet. But when I picked up the leeks, I couldn't help but see the djed tattooed on her ankle. She's a member of the Order of the Penitents of Mary of Egypt!" Her dark eyes were wide with amazement.

Peter looked puzzled. "Isis? A lady? And a member of a holy order? Where do you get such notions?"

"Because all the penitents carry that mark!"

Peter was astonished at this revelation. Surely this explained his master's continued acquaintance with the woman. And now his faith in her essential goodness might very well be borne out. "This morning Isis was talking about going home to Alexandria, Hypatia. I wonder if John has been urging her to resume her former life? Perhaps she will return to carrying out good works, comforting the poor, visiting the sick, whatever it is these penitents do."

Hypatia smiled, mischief dancing in her dark eyes. "Perhaps she will, but it's somewhat unlikely. You see, Peter, the penitents are not nearly as penitent as their alleged patroness. They belong to houses of the sort that Michael has promised to close and shutter."

Peter looked disappointed. "Then that tattoo isn't surprising at all for Isis owned just such a house, I'm sorry to say. But now that her establishment has burnt to the ground, perhaps she will lead a more chaste life."

Now it was Hypatia's turn to be surprised. Her lips tightened in outrage. "Do you mean she has been running a brothel? She was asking me to work as a whore? And I thought... Well, I wondered why such a grand lady was inviting me to sit beside her. Evidently I mistook the garment for the person!"

Chapter Twenty-five

"Exiled? But why? You are Lord Chamberlain!" Darius spoke much too loudly and John gestured him to be quieter. The sunlight sparkling cheerfully on the water trickling into the pool in John's garden provided a poignant contrast to the suddenly bleak outlook of its owner.

"Even Lord Chamberlains are not safe from Justinian's whims. You've lived in Constantinople long enough to know that."

"I'm sorry. Truly I am. Is there anything I can do to assist?"

"There is something I wish you to undertake, yes. I must leave before the emperor changes his mind and sends a detachment of excubitors to escort me into an unmarked grave outside the city. Or possibly in this very garden, for stranger things have happened. Peter and I will be departing soon and therefore I am leaving the safety of this house and its occupants in your capable hands."

"I could come with you and help guard Peter, since he insists on accompanying you," Darius offered. "He's an old man and hasn't been well. How will he survive exile and all its dangers?"

John looked at Darius, pondering how strange it was that an well educated man such as Philo could have so casually and cruelly dismissed Peter as a bumbling old fool, while the unlettered guardian of a brothel would show immediate concern for a man forced into a dangerous situation through no fault of his own except, perhaps, loyalty to the wrong person.

"Peter is thinking of the old days when he was on campaign and there's no time to argue or persuade him otherwise. Were I to order him to stay here...well, he's a free man and would follow me anyway and so pose a danger to us both. This way I can keep an eye on him until we get to a hospice far enough away where he can be left and safely cared for."

Darius bid a quick farewell and John went back inside, wondering if he would ever talk to the door-keeper again. As he went upstairs he could hear Peter clattering around, gathering up a few necessities for their flight. John's preparations were simple. Having provided himself with money, he left a pile of coins on his desk for Darius.

John looked around his study. He had left more than one place forever, as well as one life. Now he was leaving another place and a second life. He would miss its sunny austerity and his conversations with Zoe.

With a sigh, he sat beside Philo's shatranj table and let his gaze wander over the mosaic girl. He considered chipping out a bit of the colored glass to take with him as a memento. But Zoe's steady, strangely unworried gaze seemed to be telling him that that would not be necessary. He would see her again. Indeed, he would see his friends again.

"I do not know how that can be," John whispered to her, "for that would require that I be reconciled with the emperor. And as to Anatolius...I will be able to look for answers and save him only if I first preserve my own life."

It felt strange to be talking to Zoe while sunlight was still streaming in, but he did not care.

Zoe's steady gaze did not waver. She seemed to be looking not at him but at Philo's game board.

"Have you developed a fascination with this foolish game then?" he asked her.

The carved pieces on the board were arrayed just as Philo had left them. John could almost see the philosopher's hand picking up the one he had called an elephant. It stood there on the board, as still as the hand that had last touched it. Gaius would have to arrange Philo's last rites, for that was beyond John's power now.

And remembering that, John could not help thinking about the gashes on the dead man's hand, reminders of his attempts to avert death. It was a poignant last memory of a man who had loved an orderly world, who had talked so often about patterns and keys.

Yes, he thought, Philo waxed very enthusiastic about patterns and keys. Always. For what was hidden to most men might, to a philosopher, appear perfectly straightforward, since such scholars viewed the world in terms of what truths it hid.

The arrangement of the gashes was as deeply incised upon John's memory as into his former tutor's flesh. Five slashing cuts, the first three parallel, the last two slanting inward toward each other, like numerals. Three and five or two and four.

"Mithra!" John breathed.

Stepping briskly along the hall to Philo's former room, he retrieved and quickly re-examined the disorderly and rambling letter Philo had left behind.

Was it possible that Philo had left a hastily written coded message for John before setting out for his fatal appointment? Perhaps it was less his secretive nature than fear of possible derision that had kept him from voicing his suspicions. But if there was indeed a cypher, did those numbers, a message he had carved into his own flesh as he lay dying, refer to words, lines, sentences, words within sentences?

The last was the key and it took John a surprisingly short time to discover that by following the simple pattern of the second word of the first sentence, the fourth of the next, the second of the third, the fourth of that following and so to the end of the deliberately unfinished letter, Philo's message emerged.

"They are not what they say secrets inquire Michaelites find where Michael from suspect Michael beware..."

Even when revealed, the message remained cryptic. Added to that, how could he now hope to investigate Michael further?

Peter shuffled into the room. "Master, we must hurry," he urged in a fretful tone. "We must leave as soon as we can."

John took a small bundle of clothing from him. It had been many years since he had traveled so lightly.

※ ※ ※

John and Peter stood shoulder to shoulder in the dank shadows beneath a brick archway. They had just descended part way down a flight of stairs leading to the docks and had paused, ostensibly to eat the bread and cheese Peter had snatched up before their flight, but in reality to allow Peter to catch his breath after their brisk walk through the streets.

Below them, the stone quay was littered with broken crates, amphorae, bundles of straw for draft animals and other detritus. Half naked men toiled on and around several ships that rose and fell with the swell of the waves. The wind was freshening.

John drew Peter's attention to the small merchant ship he had picked out from those ranged along the dock. The squat little vessel had seen better days—and that years before—but it was still afloat. Three of its crew were busily scurrying to and fro as they stowed away the last of its cargo of amphorae. Only one gang plank was still in place. The tide was beginning to turn and they would obviously be sailing momentarily. That was why he had chosen the ship.

"Master, where are we going?" Peter asked uneasily.

"For now, wherever that vessel will take us," John replied. "If they will carry us, that is. But then again, the emperor will doubtless ensure that they do," he said with a thin smile, opening his hand to display a few coins stamped with Justinian's visage. "But remember, don't call me anything but John and otherwise say as little as possible."

Peter nodded silently, evidently resolving to begin following his master's instructions immediately.

They quickly descended the rest of the stairs and crossed to the ship John had pointed out. The sea wind gusted harder, sending straw skirling around their scuffed boots and bringing to their nostrils the pungent odor of exotic spices, a hint of far off lands and foreign commerce.

Arriving at the edge of the dock, John was suddenly aware that his feet were planted an inch or so from a sickening drop into deep, dark water. As a young mercenary he had nearly drowned in the swollen stream that had claimed one of his comrades. As a result he had, as he put it, developed a special caution when near water. He forced the quaver from his voice and hailed the crewman preparing to pull in the gangplank.

"Your captain, where is he? Two travelers here seeking passage. We'll pay a reasonable price."

The man, thickly-browed and as squat as the ship, admitted he was the captain. "Where are you bound?"

"Anywhere away from this accursed city, before it goes up in flames and takes us with it!" John spat forcefully into the water and cursed the emperor.

Beside him, Peter's bent shoulders stiffened with outrage but he held his tongue. Admiration for John's extremely inventive and grossly obscene language and sentiments beamed from the captain's face while Peter's expression changed from disapproval to barely concealed outrage as his master's disgusting tirade continued to spew forth. It was soon apparent that John had studied language much more diligently while a mercenary then he had during his studies at Plato's Academy.

Having disposed of Justinian's moral character—not to mention that of his wife—with a selection of colorful epithets concerning their preferences in bed partners, including obscene speculation as to the preferred number of legs, John spat into the sea again. Wiping his mouth with the back of his hand, he concluded in a somewhat milder tone. "And between the fires this godless holy man is calling down at will and the thieving whores infesting the place, not to mention the one living in fine style at the palace, we've decided to make ourselves scarce before we get killed."

The captain scratched his stubbled face reflectively. "Seems we see eye to eye about the emperor and that wife of his, I'll say that at least. Very well. We're taking a cargo of wine up to Lazica, so I can carry you as far as the end of the Euxine. Cash in hand and in advance, them's my terms. At least you'll get far enough away from here to keep you and the old man safe from imperial whores and fire breathing prophets. You'll have to pitch in with the crew if we hit bad weather, though. Now, let's see what a couple of vagabonds like yourselves considers a fair price."

John stepped nimbly across the gangplank, striving to conceal the weakness he felt as its half-rotted pine bowed under his weight. His negotiations lasted as long as it took the captain to realize there were three nomismata in John's palm.

"Ah," he grinned, grabbing the coins with a knowing wink. "I see why you two rascals are in such a hurry to leave. Two less ne'er do wells for the Prefect to worry about, eh? And I daresay I know where your knowledge of thieving whores comes from! Nothing worse than a thief who steals from one!"

He gave a coarse laugh and ushered Peter aboard. "You can take a corner below but don't touch the wine. It's practically vinegar. But what do they know in Lazica? I picked it up for a pittance. Before the inn-keeper that ordered it and the vineyard owner that supplied me are done wrangling about it in the courts I'll be back here spending my profits in the best house in the city!"

John heartily congratulated the man on his business sense, charitably refraining from giving him the bad news that the best house in the city was currently a heap of charred wood and smoke-blackened walls.

The two travelers stood by the ship's rail, watching as the last iron anchor was dragged up and set dripping with its fellows at the base of the mast. The ship's single square sail snapped in the wind and with crewmen straining at the sweeps the vessel slid away from the dock, bound for the narrow channel of the Bosporos and the Euxine Sea beyond.

"I could hardly believe your scurrilous calumnies about our emperor and empress," Peter remarked reproachfully. "It was remarkably convincing."

"Perhaps because it was heartfelt."

Peter, not for the first time since they had left the house, looked askance while John smoothed the shabby clothing he had donned, making certain that the knife tucked in his woven leather belt was not only easily accessible, but very visibly so.

As the small boat moved out into the crowded waterway John could discern the shape of the cramped peninsula on which the capital was situated. Beyond the sea walls by which they sailed, buildings seemed stacked one atop the next, blocks piled in a massive jumble that threatened to crash down on passing travelers at any moment.

It was a miracle that the sheer weight of all that architecture did not press the land down into the sur-rounding water, he thought, looking back at the most prominent feature of the receding city, the vast dome of the Church of the Holy Wisdom.

"Why does the empress hate you so much?" Peter suddenly asked him. "Her hand is surely in this, for I cannot believe the emperor would betray such a faithful servant as you."

John was tempted to enlighten his trusting companion as to how cold-blooded the emperor could be. But Peter, he reminded himself, often sang hymns penned by Justinian, so he held his peace.

Peter continued, his quiet voice barely audible over the splashing of waves and the creak of ropes and timbers. "I have heard it said, if you will excuse me for repeating such gossip, and bearing in mind that... well...I have heard that in particular she hates those men who are not such as may fall prey to her womanly attractions. Could that not be the reason?"

John shook his head. "Who does not distrust a eunuch, Peter? They've always had bad reputations, and in many cases with good reason if you care to study history. So it may be that Theodora, because of my condition, mistakes me for one of those treacherous creatures. But I believe there may well be a more specific reason."

He paused, collecting his thoughts, as Peter looked expectantly at him.

"Some years ago, upon the death of Emperor Anastasius," John continued, "his Lord Chamberlain, by name Amantius, had ambitions to wear the imperial purple himself. Unfortunately as a eunuch he was barred from doing so. But as it happened, Justinian's uncle Justin was at that time commander of the excubitors. It's said that Amantius had a candidate, one Theocritus, picked out to rule and thus secretly provided a vast sum of money to Justin, money that was quite possibly stolen from the imperial treasury, to buy support for the man. Justin, in a fine display of imperial maneuvering, used the money to buy support for himself and began his reign by putting the deceitful eunuch Amantius to death."

"I can see the meaning of your story," Peter said, "although I would not say it offers any moral to be drawn."

"It was a eunuch's failed plotting that brought Justinian's family to power. Who is to say whether another eunuch's more successful plot might not topple him from the throne?"

John looked down into the sea and immediately wished he had not. Their ship's foaming wake, pointing an accusing finger back toward Constantinople, lay across a darkly glassy sea, a polished mirror from Hades such as Persephone might have used during her time in that shadowed land. The gleaming surface beckoned him to gaze into it, enticed him to throw himself into its embrace. Much as he feared deep water, there was still something fascinating and irresistible about it, like those certain heights where men with everything to live for were drawn to throw themselves over the precipice to their deaths on the rocks below.

His grip on the rail tightened at the thought. With an effort, he wrenched himself away from the siren call of the water and hunkered down next to the ramshackle shed over the hatchway behind the mast.

Peter sat stiffly down beside him, gazing around as they sailed slowly into the mouth of the narrow, twisting Bosporos. Its treacherous currents formed a fitting warning to exercise caution to those traveling down from the Euxine to visit Constantinople.

The captain was much in evidence directing his crew, ever wary of the many centuries-worth of drowned wrecks waiting to claim for their own the ships of captains who were not quite canny enough. Each new victim rendered the sea passage more dangerous still. The ship's slow tacking to and fro promised many extra hours of travel.

Peter sighed. His bones were protesting already. He asked John, not for the first time, where this shockingly sudden journey would end, but his master made no reply.

✳✳✳

Darkness had fallen when John shook Peter's shoulder. The servant, dozing with his back to the cabin wall, startled awake. John quickly informed him that the ship was anchored for the night.

"Master, what...?"

John's gesture indicated the need for discretion. Light from the tiled firebox supporting the brazier on which the crew's evening meal was being cooked flickered through gaps in the cabin wall. Voices were audible, arguing about who had wagered what on the most recent game of knucklebones.

"We have reached the end of our sea voyage, Peter, and none too soon for me."

His servant looked about in sleepy confusion.

"No," John assured him, "you did not sleep for the entire journey. We have not yet left the Bosporos. Did you think I would flee, even from Justinian? With friends lying dead and unavenged or imprisoned and in danger? But be as quiet as you can, for I do not want to alert the captain of our departure. It would be better for him if he knows nothing."

Peter struggled to his feet. His eyes were wide with fear. "But if you defy the emperor..."

Though he still spoke in a whisper, John's tone was suddenly, uncharacteristically harsh. "What do I have to flee that would be more terrible than the fate that ambushed me long ago? Now hurry, Peter, please."

Chapter Twenty-six

The stout door to Anatolius' cell swung open, admitting an icy draught scented with a musky perfume he recognized immediately. He scrambled to his feet.

Theodora took the few dainty steps necessary to reach his side. Uncomfortably close to his side.

"Empress, your servant," he stammered, drawing back a pace.

Theodora looked up at him, an enigmatic smile curving her lips. Pearl-strung gold chains hugged her elaborately braided hair and the barbaric emerald brooch nestled snugly on her breast glinted in the flickering light of the oil lamp John had left behind. Anatolius wondered if it was her usual custom to visit those incarcerated in the imperial dungeons. There were those who hinted, always in whispers and inevitably after assisting in the emptying of too many wine jugs, that she was not averse to seeing jailers at their work. As to the details, even the most intoxicated remained cautious enough to leave them unsaid.

The empress glanced pointedly around the cold cell.

"These are not the sort of quarters a fine young man such as you should be inhabiting."

"Excellency, I regret that I cannot offer you a seat, for I have none to offer," was the only response the dazed Anatolius could manage.

"And yet this small cell is as large as the Hippodrome compared to those in which many of our martyrs were imprisoned," Theodora continued matter-of-factly, as if she had arrived to debate theology over a goblet of wine and a tray of sweetmeats. "Then again this little temporary lodging of yours is quite dry, I see, and seems free enough of vermin. Yes, many a beggar living on the street would consider this a fine dwelling place, preferable to sleeping under the chilly portico of the senate house or huddling in some rat-infested corner."

Theodora's smile was chilly as the ice that occasionally drifted past the harbor walls. "It is true," she continued. "that even the poorest and most miserable people in Constantinople possesses a rare treasure that you, Anatolius, for all your family connections, wealth, and high office, do not. Freedom. Although it is freedom at a price. There is always a price, is there not? In their case, it's the endless struggle to keep body and soul united long enough to recreate themselves in their miserable children. To what end, I confess, I have yet to fathom."

Theodora sighed, then went on in the same casual tones. "You are no doubt wondering if your freedom has a price and how high that price might be. Is it too high? Can a murderer such as you afford to haggle over the cost of his life?"

The empress stopped in her speech and looked at him expectantly but Anatolius remained silent. He reminded himself that he was a soldier of Mithra, that he had been anointed with the blood of the bull. He would not ask what ransom she had in mind. He would not give her the pleasure of forcing him to bargain for his life.

A look of disappointment momentarily marred Theodora's perfectly painted face. So, thought Anatolius, she had thought he would grovel, beg for mercy, kissing the hem of her robe and weeping, like so many soft young men who had found themselves on the wrong side of justice.

Theodora, seeing he would not speak, went on in that husky whisper that some, and inevitably to their bitter regret, had found seductive but that others considered akin to the warning rumbling growls of the wolves that ran in the dark forests of Germania.

"You are such a handsome young man," she remarked, "It would be a pity to see you executed. And of course the emperor speaks highly of your work for him. I know he relies upon you to keep account of his official correspondence and advise him on all those minute details of etiquette, how to address this ambassador or greet that statesman. Your duties for him are rather like those of your friend John, so far as that goes, but," her tone hardened, "I hope you have never shared John's desire to influence the emperor's decisions."

Anatolius could not hide his surprise at her mention of John.

"Ah, I see I have your interest at last! Well, then, to continue. As it happened, the emperor was originally of the opinion that it would be most unwise to allow the general populace to mistakenly conclude that a high born, handsome and," she touched Anatolius' chin lightly, "well-favored young man be permitted to murder with impunity. So he consulted those who are knowledgeable about these matters. They suggested that your punishment begin with the stripping of the skin from your knees right down to your toes."

Anatolius felt faint.

"But as all his subjects are aware," Theodora pointed out with a smile, "only Justinian as emperor has the right to wear scarlet boots, so of course he enjoyed their jest immensely. So much so that it persuaded him that, as a gesture of his renowned mercy, you will be granted a speedy death immediately after suffering the agony of being fitted for your new scarlet boots."

Anatolius' stomach heaved at her words. He silently invoked the name of Mithra, trying desperately to maintain control of himself. What was she saying now, something about signing documents giving his newly acquired estate to the imperial treasury?

"But surely it is the law that..." he croaked.

Theodora made a valiant effort to appear offended at the mere suggestion of illegality. She was almost convincing, having improved in the art of acting since her youthful years in the theatre.

"It would be a gift for the good of the empire and could well encourage others to follow your generous example. After all, who of your illustrious line will be left after you die? Your only relative now is your uncle Zeno, and he is aging and in any event rarely sets foot in Constantinople." An unpleasant smile flitted bat-like across her face. "I seem to be unable to avoid the mention of feet, don't I? But concerning your uncle, he will shortly be arriving in the city. I sent for him immediately you were arrested so he could arrange your father's funeral rites. We must always observe the proprieties, Anatolius. It is regrettable that you cannot be present at your dear father's funeral, but there it is."

Was it an indirect threat against his uncle, Anatolius wondered, recalling the kindly old scholar who spent his days pottering about in his garden, a man whom John had once described as possessing eclectic credulity?

He could not be certain, but he would strive not to reveal his fear to Theodora. He would rely upon his god to protect him from those who dwelt in darkness and to give him the courage manfully to bear whatever obscene horrors awaited. He offered up a silent prayer that he would not succumb to the temptation of begging for death. Whatever path he took, he knew he was trapped in a snare as finely meshed as the gold chains spidering Theodora's hair. He had no illusions as to his fate even if he agreed to sign over everything he owned to the imperial treasury.

It was as if Theodora could read his rapidly churning thoughts.

"Now it may be that you are relying upon the Lord Chamberlain to rescue you from this predicament, as he has done so often in the past. I hear that he visited you not long ago," she said, moving towards the door. As she opened it, she revealed what Anatolius realized was the true reason for her extraordinary visit.

In a smiling Parthian shot, she said "But my dear Anatolius, on this occasion and indeed for the rest of what remains of your life, the Lord Chamberlain can no longer assist you. The emperor, you see, exiled him. Another gesture of his boundless mercy, for he could have ordered him executed on the spot, but alas, it was fruitless. Word has just arrived that your eunuch friend was caught by the rabble. Apparently he sought to defy his emperor and remain nearby. I am supposing you begged him to help you, and perhaps that is why he disobeyed Justinian's orders. Such a pity, really, and so predictable of him. He could not have saved you and now he is dead. It appears that his life ended neither quickly nor painlessly. I will spare you the details."

The door banged behind her, the draft from its heavy closing extinguishing the small lamp's flickering flame.

Chapter Twenty-seven

Dressed in elegant clothing, Peter stood on the grassy space in front of the shrine of St. Michael, speaking with a similarly well-dressed pilgrim.

"Sarcerdus Rufus?" the man said, in response to Peter's inquiry. "His wealth is exceeded only by his piety. He followed Michael from a distant land. In fact, it's well known that Michael began his preaching on Sarcerdus' very doorstep."

Peter nodded thoughtfully and forced himself to stand upright, burdened as he felt by the unaccustomed weight of his embroidered robe.

The past hours had resembled a strange dream. First, he had fled Constantinople with his master. Then they had inexplicably disembarked from the ship taking them to safety and walked south alongside the Bosporos, back to the shrine. And finally John had insisted his servant pose as a wealthy pilgrim. At least this latter strangeness explained John's sudden and final puzzling instruction to add a fine garment in the small bundle of clothing carried with them when they left the city.

As his master had explained it, since he had been to the shrine in his official capacity on two very public recent visits, it was entirely possible that he might be recognized if he tried to question pilgrims or acolytes himself. And it was necessary that they find out as much as possible about Michael—especially about his origins.

Peter had ventured the opinion that everyone in Constantinople knew about Michael. After all, everyone in the city had talked about nobody else for days.

"Perhaps we only think we know about him and his followers," John had remarked, going on to tell Peter about Philo's cryptic message.

The servant was appalled. Why would his master risk his life because of some nonsensical letter? It was just as likely to have been some odd game the man had been playing, like the one with the board and carved pieces.

But Peter, always dutiful, had done his best, not that it had taken much craft to learn about Sarcerdus Rufus.

Peter, or rather the pilgrim he was supposed to be, had traveled a long way to pay his respects? Well, hadn't he heard Sarcerdus Rufus had traveled even further? Was Peter prepared to pour a stream of silver out for Michael's charitable works? Praiseworthy indeed, but everyone knew Sarcerdus Rufus had pledged a river of gold.

As to where this paragon of far traveling and generous virtue was to be found, Sarcerdus Rufus was staying with the acolytes and a number of pilgrims at a nearby villa.

Unfortunately, John now insisted Peter must interview Sarcerdus Rufus. Fortunately, the villa was not far down the road.

※ ※ ※

The villa's gate was guarded by a group of burly men who, Peter thought, did not look much like acolytes.

The man who stepped forward to block his path had certainly not received the scar bisecting his face from poring over scripture.

The man studied Peter, a well-dressed elderly man looking very fatigued. His tall, stooped attendant—his servant, Peter explained upon requesting admittance—stood a pace or two behind, intently studying the stony ground.

"You aren't likely to be granted an audience with Michael very soon," the guard warned Peter.

"Indeed that is not surprising, but I was advised I should bring my offering here for safekeeping," he replied. "Perhaps I might entrust a small portion of it to you immediately?"

"We do have procedures, of course," acknowledged the guard as his hand, missing two fingers, rose toward the glint of the follis Peter offered. No doubt everyone knew that Sarcerdus Rufus had given a larger bribe, but to Peter's relief the guard didn't mention this fact and simply stood aside.

"You are welcome here, good sirs," he said, waving them into the villa grounds.

Stepping through the arched gateway, Peter found himself surprised by the expanse of the gardens surrounding the dwelling. Even a cursory glance around revealed a guest house, stables, and outbuildings, all solidly built of cream colored stone and roofed with red tiles and set amidst decorative groves and fountains.

The Michaelite presence was obvious from numerous groups of people conversing as they strolled around. As Peter and John drifted among them, they passed by a fountain with a basin a woman was using to wash clothing. A ragged tunic hung drying over the shoulders of the fountain's verdigrised statue of Neptune. Rivulets of water flowed in endless streams from the conch shells held by the god's attendants.

Here and there children played outside small tents pitched beside decorative ponds. It was a peaceful scene.

The third pilgrim they consulted nodded enthusi-astically and gestured toward a small building amid a stand of oak trees.

"He'll be at the baths," he said, "You can't mistake him."

When he entered the building's caldarium Peter saw what the pilgrim had meant. Sitting in lonely majesty in the pool, Sarcerdus Rufus was the leanest man Peter had ever seen. His appearance was not improved by a head that had been shaved in the style favored by the pilgrims. His body was as hairless as a cod fish. He looked, Peter thought, like a skeleton, an animated saint's relic.

Peter greeted the man and then trotted out the story he and John had concocted. He could sense his master standing silently behind him. It was discomfit-ing to be taking his place, playing his role in life. The whole venture was madness, he told himself.

"Of course, I'm always glad to tell my tale to a fellow pilgrim. Please feel free to join me. And perhaps your servant could bring refreshments?" Peter was startled by the booming voice that echoed like thunder around the marble chamber. How could an emaciated husk produce such an enormous noise?

Peter turned toward John, unsure whether he would be able to feign ordering him to carry out such a task, but his master was already slinking off in a most embarrassingly cringing manner. John was a much better actor than he could ever be, Peter thought.

In short time, Peter had stripped and lowered himself gingerly into the small pool. He was happy enough to bathe. Hesitantly he asked concerning the stories he had heard about the man sitting opposite him.

"Yes, yes, they are all true," Sarcerdus nodded vigorously and leaned forward, causing hot water to slop in waves against Peter's chest. "I journeyed here from very far off, from beyond the eastern end of the Euxine Sea. Months it took, and it'll take months to soak off the dust of the journey." He rubbed a finger along the bridge of his nose, which was as prominent as that of a shriveled Egyptian mummy. "But such is the lot of the pilgrim. Now, what business did you say you were in, Peter?"

"I provisioned the emperor's armies." And so he had, he thought, reminding himself of the years he had spent as a camp cook.

"Ah, of course, of course. Then you will be quite a wealthy man?"

"I fear I cannot match Sarcerdus Rufus in that regard, by all I have heard," Peter replied truthfully enough.

The other man laughed much too loudly. "Nor do you need to, my friend, unless you are among those who feel any price is justified if it guarantees deliverance from the evil place!"

"But surely a devout person like yourself need not fear such a destination?" Peter did not have to mimic surprise.

"I wasn't thinking of going there, but rather of deliverance from it. It may shock you to hear that, in fact, I have spent most of my life amidst the very fires of Hell."

Peter expressed astonishment.

Sarcerdus smiled with delight at the prospect of telling his story once again. "Have you ever journeyed beyond Lazica, into the border regions?" he began. "A rhetorical question, I suppose, for few do. It's an area always in upheaval and it's such a long trip from anywhere civilized that the traveler can't be certain whether he'll arrive at his destination to find it an outpost of the empire or a recently annexed part of Persia."

He splashed some of the seething water onto his face and rubbed vigorously at his nose.

"Now, I'm a Roman myself," he went on. "My ancestors were captured by Shapur along with Emperor Valerian. I'm quite certain I am related to the latter, by the way, but that's another story. Anyhow, my family settled out there. Our neighbors were happy enough to let us practice our own religion and we were even happier to make a few nomismata off them."

Peter nodded wordlessly, trying to give the impression of being a man of the world and thus fully conversant with such situations.

"At any rate, since you haven't been to those parts," Sarcerdus Rufus went on. "I shall describe the area. I wish you could see it! There are places there where fire has burned endlessly throughout all of human memory. Mountains that smolder and give off a sulfurous stench like the pits of Hell. You would not dare set foot on them for the blistering heat, Peter, even if you had been brave enough to venture past the lakes of burning pitch boiling and bubbling at their feet."

It was certainly easy to imagine such a place, sitting half submerged in the bath's steaming cauldron. Peter wondered if someone had stoked the hypocaust too high.

"You can see the fires towering at night from many parasangs away," his companion was saying, "You could read scripture by their infernal glow, provided you could keep it from bursting into flames first. I tell you, Peter, this place is so renowned that men go there to study its terrible qualities. Why, there are not only several sorts of pitch that burn but the very stones themselves are ablaze."

"And Michael first began his ministry there, I hear?" put in Peter, who guessed the storyteller could spin out his tour of the nether regions for a long time if he was allowed to do so.

"Yes, indeed. It was on my land that he first gained prominence, and it was there also that I nearly forfeited my soul."

Peter observed that he could scarcely believe such a thing.

"Why do you think I am here? To make amends, of course! To earn forgiveness!" Sarcerdus' voice grew louder. Grape-like drops of sweat trembled, broke and rolled down the thin inclines of his face. "For when he first appeared, I ordered my servants to drive him away!" He slapped at the water as if it had offended him, sending more waves crashing around Peter.

"No! Impossible!" the latter exclaimed.

"But it was so, for I was blind, my friend. To be fair now, what did you think yourself, when you first heard rumors of his teachings, at the senate house perhaps or during one of the emperor's banquets?"

"Well..."

"Exactly my point, Peter. But then you listened to his words and finally understood what he was saying."

"That is true enough. I understood."

"I was one who did not listen at first." Sarcerdus ran a thin hand over the bald dome of his head as he stared up into the swirling steam gathering in the rafters above them.

"I own a great deal of land, Peter," he went on. "There's nothing I don't grow or raise. Wheat, fruit, goats, cattle, but most of all I favor vineyards. One morning some time ago, one of my servants came riding up to the house to sound the alarm. 'Master,' he told me, 'You must come at once, for we are being invaded.'"

"How terrible!"

"Oh, it isn't unusual to be invaded where I lived. Sometimes it's Persians, the next time it will be Romans and, if I recall aright, this particular time it was due to be Persians since there had been a Roman tax collector around the previous year, that being the usual way we know who is pretending to be in charge of the area. Aside from seeing who has the most soldiers out on the roads, of course. So I said to my man, 'Get the wagon and I will take a tribute.' As a man of the world, you'll understand that's what we call a bribe. They stop these minor skirmishes from escalating into invasions causing real damage. But he said 'No. It's not that kind of invasion'. I was intrigued, as anyone would be."

He paused for a moment and Peter, genuinely entranced by the man's story despite its length, urged him to complete the telling of it.

"As it happened, I had guests at the time," Sarcerdus Rufus obligingly continued. "After my wife died, I enjoyed offering travelers hospitality for it made my house seem less lonely. I reveled in tales of far off places and was eager to have my ears filled with exotic stories. These particular guests had journeyed out to see the fires. Nothing unusual in that, for as I told you, the area is famous for it. They repaid my hospitality with some fine codices for my library, by the way. Codices are priceless, as I'm sure you'll agree."

Peter confirmed that he did. "And were your guests as curious as I about these invaders who were not invading?" he asked, trying valiantly to keep Sarcerdus to the point of his story.

"Indeed they were. So we all rode out to my finest vineyard. Did I mention that I breed the finest horses in the region?"

Peter had no chance to reply as Sarcerdus charged ahead. "Anyway, this vineyard sits on a hillside and for as long as anyone can recall there's been a ruined temple there. It was built next to a fissure where a flame always burns, which is why I myself am of the opinion the building originally honored Zoroaster or some such fire deity. It looks picturesque enough and the only problem it causes is its attraction to amorous couples. That's understandable enough, though, what with the spectacular view and the shelter it affords, especially on cold nights."

"We were all young once," Peter said with a wry smile.

"Indeed we were, indeed we were. But to get back to what I was saying, I could tell you much about Zorastrianism and many other such things besides. You might be surprised at my knowledge of pagan sects, but I was steeped in evil, Peter. I warmed my hands at those infernal fires. I immersed myself in the words of demons and alchemists and pagan writers. I shudder to think of it now."

"This would be about the time when Michael arrived?" Peter interrupted, wiping sweat from his face.

His sparse gray hair clung to his head like honey to a spoon and he had a sinking suspicion that Sarcerdus was about to embark on another rambling digression.

"What? Oh, yes, you have guessed it! There he was, standing beside the temple and addressing a small band of followers and, although he was offering the truth as I later came to realize, all I could see at the time were my trampled grapevines."

Sarcerdus shook his head as if he couldn't believe his own folly.

"But I did notice the flame that had issued ceaselessly from the rock for all those years flickered out while he spoke," Sarcerdus said. "just as he was telling his followers that it was by fire that he would be known. And a wonder it was, too, because as he preached, the fire resumed burning of its own accord. I saw that with my own eyes!"

"So what did you do?" Peter prompted, hoping to hear the end of this remarkable account before he was cooked to the bone.

"I didn't want to wait for the authorities to act since it would take too long and so, and I am ashamed to tell you this, I armed my workers and they drove Michael and his followers away. They were easily dispersed. He didn't have as many as he has now, you see."

"Yet today here you are, a follower yourself."

"A wonder, is it not? And how it came about was this way. The following year stories began to drift back to me about a remarkable holy man who was moving west, driving the godless back like sand before the desert winds. I have business contacts in every corner of the empire, did I mention that? Well, I suddenly realized that the stories I was hearing spoke of the very man I had driven from my land."

Peter murmured some commonplace words of comfort.

"Ah," Sarcerdus said cheerfully, "but when you stop to think of it, Michael would not be about to enter Constantinople in triumph had I not forced him to flee my vineyard and take his message west. I was very humbled when I realized that I had served to set his feet on the journey."

"There has never been one so humble as Sarcerdus Rufus, as so many have said," Peter pointed out

Sarcerdus laughed heartily, raising another tempest in the pool. It was the stormiest bath Peter had ever sat in, except for one occasion when he had arranged a tryst in a similar private bath behind his then owner's house. But that had been a long time ago. Just the day before he had been sold into what became his military career, in fact.

"I thank you for relating your story so graciously," he said, beginning to get to his feet. He lurched sideways. Both legs had fallen asleep. Sarcerdus reached over and grabbed Peter's arm, steadying and detaining him at the same time.

"But don't run off just yet, Peter," he said persuasively. "I have not even begun to illuminate for you the stygian depths of the unrepeatable sins from which Michael has saved me."

✾✾✾

After Peter's lengthy immersion in steaming water, the warm sunlight felt chilly against his puckered skin as he sat next to John on a stone bench beside a tree-lined path looping behind the villa.

"If someone had poured honey or a good sauce into that bath water I'd be ready for the platter," he complained, shivering.

He had recounted his conversation to John and now his master's careful questioning was growing as wearisome as Sarcerdus' convoluted digressions.

"He would insist on telling me told me all about numerous of his guests, master. He must really have hungered for civilization out there, however blasphemous its trappings. I gather that most of his visitors thanked him for his hospitality with valuable gifts.

Which guests in particular is it you're asking about? The demon-worshipping traders from India, was it?"

"I mean the men who were visiting when Michael was driven away, Peter. I would like to know more about them, if you can recollect anything else."

"The ones who had come to gape at Satan's fires, as my wealthy friend might put it? He didn't really say too much about them, except that despite his story rambling all over the landscape I got the impression they left shortly after Michael departed. They hadn't stayed long. Sarcerdus mentioned that he was upset at the time. He'd been enjoying the conversations they had been having and he thinks that business with Michael frightened them away. Or perhaps it had been their turn to get a word into the discourse with him and they could not? Or possibly I'm thinking of the travelers from Arabia who..."

John raised a warning hand at the sound of approaching voices. Two pilgrims deep in animated discussion went by without sparing a glance at the pair sitting on the bench.

"Shaving the head and talking must be the basic sacraments of this new faith," Peter remarked when they had passed. "But truly, master, I have told you everything I know, and then repeated the same knowledge to you three more times and in different ways."

John nodded. "I believe you have, Peter. You did very well. Thank you."

"Very well? I had to say a few things I will be asking forgiveness for tonight! But what did I learn? You already knew Michael came from east of Lazica."

"I'm interested in the eternal fires out there, Peter. Those men who came to study them, the guests who traveled to that far place to see them. Did he happen to say where they had come from?"

Peter shook his head. "So far as I can see, master, we have learned only that Michael is exactly as he says." he went on. "So I fear you have risked your life for nothing because of a senseless message composed by Philo, and who can say for what reason now that he is dead?"

"I am not so certain that Philo led me astray, Peter." A new question occurred to John. "Do you have any idea when he composed that letter? Did you notice him at work on it?"

Peter had not.

John looked thoughtful. "I wonder if it could have been written while I was away those two days, pursuing my investigations?"

"To be honest, I did not seek him out when he was not intruding into my kitchen."

"Did he go anywhere during that time?"

"He was always in and out of the house. Seeking possible employment, he said."

"Nothing else?"

"Well, he claimed once to be on the way to the imperial library. I didn't believe him, but when he came back he was spouting facts in a positive flood, trying to convince me I had not seen with my own eyes the divine fire in the sky."

Peter paused, feeling lightheaded. He suspected he was beginning to ramble somewhat.

John asked him if he recalled anything else Philo had said at the time.

"Not much. He kept talking about elements. And there was also something he attributed to some historian, Livy, was it?"

John urged Peter to continue.

"The other thing I recall is that according to Philo, this historian described sacred lamps that apparently miraculously burst into flame when they got wet. In fact they were just a sham, a trick. I was offended because I took it as a sly way to say my religious beliefs are founded on a similar delusion."

Peter rubbed his face. Strangely, the bench seemed to be moving, or perhaps it was the garden, beginning to rotate around the bench. "I don't recall any more, master, and I fear that I really must lie down and rest now."

John patted his servant's shoulder. "I'm sorry, Peter, I should not have pressed you so."

But Peter was unable to reply. A dark fog gathered at the edge of his vision and suddenly he was falling forward into a pit as deep and black as Sarcerdus Rufus' former sins.

Chapter Twenty-eight

It was yet another dawn arrival. John and Peter had entered the city lounging casually in the back of a farmer's cart. If anyone had been assigned to watch against the exiled Lord Chamberlain's return, he must have been asleep at his post for the two men were soon slipping unmolested across the cobbled square between the barracks and John's house.

Although the house might not have been watched from outside it was certainly well guarded within. Darius, sworn to protect Isis' door wherever that door might be, answered John's summoning rap promptly.

"By Zurvan's beard! What are you doing back here? And Peter, why are you wearing such fine clothes?" Darius shut and barred the door after quickly scanning the empty square. "What a night this has been, Lord Chamberlain," he went on. "I was afraid your knock meant another sobbing woman seeking sanctuary!"

John gave him a questioning look. "You've been visited by sobbing women?"

"Well, only one, but that's enough for me," was the reply. "But more importantly, won't Justinian have your head removed if he learns you're back?"

"Perhaps not, after he's heard all we have learned," John said, hurrying up the stairs.

As he entered the kitchen he immediately recognized the woman whose pale patrician face was surrounded by greasy black ringlets.

"Lucretia! I am honored," he said.

She sat sobbing quietly, ignoring Isis, who was pouring wine out for her. Peter hobbled in and although he said nothing John could read his servant's horrified expression perfectly. His master's wine being freely imbibed by two women, neither of them a relative, and the sun was barely risen. The scandal of it, the wagging tongues! Thank heavens nobody outside the house would hear of it.

"Master," Peter said loudly, valiantly grabbing the wine jug and his master's honor from Isis' grasp, "perhaps some refreshment?"

The spectacle of a sumptuously robed servant waiting upon a Lord Chamberlain who was supposed to have fled at least as far as Cappadocia by now reduced Lucretia's weeping to sniffles. She rose and embraced John. He rested his face on the top of her head for a few heartbeats before gently disengaging her arms and turning away, seemingly unconcerned by the astounded expressions blooming on Isis' and Peter's faces.

"Peter, take some wine yourself," John instructed, warming his hands at the cheerily glowing brazier. He looked over his shoulder, cutting off his servant's protests. "To keep up your strength, as a soldier always should."

Darius' bulk loomed into the room. Seeing it crowded, he leaned against the door post, his muscular arms folded.

"How is Felix?" John asked Isis, who had recovered her equilibrium. After years in her profession, few things threw her off stride for long.

"He is recuperating nicely, thanks to Hypatia's ministrations. Her herbal knowledge is most impressive. She's been quite busy since you left, chopping and measuring and cooking her potions." She pointed toward the row of fragrant pots set along the base of the kitchen wall, mute confirmation of her words. "Your house is a positive hive of activity, more so than mine ever was, I do declare. But why are you here? None of us expected to see you so soon again, if indeed at all."

"I will explain later." John laid his hand gently on Lucretia's arm. "Your husband Balbinus is searching for you, Lucretia," he said quietly. "Why have you come here?"

"I came here because I was unable to see Anatolius. The house slaves would not allow me to enter and they refused to take a message to him. I suppose they thought I was some common woman, trying to cause trouble." She dabbed at her eyes. Her hands were red and rough, the nails broken.

John glanced at Isis.

"No, she just arrived. She doesn't know," the woman muttered. Lucretia looked alarmed as Isis took her hand. "My dear, your friend is under arrest, accused of murder," she said as gently as she could.

Lucretia gave a choking gasp and sat down abruptly.

Hypatia squeezed past Darius, who was still leaning on the door post. She might well have been standing in the hall listening to their conversation for some time, because she did not question John's surprising reappearance. Instead she knelt by her pots, stirring them one by one.

"There is almost always a man behind a woman's sorrow," she announced to the room at large. "Or if not a man, then men."

"How true, how true indeed," Isis said with a sigh.

Lucretia looked haggard, much older than the last time John had seen her. That had been on the occasion of her wedding, a marriage that had broken Anatolius' heart, or so Anatolius had claimed not long afterwards.

Lucretia mentioned the name almost before John had completed his recollection of the event.

"Lord Chamberlain," she said, "I had planned to give certain information to Anatolius. I felt I could trust him to see that the right people received it." She reddened slightly at this admission of that old relationship. "But since I cannot and I am among friends, I will tell you. You were at the shrine to meet with Michael. I observed you there and hid, in case you saw me and told my husband where I was. Forgive me for that."

John said there was no need to ask for forgiveness.

Lucretia thanked him and then went on. "You were there but a short time and therefore did not hear what I did. I went to the shrine because of Michael's words. How could I not be attracted by one who seeks to exalt the vessel of our humanity, used and mistreated as I have been?"

Isis gave a slight sniff of disapproval. "I appreciate your distress, child, but there are plenty who wouldn't feel too used at being matched with a prosperous senator."

Lucretia ignored her comment. "But what I heard and saw as I helped tend the sick and wounded disturbed me greatly. Michael's followers occasionally spoke of matters that did not seem entirely appropriate for men of peace."

"Certainly some do carry weapons," Peter put in. "We've seen that ourselves."

"And I have seen the results of the wielding of those weapons," Lucretia said. "But more than that, I overheard some discussing how the city would soon be at their feet and the price they would exact upon it. That did not sound much like the talk of pilgrims to me. But then came mention of supernatural weaponry."

John glanced over at her with keen interest. "Go on."

Lucretia shrugged hopelessly. "They realized I was listening and moved away. Then I recalled one of the excubitors had advised me to leave for my own safety and thinking that it was now time to take that advice,

I departed. If only he could have taken his own counsel. As I crept out, he was being carried to his grave by two of his comrades at arms."

John offered a silent prayer that Mithra would accept and reward the unknown soldier who had succumbed to wounds gained by carrying out his duty.

"But," Lucretia went on, determined, it seemed, to drain the pool of bitterness festering within her. "I do believe that aid is coming from an unexpected quarter, John. For soon the holy man, if he is indeed a holy man, will also be taking his last journey."

"I don't believe that he's in danger from Justinian mounting another attack," John assured her. "If Michael is caught he will surely die, but it will be in a far subtler way than by being put to the sword."

"As far as Michael is concerned," Hypatia put in, "I have a suspicion that Justinian cannot bribe him as he can the Persians, if you'll excuse my saying so, Darius."

Darius grunted agreement from the doorway. "I only wish Khosrow would pass some of Justinian's tribute money along to my family. Then they could live like, well, like Khosrow!"

Lucretia spoke again. "Justinian will not need to purchase peace. As I said, Michael is not long for this world. He displays the marks of shackles. He's a fraud, I'm convinced of that, but while he is now free of his chains, yet those chains still bind him, and securely at that, to an imminent death."

"Now you sound as mysterious as a prophecy from the oracle at Delphi," John said. "With Peter's assistance, I've learned some surprising things about Michael and his followers and you're certainly correct to suspect the intentions of some of his acolytes at least. But nothing we discovered suggests that Michael will die in the immediate future."

"Then I will interpret my prophecy, as you call it," Lucretia replied grimly. "Michael's leg is mortifying. I saw the creeping lines of poison radiating away from those disgusting shackle sores myself, like the rays of some dark sun. He won't be seeing too many more sunrises, that's certain."

Hypatia poured a pungent mixture from one of her pots into a clay bowl and vigorously stirred the liquid with a wooden spatula. "Isn't his leg being treated? Honey, that's the stuff for preventing infection and healing sores. At least that's what we use in Egypt, but you have to be quick with its application if it's needed. I'll wager they sent you away with honey on your ankles when you acquired that tattoo, Isis?"

Isis stretched out her leg and pulled her garment up far enough to reveal her tattoo. "They did indeed and, as you can see, it took beautifully." Neither the darkly outlined vertical rectangle with a pinched waist and flared base nor the horizontal bars across the top of the tattoo were blurred.

"But that shape, Isis!" exclaimed Lucretia. She bent down to study it more closely and then straightened. "That strange arrangement of dark lines...it almost reminds me of what I saw on Michael's ankle, half obscured by his terrible sores."

"Perhaps deliberately obscured," John put in. His thoughts leapt like the flames in the brazier.

Isis shook her head in disgust, an expression that rarely crossed that worldly madam's face.

"I have been away from Alexandria a long time," she declared. "but surely my penitent sisters have not sunk to such depths as to permit men to enter the order? To think they would stoop to defile it for the sake of a few more coins from clients whose filthy tastes cannot otherwise be satisfied. It is enough to make me ashamed of my profession!"

❊❊❊

Felix was propped up on his pallet, staring dolefully at the plaster wall, when John entered the small room next to Peter's. Felix looked, John thought, like a caged bear, too large for the cramped space in which he was confined.

"John! Thank Mithra! The emperor has come to his senses and pardoned you?"

"No, he hasn't." There being no chair, John hunkered down on the floor beside the bed.

A look of horror crossed Felix' bearded face. "If you are not pardoned, then even being here puts you under sentence of death, you know that well enough."

"We are all under sentence of death. Some of us have a better idea of when it might be carried out. Right now I need your assistance."

"Anything, of course," Felix growled. His mouth tightened in pain. "Although I fear my offer does not amount to much in my present state."

John replied that it was not Felix's skill at arms that he needed just then. "What I am going to do is catch a very subtle murderer," he continued.

"Do you mean whoever murdered Aurelius or Philo?"

"Yes, not to mention a few other people. The stylites, for example. There was nothing supernatural about their deaths, Felix. They were murdered and fire was the weapon used."

Felix's expression turned thunderous. "And fire was used against my men at the shrine. Some kind of incendiary device, do you think? I didn't actually see what happened. I was inside the building by then, bleeding half to death on the floor. But my men swore there was fire from the sky."

"That's what they would have half expected, since people have been talking about nothing else for days," John pointed out.

Felix muttered he should have guessed the truth of it even in his wounded state, since he had heard tales of the empire's enemies using such weapons on eastern battlefields. Yet he had hesitated to believe those stories. How could fire be harnessed?

John smiled thinly. "Well, Felix, consider. What if you took a divided clay pot and filled one half of it with an inflammable concoction of elements that burns when wet, and the other half with water? Then having sealed it well, when that pot is thrown..."

"...it smashes," Felix said triumphantly, "and the elements mix and burst into flame!" He frowned. "But clay pots sink, John. What about this fire on the water Hypatia keeps chattering on about?"

John admitted he did not know how that particular conflagration had been accomplished. However, since it had roared out from the mouth of the Bosporos and the shrine stood beside that very waterway he could certainly hazard a guess as to who was responsible.

"I suspect," he went on, "this or perhaps another inflammable mixture that water cannot extinguish was involved. Imagine a large amount of this substance, something that floats on water, poured into the Bosporos so that its current carries the inferno down to the city. A rare and terrible weapon indeed. Michael is most certainly involved, Felix. There's no doubt in my mind about that."

Felix winced as he shifted uneasily. "Strangely, when you think about it, Michael's trumpeted his guilt in the matter all along, hasn't he? But since he hasn't set foot in Constantinople since he arrived, who's his accomplice?"

"I believe I know," John replied, "and I intend to prove it and certain other related matters to Justinian, thus freeing Anatolius and ensuring that justice is served."

Felix twisted around on the pallet, an effort that drained the color from his face. "This is all very well, John, but surely no one knows better than you that justice is seldom on speaking terms with the truth. And as far as Anatolius goes, I fear that the emperor is more concerned right now in dealing with Michael and defusing the threat posed by him and his rabble, inside and outside the city. What's worse, by the noise I can hear even up here, your exile did little to calm the mood in the streets."

John smiled. "I am not so certain that Justinian did not send me away in part for my own safety. Theodora has, as you know, long harbored a deep hatred toward me and during such unsettled times... well, let's just say that certain very useful opportunities might have very well have presented themselves to her."

"You think the emperor cannot control the actions of his own wife?"

It was a question John did not have to answer.

"So you are willing to wager that Justinian is not so badly disposed toward you as it would seem on the face of it?" Felix went on. "Well, John, I've done more than my fair share of gaming but I've never yet gambled with my life."

"Of course you have, Felix, every time you went into battle! But more than that, I've discovered something that will immediately discredit Michael in the eyes of his followers and render him powerless to further threaten the emperor."

Felix raised his bushy eyebrows in inquiry.

"Michael is not what he appears to be, Felix. Philo hinted at that and he was correct. That's all I'll say for now. Now, about that assistance you can render me. Darius has agreed to accompany me but he's only one man, however powerful. I know there are certain of your excubitors who serve Mithra above even the emperor."

"That's true enough. At the barracks near the Chalke you will find a friend of mine, Cassius. He, and whichever men he chooses, can be trusted completely. I'll write a note for him. He'll destroy it immediately he's read it, so don't worry about that. But what will you accomplish by confronting Michael? That shrine he's taken over is not a court of law. He could have you killed on the spot."

"Your excubitors' presence will prevent that, Felix, and there will also be an impartial witness, one who can vouch for what he observes and whose sworn word will be accepted by both the emperor and the populace in general."

Felix doubted John could find such a person.

But John had already resolved the dilemma. "It will be quite simple," he replied, "for his wife is under my roof. I mean to take along Senator Balbinus."

Chapter Twenty-nine

Had he not been exhausted from his journey Peter might have recognized the furious pounding as announcing not only visitors but also grave trouble.

As soon as the elderly servant slid back the bolt, the house door was kicked wide open, sending him staggering. An elbow to the chest knocked him down. Excubitors flooded in. The hall was suddenly filled with the slap of boots on tile, the smell of leather and oiled iron.

Half-dazed on the floor, Peter grabbed reflexively for the nearest ankle. There was a hoarse yell and a man fell heavily beside him. His victim's sword clattered and slid away across the floor. Then Peter was being dragged to his feet, his arms twisted up behind his back. He was groggily aware of a blade moving toward his throat.

"Stop at once!"

The blade paused. Helmeted heads turned toward the unexpected sight of a stout middle-aged woman, standing at the base of the stairs, shaking the errant sword she'd just retrieved from the floor.

"Are these the orders Justinian is giving his excubitors now," Isis continued in a withering tone, "to slaughter old men in their homes?"

A tall man with the feral look of a hawk stepped out of the ranks to face Isis. "The servant will be spared this time, lady. However, if there is any further interference you will have to seek compensation for his loss in the courts."

Peter was shoved aside.

"And what does this unseemly invasion of a private house signify, captain?" Isis demanded.

"We are here to arrest John, former Lord Chamberlain to the Emperor Justinian."

"Have you not heard? He is gone. Exiled."

"We have information that he has come back to the city in direct defiance of the emperor's orders," the captain replied curtly, "Now, stand aside or..."

A hoarse roar interrupted the order. "You will leave this house immediately!"

"Captain?" The man looked away from Isis to Felix, who stood, swaying, at the top of the stairs. For an instant the excubitor looked as confused as he had been upon seeing the armed madam. But only for an instant.

"My apologies, captain," he said quickly, "but these men are under my command and like you I am under the command of the Master of the Offices. Our orders are to arrest the Lord Chamberlain, believed to be in this house."

"Some of you won't live to see him arrested," Isis promised grimly, raising the sword she was clutching in both hands. Its weight caused her arms to tremble with the effort.

"Don't be foolish, Isis," Felix admonished her. "You couldn't manage to inflict a scratch on any of these men, even by accident." He turned his attention back to the matter at hand. "Carry out your orders, then. But be certain you do so without damage to the house."

The search was swiftly concluded, despite the size of the building. The servants' quarters on the third floor, the second floor's bedrooms, kitchen and study and the first floor storerooms, unused dining room and offices, even the garden they surrounded, yielded no-one else apart from an irate Hypatia.

"It seems your informant was incorrect," Felix remarked sharply at the conclusion of the search. He had remained leaning on the wall at the top of the stairs, unable to step down any further. Peter had sat down on the bottom step, as temporarily as incapable of climbing up as Felix was of walking down. The two of them were, Felix thought with grim amusement, pitiful excuses for fighting men.

"It seems the Lord Chamberlain has escaped this time, but the authorities are aware of his return and the streets are being searched," the younger captain remarked before he and his men left. "He will not get very far."

❊❊❊

Some distance away, another armed detachment had almost reached its destination, although not swiftly enough for Hektor.

"Hurry up," he urged them shrilly, "or he'll escape. You hobble along like old women!"

Varus, who commanded this group of excubitors, glanced down at the boy loping along beside him, taking two quick steps for every stride taken by the marching soldiers. The man's eyes narrowed. "You may be a favorite of the Master of the Offices, child, but you do not give me orders!"

"And who was it told the Master of the Offices that the Lord Chamberlain would be found at the senate house?" the boy sneered back.

Passersby stopped to gape, perhaps wondering what poor unfortunate was about to be struck down by the emperor's lightning. Clearly these were men intent on extremely urgent imperial business, notwithstanding the garishly clothed creature flapping along beside them like some strange, exotic bird.

"What makes you think the Lord Chamberlain would be foolish enough to allow himself to be seen there?" Varus asked in return, intrigued despite himself.

"I caught him there once, plotting with that treacherous Senator Balbinus." Hektor's red-painted lips formed a knowing smile. "Who else can the eunuch go to for help now that he's a hunted man? I watch and I listen. I know things. He'll be there."

They emerged into the Forum Constantine. The throng already gathered there drifted out of their path. The power of the emperor was something the general populace preferred to appreciate from a distance.

Despite his protestations at their slow pace, Hektor was beginning to grow breathless keeping up. His flushed face prickled uncomfortably under its layer of chalk. A few men stood by the door to the senate house, but he did not recognize John or Balbinus. Perhaps that was just as well, he thought. Yes, they could be confronted inside and then arrested in full view of all the senators. How humiliating that would be! And as for what would befall the pair once they were imprisoned....

Hektor was so engrossed contemplating this pleasing prospect that he almost overlooked the figure emerging from the senate house.

Lucretia? Senator Balbinus' wife?

He had no time to speculate on why the woman would have come here. He'd spotted John.

Hektor yanked at Varus' arm. "There he is, skulking by the colonnade, look, will you? The one next to the senate house!"

Varus ordered his company to halt and his hard gaze raked the spot Hektor indicated.

"Are you blind?" the boy shrieked. "He's slouched down behind that group of Blues, trying to hide! You fool, now you've let him see you! He's getting away!"

Varus pulled his arm roughly from Hektor's grasp and shouted an order. The excubitors broke into a run. Slow or not, they crossed the expanse of the forum faster than Hektor. By the time the boy ducked into the columned arcade they were already half way down it, gaining rapidly on the fugitive.

Many of the merchants whose shops lined the back wall stepped outside to stare after the chase. Hektor had to fight his way through them. Even as he fell further behind he could see that the excubitors had nearly caught up with their quarry. But as that jubilant thought crossed Hektor's mind, the prey suddenly darted to one side, as if to seek refuge in one of the shops. Instead, an amphora smashed on the colonnade's marble floor, closely followed by the leading excubitor who crashed down, cursing, sliding in a pool of olive oil that was almost instantly suffused with a light rose tint. His bared sword had slashed open his leg.

And the Lord Chamberlain had vanished.

Hektor was first to understand.

A second row of shops sat directly above the first.

Hektor turned and ran back. Reaching the foot of the steep, wide stairway that allowed access to the upper row of businesses, he raced up, panting, his lungs burning. Echoing shouts from below announced that the excubitors had also discerned their quarry's intent to escape by taking one of the staircases to the second story and doubling back above them.

As Hektor reached the top of the stairway, the hunted figure burst into view and turned, as if to run down the steps. Hektor leapt forward, unbalancing his prey and dragging it down to its knees.

He would kill the eunuch himself!

The sharp pain of wrenched muscles exploded in his shoulder as his intended victim jerked away from his grasp.

Hektor tore a bejeweled dagger from his belt and swung it wildly, shrieking curses. The blade met brief resistance and then penetrated deeply, sinking into yielding flesh as sweetly as cutting open an aromatic melon on a warm summer night.

Hands fastened about the boy's throat. He tried to roll away from their grasp, dimly aware of fast approaching footsteps and shouting. Suddenly, shockingly, he was staring into a face.

A demon's face!

A dead, milky orb glared at him from a pool of melted flesh.

Terror gave Hektor enough strength to break the grasp of the hands on his throat.

Then he was cowering against the stairway wall as an excubitor helped the demon to its feet.

It wasn't a demon, Hektor realized, just some miserable beggar woman with one side of her face burnt away. He wished desperately that he had managed to kill her, but although she was weeping and clutching her bleeding shoulder she did not seem to be too badly hurt.

Before Varus could say anything, Hektor scrambled up and demanded of the woman what she was doing wearing the Lord Chamberlain's cloak.

"Good sirs, I came by it honestly," the woman protested, pulling her head covering back over the disfigured half of her face. "It was lent to me by a friend. He found it lying in the street."

"Lying might indeed be the right word," Varus replied curtly, "but I don't care if it was stolen or not, since we're not here to do the Prefect's job. Go and get a poultice put on that wound."

The woman wordlessly vanished down the steps.

Varus picked up Hektor's dagger. The decorative weapon looked absurdly small in his big callused hand. He held it out to the boy, laughing.

"I suggest you get yourself a man's weapon, child! And a new pair of eyes at the same time. That poor woman was nowhere near the Lord Chamberlain's height."

Hektor was realizing that Varus did not seem too perturbed at having caught a beggar rather than the fugitive eunuch. Further, it belatedly occurred to him that excubitor captains did not usually heed court pages' advice. And when had Varus realized that the person wearing John's cloak was too short? In his excitement, Hektor had missed that particular entirely. It would all require further rumination, but first he must guard against personally suffering repercussions from their lack of success in catching the man the excubitors had been ordered to apprehend.

"And I suggest you continue to seek the fugitive you were sent to arrest," the boy snapped, snatching back his dagger and wiping it clean on his tunic, "for I promise you that if the eunuch escapes I will make certain that the Master of the Offices knows exactly who was responsible for letting him go free."

✳ ✳ ✳

John thanked Mithra that the company of excubitors had been directed with uncharacteristic confusion, for otherwise he would have departed from the senate house straight into captivity. Instead, taking advantage of the situation, he and his party had been able to slip unnoticed out of the forum through its nearest archway.

The journey to Saint Michael's shrine had been less eventful but still hardly pleasant. John had apprised Lucretia of the necessity of speed and discretion in carrying out his plan and having agreed to assist, she did her part by going to the senate house to summon Balbinus out to join them. However, the couple had exchanged only the coldest and briefest of words upon meeting again, and during their ride had contrived to keep several mounted excubitors between them at all times—excubitors that did not arrest anyone but rather escorted them to the shrine, fully aware that following their captain exposed them to the severest punishments that Justinian could devise.

The only communication between the estranged man and wife had occurred after they had left the city and were riding along the shore of the Golden Horn. Balbinus had urged his mount forward in order to remark to John, loudly and pointedly, "You can see from the way my wife rides that she has committed to memory the wisdom of Xenophon on horsemanship. I of course am a villain of the worst sort imaginable, but a villain whose stables and library she would be happy to have at her disposal again, no doubt."

Lucretia had immediately pointed out from the other side of John and just as loudly, "Speaking of which, let none of us forget that the first rule of horsemanship is never to approach the horse in anger."

※※※

As he and his three companions crowded into Michael's austere room, John noted afresh the occupant's gaunt features, the eyes set like dark pools in a pale, serene face.

"Lord Chamberlain, welcome," Michael said. "I have been wondering whether I would see you again. Can it be that you bring an invitation from the emperor? Is he ready to discuss certain matters in good faith?"

John ignored the question. "I have brought with me Senator Balbinus and his wife. I believe you will recognize her," he said.

Michael's gaze moved from Balbinus to Lucretia and paused there. "You are making a terrible mistake." The words were spoken softly. Lucretia blushed and looked silently at the floor.

Balbinus glared at Michael, as if trying to ascertain what type of person this was whose hypnotic preaching had almost robbed him of his wife.

Darius shifted uneasily beside John. He had protested the Lord Chamberlain's decision to bring only two excubitors into the shrine, unarmed at that, and even then to post them outside the small room.

"When we last met you immediately expressed your regrets at the death of Senator Aurelius," John began without preamble. "I am wondering how you had come by this knowledge so quickly, being some distance from Constantinople."

Michael shrugged. "I am visited every day by pilgrims from the city."

"That may be so, but I believe word of Aurelius' death arrived on the lips of one of your bloody-handed accomplices when he reported that your orders had been carried out."

"Accomplices? My orders? What do you mean by this?" Michael's gaze met John's without wavering.

"It is my opinion that the person who murdered the senator is responsible for other deaths and, further, that all were carried out in your name," John replied bluntly.

Michael looked grim. "So, Lord Chamberlain, it seems that you are not here to represent the emperor after all, for he would hardly send an emissary to accuse me of such evil deeds. Needless to say, I do not order murder to be committed." He addressed Balbinus. "Then, senator, will you at least reveal the true purpose for this visit?"

"I agreed to be present as a witness," Balbinus told him, "and only then because my wife urgently requested it. I do not know what it is I am to witness."

John spoke again. Despite the rage in his eyes, he spoke in his normal level tone, rendering his words the more shocking.

"Then let me speak plainly," he said. "It was you, Michael, who ordered the murder of those unfortunate stylites as well as the death of the girl Adula. Those first deaths you predicted in a letter to Justinian. The death of the girl, in the house of a wealthy citizen, you prophesied in a sermon you gave here on the very evening the deed was committed."

"Is this true, Lucretia?" growled Balbinus.

She flushed with anger. "Why do you question me? I was not here on that particular evening!"

Michael shook his head wearily. "Does a prophet command the events he foretells? Of course not! Likewise, I but sounded the warning. It was the hand of God that smote those deluded stylites and a woman corrupted by the foulest of sins." He traced the ritualistic sign that Peter often made but, John noticed, used all four fingers of his right hand to do so.

"I do not believe it was the hand of any deity," John replied, noting by Darius' expression and the rigid setting of his shoulders that he did not care for Michael's characterization of Adula. "It was the very human hands of your accomplices, who soaked certain clothing in a mixture ignited by water. A heavy rain, for instance."

"Is not a human hand animated by the Lord's will His hand?" Michael asked, apparently heedless of the implied confession in the words.

"He must be very careless in the details then," John said. "Your letter predicted four deaths, but only three stylites died. Joseph was spared, but that was only because the inflammable tunic placed in his offering basket was stolen by a beggar. And so it was he who burnt to death in an alley a stone's throw away when drenched by the same storm that immolated the others. Was that beggar's thieving hand also carrying out heavenly will?"

Michael abandoned the religious debate. "I repeat I am not a murderer, Lord Chamberlain. I am a healer. You yourself saw that I cured Senator Aurelius."

"A coincidence, nothing more. You ordered him murdered also. Nor we should overlook another victim, a harmless old philosopher."

A shadow seemed to pass across Michael's pale features. "A philosopher?"

"A former tutor of mine, not one of those exiled philosophers whom you met in the east. They were traveling around, studying incendiary weapons, weren't they, looking for a tool to take revenge on the emperor who had so badly wronged them." John pressed the attack. "And is it not true that when they heard you preaching and more importantly saw the followers you were attracting they recognized in you another weapon just as powerful as fire, one that could be harnessed to it to wreak even more havoc?"

Balbinus, glancing from one to the other, looked astonished.

"I see by your expression you do not deny that part of it at least," John went on. "That's why Aurelius died, isn't it? He taught at the Academy years ago and they were afraid he recognized them when we visited the shrine. Afraid their plan might be revealed before it could come to fruition."

"We senators strongly counseled Justinian against letting those men return," Balbinus broke in hotly. "He called them toothless old thinkers, as harmless as doves."

"You are implying that I have been used, Lord Chamberlain?" Michael said sharply.

Balbinus gave a bitter laugh. "Isn't it obvious? Of course you were. The philosophers were creating an opportunity for invasion. Who knows, perhaps they were even being paid to do so. What a sweet revenge that would have been!"

"The moment Justinian's grip was loosened sufficiently Khosrow's army would have been at the gates," agreed John.

"I have never raised my hand against any man." Michael's spoke in little more than a whisper. "You accuse me of murder, yet I have never approached the walls of your accursed capital."

"But at least one of your philosophers has been to the city every market day, visiting a house such as you say you intend to shutter," John pointed out. "And I am willing to wager that while in Constantinople he also gathered information from Khosrow's spies as well as dispensing further instructions to them, just as others had done throughout the years. Nor should we overlook the fact that such visits would afford the perfect opportunity to place fatal robes in offering baskets."

"How could any of this possibly not have occurred to you?" Balbinus asked in an amazed tone.

"I am a simple person," Michael replied, sounding suddenly tired.

Lucretia finally broke the ensuing silence. "John, these accomplices, these spies, whom do you suspect?"

He had no chance to answer.

With a sweeping blow of his huge arm, Darius leapt away from John's side, knocking Balbinus out of his way. The senator shouted outraged protests, his dignity compromised more than his person injured.

The pair of unarmed excubitors on guard outside stepped uncertainly into the doorway. They had not expected a threat to come from this side.

"There's no point attempting to flee," John's voice was tinged with sadness.

Darius paused for a moment to speak quickly in his native tongue. "I had to do it, John. It was for my family. Tell Isis I'm sorry." Then he whirled around and bolted out of the room, knocking the unarmed guards aside.

John followed him into the nave as Balbinus lumbered behind, shouting "Stop him!"

But the sea of startled pilgrims had parted to allow passage for Darius, whose wild-eyed charge as he escaped through them resembled the bull to which he had so often been compared.

From behind him, John heard a woman's screams.

※※※

Crouched in a dark corner of the cellar, heart hammering an anguished tattoo, Darius rummaged through the chest of clothing. From the nave above he could hear the excubitor captain shouting orders to his men to seek the Persian outside, his voice rising above the screams and cries of pain from roughly handled patients and pilgrims being shoved aside.

Would Michael's followers manage to delay the pursuit long enough to allow him to make his escape?

They owed him that much, at least, Darius thought wildly.

At last his hand found the unnaturally stiff fabric it sought. He yanked the garment out and threw it over his broad shoulders.

He had already left the waking world. Now as he burst out of the cellar, he moved through a dream landscape where white-robed acolytes fell away from him like wisps of mist.

The grassy field outside the shrine was the dry, sandy earth of his native Persia. The sounds that trailed him were not the shouts of imperial pursuit but the wailing lamentations of his poor family, the family he had failed, whom Khosrow would surely now order put to death, if he had not already done so.

Wavy hair streaming behind him, robe flapping, Darius ran madly along the embankment where the field sloped down to the dark waters of the Bosporos. As he fled he wept.

A momentary vision of Adula passed through his thoughts. What choice had he had? If only it had been one of the other girls who had worn the fateful robe he'd been given along with orders he had tried to refuse but, reminded of his family, could not...And all the years of spying, the deaths for which he was responsible, the lies he had choked on even as he told them, his terrible betrayal of Isis' trust, in the end it had all been for nothing!

Breath laboring, he glanced back over his shoulder. The excubitors were gaining on him.

He stopped. He was a soldier as much as they. A soldier did not run away. His hands moved to discard the robe he wore. Then he remembered the justice Justinian meted out to spies unfortunate enough to be captured alive.

Turning his bearded face to the sky, Darius shrieked the terrible curse of a man about to die, calling down the gods' vengeance upon Khosrow, demanding it for the innocent blood he had been forced to shed and his dear, lost family.

Then, screaming his wife's name, he leapt into the embrace of the waiting Bosporos, into an unbearable explosion of heat that burned away the world.

Chapter Thirty

"This supposed admission of guilt was in a language no one there but you understood, Lord Chamberlain. While it was followed by self-immolation, it isn't sufficient proof of the Persian's murderous activities. Nor," Theodora stated coldly, "will it serve to free Anatolius."

The empress had perched herself with audacious impertinence on the throne in the chilly reception hall while Justinian restlessly paced its floor. The huge, echoing space around them reminded John even more strongly of a sarcophagus, perhaps because it looked increasingly likely he might soon be entombed in his own.

"After all," the empress continued, "need I point out that Anatolius arrived at your house covered with Philo's blood?"

"In a way he did, highness, since although it was mostly his own, some of it came from Darius' tunic, bloodied when he committed the deed just before rescuing Anatolius." John directed what he hoped was a reassuring look toward Anatolius, who stood in shackles a few paces away.

"We do not have time to waste on this trivial matter," Justinian put in mildly. "You are fortunate indeed, Lord Chamberlain, that I did not have you summarily executed when Senator Balbinus appeared on your behalf, seeking an audience. And you, senator," he added, with a slight nod toward Balbinus, "are lucky that that head of yours is still atop your shoulders rather than displaying its regal profile from a spike, given the dangerous company you have been keeping of late."

Balbinus made no reply. His face had begun to take on the pale tint of the ivory panels mounted on the hall's green marble walls.

The emperor paced over to the throne. With a fond smile, he put his arm around his wife's shoulders. "I know, however, that the empress is as determined as I that justice be done," he announced to the small group, "and so we will grant you a little more of our time. Lord Chamberlain, you say that this doorkeeper Darius had been a spy for years?"

"Almost certainly ever since he first arrived in Constantinople," John confirmed. "For after all, where would anyone find talk looser than such an establishment, one whose patrons included courtiers and palace officials?"

"Indeed! And now, since you've described to us this plot on the part of the philosophers and their fiendish fire weapon," said Justinian, "do you believe it was Darius alone who was responsible for all the deaths we have spoken of?"

"Not to mention those who died on the docks," Theodora put in, glaring at John.

John admitted that obviously the entire truth could never be known.

"But Caesar," he continued, ignoring the empress and addressing Justinian directly, "although it may not have been Darius who placed the murderous clothing into the stylites' baskets, it could only have been he who provided the deadly robe in which Adula died at Senator Aurelius' house. And it was Darius who poisoned the wine jug in the senator's study. He had the run of the house, assisting Isis and her girls preparing to present their entertainment. And as for Philo...." John again glanced at Anatolius but the young man was staring at the floor, shoulders slumped.

"As for Philo," John went on, "I am certain that his fateful appointment was to meet one of his former colleagues. Since he was both extremely bitter about his exile and very vocal about it, I have no doubt that colleague would have felt safe in revealing the plan to him."

Theodora interrupted to draw her husband's attention to the fact that John appeared to be criticizing his closure of the Academy. John's spirit's sank to his boots. Justice was going to prove elusive, after all. The faces of the two men beside him reflected the same grim thought.

"Not at all, not at all," Justinian said, stepping away from the throne. "The Lord Chamberlain merely reports his deductions. Not that I shall necessarily accept their truth, John, but carry on with your explanation."

John collected his thoughts rapidly. "Thank you, Caesar. As I was saying, no doubt their plan was revealed to him. A spy in the Lord Chamberlain's house would be extremely useful, would it not? And, after all, Philo had suffered too."

"Suffered?" snapped Theodora. "They should all have been thanking their pagan gods for the mercy shown by their emperor in allowing them to come home."

Justinian smiled benignly at her words.

"Indeed that is so, highness," nodded Balbinus with perhaps a shade too much enthusiasm.

Justinian ordered John go on.

"But Philo, I think, would not have thrown his lot in with them," John said. "He was nothing if not contrary. Besides, despite some of the things he said, it is obvious to me that he had really turned his bitterness on himself. I cannot see him harming others. And a man so preoccupied with beauty and order would have found no appeal in the philosophers' plans for death, destruction and chaos."

Theodora laughed. "Do you practice magick Lord Chamberlain, that you can read the thoughts of another, and a dead man too?"

"No, highness, but as my teacher he offered his thoughts to me and many of them I have made my own. I am sure he balked at the chance to work with his former colleagues. They could not afford the risk of allowing him to reveal what he had been told. So when, thanks to me, Darius arrived on the scene to bring him home, he was ordered to dispose of Philo immediately."

Justinian, seemingly lost in thought, was gazing at the hall's great bronze doors. His florid features had sagged into the unreadable expression that too many opponents had mistaken for vacuity.

John knew that his life and the life of more than one other in the room were being weighed. Finally the emperor spoke, "Although this is not exactly proof as would be acceptable in a court of law, Lord Chamberlain, your chain of deductions does seem possible. I have always trusted your insights and intelligent discussions of difficult problems. Besides, I cannot imagine my soft young secretary as a cold-blooded murderer of old men. I am certain that the empress agrees."

Theodora's venomous stare skewered John, contradicting Justinian's words even as they were spoken. Although a slight smile quirked the emperor's lips briefly, he appeared not to notice her look. "So I have decided that the matter is now closed. Guards, unchain my secretary!"

John caught the slight widening of Theodora's eyes and the flare of her nostrils. He thought her near to combustion with no need of inflammable concoctions. Perhaps she had hoped that Anatolius at least would not escape.

"That may be," the empress said, her smooth voice revealing no hint of her rage, "but there is still the matter of the Lord Chamberlain's treason in defying you, his emperor, by returning from exile. Not to mention Anatolius' complicity in all his machinations. Perhaps the young poet here was not man enough to wield a blade against one he suspected of killing his father, but he was observed copying an important and secret state document—the first message from Michael. Such an offense is punishable by death."

Justinian turned a questioning look on Anatolius.

John knew there was no use denying the allegation. "A misunderstanding, as you will doubtless have realized, Caesar," he put in quickly. "Anatolius was unable to speak with you although he knew how urgently I needed the information. He assumed you would have given your permission." As he spoke, John hoped that Justinian had forgotten his refusal to allow him to examine the document in question. "As I have explained, it was the content of that message that set me on the right track. I acknowledge that the action was rash, but it enabled the plot to be defeated."

"A knotty question to be resolved indeed," mused Justinian. "Should the emperor behead the general who wins a battle by disobeying orders or commend him for achieving the victory?"

"I am not convinced that the battle is won," declared Theodora. "Although the philosophers are under arrest, this Michael person has escaped. And while the excubitor captain whose detachment escorted the Lord Chamberlain to the shrine has been executed for his carelessness in allowing the holy fraud to get away— not to mention his assisting the Lord Chamberlain to defy your orders—yet consider. What is to prevent Michael from returning to incite the mob again?"

Justinian looked thoughtful. "Surely he would not be so insane as to come back, having escaped our wrath once? And yet it is an intriguing possibility."

His hand made an almost imperceptible gesture and the two excubitors flanking Anatolius grabbed the young man's arms roughly. Others stepped toward Balbinus and John.

"What is your answer to this most important question, Lord Chamberlain?" Justinian demanded.

"Caesar, what I shall reveal may be hard to believe," John began, willing his voice to remain steady. "It is well known that people see what they expect to see. How many of Aurelius' guests realize they observed Darius commit murder? While their attention was on the girl playing Calliope, it took but the wink of an eye to push Adula into the fountain, immediately setting her robe afire. But since everyone expects water to quench fire, what appeared to be happening when they looked around was Darius attempting to douse the flames and save the girl."

"You have already described that scene, Lord Chamberlain," Theodora pointed out.

"But I remind you of it, highness, because Michael was practicing just such a deception and also in full view. Because of that, his followers will not be pleased or inclined to remain when they learn the truth of it."

An almost child like eagerness suffused Justinian's features. "Fascinating! And what is this deception you imagine will render the heretic powerless, should he return?"

"Michael is not a holy man, excellency," replied John, "but rather a woman."

Epilogue

"So Michael's past betrayed her, like a new wife's old love letters?" mused Anatolius as he and John strolled around the Lord Chamberlain's garden not long before sunset.

John had explained that the dark lines mistaken for the onset of mortification had been what remained of a djed tattoo, the mark of an Egyptian prostitute, which Michael failed to erase.

Justinian had not been much interested in Michael's past, beyond the fact that she had left her profession to marry. The emperor was well versed in the legal rights accorded to husbands and realized she could not risk anyone revealing her whereabouts if the husband seeking her should arrive in Constantinople. She would not, he was satisfied, dare to come back. He had therefore ordered Anatolius freed and dismissed them all from his presence.

Anatolius, being more interested than the emperor in matters of the heart, prompted John to relate what he had learned.

In the darkening garden, John thought back to the words that had passed in private between himself and Michael after Darius' charred body had been retrieved from the Bosporos.

The story he had pieced together from Michael's soft, rambling words, directed as much to herself it seemed as to John, had been unremarkable, save for its strange ending. A husband who grew cold and became unfaithful. A wife who left and was pursued.

Studying Michael's delicate, pale features, so clearly those of a woman, now that he knew the truth—now that he was no longer blinded by seeing her as a despised eunuch—John chided himself for having been deceived.

"There are many stories of women who for various reasons disguised themselves as men, and of men who did the opposite," he said. "Afraid of being apprehended, she shaved her head and dressed as a man."

Anatolius frowned and abruptly stopped walking. "Had it been Lucretia I would not have wanted to see her shear off all her beautiful hair. Do you suppose Lucretia and Balbinus will be reconciled now?" His voice was wistful.

John shrugged silently. It was the only tactful answer, particularly since it did not seem to have occurred to Anatolius that in effect Lucretia had sacrificed her freedom in exchange for his.

"Did she tell you how it was she came by her religious beliefs?"

"Why should she? It was a revelation from God, as she'd told her followers, and the rest of the world, often enough."

"You believe that?"

"How do any of us come by our beliefs?"

"But what did Michael want, John? Did she truly aspire to be Patriarch? Was she merely an unwitting instrument of destruction?"

He admitted, he had not been able to fathom her motivation. "She professed ignorance of the extent of the philosophers' plot. Yet she had suffered at mens' hands and I don't think she was completely averse to the possibility of revenge, even if it could not be directed at one person in particular. Then again, it's quite possible that she also found herself swept along by events"

A chilly breeze was beginning to rustle through the bushes crowding the pathway. They resumed walking.

"What exactly did she suffer?" wondered Anatolius.

John sighed at the question. Despite recent events, the younger man still had not learned to exercise tact. "Given her old life," he replied, "much of what she underwent is easily imagined. But she did tell me that as she spoke to her followers on the night of your father's banquet, she looked out into the crowd and saw a family. A family with a young child and a woman who was close to her time. And that reminded her of the child she had lost, a loss that was the beginning of the bitter estrangement between she and her husband."

"Strange indeed," mused Anatolius, "for it is sadly true that infants die every day without their deaths threatening to bring down an empire. But it seems stranger still that she would tell you all this, John."

"Perhaps she felt the need for some human sympathy, for a holy man cannot receive very much of that." John did not add that those who had suffered greatly often sensed it, unspoken, in others. Perhaps that had been the real reason for the confidences Michael had made to him.

Their walk around the garden had led them to the pool graced by the eroded stone creature. Anatolius looked thoughtfully into the water. A few dead brown leaves floated there, heralding the approaching winter.

"And what of Michael now?" he asked.

"I hear the gossips in the marketplace have it that Michael ascended to heaven from the shores of the Bosporos. In a fiery chariot, no less!" John gave his thin-lipped smile. "That fiery chariot, of course, was Darius. But if you are a follower, it is a much more satisfactory explanation for her disappearance than the truth, which is that she fled by a more ordinary method of transport, in the back of a cart or on foot perhaps."

"But why did you allow her to escape?" Anatolius persisted.

"Everything considered, I realized if Michael sincerely believed in this matter of the body as holy vessel, to destroy such vessels was not something she would knowingly assist."

Anatolius continued to look doubtful but said nothing.

"And there again although she's free, she is not free," John went on. "So long as she's hunted, there will never be rest. She can never stop looking over her shoulder. Every day might be the day that her husband finds her. It will be the first thing she thinks of when she awakes, the last thing before she sleeps. But it is growing cold. We should go indoors."

❋ ❋ ❋

Their conversation continued in John's study.

Anatolius again expressed amazement at their escape from death. "Perhaps Justinian was in a merciful mood," he offered thoughtfully, lounging on the chair lately occupied by Philo.

"Perhaps. But if you ask me, it's much more likely that I was exiled rather than executed so as to remove me from Theodora's long reach and allow me time to complete my task," John replied. "Of course, he could still have me executed on the spot."

"Well, that applies to everyone," Anatolius cheerily pointed out, "especially if he disagrees with them. Or even if he doesn't."

"True enough. And one thing with which Justinian most certainly would not agree is my opinion that the empire does not need ungodly fire weapons," John said as he poured two cups of wine. Handing one to Anatolius, he went on, "Incendiary devices are one thing but setting water ablaze for stadia, killing everyone trapped in or on it, is another. War is a cruel enough undertaking as it is but more than that, there's no honor in such a weapon."

"But if the enemy has the secret...?"

John smiled grimly. "If they did, do you not think they would have used it long since? It would have been deployed immediately and doubtless they would have taken Constantinople by now. So, all in all, perhaps it's as well those learned academicians were found dead in their cells just an hour or so after their capture at the villa Peter and I visited. It was poisoned wine, apparently."

Anatolius had been about to put his cup to his lips. He paused abruptly. "What is this? Justinian orders wine served to those who sought to overthrow him?"

"Their guards are Mithrans."

Anatolius understood. "And Hypatia is an excellent herbalist, isn't she?"

"They knew what was in the wine and made their choice. I expected it to be mentioned during our audience, for Justinian certainly knew about it even if Theodora did not. She certainly knows by now. Hopefully she will assume that it was done on the emperor's orders and inquire no further. So let us say no more about it, my friend."

Anatolius set down his cup, wine untouched. "Your house seems very quiet, John."

"Yes, Peter is resting and Hypatia went to visit friends. Felix went back to his own home this morning, even though he still needs to recuperate a while longer. But he also wanted to mourn his fellow captain in private."

Anatolius said in a husky voice that he quite understood.

"And Isis," John went on, "well, she is distraught over Darius, of course. It's difficult to overcome affection for a person who has served you faithfully for many years, even when he betrays you. And of course Darius betrayed more than one of us. However, she went off an hour or two ago to visit the ruins of her house now that the streets are quiet again."

Anatolius wondered how Isis would manage to earn a living with her house in ruins and her girls scattered about the city.

John laughed. "If she did not have more than a few jugs of nomismata buried under her cellar floor I would be very surprised. They're safe enough for now, under the rubble. But what of yourself? You have doubtless already been informed your appointment to the quaestor's office has been withdrawn?"

Anatolius couldn't help smiling. "To be relieved of that is almost worth the time I spent imprisoned." His expression grew more somber. "Although I would burden myself with the law in the wink of an eye if it would bring my father back." There was longing in his voice. He wiped tears away.

"I am sure whatever you do, Anatolius, you will conduct your life in a manner that would have made him proud," John said.

Anatolius finally took a sip of the raw wine. "Do you think my parents could be watching us even now? I myself believe that the dead can observe and even speak to us." His haggard face lit up with a sweet smile as he continued. "Do you recall that I dreamt my mother's shade appeared in my dreams and warned me to be vigilant, to guard my back against the blade?"

John replied that he did, adding that it was certainly good advice.

"But was it more than that, John? Because what was at my back and all around me as I dozed in my father's study?"

John considered for a moment, remembering the room whose decoration had been overseen by Anatolius' mother. "The walls were painted with cupids!"

"And Darius was at the banquet in the guise of Eros," Anatolius pointed out. "Do you think...?"

John silently reached for the wine jug.

They sat for a long time, passing it back and forth to refill their cups.

A smile seemed to flicker on the face of the mosaic girl Zoe when the lamps were lit. As darkness advanced over the city, rain began to beat on the window panes.

Glossary

Glossary

ACTAEON

Hunter who accidentally saw Artemis, goddess of the chase, while she was bathing. He was transformed into a stag and subsequently torn to pieces by his own dogs.

ATROPOS

One of the three Fates, daughters of Zeus and Themis (loosely, "order" or "law"). CLOTHO, the spinner, formed the thread of a life; LACHESIS, the allotter or dispenser of time, measured its length and ATROPOS, the inexorable or inflexible, cut it with her shears at the moment of death.

BLUES

See FACTIONS

BYZANTINE EMPIRE

After the western Roman Empire fell in 476, the eastern part of the empire continued. Although Christianity became the state religion and Greek replaced Latin in everyday speech, its citizens still regarded themselves as Romans. Finally conquered by the Turks in 1453, for much of its nearly thousand years of existence the empire was one of the world's great powers. Hundreds of years after its fall, scholars derived the name "Byzantine" from the city of Byzantium, which Constantine I (274-337) had made his capital, renaming it Constantinople.

CALLIOPE

See MUSES

CERBERUS

Three-headed dog that in Greek mythology guarded the entrance to the underworld.

CHALKE

One of many structures destroyed during the Nika Riots (532) and rebuilt by JUSTINIAN I. The main entrance to the GREAT PALACE, its roof was tiled in bronze. Its interior had a domed ceiling and was decorated with mosaics of JUSTINIAN, THEODORA and imperial military triumphs.

CLOTHO

See ATROPOS

DANIEL THE STYLITE (409-493)

Born in Syria, he became a monk and spent twenty five years in a monastery. He subsequently took up residence atop a pillar near Constantinople, remaining there for over thirty years. He is said to have descended only once, in order to advise Emperor Basiliscus (d 477) against supporting the MONOPHYSITES.

DOCETISM

Early Christian heresy claiming that Christ did not have a real body during his life on earth but rather a phantom one, and thus did not actually suffer but only seemed to suffer.

DODONA

Shrine in northwestern Greece. Consulted by supplicants from as early as 500 BC, oracles were interpreted from the sounds made by leather thongs slapping against a brass plate hanging in the sanctuary's sacred tree or alternatively from the rustling of its leaves.

ETERNAL PEACE

Treaty ratified in 532 between JUSTINIAN I and the Persian ruler Khosrow I (d 579).

EUNUCH

Eunuchs played an important part in the army, church and civil administrations of the Byzantine Empire. Many high offices in the palace were typically held by eunuchs.

EUTERPE

See MUSES

EUTYCHIANISM

Religious philosophy declaring that Christ's divine nature absorbed his human side. Advocated by the monk Eutyches (c378-c452).

EUXINE SEA

Large inland sea today known as the Black Sea.

EXCUBITORS

The palace guard.

FACTIONS

Supporters of the BLUES or GREENS (chariot teams named for their racing colors). Great rivalry existed between the factions, which had their own seating sections at the HIPPODROME. Brawls between them were not uncommon and occasionally escalated into city-wide riots.

FOLLIS

Largest of the copper coins, worth 40 NUMMI or 1/288th of a NOMISMA.

GREAT CHURCH

Common name for the Church of the Holy Wisdom (Hagia Sophia). One of the world's great architectural achievements, the Hagia Sophia was completed in 537 and replaced the church burnt down during the Nika Riots (532). The structure is most notable for its immense central dome, about a hundred feet in diameter.

GREAT PALACE

Lay in the southeastern part of Constantinople. It was not one building but rather many, set amidst trees and gardens. The grounds included barracks for the EXCUBITORS, ceremonial rooms, meeting halls, the imperial family's living quarters, churches and housing provided for court officials, ambassadors and various other dignitaries.

GREENS

See FACTIONS

HIMATION

Sculptures of statesmen and philosophers commonly depicted them wearing this draped Greek garment.

HIPPODROME

U-shaped race track near the GREAT CHURCH. The Hippodrome had tiered seating accommodating up to a hundred thousand spectators. It was also used for public celebrations and other civic events.

HORSE HOOF BREASTPLATES

Mentioned by Pausanias (2nd century AD) in his Description of Greece, covering regional geography, history, folklore, architecture and so forth. The Sauromataean breastplate he describes was fashioned of overlapping slices of horse hoof sewn in a pattern resembling snake scales or unopened pine cones and was thus well nigh impenetrable. See also SAUROMATAE.

HYDRA

A kind of organ, commonly used for ceremonial rather than religious events. It appears to have been of the type fed by bellows.

JUSTINIAN I (483-565)

Justinian I ruled from 527 to 565. His ambition was to restore the Roman Empire to its former glory and he succeeded in regaining North Africa, Italy and southeastern Spain. He codified Roman law in the Justinian Code. After the Nika Riots (532) he rebuilt the still-standing Church of the Holy Wisdom (see GREAT CHURCH) as well as many other buildings in Constantinople.

KALAMOS
Reed pen.

KOHL
Powdered cosmetic used by Egyptian and middle eastern women to darken the edges of their eyelids.

LATRUNCULI
Popular Greek and Roman game involving military strategy, played on a checkered board.

LORD CHAMBERLAIN
Typically a EUNUCH, the Lord (or Grand) Chamberlain was the chief attendant to the emperor and supervised most of those serving at the palace. He also took a large role in court ceremonies but his real power arose from his close working relationship with the emperor, which allowed him to wield great influence.

MANICHAEISM
Religion founded by the Babylonian prophet Mani (c216-c276) that offered salvation through special knowledge of spiritual truth. Its basic philosophy was dualistic, viewing the world as divided between the realms of good and evil, and therefore had much in common with ZOROASTRIANISM.

MARY OF EGYPT (c344-c421)
Notorious prostitute in Alexandria, Egypt. Having worked her passage to the Holy Land by plying her profession aboard ship, she continued with her old life but eventually repented. She then retired to the desert and lived as a hermitess for over forty years. She was discovered dead by the monk Zosimus, who buried her with the aid of a lion that dug a hole in the sand.

MASTER OF THE OFFICES
Oversaw the civil side of imperial administration within the palace.

MESE
Main street of Constantinople running from the MILION to the city walls. The Mese connected, among other sites, the forums of Constantine, Tauri, Bovis and Arkadios. Its entire length was rich with columns, arches and statuary (depicting secular, military, imperial, and religious subjects), fountains, religious establishments, workshops, monuments, public baths and private dwell-

ings, making it a perfect mirror of the heavily populated and densely built city it traversed.

MILION

Marble obelisk near the GREAT CHURCH. It was the official milestone from which all distances in the empire were measured.

MITHRAISM

Of Persian origin, Mithraism spread throughout the Roman empire via its followers in various branches of the military. It became one of the most popular religions before being superseded by Christianity, perhaps in part because women were excluded from Mithraism. Mithraeums (Mithraic temples) were underground and have been found on sites as far apart as northern England and what is now the Holy Land. Mithrans were required to practice chastity, obedience and loyalty. Some parallels have been drawn between Mithraism and Christianity because of shared practices such as baptism and a belief in resurrection and the fact that Mithra, in common with many sun gods, was born on December 25th. Mithrans advanced within their religion through seven degrees. In ascending order, these were Corax (Raven), Nymphus (Male Bride), Miles (Soldier), Leo (Lion), Peres (Persian), Heliodromus (Runner of the Sun), and Pater (Father).

MONOPHYSITES

Adherents to a doctrine holding that Christ had only one nature (a composite of the divine and the human) rather than two that were separate within him. Although condemned by the fourth ecumenical council in Chalcedon (451) it nevertheless remained particularly strong in Syria and Egypt during the reign of JUSTINIAN I.

MUSES

Zeus' nine daughters by Mnemosyne ("memory"). The Muses' names, spheres of influence and emblems are generally agreed to be:

Calliope (eloquence and epic poetry); wax tablet and stylus. Considered the eldest Muse.

Euterpe (lyric poetry and music); a flute, which she is said to have invented.

Erato (erotic poetry); a lyre.

Polyhymnia (sacred poetry and hymns). Usually depicted pensively leaning her elbow on a low pillar.

Clio (history); a scroll.

Melpomene (tragedy); tragic mask. Often shown wearing cothurni, the height-enhancing boots worn by actors in tragic plays.

Thalia (pastoral poetry and comedy); shepherd's crook and a comic mask.

Terpsichore (dance and choral singing). Commonly represented as dancing while holding a lyre.

Urania (astronomy); celestial globe. Shown wearing a starry cloak.

NOMISMA (plural: NOMISMATA)
Standard gold coin at the time of JUSTINIAN I.

NUMMI (singular: NUMMUS)
In the early Byzantine period the nummus was the smallest copper coin, worth 1/40th of a FOLLIS. Although suspended in 498 the minting of nummi was resumed in 512.

ORACLE AT DELPHI
Most famous oracle in Greece. Priestesses serving in the temple to Apollo on Mount Parnassus prophecied in a semi-conscious and incoherent state after inhaling vapors escaping from the earth and chewing laurel leaves. Their ramblings were interpreted by a temple priest.

OROPOS
Famous healing shrine in Attica, east central Greece. The sick slept there in hopes of dreaming a cure for their illnesses.

OVID (43BC-I7AD)
Roman poet best known for his erotic verse. Author of the Art of Love and also The Metamorphoses, a mythological-historical collection.

PARASANG
Ancient Persian unit of distance based upon ground covered in an hour's march. Usually estimated at 3.5 modern miles but not altogether fixed.

PARTHIAN SHOT
One delivered whilst in retreat.

PATRIARCH
Head of a diocese or patriarchate. In the time of JUSTINIAN I these were (ranked by precedence) Rome, Constantinople, Alexandria, Antioch and Jerusalem.

PLATO'S ACADEMY

Plato (?428BC-347BC?) founded his academy in 387 BC. Situated on the northwestern side of Athens, its curriculum included natural science, mathematics and training for public service. Along with other pagan schools it was closed in 529 by order of JUSTINIAN I.

PLOTINUS (c204-270)

Egyptian philosopher who went to Rome in 244 and taught there until about 268. His writings were edited by his student Porphyry (234-305) into six sets of nine books under the general title of The Enneads (from "ennea", nine)

PYRRHIC VICTORY

Pyrrhus (319-272BC) ruled Epirus in northwest Greece. His victories over the Romans were so hard won that when congratulated upon them Pyrrhus is said to have replied that one more such victory would ruin him.

QUAESTOR

Public official who administered financial and legal matters as well as drafting laws.

SALUS

Roman goddess of health. Her Greek equivalent was Hygieia.

SARACENI

Nomadic tribe living in the Arabian desert regions. Their unusual wedding customs were described by Roman historian Ammianus Marcellinus (4th century AD).

SAUROMATAE

Scythian tribe said by Herodotus (c485-425BC) to be descended from intermarriage between local warriors and shipwrecked Amazon women. See also HORSE HOOF BREASTPLATES.

SHAPUR I (d 272)

Persian ruler who in 260 defeated the Romans at Edessa (now Urfa, Turkey) and captured Emperor VALERIAN, who died whilst in captivity.

SHATRANJ

Ancestor of chess, originating in India.

SILENTIARY

Court official whose duties were similar to those of an usher and included guarding the room in which an imperial audience or meeting was being held.

SINOPE
Now known as Sinop. A port on the southern shore of the EUXINE SEA.

SPATHA
Long-bladed sword.

SPATHOMELE
Spatula-like instrument employed in mixing, stirring or applying medication.

STADIA (singular: STADE or STADIUM)
Ancient Greek measure of distance. As adopted by the Romans a stade equaled 606 feet 9 inches, the length of a footrace at the Olympic Games.

STYLITES
Holy men who often spent years living atop columns. Also known as pillar saints, from "stylos", pillar. Constantinople boasted numerous stylites.

THEODORA (c 497-548)
The influential wife of Emperor JUSTINIAN I, whom she married in 525. It has been alleged that she had formerly been an actress and a prostitute. When the Nika Riots broke out in Constantinople in 532, she is said to have urged her husband to remain in the city, thus saving his throne.

TYANA
Town in Cappadocia, a region in east central Turkey.

VALERIAN
See SHAPUR I

WALLS OF CONSTANTINOPLE
Constantinople was protected by a series of sea and land walls, the first of which were built by Constantine I (274-337) who made the city the empire's capital in 324. In 413, to accommodate its expanding population, Theodosius II (401-450) added another set of fortifications, an inner and outer wall and a moat, west of Constantine's wall.

ZEUXIPPOS
Thracian deity whose name combines "Zeus" and "Hippos". The public baths named after Zeuxippos were erected by order of Septimius Severus (cl46-2ll). A casualty of the Nika riots (532) they were rebuilt by JUSTINIAN I. Situated to the northeast of the HIPPODROME, they were generally considered the most luxurious

of the public baths and were famous for their classical statues, numbering between sixty and eighty.

ZOROASTRIANISM

Religion founded by Zoroaster (c628BC-c551BC), of whom little is known. Its focus is the cosmic struggle between light (good) and darkness (evil).

ZURVAN

Persian god of destiny and time and father of the twins Ahura Mazda and Angra Mainya, who represented good/light and evil/darkness respectively.